Peter Bridgford

Where Eagles Dare Not Perch

Black Rose Writing | Texas

The final approval for this literary material is granted by the author.

First printing

This is a work of fiction. Names, characters, businesses, places, events and incidents are either the products of the author's imagination or used in a fictitious manner. Any resemblance to actual persons, living or dead, or actual events is purely coincidental.

ISBN: 978-1-68433-107-9
PUBLISHED BY BLACK ROSE WRITING
www.blackrosewriting.com

Printed in the United States of America
Suggested Retail Price (SRP) $20.95

Where Eagles Dare Not Perch is printed in Chaparral Pro

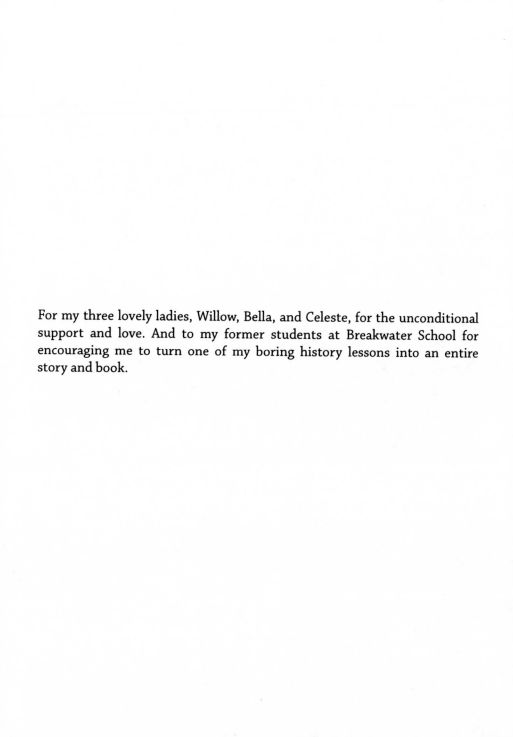

For my three lovely ladies, Willow, Bella, and Celeste, for the unconditional support and love. And to my former students at Breakwater School for encouraging me to turn one of my boring history lessons into an entire story and book.

Where Eagles Dare Not Perch

"The Corps of SharpShooters will be used not in the midst of battle, but on the outskirts, where, beyond the smoke and fury of the engagement, they will act independently, choose their objects, and make every shot tell. Posted in small squads at from one-eighth to three-eighths of a mile from the field, firing a shot a minute, and hitting their mark with almost a dead certainty, they will be a great annoyance to the enemy. They will continue their attention to the officers, and by picking those off, will bring confusion into the enemy's line."

-An excerpt from a June 4, 1861 article in the *New York Post*

"What a terrible thing war does; it takes young men in the flower of their youth, it demeans them, it humiliates them, it destroys the last vestige of dignity. It sometimes kills or maims them. Those who survive are not quite the same."

-Belton Y. Cooper, in
Death Traps: The Survival of an American Division in World War II

"It is well that war is so terrible, or we would grow too fond of it."

-General Robert E. Lee

Chapter One

Zachary Webster crossed the snow-covered fields with the purposeful movements of an apparition searching for something it had lost. Because the wind was from the north, he snowshoed around the southern edge of the fields and along the stone wall toward the site he'd scouted a few days earlier. The cloudless sky was completely impotent against the achingly frigid temperatures of the day. However, the intense sunlight reflected off the snow with such force, he walked with the bill of his winter hat pulled down low to shade his eyes. This made him look like some kind of miscreant. As he continued on in this manner, Webster reflected how a Wabanaki farmhand had once told him that the tribes in the North used bone goggles to prevent snow blindness in the winter, and he wished he had a pair of those now. Instead, he trudged along with his head downcast as if he walked in shame.

As soon as he found his spot, he began to tramp down the windblown drifts. Skillfully and quickly, he made a platform on which he could lie prone with his rifle resting on the stones of the wall in front of him. The winter had been a particularly harsh one, complete with arctic-like temperatures and unusually heavy snowfall, and it had taken its toll on the humans and animals of Maine alike. Even the moose, which usually only moved during the hours just before dusk or dawn, were now too pressed by their impending starvation to be cautious anymore. Their desperation forced them to leave their hiding places and move at all hours of the day to get at any available food. Because of this, Webster was sure that one would come through the opening in the woods in front of him to get at the willows by the pond. When it did, he would shoot it and butcher it for his mother and brother to supplement their meager food stashes.

As Webster waited, the frosty air nipped at his cheeks, but his woolen clothing kept his body warm. He looked down at the special mittens with the moveable finger flaps that his mother had knit for him, and he was particularly grateful. With the flaps down now, he could keep his fingertips warm until it was time to use them on the rifle's trigger. When he'd first received them in the mail from his mother, the other men in his company were so envious of the mittens that they'd stood in line to propose outrageous and irrational trades for them. Even though he refused their offers, he immediately wrote back home to ask his mother to make enough for the rest of them. She and the other women of her church began to churn out pairs like a factory, and soon the men in Company D of the Second U.S. Sharpshooters Regiment had the warmest hands in the entire Union Army.

He pulled his Sharps rifle up to his shoulder and looked through the brass scope that ran its length to scan the woods for any movement. There was a sudden commotion above him, and he looked up to see a bald eagle being chased by a murder of crows. At first, the giant raptor's wings were spread wide as it tried to gracefully soar away from the trouble, but as more onyx pursuers joined in, it was forced to flail awkwardly in its panicked attempt to escape. Webster thought the ongoing ruckus overhead was likely to spook any nearby game, and his temper began to flare. He tightened his mittened hands on the stock of his rifle and clenched his teeth as he fought to regain his calm. He knew from experience that an emotional shooter was never accurate, so he closed his eyes and tried to empty his mind. When he did this, an unpleasant war memory barged its way in, and he was helpless to stop himself from reliving it.

During the late summer of '62, Company D had been ordered to set up an ambush outside of Rappahannock Station to hit a small Confederate force that was advancing toward them on a dirt road. He and John Tilden were sent out to find a good spot on the eastern side of the road, while the rest of the men took up position on the other side behind a stone wall. The plan was for the two sharpshooters to start picking off the leaders and drawing the enemy's fire before the rest of the company caught the rebs in a murderous crossfire. As the men settled into their places to wait, they felt the unholy warmth that comes from knowing they were in the middle of a perfect situation to kill the enemy. The men even quietly joked that any rebs that survived the melee would be like chickens running right back to the coop!

While Tilden was only a couple of years younger than Webster and was from nearby Bangor, they hadn't known each other before the war. But all the men of the company liked the young boy immensely. They joshed him incessantly because his blond hair was so fine he could never sprout enough growth on his chin to be considered a beard, and the resultant flaxen fuzz whenever he tried looked more like mold on an apple. Although they kidded him about this, the men respected Tilden because he was a good shot and nearly as unflappable as Webster in a gunfight. It was often said that both boys not only seemed absolutely fearless but were apparently charmed to survive any fray that came their way.

There was another reason Tilden was loved—he provided moments of comedic relief. He was always cracking jokes and making everyone guffaw, even when their eyes were sunken into their skulls with the fatigue and despondency the war exacted upon them. Without ever being an annoyance, the boy just knew the best time to say something humorous to brighten up their lives. And no matter what horrors the war put forth, Tilden never seemed to let the burden of them weigh him down. In fact, many commented on how bubbly his spirit still appeared after even the worst battles the sharpshooters had endured. Some of the men were even so cavalier as to suggest that they hoped all would survive to the very end of the conflict, for Tilden seemed to be just the kind of fellow who could become a lifelong friend.

The ambush was set up so perfectly, Webster had even allowed himself to daydream about how he and Tilden would whoop it up and laugh as they skedaddled back to the safety of their lines once the shooting got too intense. It was ridiculous for a sharpshooter to expect to survive an upcoming battle, but thinking that any of the soldiers in the company would laugh and skip back to their lines like they were playing games on a Sunday afternoon, well, that was an impropriety that Webster felt embarrassed about, even now. He'd seen enough of the war to know that true happiness did not exist amongst unceasing violence and death.

The day was very hot and humid. As Tilden and Webster aimed their rifles at the road in their tree-bound snipers' nests, sweat began to drip down their faces and drench their green uniforms. Both were seasoned sharpshooters, so despite their discomfort, they remained as still as statues as they waited for the rebel force to get closer. Then the crows started in on them. The noisy birds began cawing and diving down at their trees, and like loud, ebony pointers, they revealed the sharpshooters' position to anyone with a pair of half-decent eyes and ears. Webster could still feel the depth of the nausea that overwhelmed him as soon as he'd realized those crows were going to spoil everything.

Tilden quietly chuckled at the birds, dramatically shook his fist, and then stuck his tongue out at them. Even though his silly reaction diffused Webster's anger a little, he watched in horror as the boy suddenly got up to aim his rifle at the crows. Webster started to rebuke Tilden for being so careless, but before he could say anything, the boy's movements caught the eye of a rebel sharpshooter hidden somewhere in the surrounding trees. There was a distant puff of smoke, followed by the sound of the percussion, and then the delayed snapping sound of the Minie' ball as it went through the young boy's throat. Tilden's body spun and fell chest-first to the forest floor. The shot had nearly severed his neck, and the boy's head was turned completely around with eyes opened wide and his mouth in a gaping O of surprise. He looked back up at Webster like he'd just heard the most unbelievable truth.

Fighting the shock of seeing his friend killed in front of him, Webster tried to stay disciplined enough to find where the enemy shot had originated. But the targeted rebel force quickly left the road and scattered for cover to return fire. There was such a great volley at his tree that Webster was forced to jump down and take up position in the safety behind the main trunk. The rest of Company D began shooting from their positions across the road, but the perfect moment had been completely lost. With the rebs fanning out and overrunning the whole area, a general retreat was called by buglers.

Before Webster turned to run to safety, he went over to see if he could gather up Tilden's body to bring it back to camp. However, the scant thread of skin attaching the head to the body stopped him from even trying. The macabre thought of finishing the decapitation to bring the head back went through his mind, but he thought better of it. As he ran from tree to tree in retreat, the splinters of bark from the enemy's fire pelted him like hail. He found a group of large boulders on a rise to take position behind, and he waited for the first rebs foolish enough to pursue him. He calmly killed three of them before the rest of the unit decided that the direct approach was not worth it, and by the time the reb soldiers finally worked their way up to those boulders, Webster was long gone.

Afterward, Captain Small was furious and wanted to know what the hell had happened to make such a perfect situation turn out so badly. Webster almost told him about Tilden's foolish mistake, but he could not soil the boy's reputation. Instead, he made the rebel sharpshooter out to be the real culprit, purposefully overestimating the distance and skill needed for such a shot. His secret hope was that, if he inflated the shooter's lethal reputation enough, the captain would send him and some other men back to get him. But in the end, the company was ordered to another part of the battlefield, and Webster never got another chance to avenge Tilden. This missed opportunity to exact retribution upon the enemy greatly irked him—the boy from Bangor with a good sense of humor and a steady nerve deserved much more than he got in the end.

With these crows now threatening to ruin another perfect situation, Webster felt the sharp pangs of nausea rising in his stomach again. Instead of getting angrier, however, he suddenly turned to shake his fist and stick his tongue out at them. The reenactment of Tilden's silly gesture made him chuckle and refocused him. When he looked back through the scope again, he caught some movement in the small trees at the edge of the forest. He carefully pulled the mitten tips back so that his fingers could work the second trigger to make the main one into a hair trigger. He didn't need to do this, since the situation did not require that kind of quickness or precision, but he allowed his sharpshooting instincts to kick in without fighting them. He slowly cocked the hammer and made sure the cap was dry and ready to go.

The moose was struggling in the deep snow. Webster could see the large bell on its throat and knew it was a young bull. Not that this detail really mattered—he was going to shoot the animal for his family to eat, regardless of its age or gender. Even at this distance he could see that the moose was very skinny, and he pursed his lips because he knew it wouldn't provide too much meat. It was clearly starving, and if it survived the winter, it'd be much more fattened up by the fall. However, his family needed the food right now, and some moose meat was more than none.

As he watched the animal slog its way toward the opening, Webster cleared his mind. He could not think about Tilden and the crows anymore. He could not think about how his father's body was currently in its coffin in the family barn waiting for the ground to thaw enough to dig his grave. He could not think about his need to convince his younger brother, Elijah, not to enlist in the war. He especially could not think about how strangely his beloved Catherine was acting toward him, nor the rumors swirling about her and Jonathan Stiller. Even the fact that his month-long furlough would be over in three days and he would be headed back to the fighting could not distract him—he needed to think about the moose and the moose alone.

When the animal cleared the tree line, it stood still for a moment and pivoted its substantial ears around to listen for any threats. Webster exhaled and then inhaled a gradual and sustained breath to calm himself. The moose, convinced of the safety of its situation, snorted loudly like a racehorse before resuming its struggle through the snow. Webster let his breath flow out slowly and steadily as he pulled the trigger. The cap went off, the rifle kicked, and the moose went down on its knees. In one fluid motion, Webster stood up, slung his rifle, bounded over the wall, and began snowshoeing over to the wounded creature. As he neared it, he instinctively pulled his bowie knife from its sheath under his clothing and held it in his hand like a sabre. Once upon the now prone and helpless moose, he effortlessly slit its throat and then stood reverently as he watched the redness of its blood seep into the alabaster snow.

Now that his ears had stopped ringing from the percussion of the rifle, the subtle sounds of the winter woods came back to him with a renewed volume. He could hear the haunted whisper of the winds as they swayed the tops of the towering white pines, the eerie cracking and popping of the ice on the nearby frozen pond, and the sounds of his own rhythmic breathing as he caught his breath from the exertion of reaching the wounded moose. He hoped that Elijah had also heard the shot and was on his way down with the horses and the sled. This moose, albeit a skinny one, was going to be a hefty amount of weight for the two of them to carry back to the house, and the sled would make the unpleasant job of getting the meat up there a lot easier. He also felt some urgency to cut the animal into pieces and get the meat stored quickly, since it was not currently moose-hunting season in Maine. He was pretty sure the moose warden, Mr. McArthur, was probably comfortable in front of his warm fireplace right now and would never know about the shooting of this animal, but he wanted to avoid detection nonetheless. When he couldn't wait any longer, he bent down and began to eviscerate the moose with his knife.

Chapter Two

About twelve miles down the Kennebec River from Augusta, Captain Ephraim Small was looking at the winter landscape outside his window. Because his house sat atop the hills surrounding the town of Gardiner, he was able to gaze down upon the town's main street and across the wide river valley. The winter had been so cold that the river was nearly frozen solid, but the tidal ebb and flow had cracked the ice into thick slabs that were stacked now like snake scales. Some of the village's old-timers warned that, once the river became engorged with snowmelt in the spring, these pieces of ice would form a dam that would clog the river and flood the town worse than ever before. And even though Captain Small knew his house and family would be safe up high, he worried that there would be no town to return to after this war—if he was lucky enough to survive at all.

As the captain of a company of sharpshooters, he had to go through an almost endless supply of paperwork, and he was at his desk in the study to do so again now. He'd enjoyed his month-long furlough, but he wanted to spend these last few days with his wife, Martha, before returning to the front. He could hear her now, near the fireplace in the living room, as her knitting needles clicked and clacked in a miniature tattoo. And, as he listened to the cadence of this play off the ticking of the grandfather clock in the hallway, he wondered to himself if the Union soldiers who received her handmade socks would fully appreciate the rhythms of the household that were woven into them.

He looked over the papers again. According to the latest muster roll, nearly all the men of his company had reenlisted for another three years, and this made him smile. The actual number wouldn't be known until the men arrived at the Augusta train station in three days, and that was certainly enough time for some of them to have second thoughts and not show up. After what they'd seen over the course of the last three years, who could blame any of them for getting too comfortable in their own beds to want to go back to the war? The captain wouldn't begrudge any of his men if they made that choice, but he didn't want to be embarrassed by standing at the train station with only new recruits behind him.

He knew most of the men would show up. That being said, they all understood that the rest of the war was going to be a bloody affair. As soon as they could push General Lee back to Richmond, the Union Army would be able to drive the final stake into the heart of the Confederacy. But the old Virginian had proved to be more than a worthy adversary, and to get the better of him and his army was going to require much more killing and dying on both sides. If the Army was going to win this war, the sharpshooters would have to play a crucial role in applying the coup de grâce, and they all knew this was going to cost them dearly.

Captain Small shook his head. While he was buoyed by the announcement that the infamous General Ulysses S. Grant was taking charge of the Army of the United States, he was worried that the man's reputation for being reckless with the lives of the soldiers to win at all costs would result in even more deaths in his company. There was a subtle irony in that the men who were now reenlisting might finally have the leadership to win the war, but many of them wouldn't live to see that day. As a matter of fact, for some of his men, this furlough would be the last time they would ever see their loved ones or their homes. And the captain understood that this startlingly clear picture of their irrevocable mortality could make every man clench in fear. But he knew from experience that the soldiers of his company were exceedingly brave men, and he felt confident that nearly everyone would be there at the train station, ready to go back and finish off the Confederacy once and for all.

As a natural worrier, he scanned the names on the muster again to assess the likelihood that each man would show up. When he got down to the bottom and found the name of Zachary Webster, he stopped. He knew that this young man had just lost his father, and his mother and younger brother would need extra help on the family farm in Augusta. This worried the captain enough to make him tap his finger on the name a couple of times. Webster was the kind of soldier who made his commanding officers look good, and yet he did so without needing to draw attention to himself. And although the official reports of the battles would never reveal all of the man's accomplishments, the captain had heard enough of the men's tales from the battlefield to know that once Webster stepped foot onto the arena of conflict, he transformed into something to be wholly feared by the enemy.

That being said, there was also something unnerving about Webster. At the very beginning of the war, one of the greatest challenges the leaders of the newly formed Union Army faced was that most of the recruits needed to be convinced that it was acceptable to kill. After all, those young boys and men had been taught since birth that killing another man was ethically wrong or a mortal sin. It took some effort to persuade law-abiding men that it was okay to shoot at the enemy. Once they understood that they were involved in a fight to keep the country together and it was justified to fire their weapons to accomplish this, most men only needed some strict military training and a little time to complete their transition into soldiers. The shockingly bloody violence of the Battle of Bull Run made this transition irreversible for all. After those first horrific days of true battle, no one needed any more convincing, for the realities of war were startlingly clear to everyone.

But from the moment Zachary Webster stepped off the train in Washington and began training with the raw recruits at the Camp of Instruction, it was clear that he was quite different from the other men. He not only seemed to enjoy the training, but when he got the chance to fight and kill, he did so without hesitation or remorse. The other men in Company D marveled at his complete indifference during a battle. Whether he was stabbing enemy soldiers in the heart with his bayonet, slitting their throats with his knife, or shooting the tops of their heads off with his rifle, Webster always acted as if he were as troubled by his actions as a farmer is after planting a field of corn on a beautiful spring day.

Whereas some of the men in the company loved to hear themselves broadcast their own accomplishments and accolades after each battle to make themselves feel better about what they were doing, Webster never wanted to talk about any of his own actions. He'd sit with them as they gathered around the fires to chat, but never once did he speak without being prompted. And he would get so irritated when asked about the specifics of his deeds in battles, that the other men learned not to do so to avoid a black scene. Only when he was back in his tent or away from the fire could the other men freely talk about Webster's legendary exploits, and then only in guarded whispers.

A tiny black-capped chickadee now flitted on the branches outside, and the captain watched the songbird's movements. It seemed so delicate and vulnerable as it jumped to get closer to the piece of fatback that was strung in the bushes, and he marveled how the little bird happily went about its business without a care. Neither the extremely cold temperatures nor the nefarious house cat that lurked nearby in the evergreen shrubs seemed to cause the bird any concern, and the captain had to wonder if the little creature was extremely brave or just plain insane. Or both. Either way, he secretly wished he could be more like the little bird these days.

The chickadee reminded him of a story about Webster. During the early moments of the Battle of Chancellorsville the year before, the sharpshooters of Company D had been sent out with the 26th Pennsylvania to help occupy the skirmishers in front of the main body of General Sickles' troops. Their small attack initially overwhelmed the enemy, and they captured many prisoners. But then Stonewall Jackson's surprise flanking movement routed the main battle line, and the sharpshooters found themselves cut off behind a wave of enemy forces. Some men had panicked and were either killed or captured when they tried to flee—but not Webster. Instead of trying to retreat to the safety of the Union lines, he was last seen heading directly into the smoke of the oncoming forces. His movements were so purposeful that several of the men were certain he was committing suicide by choosing to die in a hail of bullets. Afterward, even the captain sat heavy with a heartfelt sadness over the young man's apparent demise.

But that night, as the company was positioned in pickets on the banks of a stream and the captain was in his tent writing up the reports from the day's events, Webster appeared out of the shadows. Somehow, the man had not only escaped the Confederate forces, but had avoided the Union provost marshals that were patrolling the camp to ensure no enemy spies could infiltrate the ranks. The men of Company D, who were bandaging their wounds as they prepared their suppers, swarmed him with attention. They wanted to know how he had escaped, but all he would tell of his ordeal was a simple statement: "Ah, boys, I've been either treed like a coon or slithering through the dirt like some kind of serpent while you've been relaxing back here, eating your fill of warm food."

He wouldn't give any more details of his escape, but he did have a lot of information about the army they were now facing. He knew the units and what states they were from. When asked how he had come to this information, he replied, "I just asked them rebs to tell me, polite and all."

When pressed for more, he merely shrugged. "I can be somewhat persuasive when I need to be."

While reporting in the captain's tent, Webster pulled some folded papers from his belt that turned out to be enemy orders. These not only revealed the strategy for some of the upcoming battles, but also had the signatures of several Confederate generals who were leading the opposing forces. After giving the papers to the captain, Webster saluted and headed out to get some food and settle in for the night. And as he walked away, Captain Small noticed that the man's gait seemed to be more from a mildly tiring journey, not a life-or-death struggle behind enemy lines.

The next day, Webster's tentmate, Samuel Worthington, quietly confided to the rest of the company that, before falling asleep, Webster had taken out a Confederate Colt 1851 Navy revolver from his waistband. When asked about it, he'd said nonchalantly that he'd gotten it during his time behind enemy lines. This type of revolver was commonly used by Confederate cavalry, and this one had the initials of the previous owner elaborately etched upon it. Samuel wanted to hear how he'd acquired it, but Webster simply stated, "I liberated it from a Johnny Reb on a pretty chestnut mount. He was quite a fighter, but I was just a little better."

As the captain thought about this memory, the house cat made a mad dash through the deep snow to get at the chickadee. But the little bird easily flew up to the lower branches of a nearby pine tree, where it taunted the cat from the safety of its new perch. The captain smiled at the songbird's guile, and then his attention returned to the muster roll. He knew he didn't need to worry about Zachary Webster returning. Of all the men in his company, he was sure that this one man was made for this war. And that made the captain shudder slightly because Webster was killing very effectively and without emotion. This brought up several troubling questions: What would a man like Zachary Webster do after the war? Could someone who was capable of killing so effortlessly during wartime resume his life as a humble farmer? What if the man survived the war and was unable to halt his murderous ways? The captain shuddered again. If the horribleness of this war had unlocked some murderous traits within Zachary Webster, and he came back home and unleashed it on the people around him...the captain almost hoped the man wouldn't survive the war.

The rawness of this thought made him stand up abruptly and walk over to the window. The cat, still struggling through the deep snow, looked over at him scornfully, but the captain did not notice because he was too focused on the tempest of disturbing thoughts inside his head. This war—this horrible, costly war—was turning everyone, including himself, into the worst kind of men. The world seemed to be filled now with nothing but the broken and corrupted versions of their former selves. And as much as he was sick and tired of the wasteful slaughters on the battlefields, he was more fearful of the days that would come after the war. For it would be then that these grotesquely distorted men would return to lead the country again. And when that happened, the populace would have no choice but to follow them. What kind of future was that?

The lone chickadee was joined by more of its kind now that the cat was no longer a threat. As they hopped along the branches, chirping their rebukes onto the invisible enemy who lurked elsewhere, the captain remembered a line from his favorite Shakespeare play, *Richard III*. He said it now aloud as if the birds were his audience: "The world is grown so bad, that wrens make prey where eagles dare not perch."

Chapter Three

Elijah Webster heard the report from his brother's rifle from down at the edge of the fields, and he slapped the horses' backs with the reins again to urge them on. The snow was so deep in places, the team seemed to disappear as they struggled through it, and he knew Zachary would be upset with him if he worked them too hard to get the sled close. But he also didn't want to miss the butchering of the kill. His brother was such an expert at dressing out game, it was almost like watching an artist at work. Plus, Elijah was keenly aware that their time together was coming to an end, and he didn't want to waste any of that time trying to get through the damn snow!

It was nice to have Zachary back at home, but it was clear that he was changed from when he'd first left for the war. He looked the same—he still had the light-brown hair that became blond in the sun, the clean-cut face he religiously kept closely shaved, and the deep-blue eyes that were intense enough to penetrate your skin. But there was something different about his brother. While Zachary had always been more reserved, his quietness now seemed to have a new source. It was either a shield to protect himself or a fence to keep people away, and Elijah couldn't figure out which. Everyone had been excited for him to come home so they could hear his stories from the war. Throughout the area, the locals were starved for the details of valor and heroism that the war undoubtedly unlocked in the young men fighting it. But with Zachary, unless someone forcefully pulled the information out of him, he remained completely tight-lipped about it all. Instead of being the anticipated fountain of exciting tales, he acted almost irritated when he was asked about the war.

His marksmanship target was an example of this. To even be eligible to join one of Hiram Berdan's sharpshooter units, each prospective candidate had to prove he was worthy of the honor by passing a rigorous marksmanship test from various distances and positions. All shots had to hit the target, of course, but their grouping was equally important. Several months after Zachary passed the rifle test and headed off to Washington City to join the sharpshooters, the Webster family had received his test target in the mail. As soon as they had it in hand, they took it into town and spared no expense to have it framed. Then they hung it proudly over the fireplace mantel for all to see. Zachary's target was shot through by the required twenty bullets, but they were in a tight circle less than four inches wide. On the paper of the target, down by the right-hand corner, none other than Brigadier General Hiram Berdan himself had written a short note:

Dear Mr. and Mrs. Webster,
Thought you might like to have this. This is one of the most impressive displays of shooting I have ever seen. Let it be known that the shot nearest to the center was from over 300 yards away! Zachary is quite handy with a rifle—the enemy certainly has a new talented sharpshooter to contend with!
Sincerely yours,
General Hiram Berdan
November 30, 1861

Whenever visitors came to the Webster homestead, they were ushered over to see this display first. The target shooting was impressive, but the personal note from General Berdan was nothing anyone had ever seen before. Yet when Zachary came home and was shown the shrine, he acted as if he was unable to look at it and walked away without comment. His negative reaction had completely surprised his mother and brother, but after a while, they saw his deep-seated pain whenever they asked him about the war, so they stopped altogether. They'd hoped he would begin talking about it if they left him alone, but quickly realized that his silence on the matter was never going to be broken. And that was when they'd begun to grasp the changes the war had made in him.

But their friends and neighbors were not so quick to learn this. As soon as they heard Zachary was home, they had unabashedly invited themselves over, parked their buggies in the yard with great fanfare, and come into the house to sit down in the parlor chairs like eager children ready to listen to his war stories. Without awkwardness or embarrassment, Zachary remained either absolutely silent in front of his audience or answered questions in such a reserved way that it was clear he was only telling people what they wanted to hear. There were no stories of adventure and conquest, just facts and figures that could have been gleaned from any newspaper account. And, as these disappointed guests left the house unfulfilled, they looked as if they'd just endured a bad meal.

From time to time, their mother would make snippy comments about how she wished Zachary was more like Andrew Hopkins from the neighboring town of Vassalboro, who had come home early after being shot outside New Orleans in '62 while fighting with the 15th Maine. It was known around the area that Hopkins captivated listeners with his exciting and heroic war stories. However, whenever she mentioned this, Zachary would nod in recognition and then coolly recommend that the next time anyone invited themselves to their house to hear his stories, she should feel free to immediately forward them on to the Hopkins residence. And that was all he would say on the matter.

Elijah knew that people were beginning to speak negatively about his brother for his refusal to tell war stories, and he figured his brother knew about this, too. But Zachary didn't seem to care in the least about it—no coercing or cajoling made him talk about the war. Gradually, though, Elijah understood that his brother was not merely being stubborn, but was protecting them all from things they might not have the ability to fully grasp. And whenever he hinted as much to his mother, the two of them would silently nod in agreement. After a while, they both understood that Zachary was sparing them the unthinkable details of the war, and they were grateful for his silence. Eventually, the uninvited guests found other sources to satisfy their curiosity and just stopped coming to the Webster house. And although this hurt their mother's pride, it allowed the three of them to breathe a sigh of relief that they did not have to participate in any more awkward performances before an unwanted audience.

That being said, Elijah could not pretend he wasn't curious about the war; truth was, he was nearly obsessed with it. He wanted to know more about it than he could get from the newspapers, and more than once, he gave some thought to visiting one of those households where the more talkative veterans were extolling their stories. In a fit of curiosity, he'd been so bold as to ask his brother how many men he'd killed in the war. Zachary had turned those intense blue eyes upon him and made Elijah's skin feel scratchy, and after what felt like an hour of silence, he'd finally responded in a low voice, "As many men as I've been asked to. And more than that."

The tautness of his brother's voice was enough to signal he wouldn't be taking any more questions, and they began to talk about something else. But for Elijah, his brother's answer was most unsatisfactory. With his interest only piqued, he'd waited for Zachary to go over to Catherine Brandford's house one day so he could head up to his brother's room and look at the wrapped Sharps rifle that stood like a sentry in the corner. Elijah carefully unwrapped it like he was freeing a religious relic from a shroud. He held the gun up in the bright sunlight, and sighed deeply at the inherent potency and beauty of it. There were numerous and organized notches in the wooden stock of the rifle, and as he drew his finger over each one, he counted them. The number seemed too high, so he went over the notches again until they stung his fingers. He rewrapped the rifle, put it back in its original position, and scurried out of the room in a growing panic. He held onto the number of notches in his head, and he hoped that before his brother went back to the war, he'd get a chance to ask about them.

Now, as Elijah whipped the horses onward, he allowed himself to ask the question that was starting to form in his head: Just who was this person who'd come back from the war? When his brother left three years prior, there was no indication that he'd be an overly successful soldier. As the older brother, Zachary was always bigger, braver, and stronger than Elijah, but he certainly wasn't the biggest, strongest, or bravest of all the young men from Augusta heading off to war. Yet the number of notches on the rifle spoke of something extraordinary. None of the war stories Elijah had ever heard involved specific killings—*inferred* killings perhaps, but never any of the gruesome details. However, his brother's rifle boldly proclaimed a real number—a very large number. And Zachary's silence only amplified its magnitude, which scared and bewitched Elijah at the same time.

When the horses reached a curve in the road and the snowdrifts became too deep for them to power through, Elijah had to concede defeat. Although he hadn't made it all the way, the sled was close enough to make their job easier. He hopped down into the snow and began snowshoeing toward where the shot had come from. By the time he found the kill site, his brother had already skinned the moose and the hide was lying in a bloody pile next to the carcass. In his hand was a very large bowie knife, and the ease with which it sliced into the remnants of the moose's neck to take out the windpipe indicated that it was razor sharp. Elijah was mesmerized by the smooth motions of his brother's hands and the size of the blade, and he said with a grunt, "Been meaning to ask you about that knife. I've seen it lying around with your clothes."

His brother looked up at him. "Yuh?"

Elijah waited for his brother to say something more, but he remained stone-faced before he resumed cutting the moose carcass. Elijah cleared his throat and added, "So where did you get it?"

Webster looked up again and held his young brother's gaze. Finally, he said, "Down in Virginia, a while back."

"You buy it?"

"Nope."

"Trade for it?"

Webster let out a sigh. And then he chuckled. "Yes, I reckon you could say that. Yes, you know what, Elijah? I did trade someone something for this-here knife."

"With someone in the company?"

"No, with a reb soldier. Now, before you ask me any more asinine questions, I got to remind you that we need to finish dressing out this moose and get it up to the barn before sundown. We can talk about the knife later, if you're still so inclined."

Elijah started to ask another question, but he sensed that his brother was about to lose his temper with him. But it made him sad to think he might never know the full story of how his older brother traded with a Confederate soldier for a knife. He thought it might be a funny story to hear.

The two brothers worked without speaking as they wrestled the heavy carcass so that Webster could get at the vitals and cut apart the joints. The meat of the moose was startlingly red in the colorless winter world, but the whitish-gray pile of entrails off to the side looked more like a mound of soap. Once Webster neatly sawed through the hip joints and sternum of the moose, he spat into the snow and said, "How old are you now, Elijah? Sixteen?"

"Yep, I will be this spring."

"March twenty-fourth, right?"

Elijah nodded with a proud grin. His brother undoubtedly had a lot on his mind, and the birthday of a younger brother seemed too trivial a fact for him to know. "Yep, I'm gonna be sixteen on March twenty-fourth. Why?"

"Have you thought about enlisting?"

The question created a void of silence between the two brothers which filled with the sound of their own breathing. Elijah was unsure how to answer. If his older brother was looking for a moment of pride, then he should tell him that he did plan to enlist. But if Zachary was feeling protective, the correct answer should be that he hadn't given it any thought. His voice had been soft when he asked the question, but Elijah couldn't tell which answer his brother wanted, so he decided to head right straight down the middle. "It's crossed my mind some."

"You gotta be your own man, Elijah, but I hope you don't."

The renewed silence of the moment was broken by the caw of a single crow overhead. Elijah looked up to find the bird, but when he looked down again, his brother was staring back at him with such force, he nearly lost his footing. After he recovered, he cleared his throat. "You remember Frederick Higgins? He was in school with me and lives over closer to the river."

"I remember him."

"Well, he went and enlisted the other day. He put a piece of paper with the number eighteen written on it in his shoe. When they asked him his age, he said, 'I'm over eighteen.' He's down south right now, fighting in the war."

"If he ain't dead."

"He ain't dead. Not everyone who goes to war dies. You're doing fine. Lots of men are down there, fighting and getting glory, and are quite alive."

"A lot are dead."

"You know, this war ain't gonna last forever—don't I get my shot at it?"

"No, you should stay here on the farm and help Ma."

Elijah shook his head. "I thought you weren't gonna tell me what to do."

Webster grimaced. "I'm not. I'm just hoping you stay on the farm, that's all."

"But why?"

"For a lot of reasons. Namely, Ma needs you. And this farm needs you, now that Pa's gone. Aren't them reasons enough?"

"Uncle Thomas and Aunt Clarice are around to help. And they can always hire some more hands to work this spring. Why should this farm be my prison?"

"Ma needs you more than the Union does."

"What does that mean?"

Webster stacked the two hind moose legs next to each other like giant pieces of firewood. "No one is gonna say it out loud, but the war is over, Elijah. The rebs are too damn proud to admit it, but their defeat at Gettysburg broke their spine. Sure, they have the fight left in 'em, but now they know they can't win this war. It's just a matter of convincing them that it's over. The Union Army's got more men than they know what to do with; they don't need you, Elijah. But Ma *does* need you here, making this farm work. Wars come and go, but this farm will be here forever."

"The newspapers ain't saying the war's over. Matter of fact, they say it ain't nowheres near to being finished. Until we're marching through the streets of Richmond, the Union Army's going to need more young men like me."

Webster spit forcefully into the snow. "Yeah, they might be saying that, but Ma needs you more."

Before Elijah could respond, Webster pulled a couple of burlap bags from his haversack. He handed one to his brother, then put the other onto his shoulder. He grabbed one moose leg and flung it onto this and started snowshoeing away. When Elijah finally heaved the other moose leg into position, his brother was already far ahead of him. He tried to catch up, but he couldn't make any ground. Webster threw the leg onto the sled and turned around to head back to the carcass. As the brothers passed each other, they barely nodded, just trudged along silently in their task.

After they'd loaded the front legs into the sled, Webster finally spoke again. "Elijah, do what you gotta do. But please think about staying on the farm through this summer and fall. Ma does need you, and if your newspapers are right, the war won't be over by then. You could still enlist, if that's what you really want to do."

Elijah nodded, but he didn't say anything at first. The snow path was now well packed down and freckled with drops of the moose's blood. All that was left to carry to the sled was the pelvis of the animal, but the sun was getting lower in the sky, so there was an urgency to their movements, though both were tired and blood-covered from their chores.

"I gotta ask you something."

Webster coughed and spat. "It ain't about the knife again, is it?"

"Naw, it ain't about the knife."

"What, then?"

"It's about the rifle."

"Aww, Elijah!" Webster moaned.

"It's got notches on it. And I was wondering—"

"How do you know my rifle's got notches on it?" Webster asked harshly.

"Well, I can see it right now."

"You can't see if it's got notches on it or not, Elijah."

"What does it matter whether I can see it or not?"

"'Cause the only way for you to know my rifle's got notches is if you've been going through my possessions. And if you're going through my possessions..."

His sentence didn't need to end. Elijah felt the hairs on his neck go straight at the implied threat. "I swear, brother, I saw it today and another time when you were headed out to the barn to chat with Pa."

Zachary Webster stopped moving and looked his brother up and down from head to toe. He loved the boy, but he could not have him going through his belongings without permission. That was unacceptable. Something like that was worthy of a good drubbing or worse from tentmates on the front. He had half a mind to administer that kind of punishment right now to teach the boy an important lesson. He put up his hand. "You are never to go through another man's possessions, Elijah. In this war that you're so chafing to get into, that'd be a good way to get beaten or shot by your own men."

"I swear I didn't go through your things, Zachary."

Webster could see the agitation his accusation was causing, and he could see the boy's fear...and he realized it was a good thing his furlough was coming to an end. It would be a relief to be away from these people he held so dear, if for no other reason than to save them from the truths they were so desperate to hear from him. After all, the answers to their questions would only cause other questions to topple down in a crushing avalanche of dark sins. How many notches *were* on his rifle? How many men *had* he killed? How many throats had he slit with that bowie knife which he gutted that Alabama farm boy to get?

Webster exhaled loudly. He knew there were half-truths horrible enough to stop further questions, so he said, "The notches are for all the soldiers I know I've shot and killed. I've fired my rifle at many more rebs than that, but I cannot be sure if the bullet from my gun killed them or not, so I don't put a tally for those. I started doing this early on in the war because I realized that I owed those men the respect of acknowledging that their deaths were caused by me and my rifle. Even if they're my enemies, they should get the chance to have a memorial to their sacrifice in this war. It's the least I could do after taking their lives."

The last comment hit Elijah like a punch to the stomach, and he looked at his brother with a wounded expression as he thought about how many notches he had counted. If those were just the men his brother knew he'd killed, and there were many more he wasn't certain about, the total number was appallingly high, and the sudden comprehension of this made sour bile gather in the back of his throat. Suddenly, going off to fight in this war didn't seem to be such a good idea anymore.

Chapter Four

Webster headed off the porch with the lantern in his right hand. The nighttime air was so cold it was painful to walk through. He could hear the gunshot-like sounds of the frozen trees popping in the nearby woods as he walked the packed-down path toward the barn, and he fought the instinct to flinch at each report. He was headed for his nightly visit with his father's body, and as the lantern's light gave him an illuminated haven in the abyss-like darkness of the moonless night, he felt the familiar comfort that came from having his rifle balanced on his shoulder as he walked along. He turned to look back at the few lit windows of the house to see if anyone was watching his progress, but no one was.

When he arrived at the barn door and undid the latch, the winter's frigidness seemed to have shrunken the whole structure. The hinges creaked jaggedly in protest as he opened the door, and the floors and walls groaned as he made his way into the center of the barn and past the stalls with the cows and horses. The animals all snorted at him for his intrusion, and he stopped to check their food and break the thick ice that had formed on their water troughs. After accomplishing this task, he continued on his way toward the small storage room where his father's body lay, the light from the lantern dawning his arrival around each corner.

His father's coffin sat on two newly constructed sawhorses, and Webster gathered the piece of black material that covered it, and he folded this and laid it down carefully on a nearby hay bale. Uncle Thomas, who sometimes worked as a carpenter in town, had constructed the pine box with lines that were so straight and with wood so beautifully grained, the sarcophagus seemed far fancier than the casket of a mere country farmer. This made Webster wonder what would happen to the countless dead from the war who hadn't been given proper burial. Unfortunately, over the last three years, he'd seen enough unburied corpses rotting on the ground to know the answer to that question.

When he first received the news that his father had died and that the ground was too frozen to bury him, he was slightly bothered by the idea that the man's body would be in the barn until the spring thaw. But now that he was getting the chance to say good-bye to his father during his furlough, he was glad it had come to pass this way. It was pretty clear that the dead man didn't care now, one way or another, but it turned out to be a good thing for him to have these last chances to talk with him. During their times together, Webster told him everything. He hadn't known how much he needed a confessor and an absolver who would listen without judging, but he found himself almost unable to stop telling Pa his long list of sins. It seemed completely plausible to him that if anyone could truly understand the contradictory nature of warfare, surely a dead man would.

"Hello, Pa," Webster said softly to the closed coffin.

He put the lantern on a nearby wooden crate and stood the rifle against the wall. Now that the room was illuminated, he set about going through his nightly routine. First, he took the lid off the coffin and put it down carefully on the floor. It was only loosely secured because the family felt that others might want to see William Webster before he was buried in the spring. Webster looked down at his father's corpse. The man wore a new suit that had been purchased for his burial, and his wan face was set like a stone statue. His beard was meticulously groomed and his hair was neatly combed back. His eyes were closed, but his frozen eyelids had contracted with the cold, so they were both open now just a slit. His father's hands were clasped together at his waist. On one of his earliest visits to the barn, Webster had made the mistake of grazing the dead man's hands, but the burning sensation that came from touching something frozen made him step back, and he never tried to touch the body again.

"Shot a moose today, Pa. It was a skinny bull, but it'll feed Ma and Elijah for a little while. Not too long—not with the way that boy eats these days! But at least it's something to tide them over."

The mention of his brother's name made him shake his head. "I tried talking Elijah out of volunteering for the war today, but it went very badly. I'm not sure he heard what I was trying to say. I described some of the horrors of war to scare him, but I think I did it too well. Now he looks at me a little differently. 'Course, I am different now, Pa, but I don't want Ma and Elijah to think too much on that fact. And, even though it's been good to be back home, I must say I'm looking forward to getting back to the war. I feel out of place here. I seem to spend all my time trying to explain myself, and that gets tiring. I gotta say, it's far simpler for me back down there at the front. I don't have to explain nothing I do down there—I just do it."

He glanced down at his father's body in the pine box. It was a body well suited for the hard labor of working on a farm. Webster bent down to feel along the seams around the base of the coffin. He knew it was far too cold for any rats or mice to be active this time of year, but he checked the coffin for holes each time he visited the barn to make sure no rodent had attempted to get inside to gnaw on his father's body. Even though he'd seen countless dead bodies chewed on by animals on the battlefields and never lost any sleep over that prospect for himself or the other soldiers, the illogical fear that that fate might befall his father in the barn kept him up at night.

"Going to see Catherine tomorrow," he blurted out suddenly. "Before I leave to go back, I want to talk to her one last time. There's something different between us, and I need her to tell me what it is." He inhaled the cold air that was tinctured with the aromas of manure, animal sweat, leather, and dried hay, and he scanned the dimly lit storage room. Then he continued in a controlled voice, "I need to ask her if those rumors I told you about are true, and I'm going to ask her to her face about it tomorrow. Not sure how it will all turn out. But that conversation has to occur."

He went over to his rifle and picked it up. He began to clean and oil it again, though it didn't need it. He was silent for a while, savoring the quietness of the barn and his father as he vigorously rubbed the oil into the steel barrel. Then he looked at his hands and said, "I haven't told you the story about me shooting the reb officer, have I, Pa? After that unfortunate incident that claimed the life of my friend Tilden, my company was about to be placed in another skirmishing role to probe the Confederate lines. But just before we were sent out, Captain Small called me over to talk to him. He ordered me to go off to the far left flank of the action by myself to cause as much trouble as I could. It was commonplace for the captain to give us such orders, so the solitary nature of this assignment didn't bother me none.

"As I grabbed my rifle and headed off, I could hear thunderous gunfire in the distance, but I felt at peace as I worked my way around the trees toward the action. When I heard the sounds of enemy soldiers in front of me, I dropped to the ground and slithered forward for a better view. On a little knoll, I found shelter behind some large stones that overlooked a place where some reb pickets had felled a big tree across the road. The soldiers thought they were alone, so some of 'em even had their heads above the trunk of that tree. I was in the perfect spot to cause the trouble I'd been ordered to, and I figured I'd pick off a couple of 'em before hightailing it out of there to find better shelter. After that, I'd double back to pick off some more of 'em. And by the time any Union force encountered that picket, they'd be so flustered and out of place, even a weak attack would drive them back. That's the way we sharpshooters fight, Pa, hit and run to create confusion.

"Anyway, just as I was looking through my scope at all the heads of the soldiers in clear view, and I started to pick out a particular one to shoot, some other motion off to the side caught my eye. I took my finger off the trigger to wait and see what it was. A young rebel officer on a beautiful sorrel came over to inspect the picket, and he not only rode right around the fallen tree, but stopped his horse in the middle of the road and glanced around the woods. To this day, Pa, I don't know why on earth he thought he could do this. He was either brave, naïve, or just a damn fool, but he made such a helluva target that the sight of him through the scope gave me goose bumps as I shot him from his horse."

He stopped talking and let the images replay in his head for a moment before resuming. "Even though I had a clear shot at his head, I gut-shot him on purpose, Pa. I was still angry about Tilden, so I aimed right for his stomach. The soldiers of the picket started firing panicked shots in every direction, but they didn't come nowhere close to me. When I didn't fire again, they all stopped their shooting to conserve ammunition. The young reb officer was moaning and groaning on the ground, and when he tried to yell to his men to help him, the combination of his wound and his fear made it hard for him to get enough air out to do so. When I heard him struggling like that, I knew I was gonna stay as long as I could just to watch him die."

Webster walked away from the coffin, rewrapped his rifle, and propped it up against the wall. He turned to look at his father and then sat down on a bale of hay. He was silent for a moment before continuing. "I rolled over and reloaded my rifle like we usually do when we're hiding behind boulders, and I waited to hear what those rebs were going to do next. They must've thought I'd skedaddled, 'cause they started sending some men over the tree trunk to get at the fallen officer. I spun back over and shot the lead soldier in the head. The rest of the men ran behind the tree, scurrying and shrieking like mice. They fired off another tremendous volley, and since that second shot gave my position away, they peppered my boulder with shot. I reloaded again and waited for them to stop shooting.

"I heard one of 'em get up on the young officer's horse and start to ride like one of Hell's horsemen to get to their headquarters to tell their leadership about the situation. Them rebs started a fearsome fire at my spot, and I crawled around so I could take better aim at the man as he rode away. I was about to shoot him, but then I came to the conclusion that I could cause more trouble for the rebs if I let him take the information of my attack to their headquarters. That way, they might even shift some of their men away from the main battle lines to bring them over to where we was."

He stood up again, went back over to the coffin, and picked up a few stray pieces of sawdust with the tips of his fingernails, careful not to make contact with the frozen body. Satisfied, he continued to speak. "Well, Pa, it turns out I ended up succeeding even more than I was hoping. I was told afterward that the rebs thought I was an advancing force, and they sent an entire regiment over to that picket. I had caused the trouble I was ordered to, and after letting them rebs waste some more ammunition on me, I got ready to go boil my shirt.

"But the young officer was starting to truly suffer there on the ground, and I could not tear myself away from the scene. When he ripped his shirt open to find the wound, he yelped when he realized that his innards were bleeding out of that bullet hole into his hands. Then he started pleading for his men to get him some water. Getting gut-shot makes you thirsty, so I'm told. His men tried to get him some, but I scattered them every time with a shot. The officer kept asking, but every time I heard him do so, I would spin over and shoot at them. They'd shoot back at me, but the boulders were good protection, and none of their shots came close. They were too scared of me to come and rout me out of my hiding place, so I had them pinned down. I was occupying an entire picket, which was what I was supposed to do.

"When the officer started calling out for his mother and then begging for mercy from God, I felt some regret that I had not shot him in the head in the first place. But Tilden never got a chance to beg for his life, so there was a side of me that was happy this reb officer was suffering. That's something I ain't too proud of, Pa."

His voice trailed off as he listened for any sounds in the silent barn. The scene from that day played over again in his head. The way the rebs had shouted at him and called him names made him grin at the time, but now they made him grimace. He continued, "When I heard troops advancing toward me off in the distance, I knew their reinforcements were coming and it was time for me to go. I figured a reb sharpshooter or two were probably taking position nearby, so I knew I needed to be careful not to give 'em any good shots. I guess them picket soldiers were waiting for the reinforcements to get there 'cause there was a long lull in the gunfire. I spun a different direction than before, and I shot that wounded young officer in the head. I kept rolling and was up and running before the plume of my rifle smoke cleared.

"The hail of bullets that followed me was like a hornet's nest of lead, Pa. Trees were splintering all around me as I raced through the forest. One shot—I know it was from a rebel sharpshooter somewhere nearby—grazed my elbow. It actually pierced my tunic and plowed a furrow through the skin there. It hurt bad, and I felt the trickle of blood, but I didn't stop running till I was safely back with my company. They were engaged in their own skirmish near a fence, and we fought there for the rest of the day. That night, my captain asked for a report of my actions and I told him that I exchanged fire with a reb picket on the road and had shot an officer on horseback, but I didn't tell him about the gut shot, Pa. Truth is, I've never told *anyone* about it!"

He stood up and gently grabbed the coffin's lid. He put it back into place and dusted it off with his hand. Then he said in a reverent whisper, "But that's the thing, Pa—even though I can still hear that young reb officer in my head, it doesn't haunt me none. War is a ripely unpleasant business, but it don't trouble me much. Truth be told, I actually find myself enjoying it. And I guess that makes me not right in the eyes of a good many people, Pa, but I can't say that that worries me none neither."

Chapter Five

The raging blaze in the fireplace made the sitting room of the Brandford house too warm to be comfortable, and Zachary Webster and Catherine sat in the midst of a stony silence with their foreheads glistening with sweat and their apprehensive eyes scanning the room. Their conversation had begun pleasantly enough, but once it became harder to get the right words out, they both had stopped talking. When one of the logs suddenly popped and sent sparks onto the stone hearth, Webster looked down at the embers dying slowly and thought to himself that they were a fitting image for this exact moment. He looked back up at Catherine to see if she was startled by the invasion into their silence, but her face showed no change. She remained rigid and facing him, so he said quietly, "I cannot remember a time when it has been so cold for this long."

She nodded. "It has most definitely been a long, cold winter here in Maine, Zachary."

He waited for more, but that was all she seemed ready to say. He tilted his head and felt himself slow his breathing. He wasn't prepared for his Catherine to be so distant and stoic on their last visit together, and her continued silence slightly unnerved him. Then again, perhaps it was the answer to his unasked question.

"It *has* been a long, cold winter here in Maine," she repeated.

He nodded. "It's been a long, cold winter everywhere, Catherine."

Silence rushed in to fill the space again, and he looked around. He'd been a frequent guest in this very room before the war, but now he felt as if he were trapped behind enemy lines. Catherine's expression was no different from the defiant glances the Union soldiers received from those Virginians who watched them march past. He decided to charge right in, saying, "I was wondering how come you stopped writing to me, Catherine."

She continued to look at him with impassive eyes, but then she finally spoke in a soft but certain voice, "But I didn't stop writing you, Zachary."

"Well, no, not completely. But it weren't as frequent as it once was. I guess I just got to wondering if I did something wrong."

She snorted and looked up at the ceiling. "No, Zachary, you didn't do anything."

"Getting your letters was always the highlight of my days, so when I didn't hear from you..."

"I'm sorry, Zachary, but I *have* been writing to you. Maybe they just haven't been delivering all of your mail."

His shoulders slumped slightly. "Sure, that's probably it. I guess what I'm really trying to say is, if there ever was a reason you didn't feel like writing me, I'd hope that you'd let me know what I did to make you feel that way."

She let the silence surround them again and then her head moved subtly, but he could not tell if it was a nod or a shake. Webster knew that he should excuse himself and leave, but he needed to hear the answers to his questions. He continued, "It's just that, since I've been home, things have been different between you and me. And I've heard things—"

"Oh, pray tell, Zachary Webster, what exactly have you heard?"

He stammered at the sudden venom in her voice. "Well, uh, I'm sure it's nothing, really."

"Come on, Zachary, it must be something. Why else would you have brought it up? Do tell me what you've heard."

"Just that you might have a new...interest."

"An *interest*?" she asked with a toothy leer. "You mean like knitting?"

He looked down at his feet. "No, like a new beau."

She was suddenly standing up in front of him with her hands on her hips and a snarl on her face. "Oh, really? And when did the great Zachary Webster start listening to the idle chatter of foolish old toothless women spreading malicious rumors?"

He shook his head and put his hand out to touch her wrist, but she pulled away from him. "I don't, Catherine. But it got me to wondering. You didn't seem to be writing me as often. Then, when I got home, you didn't seem to want to spend as much time together as I was hoping for. So when I heard the rumors about you and Jonathan Stiller, I started to wonder about you and me."

"Ah, Jonathan Stiller. So the old women are chattering about Jonathan and me, are they? What exactly are they saying, Zachary?"

"Please, Catherine, why don't you sit down and we can just talk about something else. I didn't mean to upset you—I just thought it might be good to discuss these things before I head back to the war. I'd like to leave here today knowing that things are fine between us, that's all."

Catherine hesitantly sat back down, but she now glared at him. "Yes, Zachary, let's discuss these things."

"Well, is Jonathan Stiller your new beau?"

Catherine was up again, pointing straight at his heart. He could see her finger trembling. "You have no right to come into my house and ask such questions as these, Zachary Webster! You have no right!"

And he knew. He'd known it all along, but he was trying hard to fool himself into thinking that the worst ideas in his head were not true. But Catherine's rage told him they were. It was clear now that she'd fallen in love with Jonathan Stiller while he'd been away fighting. Before the war, the discovery that the woman he planned to marry was in love with another man would have broken his heart so badly he would have excused himself to drive home and cry his tears in the privacy of his own bedroom. But now, he felt no emotion. As a soldier, he'd been forced to calmly accept everything at face value, so there was no more room in his world for sentimentality. He stood up easily. "You're absolutely right, Catherine. I have no right to ask these questions of you in your house. I apologize for that, and I thank you for taking the time to visit with me today. I wish you well in the future."

The sudden casualness of his motions and voice caused a shiver to run up Catherine's spine. He was not getting up to produce more drama; he was merely standing up to leave. She spoke soothingly to him. "Oh, Zachary, you don't have to go. I'm so sorry I'm being argumentative like this today. All those people who've been talking behind my back have me mad as a wet hen. Why don't you and I just sit down and talk about something else? I will behave, I promise."

"Naw, I need to get back to the farm, Catherine. I've got some things to take care of. I do truly appreciate you taking the time to talk to me today."

She shook her head. "Don't go, Zachary. I was just being snippy."

"But I do have to go. Good-bye, Catherine."

"You don't have to give up so easily, Zachary."

"Give up?"

"What I mean is, you could fight for me."

Webster's smile became as tight as a piano wire. "You know, this war has taught me so many lessons about life, Catherine, it really has. In a mere span of three years, it has erased and eclipsed everything I've ever known and understood. One moment, right was right, left was left, up was up, and down was down. Then this war showed me that none of that's true. I keep hoping it's all some kind of lens that's distorting reality for its own purposes, but I know, deep in the marrow of my bones, that the world has changed and it will never go back to the way it was. Nowadays, my right is war, left is war, up is war, and down is war. And it ain't ever gonna be any different for me—not even when the fighting stops."

"Life changes us all, Zachary. That doesn't mean we shouldn't fight for what we want or for what we believe in, does it?" Catherine said as she slowly sat back down in her chair.

"For example, last year I found myself face-to-face with a reb soldier just outside of Fredericksburg. I was reconnoitering behind enemy lines, and while I moved from tree to tree in that lush Virginia forest, I stumbled right onto the man. His uniform was gray and tattered, and I could smell cigar smoke on him. I have no idea what he was doing out there by himself. He could have been picking blackberries or foraging for food. Maybe he was looking for a dignified place to go to the bathroom with some privacy. I don't rightly know. But I came upon him and I knew that if he got a chance to yell out, I'd be in hot water with a bunch of swarming, shooting rebs descending upon me. But he'd already seen me, so I had to do something right quick. Without thinking too much, I swept his legs with my rifle, got him on his backside, and then brought my rifle butt down onto his face."

Catherine was so riveted by his story that her body leaned heavily against the chair as if prepared for some unforeseeable collision. Webster barely acted as if she was in the room with him anymore, and he continued speaking to no one in particular. "He started to beg, 'Please, don't kill me. Please, don't kill me.' So I hit him with my rifle butt again as hard as I could manage, and it made the sound of a ripe pumpkin being broken open on the ground. When he tried to beg a second time, the broken teeth and blood made him sputter and lisp. It was hard to understand what he was saying, but he kept trying. He even got out that he was a father of four back in Mississippi, and he begged for his life again and again. Like that mattered at all!"

When Catherine grabbed his wrist, she realized there was no more life or warmth in it than a dry piece of firewood. She let go of it suddenly and dropped her arm as if it were too heavy to hold aloft. "Oh, Zachary, please tell me you showed the man mercy!"

His eyes suddenly bored down on her, and she felt a tingle in the pit of her stomach. He gave her a patronizing grin. "We are fighting a *war*, Catherine! You people, living up here in this peaceful garden of nonviolence in Maine, far away from all the killing, sometimes you forget that. To you, the war is nothing more than exciting stories and tales of heroism that you want to sit around your warm parlors and swoon romantically about. But war is nothing like that! It's the coppery taste of blood, the smell of shit and death and brimstone, the constant ringing in your ears from the firing of guns and cannons. It's the moaning of the wounded as they beg to die! There are no good qualities in war, Catherine. There's no mercy, no heroism, no kindness or beauty in war—there is only kill or be killed. And the day a soldier forgets that and looks for noble qualities is the day he dies. So, no, Catherine, I did not show any mercy to that reb; I finished the job at hand. He didn't give me away, and I continued reconnoitering until I had enough information to give my captain to help us win the next battle.

"Much later, I gave some thought to what happened in those woods with that reb. From an experience like that, I learned that it makes no sense to beg in this world. Begging doesn't get you nothing but shame. In the end, there was not one thing that reb could have said to me or done that would have kept him alive. Not one. You see, no matter how much you want something or how much you think you deserve it, begging can't get it for you. In the end, it's better to accept your fate with dignity."

"You could have spared his life, Zachary. You could have shown mercy."

He snorted with contempt. "There weren't no possibility of that, Catherine."

She waited for him to add something more, but he seemed content with what he'd already said. She look down at the floor and asked, "So, Zachary, what does that story mean for you and me?"

When he looked at her, his blue eyes seemed to evaluate her like a man surveying the best tree to fell in a woodlot. His voice was even and flat when he finally replied. "Well, Catherine, I think it means that I won't be begging for anything, today or ever again."

"But what if you were asked to fight for something? You could do that, right?" Catherine asked with passion.

Webster shook his head and clicked his tongue. "I was fighting for the Union when I killed that begging reb outside of Fredericksburg. Do you really want that side of me to come out...for you?"

When she was silent for too long, he said with an awkward smile, "So, Catherine, I thank you for taking the time to talk with me and I bid you a good afternoon."

Catherine Brandford started to say something, but Zachary Webster was already walking out of the room without another glance at her. As she heard the door close quietly and the crunching of his footsteps in the snow outside, she wondered what emotion was keeping her anchored in her chair rather than pursuing Zachary to smooth things over with him—fear, anger, or pride. She sat and listened to the clock tick, the fire pop, and the sounds of Zachary Webster getting farther and farther away. When she finally took a deep breath and felt the overwhelming sense of relief wash over her, she instantly knew that the emotion she'd felt was fear.

Chapter Six

As he put the horse away in the barn, Zachary Webster was still processing his visit with Catherine. He knew that losing the woman he hoped to marry should make him angry, but he felt no umbrage. Instead, he was consumed by the burgeoning eagerness to get back to the war. For, as he had told his father, he did not seem to fit in around here anymore. He belonged back in the war. He was so deep in these thoughts as he strode toward the house that he hadn't noticed the presence of an unfamiliar buggy in the dooryard until he was nearly upon it. Although he wanted nothing more than to pack up his gear, he felt an almost paternal responsibility to check on who was visiting the family farm at this time of day.

Inside, there were strong aromas of freshly made coffee and bread. He hung his heavy coat on one of the hooks by the door and walked into the parlor to see who was visiting. His mother, Elijah, and Angus McArthur were seated and comfortably chatting with coffee cups and saucers in their hands. He quickly assessed the situation—his mother looked excited for the company, but Elijah looked as edgy as a trapped animal. Mr. McArthur was an older man with white hair parted in the middle and a bushy white walrus mustache. He was wearing a brown suit with thin blue pinstripes and a Moose Warden copper badge on his left lapel. When the old man stood to offer his hand, Webster instantly knew why he was there.

"Look who stopped for a visit, Zachary. It's Mr. McArthur!" If his mother understood the implications of the man's visit, that comprehension was overshadowed by the excitement of an unannounced guest in her house.

"Hello, Zachary. It's been quite some time since I've seen you."

"Yes, sir, it has, Mr. McArthur."

"Oh, please, call me Angus. Any man who is a celebrated war veteran like yourself has the right to call me by my first name," the old man said with a grin as he sat back down into the comfortable chair. Mrs. Webster was seated on the sofa with Elijah next to her, but Webster remained standing.

"That's right, Zachary, Mr. McArthur came to hear some stories from you about the war." Her voice took on a pleading softness. "Please indulge us with a story, won't you?"

Normally, he would have gracefully declined or found some benign anecdote to satisfy the inane request, but Catherine's response to his ugly story had opened a vault in his heart, and cruelty seemed to be seeping out of him now. He looked at the expectant faces of his mother, his brother, and Mr. McArthur, and he no longer felt any need to protect them. He smiled as he said smoothly, "Of course, Mother. I just finished telling a rousing story to Catherine, and she was spellbound by it, or so it seemed. Two war stories in one day—that's certainly a full day for me, huh? Hmm, well, let's see... Which story should I tell? How about the action at South Mountain? It was an important battle before Antietam. Does that sound good, Angus?"

"Oh, yes, I've read quite a lot about Antietam. McClellan really licked Lee in that battle, didn't he?" Mr. McArthur asked as he leaned forward to hear Zachary's tale.

"Well, war isn't quite the same in the midst of the action as it reads in your newspapers here, Angus. We common soldiers have such a limited view of it all. We only see what's in front of us. I guess you could say we only get to see what we're pointing our guns at. Now the generals, they get the big picture. With their giant maps in front of them in their spacious tents, they have the opportunity to see the entire battlefield. But for us soldiers, we only go where the captains tell us to go. And during most battles like at Antietam or Gettysburg, we do what we're told—march here, march there, fight here, kill there, die everywhere. So it's hard for us to tell if the battle is being won by the Union or by the rebs when the shooting and shouting start. Actually, the only thing I try to keep in mind is not getting killed. So I wouldn't know if McClellan gave Lee a good licking or not at Antietam. But I can tell you it was one of the most brutal battles I've ever fought in, that's for sure. I saw a lot of good men die there."

Elijah, who was watching his brother tensely, now seemed to relax as a long-awaited story was commencing. There was an evenness to Zachary's voice, and he was less worried that something bad was going to happen. He wanted to hear the story, so he found himself listening wide-eyed like an eager child.

Webster went on, "After the fight for South Mountain, where even some regular units were turned into skirmishers so they could fight our way for the day, I guess we sharpshooters thought that the Battle of Antietam was going to be one of those times when we were used properly. Ah, I will never forget how we all made our way up that mountain just looking for someone to shoot at! We moved boulder to boulder as we watched for any target. A head would pop up above the rocks like some kind of groundhog, and we'd put a bullet into it—*boom*!—and there'd be that pink cloud of spray where the man's head had been. There was so much killing that day, the sides of the mountain looked like it had patches of pink lady's slippers on it. Oh my, it was good hunting! I almost lost track of just how many rebs I killed. Well, almost.

"When a few of us found a reb mountain howitzer pulled by a team of mules—which most men call a 'Jackass Gun'—that was firing down on the nearby Pennsylvania Bucktails, we all took aim and picked off the men working the gun. So many bullets hit their bodies at the same time, they would palsy and shake before falling to the ground! We even shot the mules pulling the gun before we moved on to the next target. It was a complete waste of ammunition to do this, but we were having so much fun, and it made moving that gun so much more difficult, so we kept firing away until everything was dead. We continued up the mountain that way and swept the whole thing clean!

"I guess that's why our spirits were so high when we were ordered to the battlefield in Miller's Cornfield the next day. We were ready to continue doing what we do best, but we were suddenly commanded to take our place in line like ordinary infantry. You see, on that day and in that battle, we were considered nothing special. We were just regular forces to be led to slaughter like the rest of the Blue Coats. *Tsk-tsk*, what a waste!

"Anyway, we headed into that cornfield to support Gibbon's Iron Brigade, which was made up of good Wisconsin and Indiana boys. We walked into those tall stalks of corn and were ordered to lie down and take cover. After a short time, we were told to stand up and engage the enemy to our right. We could see there was action in the cleared fields beyond, and the bullets and shot were as thick as black flies. Almost immediately after we emerged from the protection of the cornstalks, several members of my company were hit. We returned a withering fire, and this set the rebs to running! We gave chase. It was like shooting fish in a barrel! We could see the dust from the uniforms puff off of them as we hit 'em, and we watched their bodies twist in the air with each successful shot. Then we ran smack into their reinforcements, which we continued to push back with fierce fire from our rifles. I tell you all, it looked like we had won the day.

"Then we were overwhelmed by a huge contingent of fresh reb troops. They said it was the infamous Hood's Texans and Law's Brigade, but I don't know for sure. All I know is that the air was full of their lead. We tried to hold them off, but their shots were hitting home too often. Men on both sides of me fell dead onto the ground. The withering volleys of the enemy stopped us in our tracks and then started to brush us back the way we'd come.

"We were given the order to fall back. Those fields were suddenly aswarm with rebs, and we ran back toward the cornfield, firing all the time at those bastards as they tried to catch up to us. There was no time to stop and help the wounded—we just left 'em there, mewing like kittens. Then those rebs began shrieking like banshees, hollering that damn noise of theirs. You all, of course, know about the 'rebel yell,' right?"

He stopped and looked at them. His abrupt question had caught them off guard, and they were not able to answer. He shook his head in annoyance. "Them rebs have this scream that they use when they throw themselves into battle. It's unlike anything I've ever heard in my life, and I've heard it now over a hundred times, I suspect. It still cuts to the quick. I have dreams sometimes of the sound of shrieking men, thousands of them, hollering at us with fear and savage contempt, as they get ready to plunge into the fray. I've met more than a few veteran soldiers who piss their pants whenever they hear that yell.

"Anyway, them charging rebs were right on our tails as we came upon Campbell's Battery B. The men in that unit were just about to skedaddle, but we rallied 'em. We all continued to fire at the advancing rebel flood, and it looked less than hopeful. But then General Gibbon himself noticed that the battery was overshooting the mark, and he came over and adjusted several of the elevating screws and ordered the Napoleons loaded with canister. Of course, you've read the newspapers and know all about canister, huh?"

His question had such a subtle sharpness to it that, although Mr. McArthur and Elijah had some idea of what it was, they merely shrugged. Webster showed his contempt for their lack of knowledge by rolling his eyes. "Canister is like buckshot for cannons. It's a tin canister with dozens of iron balls the size of plums inside. This particular ammunition is extremely effective when fired upon soldiers at close range. I gotta tell you, seeing the reaction of the human body to a load of canister hitting it is awe-inspiring! Those metal balls chew everything up in their path, turning men into pieces of pulp in a matter of seconds. It's truly amazing when seen firsthand!

"Fact o' business, after General Gibbon's corrections, that battery started pumping their canister fire onto that advancing rebel force with devastating results. We watched as entire groups of men were thrown up in the air, their bodies split in two like twigs and their hats thrown even farther like some kind of celebration. As the shells landed in that cornfield, we could see their groundswell lifting the bodies and spreading them like grass seed. One man in my unit swore that he saw an arm, cleaved from its body like it was done by a professional butcher, thrown into the air as high as the crown of a young tree!

"We sharpshooters continued to fire our rifles into the bloody massacre and take out any individuals that survived the torrential shelling, and the battery kept blazing away until they had almost no ammunition left. Once fresh troops arrived, us surviving members of the sharpshooter regiment and the men of the battery were ordered to fall back. Our reinforcements then pushed the enemy back across the Pike and past the Dunker Church. Since we'd lost nearly half of our men, we were kept in reserve for the rest of the day and didn't get back to the battlefield again. But I hear tell that they had one helluva time cleaning up that cornfield afterward. All the cornstalks were cut down to the ground as neatly as if a giant razor-sharp scythe had been used. But the ground was covered with a mixture of body parts, lumps of flesh, random piles of guts, and a slick layer of blood. They couldn't actually bury individual bodies and had to dig giant trenches to scoop the mess into and bury it all together. I guess you could say that Miller's Cornfield is now fertilized by the dead from both sides.

"So, you see, Mr. McArthur, when I think back on the Battle of Antietam, I don't think about General George B. McClellan or General Robert E. Lee. I don't think about the Army of the Potomac or the Army of Northern Virginia. When I remember that battle, my memories are all about the men I fought alongside and had come to love like family who are still there, their pulverized bodies now part of the soil of that battlefield."

Webster stopped talking; his story was done. He glanced at the expressions of his audience, and the horrified and shocked looks on their faces made him grin. They had asked for something, but were ill-prepared to hear the truth, and he felt the satisfaction of knowing that their perspective was now vastly and irreparably changed.

Finally, Mr. McArthur cleared his throat and said quickly, "Well, that is certainly an interesting story, Zachary. It's unlike most stories I've heard about the war."

"I've got others, Angus, if you want me to tell them to you."

"No, not today—I really must be going. Abigail expects me home for dinner. I just came over to hear a story from you before you head back down there."

"Oh, okay, Angus. Maybe I can come over to your house sometime and tell you and Mrs. McArthur some more of my stories, huh? I've got hundreds of 'em."

The old man looked panicked. "Oh, I don't know about that, Zachary. I'm not sure Abigail is up to hearing much about the war. But maybe you and I might get together to talk more in the future."

"If I survive this war, Angus, I promise I will come over and tell you many more stories of killing and dying in battle."

The older man appeared horrified by this offer, and he looked around at Mrs. Webster and Elijah to gauge their reaction to the story. When he saw they were equally discomforted by it, he stated evenly, "Uh, before I go home, I do have a question I need to ask."

"What is that, Angus?"

"Well, I was wondering if any of you have knowledge about a moose being shot around these parts?"

"No, Mr. McArthur, why would you ask?" Webster questioned, arching his eyebrows.

The old man looked directly into his eyes, but he looked away quickly when their sharpness scared him. "Oh, never mind. I'm sorry I even mentioned it. I'm sure it's just a little confusion, that's all. Well, I better be going. It's been wonderful visiting with you all."

"Oh, thank you for coming today for a visit, Angus!" Mrs. Webster said sadly.

"A little confusion?" Webster spoke with metal in his voice. "What kind of confusion, Mr. McArthur?"

"Oh, I'm sure it's nothing, Zachary. I'm truly sorry I brought it up."

"But you did bring it up, Mr. McArthur. Clearly, you wanted some kind of an answer from us."

"Well, it's just that I received a report about a moose being shot and butchered on your property. And apparently there was also some evidence that the meat was brought up this way."

"Hmm. Did you see the moose in question?"

The tense silence of the room was interrupted by Elijah's sudden sneeze. The three adults turned to look at him, then Mr. McArthur muttered, "No, I didn't."

When Webster spoke again, his voice was thin and taut. "I'm sorry, Mr. McArthur, I'm a little perplexed, then. You asked us if we knew anything about a moose being taken out of season, but you personally did not hear the shot or see the animal that was supposedly killed, right?"

Mr. McArthur looked hard at him. "That is all true, Zachary."

"Oh. And who was this report from, Mr. McArthur?"

"That's not really important, is it, Zachary? As Moose Warden, people notify me about all sorts of things. And I think this time there was some confusion about the facts. Let's leave it at that."

"This report came from *who*?" Webster asked, his voice getting more powerful. "I think if someone is accusing me of doing something wrong, I have the right to know who my accuser is. Don't you, Mr. McArthur?"

"Now, now, Zachary, I never said anything about an accusation. I merely asked—"

"You merely *asked*, Mr. McArthur, if I knew about a moose that was shot out of season on our property and then transported toward this house. That is what you asked me, isn't it?"

Mr. McArthur fidgeted nervously and looked to Mrs. Webster for some kind of support. She looked back earnestly but said nothing. He sighed. "Yes, I guess that is one way of looking at my question to you. But I did not mean to upset you."

"You haven't upset me, Mr. McArthur, not in the least. What you have done is accuse me and my family of doing something illegal."

As if suddenly realizing that her son was getting agitated, and feeling some concern as to what he was capable of, Mrs. Webster said meekly, "I'm sure Mr. McArthur didn't intend to accuse anyone, Zachary. He's merely following up on something that someone said, that is all."

"Quite right, quite right. I'm just doing my job, Zachary. Following up on something I heard."

"From *who*?" Webster repeated his question menacingly.

Mr. McArthur scratched his head and shrugged his shoulders. "It doesn't really matter, Zachary, does it?"

"It does to me. I do not take kindly to anyone spewing false lies about me or my family."

Mr. McArthur exhaled loudly. "I'm sure it is just a big misunderstanding. All I can tell you is that Jonathan Stiller was setting traps over on Walker's Point on the pond the other day and he thought he heard a shot come from around here. When he went over to investigate, he said that he'd come to a place between your fields and the pond that looked like a moose had been butchered there. He said there were sled tracks headed up this way."

"Well, Mr. McArthur, we could go out there right now, just you and me, and you could see for yourself if Mr. Stiller is right with his allegations."

Mr. McArthur looked out the windows of the parlor. By the way his head drooped and he clucked his tongue, Webster knew the old man was not going to snowshoe in the darkening afternoon. He shook his head and clucked his tongue again. "No, Zachary, I don't need to head out there to check right now. I'm just following up with a complaint I received."

Mrs. Webster gasped, and then asked pathetically, "So you didn't come here today for just a visit, Angus? You came here to accuse us of poaching?"

"No, no, Mrs. Webster, I wanted to see you and your boys. But I am the Moose Warden for this area. So when I'm told that a moose might have been taken out of season, I have to at least inquire about it. I thought that by coming here I might kill two birds with one stone, so to speak."

"So now you're going to talk to Jonathan Stiller, right?" Webster hissed.

"I am?"

"Well, of course, Mr. McArthur, you need to follow up on the fact that he admitted he was trespassing on our property."

"Walker's Point is not on your property, Zachary. If he was setting traps there, he was perfectly legal in doing that."

"That's very true. But if, as you said, he came over to investigate this supposed butcher spot and saw sleigh tracks coming straight up to this house, I believe when he did that, the man trespassed grossly onto my family's land. And I want there to be the normal consequences for that transgression."

No one spoke. Elijah, who was amazed at the way his brother was now commanding an older authoritarian like Angus McArthur on how to do his job, looked back and forth between the two men and his mother to see who was going to respond first. His brother looked like he was awaiting a reply and his mother seemed too shocked to say anything. Finally, Mr. McArthur coughed and said, "No, Zachary, I am not going to speak to Jonathan Stiller. I'm the Moose Warden, so I only have the authority to do something about moose taken out of season. Matters of trespassing are out of my jurisdiction. If you want to pursue that, you will need to talk with the sheriff about it. As for Mr. Stiller, I will let him know that I've spoken to you about the moose and there must have been a misunderstanding. *That* is what I am going to do."

"I see. So I need to go over and speak to Mr. Stiller myself, huh?"

"Now, Zachary, I've known your father, God rest his soul, and your mother for so long, I feel I can speak to you more directly than most. Do *not* confront Jonathan Stiller. He thought he heard and saw something egregious and reported it to the proper authority. I have followed it up according to the extent of my position, and I've come to the conclusion that there's no need to pursue it any further—for me, this matter is closed. Now, if you do feel that another crime happened, like trespassing or such, then it is your prerogative to pursue the matter with the proper agent of the law, namely, Sheriff Brackett. However, confronting Jonathan Stiller directly would be very foolish and inflammatory as well. Nothing good could come of that!"

No one spoke for another tense moment or two. Finally, Mr. McArthur stood up. "Well, I must really be going. Abigail does expect me."

Mrs. Webster stood and began talking hurriedly, "Well, thank you for coming. It was good to visit, nice to see you. Please give my best to Abigail."

Mr. McArthur could not take his eyes off of Zachary Webster. The boy's blue eyes crackled with energy and the smirk on his face was disconcerting. The old man turned his head just a little and nodded to the Websters, but he positioned his body in such a way that he was able to walk out without completely turning his back on them.

Chapter Seven

When Zachary Webster saw Jonathan Stiller in downtown Augusta the next day, it was purely happenstance. Both men had gone into town to run errands—one getting supplies for the farm before he headed back to the war, and the other taking care of some personal business. As a matter of fact, Webster would not have known Stiller was nearby if he hadn't heard Mrs. McKnight call the man's name as he was leaving the General Store—at which point no one was more surprised than him.

Just the night before, as he'd relayed to his father how his beloved Catherine had been stolen from him by the very man who was also accusing his family of poaching, Webster had come to a momentous conclusion: he now considered Jonathan Stiller his enemy. The deep impact of this statement made him pause for a moment, but when he resumed speaking again, he quickly relayed to his father the battlefield deduction that followed such a conclusion. It was the simple truth which all soldiers lived by—once the enemy was located, they were to be killed wherever and whenever the opportunity arose. Webster had pledged to his father that, although he had no intention of confronting Stiller before heading back to the fighting, if he was lucky enough to survive the war and return to Augusta, he'd kill the man the first chance he got.

But now, as he carefully trailed Jonathan Stiller and watched the man go inside Sutler's Tobacco Shop, he knew this was exactly the right opportunity. And, although downtown Augusta bore no similarity to the dense woods or the rolling fields that made up the battlefields he was used to fighting on, Webster found himself unconsciously reverting to a sharpshooter again. His senses became so acute, he was aware of the sights and sounds of his surroundings with an alarming vividness. He instinctively knew from which direction the wind blew and where the sun was in the sky, and he could feel the even beats of his heart and the steady rhythm of his breathing. He was no longer a man buying farm supplies; he was now a veteran soldier hunting an enemy. And as such, he was programmed to continue scouting his target, avoiding detection, and waiting for the most advantageous time to kill and get away.

When he saw Stiller leave Sutler's Tobacco Shop and head down the snow-packed sidewalk toward Mulkern's Tavern, Webster touched the bowie knife in its sheath on his back. Just the knife's presence reminded him that he needed to come up with a proper tactical assessment of the battlefield to develop the appropriate strategy. The current conditions were unacceptable. Even though the street was nearly deserted, killing a person in broad daylight and in such a public place could not be accomplished without a witness. So he needed to continue following the man until they came to a place that presented a better ambush site. How many times had he done this during the war? Too many. As a sharpshooter, he constantly had to bide his time in the field for just the right moment to kill his enemy and get away safely to do it again another day. As they were told repeatedly, a live sharpshooter was far more important to winning the war than a dead one. If the conditions were not right for taking care of Jonathan Stiller at this very moment, there'd be plenty of time to wait for them to develop. When it came to killing, Zachary Webster was a patient man.

When Stiller went into Mulkern's Tavern, Webster crossed the snow-covered street and entered an alleyway to wait until the man came back out. This was the perfect location for stalking his prey, as Webster could clearly see the main entrance of the tavern and yet be sheltered from the view of any random pedestrian whose misfortune it was to be out on such a cold day. He took up position behind a stack of pallets. It began to snow, and the small gritty flakes gathered on his shoulders and his hat. He felt neither the cold nor the snow, but remained wholly focused on the doorway of the tavern across the street.

When Jonathan Stiller finally came back outside, he had the collar of his jacket pulled up almost to the brim of his hat to keep the warmth close to his body. He turned and headed down the main street away from the center of town. Webster was out of the alley and behind the man before he'd even left the block. By the way Stiller ambled along, it was clear that he was completely unconcerned with anything going on around him. Truthfully, he wouldn't have known if he was being followed by a marching band because his mind was so occupied by thoughts of Catherine Brandford. The two pints he'd just had in the tavern were not only warming his insides, they were making his thoughts too fuzzy to effectively plan how he was going to win the girl's heart outright after her beau returned to the war. He looked forward to chatting about the details of that pursuit with his older brother, Jedediah, during their next conversation.

When Stiller suddenly turned onto a side street that ran up the hill and away from the river, Webster instantly knew they were headed toward an area occupied mostly by warehouses. This made his heart beat quicker because it was the perfect location to kill the man and get away without any witnesses. As Stiller neared an alley between two brick warehouses, Webster pulled the knife from its sheath and began to run toward him.

Jonathan Stiller was caught completely off guard by the assault. After being knocked to the ground, it took a moment for his senses to recover from the brutal attack. But when they did, he saw a man standing menacingly in front of him with a huge knife in his hands. He did not recognize his attacker at first, but it was apparent from the man's stance that he intended to kill him. Any pain from the ambush subsided quickly with the understanding of the severity of his situation.

Webster snarled, "Do you know who I am?"

Stiller shook his head. "Can't say that I do."

"My name is Zachary Webster."

Jonathan Stiller stood up and carefully swiped the snow from his pants. "Well, this is a very interesting way of introducing yourself, Mr. Webster."

Webster growled, "So now you know why we're here, right?"

Stiller nodded. "Catherine Brandford."

"Yes, that's right."

Stiller tried to surprise his attacker by suddenly throwing himself at him. He had hoped he could dislodge the giant knife, but Webster not only deftly avoided the charge, he thrust his knee into Stiller's gut, effectively knocking the wind out of the man. While he was down on his hands and knees, Webster brutally struck him with the butt of his knife handle above the left eyebrow. This blow split the skin open, and blood flowed down into his eye and off his downturned cheek into the white snow.

"Get up!" Webster roared.

Jonathan Stiller was suddenly scared. The ease with which Zachary Webster had stopped his attack told him he wasn't just up against a farm boy in a small-time scrap. He'd been in enough fisticuffs to have confidence in his ability to handle himself in one of those, but he was now facing someone who could fight effectively and lethally. Instead of taking on this soldier who was waving a knife with a blade as big as a canoe paddle, he decided to talk his way out of the situation. He got to his feet and shook his head. "I know you're angry. I'd be angry, too, if I was you, Webster. But you need to know that we didn't plan any of this, Catherine and me."

"Oh, I'm not angry. This isn't about anger, it's about the rules of war."

Stiller was confused by this response, but he continued on quietly, "Naw, it just happened, really. When Mr. Brandford wanted some of his land cleared last fall, I made a deal with him that I'd cut the trees and transport the logs to the sawmill if we would split the profits from the finished lumber. I went over there to cut them trees down, and Catherine brought out a pitcher of lemonade. We chatted, mostly about the weather and the hot temperatures. But the lemonade break became a daily occurrence. After the job was done, I found any excuse to come over to the house and talk with Catherine some more. But we didn't plan for any of this to happen."

Webster leveled his knife. "So is it a common occurrence for you to prey on the sweethearts of soldiers off fighting the war? A war that I cannot help but notice you are not currently taking part in neither, Mr. Stiller."

His insults stung, but Stiller tried to remain as calm as his assailant. "No, it's not a common occurrence in any way, I can promise you that. But it happened. If you care for Catherine, don't you want her to be happy? Why don't you let her decide what she really wants? Let her choose her own future."

If these comments registered at all, Webster's face didn't show it. He wiggled the blade at Stiller again and said, "Ah, she made it abundantly clear that she's already chosen. She told me as much yesterday. But that ain't why I aim to kill you today."

"For the love of God, what other reason could you possibly have?"

"You told Mr. McArthur that we shot a moose out of season."

Stiller was stunned by this revelation. "I did no such thing, Webster! Angus and I were talking about the severity of this winter and how people are having to scavenge from the woods and lakes to get enough food to eat. I merely mentioned to him that I had heard a rifle shot and seen where a moose had been butchered. But I never thought he'd do anything about it."

"Well, he came to my house to accuse me, my mother, and my younger brother, and then he informed us it was you who told him about it."

Stiller shook his head at that foolish old man. Who in their right mind went up to people to accuse them like that and then revealed the source of his information? It seemed irresponsible, to say the least. He shook his head again. "It weren't my intention for Angus to go up to your house and confront you. We were merely talking about—"

Webster cut him off. "So, Jonathan Stiller, by preying on the innocence of my girl while I was away fighting this war, by trespassing on my family's land, and by accusing me and my family of poaching, you have become my enemy. Do you understand what that means to me as a soldier?"

The cold, emotionless tone of the man's voice caused the hairs on Stiller's arms to stand up. It was clear that Webster was about to kill him, and he began pleading for his life. "Please don't kill me! For the love of God, this can all be made right without resorting to bloodshed. I'll talk with Angus and tell him how mistaken I was about it all. And, as for Catherine, we can—"

The attack was so fast and savage that Jonathan Stiller didn't have time to react. One moment he was trying to tell Webster he would not see Catherine anymore, and the next he was pinned against the brick wall of a warehouse with a giant bowie knife thrust deep in his abdomen. At first, he thought he'd just been pushed up against the wall, but when the pain suddenly registered, he knew that the knife was embedded up to its hilt and he was going to die. When Webster extricated the blade, Jonathan Stiller fell face-first onto the snowy ground. And as he lay there and felt the coldness of the air and the burning sting of the snow on his face and the flashing pain of the knife wound, he became keenly aware of Zachary Webster's movements as he wordlessly grabbed a shock of his hair, lifted his head, and slit his throat. He watched his lifeblood stain the snow a bright burgundy before he lost consciousness and died.

Webster looked down at the corpse without emotion. He had accomplished his task, but he felt the absence of anything—neither remorse nor happiness. He no longer seemed capable of feeling those these days. Remorse was a human emotion that did not serve soldiers who were asked to kill each other and stack the bodies like cordwood. And happiness only came from winning battles and living another day. As Webster pondered this, he thought about the nation as a whole, and he truly hoped it still had the ability to feel both remorse and happiness. Maybe those feelings were on a storage shelf in the pantry of humanity for the long, cold winter that warfare represented, and when the battles and the killings were finally ended, they could be brought back to help with the rebirth of the entire nation again. He knew that *he* might be a hopeless case, but he still had hopes for the country.

Big lacy snowflakes started to fall. He looked up at the dark and menacing clouds overhead and knew it was time to get home. Because there were no witnesses and the location of the alley was far enough away from the main part of town to prevent discovery for some time, he knew he could get away without a problem. And if these flakes were evidence that another prolonged winter storm was about to hit, the resultant snow would completely bury the body and ensure that he'd be able to get back to the safety of the war before it was found.

Webster sheathed his knife, turned, and left the alley, heading back toward the street where he'd left his horse and sled. If he drove home quickly, he'd be in time for supper with his mother and brother. He was already packed up for tomorrow's mustering at the train station, so after his last visit with his father in the barn, he'd have plenty of time tonight to put another notch on his rifle.

Chapter Eight

The tiny ice crystals reminded Captain Small of shards of glass as they fell upon the dark woolen overcoats and bedrolls of the assembled men of Company D at the Augusta train depot. As the captain surveyed his troops, he smiled with satisfaction that all were present and accounted for. From the condition of their clothes and gear, it was clear that lots of mending had been done during this furlough, and he hoped the men themselves had been mended by their time off. He also worried that it'd been long enough for the men to have grown too soft and comfortable during their time away from the war. They were all headed straight down to Brandy Station, Virginia, where after a brief stint in winter quarters to let the weather improve enough for major battles, they would be thrust back into a new campaign against the Confederate Army of Virginia. This third year of the war looked to be the most pivotal. With their great General Stonewall Jackson dead, the Mississippi River now completely under Union control, and Lee set back on his heels in Virginia, the Confederacy was ripe for the plucking, and Captain Small was eager for the men of Company D to play an integral role in this.

While other units who massed at this train depot during more pleasant weather were given a send-off that included cakes and coffee made by the local ladies and an accompaniment from a military band, the harshness of the weather dictated that none of the pageantry would happen on this day. The men of Company D awaited the order to board their assigned train cars with wordless resignation, and when this was given, it happened without ceremony.

Once the soldiers were in their seats, however, the real socializing commenced. Webster and his tentmate, Samuel Worthington, found each other and sat together. Even though he felt comfortable with nearly every man in Company D, Webster had the strongest bond with Samuel. They'd been friends since the first days of training, and over the course of the last three years, their relationship had grown to the point of brotherhood. The two men were polar opposites—Webster was quiet and aloof, while Samuel was talkative and personable—but they had a trust and familiarity that breached their differences. While Webster's silence unnerved many men, Samuel appreciated it and found ways to communicate with him that required few or no words.

As the train began to pull away from the station, some of the men waved at their loved ones huddled together on the platform outside, while others sat stoically and expressionless to prevent their emotions from bubbling over. Webster glanced over at Samuel's reaction to their departure, and saw that he was not looking out the window or waving. His family had said their good-byes just before he'd taken the stage from their home in the coastal town of Rockland, and no one was there to see him off in Augusta. As for himself, Webster wasn't waving to his mother and brother because there was simply nothing left to say. He loved them, but he felt he'd never see them again. Whereas most of the men gave a collective involuntary groan as the train cars bumped and jumped into movement, Zachary Webster let out a sigh of relief.

Down on the platform, Mrs. Webster also exhaled loudly as she watched the train pass out of sight. Elijah looked closely at her and she returned his gaze without saying anything. In that moment of silence, however, their complicated feelings were shared. They knew in their hearts that this was an unconditional good-bye. And although this created a burning despair and made their stomachs feel like they were full of acid, both of them had come to the conclusion that Zachary was not the same young man they had known before. Elijah nodded and closed his eyes with the full understanding that his mother's sigh came from a sense of relief rather than sadness, and he wanted her to know that he shared that feeling with her. Because there was no good way to express any of this, he did what felt most natural. He put his hand on her shoulder and said, "Hey, Ma, we better get going before this storm picks up. We need to get the animals ready."

Zachary Webster felt more at ease with each mile the train chugged away from Augusta. He was glad to be wearing his green uniform tunic and pants again, and he chuckled to himself that his time at home had been akin to being forced to wear ill-fitting, scratchy clothes for a month. There did not seem to be one part of him that wasn't chafed from the experience. As for any regrets about his murdering Jonathan Stiller the day before, he was merely relieved that he'd gotten away without a single repercussion. Otherwise, he gave it no more thought. After all, if he chewed himself up over every man he'd killed on the battlefield, there'd be nothing left of him—he would have eaten himself up from the inside out by now. For him, the killing of Jonathan Stiller on the streets of Augusta was truly no different from any other killing he'd done in the war: he'd identified his enemy and dispatched him. There was no need for further thought—what would be the point of that, after all?

•   •   •   •   •

This trip back to the war was going to be a long and arduous journey. The men of Company D were scheduled to travel on this train to Portland, take another one to Boston, and then another one to Stonington, Connecticut. There, they'd board a steamer and sail overnight to New York City. Then they'd take a train from New Jersey through Baltimore to Washington. The final leg of their journey would require them to take a ferry across the Potomac to the city of Alexandria, where they would catch their final train to Brandy Station. All the men knew the trip was supposed to take only three days, but it would feel more like three months.

There was excitement among the new recruits about traveling through the almost mythical cities of Boston, New York, Baltimore, and Washington City, since many of these young boys had never been out of the state of Maine. And, like puppies, they were restless in their train seats. The veteran members of the company kept having to settle them down with reminders that they were traveling as soldiers of the Union Army, which was like riding atop a painfully slow caterpillar. First the head would move...and then the back parts would follow in a delayed and clumsy effort. Although they might know the basic steps of the trip, the men themselves would be the last to be informed when they were moving out or where exactly they would be going, so they needed enough patience to make the journey without erupting in frustration. With that in mind, the recruits were commanded to get some sleep to prepare for the coming ordeals. Some men took the advice and snored away in their seats, but a few continued to whisper among themselves with a shrill fervor, while outside, the river, like a frozen snake, slid past their frosted windows as the train chugged back to war.

Chapter Nine

As their train reached Kittery and trundled across the Piscataqua River and into New Hampshire, the men of Company D became eerily quiet. The state line marked the exact point where these men had just spent the last month, perhaps their very last one, being husbands, fathers, sons, and brothers again. Now they needed to shed those sentimental roles and become soldiers, once and for all. With the wintry New Hampshire countryside streaming past their windows, all were keenly aware that many of them might never see their home state again, and they rode the rest of the way to Boston awake, but as silent and uneasy as livestock.

There was one man who was not quiet. His name was Ellison Wentworth III, and he was the company's new lieutenant. He'd been talking to the captain since boarding in Portland, and as the train continued on its way to Boston, he showed no signs of stopping. He was replacing Samson Butler, the former first lieutenant who had been wounded during the battle at Locust Grove just before the furlough. A rebel sharpshooter had shot him below the knee, and the bullet had shattered his lower leg bones as thoroughly as if someone had taken a hammer to them. Even though he had survived the required amputation in the Union field hospital, he'd succumbed to the infection that followed. He was buried a week and a half later without ceremony in a makeshift cemetery nearby. When the men of Company D learned of his fate, they were too excited about their imminent furlough to properly mourn the man's death. In fact, when Wentworth was introduced as the new lieutenant, most of the men were surprised that the company was in need of one. But that was the state of affairs in a war—men died and then were quickly forgotten.

Ellison Wentworth III was a graduate of the prestigious Bowdoin College. As a member of the wealthy and powerful shipbuilding Wentworth family of Bath, Maine, the young man received a glowing recommendation from none other than the heroic Commander James Aldin, Jr. However, instead of accepting a guaranteed commission in the Union Navy, he had opted to enlist with the sharpshooters. His family was certainly surprised by his choice, for they had assumed he would want to serve his country by commanding a ship his family had constructed. But throughout much of his life, Ellison Wentworth III went out of his way to be his own man, so, although nearly worn out by his fervent determination, his family silently accepted his choice. They knew they couldn't change his mind in this matter, and finally resigned themselves to the fact that he would bring the family honor and pride in any pursuit he undertook. But they worried mightily because there was far more risk as an officer in a sharpshooter company than serving safely on a ship enforcing the blockade or patrolling a Union-controlled river. The family had big plans for him after the war, so they actively prayed that his service would leave him unscathed.

From his endless chatter with the captain, it was clear that Lieutenant Wentworth was too full of excitement to sleep. The veteran soldiers of Company D were amused by the captain's facial expression as he forced himself to listen to the new lieutenant prattle on excitedly about minute details. And even though Captain Small had many official tasks needing to be done during the train ride, he looked calm as he listened patiently to the man. It was a well-known fact that greenhorns always talked incessantly until the shooting started, but they went silent when the killing and dying began. So, although the new lieutenant's constant talkativeness was somewhat annoying, the men granted him this one chance to vent his nervousness, for they would soon see the man under fire and know very quickly whether or not he was cut from the good cloth.

But there was something about him that made all the men of Company D do a double take as soon as Lieutenant Wentworth stepped aboard their train car in Portland—he looked so much like Zachary Webster that the two men could have been twins. And while Captain Small could see the resemblance, he began to see the differences even more clearly. Both men had the same facial shape and the same hair color, but the lieutenant wore his mustache and goatee in the manner of General Winfield Scott Hancock—the style often referred to as "Van Dyke." Webster, on the other hand, was always clean-shaven. They were of the same height, had the same build, and shared a similar eye color, but the captain could see that Zachary Webster's presence was much different than Lieutenant Wentworth's. One put you on edge, like you were too close to a feral animal—and the other put you at ease, like you were next to an innocent, chatty little boy.

The men of the company did not pick up on the differences as quickly, and they whispered jokingly that the lieutenant must be a younger brother of Webster's that he never spoke about, because the younger sibling so obviously outshone the older one. Some also said that the man was a not-so-distant cousin who clearly came from the good side of the family tree rather than the dark and shadowy side of it. Webster was able to joke about this with the other men, but even he had to admit that he was somewhat unnerved by the physical similarities between himself and the new lieutenant. He stared at the man and tried not to get caught doing so. But as their train left Maine and passed the point of no return, all joking and joshing instantly ceased, and they rode the rest of the way in silence. Interest in the two men faded away as the soldiers accepted their war-bound fates.

But Lieutenant Wentworth did not stop talking, and Captain Small eventually began to lose patience with him. There was too much paperwork and planning to do before the Company reached Boston, and the new lieutenant's endless discourse on earlier battles and exciting new strategies kept him from that. It was clear that the man was knowledgeable about the tactics of war and the historical lessons of earlier battles, but the captain had lost his ability to concentrate on the man's ramblings. He started to think about his wife and her perfumed neck, and how he missed his house and the peacefulness of being alone in his office. When he looked around the train car, he could tell the men were transitioning into soldiers once more, and he wished he could have his own private moment to do the same. He would soon be ordering these men into situations from which some would not return, and he wasn't sure he was mentally ready to resume that ultimate responsibility.

"It is incompetence on both sides that's drawing this conflict out, don't you think, Captain Small?"

The captain was startled that the lieutenant had asked a question that required an answer, and he shivered with his attempt to remember what they were talking about. He nodded slowly, trying to regain the thread of conversation they were engaged in, before he was sucked into thoughts about his home and his wife.

"There have been mistakes on both sides, Lieutenant, but I'm not prepared to say there's been outright incompetence. That is far too deep an accusation for any of us to make."

"But look at General McDowell, for example. The man cost us a victory at the first Battle of Bull Run by sending inexperienced troops in with overly complex orders. In the end, they ended up running away with their tails between their legs! Then, a little more than a year later, at the very same location, his failure to communicate with Pope and his rather flawed decisions led to yet another embarrassing defeat. Now, to me, that's not only the very definition of incompetence, but also justification for the man to be brought up on charges!"

The captain scanned the train car slowly and subtly like a serpent seeking prey. When he was certain no one had been listening to the lieutenant, he leaned toward the man and whispered harshly, "Ellison, you're extremely fortunate that none of the men heard that last comment of yours, and I can address you as one officer to another. For if they had heard you, I'd be forced to publicly reprimand you as your commanding officer, and that rebuke would leave a stain that would take some washing to get out. Listen to me and listen to me well, Ellison—you must never, ever criticize the leadership, make accusations of wrongdoing, or mention specific failures of any decisions or actions aloud in front of the men again!"

"I was just..."

Captain Small's eyes narrowed and the skin on his face grew taut, and Wentworth knew enough to stop talking. He looked down at the armrest of his seat and awaited what was coming. The captain scanned the slumbering men in the train car again. Still satisfied that no one was listening to their comments, his voice took on a paternal rigidity. "Ellison, our job is to follow the orders we're given and lead these men in battle. We can never give them any fodder for doubt or allow the fear of failure to reach them. If we do that, we won't have anyone behind us when we give the order to charge. As soon as you lose their confidence or loyalty, you've lost the battle. I know I have the complete confidence and trust of these men. I know this because I have seen it with my own eyes. I've ordered them to jump up and run into the fires of Hell, and they have. But any talk of incompetence or flawed decision-making by the leadership only spreads the seeds that will weaken that resolve to the point of ineffectuality, and I will not tolerate that happening to my company!"

"Yes, sir. I understand. I just—"

"You haven't seen any of this war yet, Ellison, so it's easy for you to make academic statements. I'm sure you and your colleagues sat around the parlor talking about how Pickett's Charge at Gettysburg was a foolish waste of a division of good men. I know I've heard other educated men say it was. But I witnessed that event. These men witnessed that event. We stood on that ground that President Lincoln has since called 'consecrated,' and we watched the soil struggle to soak up the blood that was spilled there. Yet I still marvel at how that one single moment revealed the true strength of our enemy.

"General Lee ordered his generals to take their men across an open and exposed field to attack a superior army, and they did so without question. And although they came close to winning that battle, ultimately they failed, and a good many seasoned soldiers died in the process. But that is not a topic for you to discuss in the smoking salon with your friends, Ellison— that is now an example of the power of the foe we are fighting against. Make no mistake, General Lee still has his men completely and unquestionably behind him. What that means to you and me is that we must make the men on this train match the reb's fervor, ferocity, and loyalty. For if we cannot match them, we will lose this war. Do you understand that, Ellison?"

"Yes, sir. I will try my best to do better in the future."

The captain nodded, but added, "You need to do more than just try. If the men hear you spouting your opinions about the potential incompetence of our leadership and bringing a general up on charges, they'll start to doubt us as leaders. Men full of doubts are less likely to commit acts of sacrifice, and we need our men willing to sacrifice everything if we are going to emerge victorious in this conflict."

"I understand, sir."

"Good, Lieutenant Wentworth. I hope so, for your sake. To quote the great William Shakespeare, 'To be furious is to be frighted out of fear.'"

Chapter Ten

Like a big he-bear emerging from its hidden den, Jedediah Stiller's arrival at the wake was met with a combination of excitement, fear, and caution from the rest of the family. For longer than most could remember, they had not had any contact with the eldest son, so when he walked wordlessly into the front parlor to view his brother's body, there was an audible gasp and a genuine moment of pregnant silence. How exactly he'd heard about Jonathan's death no one knew.

As he walked over to the coffin, he was greeted with subtle and ambiguous nods from various family members, several of whom moved back a step or two to give him a wide berth as he passed. The giant man looked down at his brother in the coffin, then leaned in and spoke quietly into his ear. Those near enough to hear him said it was something in a language they could not understand, be it a foreign tongue or just crazy gibberish. Whatever it was, he spoke with intense emotion and then touched Jonathan's forehead and made a strange mark upon it. When he turned to leave as silently as he'd come, it was Mrs. Stiller, eyes swollen and raw from weeping, who came forward and gently grabbed his huge forearm. Without speaking, she looked into his eyes and then steered him toward the room in which the food was set out. Like a beast of burden, the man followed without resistance.

Jedediah was the first-born of the Stiller family. From an early age, it was quite clear that he was a quiet, kind, and intelligent little boy. But when his growth spurt began, the family quickly realized it wasn't going to stop. He grew bigger and bigger until, by the age of sixteen, he towered over everyone, including his largest male relatives. When his muscles continued to fill out and the skinny beanpole turned into a mighty man with a very thick neck and broad shoulders, people whispered that he was a creature built by God for laboring on a farm. But the Stiller family knew Jedediah was far more complicated than that. For although the young man possessed great size and strength, he clearly had the sensitivity of an artist, a poet, or a philosopher. In this, they could see the contradiction that would haunt him his whole life. Due to his physical size, most people would expect a toughness and ferocity befitting his grand stature—qualities that simply were not there yet. The truth was, the boy was emotionally fragile when it came to his interactions with other people. And so, to prevent this gentle and innocent soul from being hurt, his family became fiercely protective of him. Uncles and male cousins jumped in to prevent any kind of potential fisticuffs, and aunts and female cousins formed a virtual blanket to keep rumors and ill will from hurting him.

That all changed when he fell in love with the papist Quebecois girl. As soon as he announced their romance, his father declared forcefully that, emotionally fragile or not, no boy of his was going to associate with some Catholic harlot from a mill-working family who lived on the other side of the river. Jedediah tried to debate the issue, but the argument was ended by the parental decree forbidding him from seeing the girl ever again. And while his mother spent many a sleepless night over the issue, her silence was viewed by her son as apparent consent. And for the first time in his life, Jedediah was confronted by an unwinnable situation. His heart was overwhelmed with the power of his first true love, yet his soul was gripped by the strength of his family. But in the end, his love for Marie Brousseau trumped his father's edict, and he chose her over them.

Later, Jedediah would joke bitterly that the following period of his life was a time in which he lost everything, gained everything and even more back, and then lost it all completely. Not one member of the Stiller family attended the Catholic Mass of Marriage between Jedediah Stiller and Marie Brousseau at St. Mary's Roman Catholic Church that hot and humid summer day, and each and every attempt at reconciliation with his mother and father was quickly and coldly rebuffed. He was told, in fact, that the Stillers no longer had an older son. Although stung by this perceived abandonment, he quickly concluded that his new Quebecois wife and her extended family were now his real family, and he threw himself into their lives and into working with them at the mill. His enormous strength and physical prowess were well suited to this industrial environment, and he soon found himself laboring more hours than there was daylight. Whenever he wasn't working, he was living, loving, and laughing with his new wife and her people. Through their music, joy, and companionship, the wounds from his own family's spurning were cleansed enough to begin healing. He found himself happier than he had ever been.

Marie Stiller's pregnancy marked the high-tide moment of Jedediah's life. As the young couple basked in the attention from the rest of Augusta's Franco-American community, they were showered with gifts and salutations for the fulfillment of the new marriage that the unborn baby represented, and their social status in the millworkers' neighborhood rose substantially. At the same time, they received nothing—no news, no congratulations, no signs of endearment—from the Stiller family. Indeed, they remained staunchly indifferent. Undaunted by this, the young couple remained very happy and content in the world they made together. While Jedediah was working very hard at the mill and becoming a natural leader in his new adopted community, Marie continued to be swooned over by the other *memeres* in the mill. And after a small collection was taken up from the other millworkers, they had enough money saved to rent a tiny apartment to live in after the arrival of the baby.

That spring was marked with unusually heavy rains and warm temperatures as Maine awoke from its winter slumber early and with great energy. Trees leafed verdantly, flowers bloomed confidently, fishermen saw massive sturgeon jumping on the Kennebec River, and a mating pair of bald eagles hunted successfully from the tallest trees on the shoreline. The world seemed alive and charged with unlimited possibilities. In the very midst of this incredible season of rebirth, Jedediah Stiller's world ended when his beloved wife and their baby boy died during childbirth.

Almost immediately, those around him waited for repercussions. Like a massive lightning flash that illuminates the entire summer sky is usually followed by a bombastic thunder crash, the stunned Franco-American community fearfully awaited an explosive reaction from the giant man. But it never came. Jedediah calmly arranged for his wife and child to be buried in a simple grave in the Catholic cemetery, and he continued to function at his job. The Stiller family did not contact him with their condolences or come to the funeral, but he did not appear to notice this. Indeed, it seemed as if all of the man's actions during those days were made in an eerily calm way.

The Brousseau family knew better. They heard the man's heart and spirit being shredded each day with the precision and obsession of a small child tearing paper. Big pieces were torn into smaller, skinnier pieces and then slowly, deliberately shredded into tinier and tinier strips. Rip. Rip. Rip. By the time it was over, most of them agreed that the most notable outward change in Jedediah was in his eyes. They used to be full of compassion that invited you in and warmed you like a summer day. But the despair from the deaths of his wife and child caused the pupils of those eyes to shrink down and become hard obsidian pebbles. In fact, due to his large size, his black marble-like eyes, and his lumbering gait, the man was often and openly compared to a wounded black bear. Because of this, it was common for those near to give him room as he passed by.

Then Jedediah Stiller simply disappeared. Without any warning, he packed all of his possessions from the tiny apartment, quit his job at the mill, and left town. Over the course of the next ten years, Marie Brousseau's family received mere wisps of rumors about the man that floated through town like the fibrous seeds of cottonwoods on the whim of the winds. Whenever they heard a bit of news, they made every attempt to relay the new information to the Stiller family, but after no response from them, they eventually stopped. Instead of disseminating reports about the man's activities, they devoted their energies to creating a story from fragments of the accounts which they transformed into the complete myth of Jedediah Stiller.

From these early reports, they learned that, after leaving Augusta and making his way down to New Bedford, Jedediah had signed on as a crew member on a whaler that was headed out on a 'round-the-globe journey. His great physical strength made him such a legend in the whaling fleet that Quebecois whalers on their way home to their families would stop in Augusta just to seek out the Brousseau family and tell them about some of the man's incredible accomplishments. And like all myths, the truth and fiction of the various stories were woven together to create a tapestry that the family needed to hear more than to validate. Jedediah could throw a harpoon with such force it could go through a tree. He could single-handedly row a whaleboat faster than a ship under full sail. He could fearlessly stand on a floating whale carcass and flense up the blubber while the sea boiled with ravenous sharks longer than two grown men. He could carry huge casks of whale oil on his shoulders the way most men carried a sack of potatoes. He could kill a man with one punch in a fight. On and on, the stories trickled back to the Brousseaus, who hungrily feasted upon them and sated their familial pride.

But as the years passed, the visitors became less frequent. The last bit of news they received was that Jedediah had jumped ship and boarded another whaler bound for places with names that sounded like the babbling of a baby. Without fully comprehending why, the Brousseau family seemed to understand that once a man went around something called Cape Horn, he would never come back home. So they went on with their lives and spoke of Jedediah Stiller with less frequency and less passion. Soon, the continuing cycle of births and deaths of their living family members gradually supplanted the legendary tales about the ghostlike man they had once known. He wasn't forgotten, but since he was never going to return, they needed to face their own realities and move on with their lives.

But eventually Jedediah Stiller did come back. The man was suddenly seen walking the city streets. He was hard to miss—a giant with exotic black-blue tattoos on his cheeks and chin, his long hair tied back with a strip of leather, and both ears pierced with golden earrings. He was a person who certainly stood out in quiet Augusta. His odd appearance put the entire town on edge, and panicked citizens reported the daily sightings of the man and his movements with increasingly inaccurate fervor. When he was first seen going to the millworkers' neighborhood, most assumed he was going there to stir up trouble with the downtrodden laborers. Then he was seen heading into the cemetery, and stories began to circulate that the man was a devil who feasted on the flesh of the newly dead. There were no bounds to the incredible accusations and untrue accounts, and many households of the capital area locked their doors and loaded their weapons for protection during that first week of his return.

The truth was far less spectacular. Jedediah wanted to find the Brousseau family and reconnect with them. But when he got to the familiar neighborhood, he was told that the people he sought had all moved to the nearby town of Lewiston to work in the mills there. With no living Brousseaus to reconnect with, he went straight to the graves of his dead family. The tiny plot of his wife and child's grave looked particularly neglected, so he spent the next several days working on it. He slept next to the gravestone, lying under the stars of the nighttime sky and humming never-ending songs. When he finally walked away, the site was as manicured as those of the nicer sections of the cemetery.

With those tasks finished, Jedediah headed across the bridge that spanned the river and right to the Stiller farm. He had no false hopes of reconciliation or any interest in seeing either his mother or father, but he was curious to see how his younger brother had grown. When Jonathan Stiller saw the massive hulk of his older brother standing at the edge of the fields like some kind of gigantic stone cairn, he instantly threw caution to the wind and trotted directly over to him. The two stood facing each other wordlessly for a moment that seemed too long, but then they surprised each other by embracing in a series of crushing hugs. The silence between them was broken, and the news started to flow—mostly from Jonathan. Jedediah learned that his father had died many years earlier and that Jonathan was running the farm now; that his mother, who lived on the farm as a widow, only spoke of her eldest son with a loving voice full of forgiveness. When Jedediah did not respond to this, Jonathan extended an invitation to stay at the farm. This offer was firmly declined, however, and after exchanging another heartfelt but quick embrace, Jonathan watched his older brother lumber away and fade into the forest. He wasn't sure he'd ever see him again.

But for reasons no one could fathom, Jedediah decided to settle in the area. Just north of town, he found a remote and nearly inaccessible parcel of land for sale, which he purchased outright. The local gossip was that he paid for it with strange golden coins that he pulled out of his seabag. Once the land was officially his, Jedediah built a small shack in which to live. From the outside, it looked rough-hewn and simple in design, but the interior showed that the man had learned from the rugged construction of the wooden sailing ships during his whaling days. With his dwelling finished, he began to build a life with its own schedules and trends. He spent his winters trapping and fishing on his land, and during the summer seasons, raised pigs and goats to sell in town. He remained so secluded from the other residents of Augusta that they began to refer to him as the Hermit of Kennebec Valley. When he did come into town to sell his pelts or some of his exotically spiced pork, which he cooked in an underground stove just as the savages of the South Pacific had taught him to do, the conversations on the streets were about nothing but the sightings of the hermit.

Although he did nothing to warrant a negative reputation, Jedediah

Stiller became the tattooed monster of the woods that parents conjured up to frighten their children into good and proper behavior. His supposed ability to come silently into town and grab naughty children and drag them back to his land to cook them in his *umu* caused many a child to check under their beds before falling asleep at night. Adults and children alike kept their distance from the giant whenever he came into town and waited until he was long gone before they whispered to one another about his actions.

What no one knew, however, was that the hermit was not completely alone. Jonathan Stiller secretly visited his older brother as often as he could afford to get away from the farm. At first, the two men sat silently smoking their pipes and drinking a mysterious steeped concoction, but gradually their conversations began to take shape. Jedediah initially resisted any attempts by his brother to drag out the stories of his voyages, and he skillfully deflected the unwanted attention by insisting on listening to the news and events of Augusta from Jonathan instead. Eventually, he relented and began to tell stories of those years he was at sea.

In this way, Jonathan became Jedediah's confessor. The quiet, peaceful, and sober recluse who now lived in Augusta had exorcised his demons by committing shocking acts of debauchery and violence in port towns around the globe. The grisly details of his stories were horrible enough to make Jonathan feel slightly sick to his stomach and have just an inkling of fear for his own safety. But he came to realize that the death of his brother's wife and son and the way their own family members had turned their backs on him had created a noxious, pus-filled wound inside Jedediah where his heart had once been. He also understood that the only way for such a deep lesion to be evacuated was through drinking and brawling. Although it was difficult to hear about all of the beatings, stranglings, breaking of bones, stabbings, and deaths that Jedediah had meted out during those years, Jonathan knew they were just vehicles to his healing. And once this wound was completely emptied of its pus, Jedediah had come home.

The two brothers never spoke more of the future than the next day, the next crop, the next trappings, or the next hunt. They came to the unspoken agreement that true reunification of their family was never going to happen, so both men savored their visits together for as long as they could. They accepted that the future of their brotherly relationship was tentative at best. After all, Jonathan was tied to the family farm, where he would live out his years. And although Jedediah was comfortable enough in his momentarily sedentary life to think he might stay in Augusta for some time, the fact remained that the man was not anchored to the place by anything or anyone. He and his brother both knew that if he ever got a sudden dose of wanderlust, he would head out for distant lands without looking back. For the time being, they were both very happy to have each other's companionship, and they looked forward to their conversations.

On the fateful day that he learned of Jonathan's death, Jedediah had come into town to sell a bundle of rabbit pelts from his traps and buy some salt pork and coffee. As was his manner, he never spoke more than a few sentences to the merchants as they conducted their transactions. But he noticed that they were acting as if they were handling a poisonous serpent as they waited on him, and he began to wonder exactly why they were behaving so strangely. Finally, an Augusta policeman felt brave enough to tell him the news. People nearby watched and waited for his reaction. They all assumed the man would explode in a beastly rage when he learned his young brother had been murdered, and they stood at their store windows preparing themselves for the fury that the monster before them was about to unleash.

But the hermit did not react at all. His face remained completely unchanged as he nodded and learned that his brother's body had been found in an alley in the warehouse district after several local dogs had begun to feed on it. When the police officer finished telling him all the horrible details, Jedediah Stiller merely thanked him and then turned and galumphed away without another word. After this, the policeman quickly warned the townspeople to brace for the reaction of Augusta's infamous bogeyman. He had seen the rage in Jedediah's beady little eyes, and he warned them that the hermit was going to lash out eventually.

The news of his brother's murder, however, hadn't caused Jedediah to feel the need for immediate vengeance. Instead, he knew he needed to get over to the Stiller farm to see his young brother one last time. But as he trudged along, the memory of his wife and child's death, which he had tried so hard to put into an untouchable crypt within himself, fought to resurface and reignite his rage. After their deaths, he'd managed to suppress that bottomless anger until their graves were filled with dirt. Only after his beloved ones were buried had he surrendered to it and let it rise within him like the swelling river during spring flood season. Soon enough, it eroded his sense of reality and ethics, and then it completely consumed him. As he made his way through the violence of his whaling years, the rage made it feel as if someone else was driving his body. But each deplorable act of brutality Jedediah perpetrated during that time was nothing more than a sluice to release the pressure from this anger, and eventually, when he was finally emptied of it all, he found himself back in control.

But, as he made his way to visit the body of his dead brother, he could feel that rage once more. Like a reversing falls, it stormed back into him, and he knew he would ultimately lose control. He silently resigned himself to the fact that he would have to go out into the world again and do horribly violent acts in an attempt to recover himself once more. This time, however, his brutality would not be directed against random strangers—it would be focused wholly upon the man who had murdered his brother. He would spend each waking moment finding the fiend who had done the heinous act, and whenever he found him, he would flense him with one of his blades and eat his heart. He'd even cook it the way he'd been taught by the Maori. His brother's killer was now Jedediah's biggest enemy.

He had many tasks to do before he could begin this quest, however, and he hoped that the floodwaters of his vengeance wouldn't overwhelm him before he was able to complete them all. He needed to see his brother's body one last time, clean up his affairs, and get the clues he needed to track down the man he was going to kill. As he lost himself in the rhythm of his powerful steps, he also silently prayed to no particular deity to keep any innocent souls out of his way on the path to his brother's killer, for he knew from experience that once the rage took hold of him, no one would be spared his fury, whether innocent or guilty.

Chapter Eleven

Jedediah looked back at the Stiller farmhouse one last time. The whiteness of the clapboards reminded him of sun-bleached whale bones on white sand beaches, but the smoke spiraling up from the chimney drew his eyes to the cloudless blue skies. Although it must have appeared to everyone in the house that he and his mother had just reconciled, Jedediah knew he would never see her or any other family members ever again. Once he found and killed his brother's murderer, he would just keep moving. There was nothing in Augusta for him anymore, and he knew that his fate lay somewhere else. He turned his back on the farm and resumed walking with a quicker pace. He felt the growing urge to allow his rage free rein, but he needed to get some things done before that could happen.

Finding Jonathan's killer would not be easy. There'd been no witnesses nor evidence that hadn't been buried and effectively erased by the snowfall. An Augusta policeman had told Mrs. Stiller that there were no solid suspects, although he proudly reported to her that all of the Catholic French-Canadians of Augusta were questioned, as were several unsavory-looking strangers who'd been in Mulkern's Tavern the same day Jonathan had been there. Unfortunately, they were no help. And since the Stiller family could not imagine anyone who might want to hurt Jonathan, let alone viciously kill him, they were no help either. Jedediah didn't know who would want to kill his brother, but from their conversations, he'd learned that the young man had kept more than a few secrets from the rest of the family. For instance, Jonathan was discreetly courting a young woman who was already spoken for. Not only had he told his older brother this news, more importantly, he'd told him the woman's name. And since Jedediah knew that secret relationships were rarely without some bitterness, he figured that talking to this Catherine Brandford would confirm his hunch as to who might have had ill will toward his brother.

He went into his shack and quickly packed his canvas seabag with all the gear he would need for his journey. There wasn't much. He'd made all of the furniture and utensils he owned, and although he took pride in the quality of the work, none of them were sellable or salvageable. So after slinging the seabag comfortably onto his back, he went out the door and walked a short distance to look at the outside of the dwelling he'd built. As with the furniture on the inside, he was proud of its construction, but it was not worth saving. He set his seabag on the ground and lit a torch. He walked forward with this in his hand, opened the door of the shack, and carefully tossed it into the midst of his bedding. He knew the flames would race up the dry wooden walls and engulf the roof. Ultimately, there would be nothing left but a pile of ash.

The burning of his shack came with no sentimentality. It was not a place he associated with anything overly important or happy in his life. No family was started or raised in it, and nothing great was accomplished there. He'd merely lived within its comfort. And while he was grateful that he'd had a chance to converse with his brother while living there, now that Jonathan was dead, the cabin, the land, and the very town of Augusta now held absolutely no meaning for him. Ironically, he had hired a lawyer a few months earlier to write up a will that bequeathed the shack and property to Jonathan, but his brother's death had made those arrangements moot. He couldn't take the time now to make amendments to that original will, which meant it might go straight to his mother. If that was the case, he wanted to make damn sure he did not give her any more than a pile of ashes in the midst of a swampy woodlot.

Jedediah strapped on his snowshoes and headed toward town. The snow from the last storm made the going slow, but the big man powered through with silent determination. As he walked, he kept to the woods and frozen streams as much as he could. He wasn't purposely avoiding people, but his path needed to be as direct and quick as possible. He wanted to finish everything before the sun set. His first stop was the Brandford farm. He sensed that the young woman was the lynchpin of his whole journey, and he quickened his pace.

• • • • •

When Catherine Brandford opened the door and saw the menacing form standing there, she was convinced momentarily that her house was under siege, and she let out a short, fear-filled yip. The man-monster lifted his head so she could see the tattoo lines on his face and said in a deep but peaceful voice, "Miss Brandford, I am Jedediah Stiller, Jonathan's brother. May I please come inside to talk with you for a moment?"

Catherine knew that Jonathan's older brother was the infamous hermit, but she had never laid eyes on him before. Now that she looked up at his face, she could see the family resemblance. However, the man's onyx eyes unnerved her, and she hesitated long enough that Jedediah said soothingly, "This won't take long, Miss Brandford. Please, I just need to talk with you very briefly. I will leave my pack and snowshoes outside. I promise I will be on my way henceforth."

The man spoke with such intelligence, Catherine shuddered with embarrassment for keeping him outside in the frigid wind longer than was necessary. She stood back and gestured to let him enter. When he tried to fit past her, she was overwhelmed by his sheer size. He towered over her, and his wide shoulders forced him to turn sideways to go through the doorway. After she shut the door, she could smell him. It was not an unpleasant odor—a combination of woodsmoke, sweat, and the earthen aroma of animal skins—and it was beginning to dominate the greeting space of the house. She scooted around him, saying, "Let's go into the parlor to be near the fire."

The giant man did not move. He looked around doubtfully and stood fixed where he was. He said softly, "I don't want to take too much of your time, Miss Brandford."

"Mr. Stiller, I have plenty—"

"Call me Jedediah, Miss Brandford," he said firmly.

"All right, Jedediah. But then you need to call me Catherine."

"I will do that."

She took a seat on the sofa to wait for him to come in, but he remained rooted in the front hallway. The way his black eyes scanned the room made her uneasy. "Come into the parlor and sit down, Jedediah."

He finally stepped into the room, but when he neared the comfortable chair she was indicating for him, she suddenly realized the man's hesitancy was because he knew he was too big to fit in it. So she quickly moved over and settled into it while motioning for Jedediah to sit down on the sofa. He seemed to grimace or grin, she wasn't sure, and he lowered himself down as delicately as if he were nurturing a clutch of eggs. They sat in silence for a moment. Catherine looked over at him and took him in. He was clothed in an outfit made from the skins of animals, and she could see that the sewing on the seams was well done and intricate. She knew he had probably made the clothes himself from animals he'd trapped or hunted, and she admired his skill. She waited for him to speak first, but he appeared to be mulling something over in his head. She said quietly, "I'm so terribly sorry about Jonathan's death. He was a good man."

Jedediah nodded silently. Then he took a breath and said, "That is partly why I came to talk to you today. There is something I need to ask you, Catherine."

"Oh?"

"About Jonathan."

"Yes?"

"And you."

"Oh?" she said again.

Jedediah stared squarely at her, but she did not avert her eyes. He was accustomed to people glancing away when he looked at them, so he was surprised by the strength of her returned gaze. His brother had not told him much about Catherine Brandford, but now that he felt he was being held at bay by this petite woman, he wished he had. He'd half expected to find a sobbing emotional wreck who had just lost her secret love, but she was staring him down so efficiently, he was not sure how to proceed. He needed the information he thought she had, so he said softly, "No one knew, not even our own mother, that Jonathan and I met to talk together nearly every week, Catherine."

"That's good to hear. He talked about how important you were to him, so it's good that you two were able to get together and speak your minds."

He grimaced. She was not making this easy. He cleared his throat. "Well, during our times together, he talked about you. About you and him."

Catherine tensed and leaned forward in the chair, and for a brief moment, Jedediah Stiller clenched his fists to defend himself. Her eyes narrowed and she asked with some spice, "And what did your brother tell you...about me and him?"

Jedediah heard the hint of challenge in her voice, so he shrugged his shoulders. "Truthfully, he never went into specifics. He just told me he was smitten with you, Catherine."

"Is that so?"

He tilted his head to try and read her cool expression. "Yes, it is. He said repeatedly how he hoped you two would have a future together."

Catherine let out a short sigh, but then she said nonchalantly, "Is that all your brother told you about me and him?"

"What more does one brother need to say to the other?"

The two stared at one another for an uncomfortable moment. Finally, Jedediah rolled his eyes and exhaled loudly. "Catherine, I'm not sure what you think I have to say to you today. You seem prepared for some kind of battle, but I only want you to know that I am going to do everything in my power to track down my brother's killer."

Catherine's eyes opened very wide. "Do you know who that is?"

He shook his head slowly. "No, not yet. But that's why I'm here to talk with you today."

"I don't understand, Jedediah."

"From what Jonathan told me, I think you know far more than you are saying."

Catherine jumped up and stood very erect. "What, exactly, are you insinuating, Mr. Stiller?"

Jedediah looked at her with admiration. The woman was bristling for battle against a man who could snap her neck with one hand, but she was exhibiting enough strength, passion, and fieriness to make him a little scared of her. All of a sudden, he fully understood why his brother was so attracted to her, and he felt a jolt of warm energy start behind his knees, circle around his groin, and force its way into his stomach and throat. He pushed it back down and felt a cold sense of shame with the knowledge that he had just harbored an attraction for his dead brother's love interest. His anger flared and his voice boomed in a clap of thunder. "Sit down, Catherine

Brandford! I didn't come here to upset you or accuse you of anything. I just need to ask you some questions."

She sat down slowly. She did not like the power in the man's voice and she didn't want to obey him, but felt compelled to. Her eyes remained fixed on him, but her legs shook a little as she recognized the magnitude of anger inside him.

When he spoke again, it was in a much softer voice, but there was no apology for his outburst. "From my conversations with Jonathan, I learned that he was in love with you but you were true to a beau who was fighting in the war. My brother wanted nothing more than for you to be happy, but it was clear to me that he hoped your happiness was going to be from living a life with him. That's all he ever said about you, Catherine. He always spoke of you in the fondest and most respectful of ways, and I apologize if I gave you the impression that he said anything otherwise."

Catherine gave a quick bob of the head to convey her appreciation for his clarification, but the man's face was now darkly solid, the tattoos swirling like vapors on his chin and cheeks. When he spoke again, it was as if he was speaking through an inhalation of breath. "I guess there is no way to say what I need to say with enough subtlety, Catherine, so I am going to just say it. No one knows anyone who would have wanted to hurt Jonathan, but I can think of one man who might—your beau."

Catherine shook her head frantically. "No, no! There's no way Zachary could have killed your brother!"

"Zachary? Zachary who?"

"No, there's no way he's responsible!"

"I didn't come here to tell you that he did or he didn't, Catherine. I only came to get his name from you so that I may speak with him. I could've just started asking around town to get it, but I didn't want to violate your or my brother's privacy in any way. So instead I'm asking you, face-to-face—what is the last name of your beau?"

"You don't understand. It's just not possible that Zachary had anything to do with the murder of Jonathan."

"Catherine, my brother told me your beau was just here on furlough from the war. Jonathan spoke with such sadness about the fact that you two were not seeing each other while he was around, but he was willing to wait until the man went back. Now if your Zachary learned about your blossoming relationship with my brother, he would have had more than enough reason to want to get rid of him. All I'm asking for is his last name so I can talk to him."

"That's just it, Jedediah. He's not here anymore. He left town to go back to the war several days before Jonathan was murdered."

Jedediah looked at her as though examining her frame for cracks, then he said, "So you've given this some thought, haven't you? Of course you have. You've been asking yourself what a young soldier who's been off fighting a war would do if he came home to the rumors that his sweetheart had gotten close with another local young man. I can tell you have. A man in that situation would definitely want to kill off his competition before he headed back to the war. And now that I've met you, Catherine Brandford, I know for a fact that your Zachary had enough motivation to kill my brother Jonathan. So please, just tell me his last name so I can try to track him down and make him pay for what he has done."

The man's last comments hit Catherine like a concussion, and she shook her head even more vigorously. "No, Jedediah. I don't think Zachary could have possibly killed Jonathan. He did come over here just before heading back to the war to ask me about the rumors. When I had nothing to tell him, he got up from the chair I'm sitting in now and left this house without even a glance back. He did not storm off or yell or make any commotion whatsoever. Actually, he showed a complete lack of emotion. And because of this, Jedediah, I do not believe Zachary had enough hatred toward Jonathan to do what you're saying he did."

"He is not the same boy you knew before the war, Catherine. He's a soldier now, and that changes everything. While I was a whaler, I had the displeasure of meeting many soldiers along the way. And I will tell you they are a different type of man. They are trained to kill on command, and once they're allowed to do that, they can't stop. Men who have lived through that life are no longer the obedient and law-abiding creatures they were before there was blood on their hands. For them, there's no longer any right or wrong—there's only kill or be killed. Your beau, Zachary, is no longer an innocent farm boy from Augusta. He's a soldier who's been killing for the last three years. So, I am going to respectfully disagree with you that he could not have killed my brother. He may have walked away from your last talk not showing any emotion over the fact that you and he were done, but I know in my heart that your soldier would want to punish the man who had taken his beloved. And I think Zachary got that chance and Jonathan never saw him coming."

"Even if everything you are telling me about soldiers is true, Jedediah, Zachary and his entire company boarded a train to head south several days before your brother's murder. His mother and brother went to the train station to send him off, so I'm quite sure he didn't miss that train. He wasn't even here in Maine when your brother was killed!"

Jedediah shook his head thoughtfully. "My brother's body wasn't found right away because of the snowfall from that last big storm. It appears the murder happened several days before his body was discovered in that alley. So you can't equate the time of Jonathan's murder with the date that you were first informed of his death. My brother was in town, running errands, just before your beau and the rest of those soldiers headed back. The fact is, your Zachary was still here in Augusta on the day my brother was killed, and I'm fairly certain he's the murderer."

He noticed that Catherine had a tight grip on the armrests of the chair as she continued to shake her head emphatically. A wave of pity for her hit him, so he continued quietly, "Catherine, I know this is hard to hear. But I'm just trying to get some justice for my brother Jonathan. Help me do that."

When she simply continued to shake her head, his voice took on a honed edge. "Jonathan was murdered, Catherine, and was left for the dogs to eat! Doesn't he deserve some kind of justice? I am going to be the agent of that justice, one way or another!"

Her eyes were watering as she answered, "You can't be sure it was Zachary who killed your brother. You are putting these connections together, but you have no proof. If you are so hell-bent on justice, tell the Augusta police about your suspicions and let them pursue the matter. Let the justice happen in a courtroom."

Jedediah raised his head and laughed loudly. "The police? Do you really think the Augusta Police Department has the resources to track down a soldier in the Union Army? No, I need to do this myself. So give me his last name and any other helpful information so I can find him."

Catherine tried to reason with him. "But you could head off and chase Zachary, only to find he had nothing to do with this heinous act. Wouldn't that be a horrible waste of your time and effort, Jedediah? And what if, in your blind pursuit, you either kill Zachary or get yourself killed—and it turns out you were wrong? That would be just plain tragic, wouldn't it?"

The black and blue tattoo lines on the giant man's chin and cheek curled in on one another to form a knot. Catherine's eyes were so transfixed by this that it took her a while to realize he was smiling. She tilted her head, preparing to ask *why* he was smiling, but Jedediah shrugged his broad shoulders and the smile faded. "Isn't it tragic enough that my brother Jonathan was attacked, stabbed, and left in some alley for the dogs to find?"

"Yes, of course."

"Catherine, if you cared for my brother at all, you would want justice for him."

"You don't want true justice, Jedediah, you want revenge. I can see the rage in your eyes. You're going to follow him, and if you find him, you're going to kill him to get vengeance—not to look for justice!"

The comment about his eyes made him look down at the carpet. He said, "But don't you think Jonathan deserves justice?"

"You keep asking that. Yes, yes, I do think Jonathan's murderer needs to be captured, put on trial, found guilty, and punished according to the rules of the law. But I cannot condone vigilante behavior. And I will not be a party to a senseless murder."

The man's face tightened frighteningly. The wildness and the intensity of his gaze scared Catherine, and she realized that if he wanted to hurt her, he could easily do so. She licked her lips and got ready to ask him to leave.

Jedediah nodded to himself and sighed heavily. "Catherine, I'm a desperate man. So after we are done talking here, I plan to head off to find my brother's killer, one way or another. If you don't help me, I will get my information in a different way. I'm quite sure that someone knows your Zachary's last name, and I'll get it just by asking around. And when I do, I will go to the man's family and get more information about his unit and its destination. That all could be quite messy. And it doesn't have to happen that way."

Jedediah Stiller's thinly veiled threats made Catherine gasp. She could see Mrs. Webster and Zachary's young brother, Elijah, in her mind, and the thought of them being harmed by this gigantic wild man on his quest for vengeance made her shudder. If she was the one who caused him to hurt them, she'd never be able to live with herself. But she did not want to be the prime instrument of Zachary's death either, and the resulting confusion confounded her enough to give her pause before speaking again. She needed to make a quick decision, and she sat frozen in place while she made it.

The horrible story that Zachary had told her during their last visit made it easier for her. The fact that he hadn't shown mercy to that enemy soldier had revealed just how much the war had transformed him. It was clear to her he was now the type of creature that was more than capable of handling a vengeful beast like Jedediah Stiller. She spoke clearly and succinctly when she finally said, "His name is Zachary Webster. He's a sharpshooter in Company D of the 2nd United States Sharpshooters Regiment. His company was headed down south to get back into the war. And now that you have your information, Mr. Stiller, please leave my home and never come back. Also, leave the Websters alone. Go on your deadly mission of vengeance, but spare them. And I pray that God will have mercy on your soul."

The giant stood slowly. He was so tall that it hurt Catherine's neck to look up at him. She wanted to stand, but his immense size pushed her back into the chair. He seemed unperturbed by her send-off as he gazed down at her. "One thing I've learned about the Almighty is, you only get from Him what you give Him, ma'am."

She pointed fiercely at him and commanded, "Get out of my house!"

"You've been most helpful, Miss Brandford. I do wish we could have met under different circumstances, but I guess that wasn't our fate. Good day."

Chapter Twelve

The frigid temperatures and the biting wind made his sleep far from comfortable, but Jedediah was not seeking comfort by spending the night at his wife and son's grave—he was rediscovering the headwaters of his rage. He didn't feel compelled to explain anything to himself or to anyone else; he merely wanted to tap into the excruciating suffering to trigger the transformation he sought. If he was going to get justice for Jonathan— pure, cold, and true justice—he needed to wholly embrace his vengeful side. Seeing the names of his wife and son etched on their gravestone and picturing their lifeless bodies beneath the frozen ground broke the dam of his resistance. As the minutes of the night ticked off with the popping of the trees, the howling of far-off dogs, and the fierce gusts of wind, he felt the completion of his transformation.

When there was the faintest blue-orange haze over the tops of the trees on the eastern horizon, it was time for him to go. He knew he would never see his wife and son's grave again, so he reached out and touched the stone with his bare hands. His fingers prickled and then went numb in the extreme cold, so he quickly re-donned his mittens before he picked up his pack and headed off. He hesitated a moment when he suddenly comprehended that his rage was different this time. With the death of his wife and child, it had felt like flames engulfing a house in a swirling tempest out of control. This time, however, there seemed to be still an iota of his humanity left in it. He could tell there was some doubt, fear, hope, and regret already folded in with his rage, and although he was glad not to have lost himself completely in the fury, he hoped it would not turn into weakness.

When he started to walk again, his strides were long and strong. Before leaving town, he felt compelled to do one final task, and it required him to cover a fairly good distance. If he kept up this hurried pace, he'd be able to accomplish it and be back at the train station with plenty of time before his scheduled departure. The sense of urgency was further fueled by the knowledge that Zachary Webster already had quite a head start on him. Jedediah knew he would have to do some time-consuming searching, but he felt confident that he'd be able to track down the man by following his company's path. All he needed to do was meet the right people who could tell him the right information at the right time, so he had to be prepared for a frustratingly slow process. He just hoped he could get to Zachary Webster before the Confederate soldiers did. He was more than hopeful about this, but he needed to punish the man's family before he set off.

Chapter Thirteen

Elijah Webster walked out to the barn to check on the horses. One of them had developed a dry cough recently, and he and his mother were worried that the animal was getting sick. He had taken to going out to the barn several times a day to check on the horse and see if the cough had worsened. This was not the time of year for farm animals to fall ill, for those that did usually died. And since it was common for livestock to die in pairs, the Websters found themselves at risk of completely losing their ability to get around, and the thought of this greatly troubled Elijah and his mother.

As the young boy loped his way along the icy pathway, his head was awhirl with thoughts. He continued to be somewhat shocked at how much relief he and his mother still felt since his brother's departure. This was a new feeling, and he didn't like it. Before the war, the two brothers had been so close they were more like friends, and they never seemed to have the issues most siblings had. During this last visit, however, things between them had been much different. From the moment Zachary had walked into the house, it was obvious the war had changed him into a cold and distant person, and Elijah had to admit that his brother was no longer someone he could trust wholeheartedly. Those notches on the rifle and that horrible war story he told before leaving made it abundantly clear that he was now a man who had grown too comfortable with killing. And even though he knew it was naïve, he held out some hope that, once this terrible war was over, Zachary would come home and change back into the brother he had once been.

This last thought made Elijah stop in his tracks. Before his brother's visit, it was a foregone conclusion that he would enlist as soon as he reached his next birthday. But now he wasn't so sure. The war was being hailed as a glorious chance to become the hero that every young boy dreamed of being, and that had beckoned Elijah like a Siren. But seeing the way the war had changed his brother gave him second thoughts about wanting to save the Union or have people call him a hero if it meant the experience would transform him into someone dark and murderous like Zachary. This moment of self-discovery stunned him enough to freeze him in place.

Elijah Webster never saw Jedediah Stiller until the giant man was already upon him. With the ease of a small piece of lint being flicked by a strong finger, the boy's body was flung into the air by the collision. The softness of the snow cushioned the landing, but there was no chance for recovery as the attacker, a huge tattooed man clothed in animal skins, grabbed him by the throat and pushed him down with his knee on his chest. Gasping under the crushing weight, Elijah could see a darkened face of anger with blue-black lines twirling up the chin and cheeks below blackened marble-like eyes. The disorientation from the ambush and the unknown identity of the attacker paralyzed Elijah. He was a strapping young boy, his arms strong from all the manual chores of the farm, but he now lay as helpless as a beaten dog in the snow, his legs spread wide in submission. His eyes were white with surprise, and his overwhelmed and frightened brain could not make his mouth work. He hoped his mother had seen the attack from the window and was getting the shotgun ready, but he couldn't count on that.

"Do you know who I am, boy?" Jedediah Stiller bellowed.

Because he still couldn't get his mouth to function properly, Elijah wordlessly shook his head, which seemed to anger his attacker more. The giant pushed down harder and with more weight, and the boy struggled to breathe. It was then that Elijah saw the man held a large wooden mallet in his other hand. It was the pin mallet Jedediah had obtained during his whaling days, and he had found it as useful in pulverizing human bones in a fight as it was in pounding caulking in the boatyards. It now hovered in a perfect position to smash in the boy's head.

"I am the brother of Jonathan Stiller! My name is Jedediah Stiller!"

Elijah's fear grew with the booming volume of the man's voice, but his brain struggled to recognize the names just mentioned. He'd heard of the Stiller farm, but he'd never been there. The last name wormed its way through the haze in his brain, and it tapped him with a sudden fleeting familiarity. Stiller? That was the name of the man killed in downtown Augusta recently! Because Zachary had done all the chores before leaving for the war, neither Elijah nor his mother had been in town as of late to get much news. If it hadn't been for a random encounter with Oliver Jacobsen as he took a load of logs down the road, Elijah wouldn't have heard about the murder of Jonathan Stiller at all. Even then, Elijah wasn't sure he had ever met the man, so he was not able to see the victim's face in his mind. He was totally aghast as to why the man's brother was now smothering him in the snow with a mallet poised to strike.

For Jedediah, the boy's overall lack of a response only angered him. He wanted nothing more than to crush the boy's skull with the mallet, but he needed him to acknowledge the sins of his brother before he could exact his vengeance. He leaned closer to his face and growled, "Your brother Zachary murdered my brother Jonathan."

The boy merely blinked at this accusation, but then he started shaking his head enough to create a shallow hollow in the snow that Jedediah now imagined filling up with the boy's blood and brain matter. The giant man nodded his head, saying fervently, "Oh yes! Oh yes! Your brother Zachary killed my brother Jonathan. Stabbed him to death and left him in an alley to be found by the dogs!"

The boy continued to shake his head with the rhythm of a pendulum, and this started to bother Jedediah and usurp his anger. He eased his grip on the boy's throat—but only slightly. "Do you know Catherine Brandford?"

The boy furrowed his brow sharply and nodded.

"Well, my brother and she fell in love. They were going to get married. Your brother killed Jonathan because he found out that Catherine chose my brother over him."

The look of understanding that suddenly took over the boy's face disarmed Jedediah. With only the smallest of facial movements, he signaled that he not only knew this accusation was plausible, but likely. And what was even more disturbing was the faint new look of contempt on his face. Jedediah knew nothing about the Webster family, but he now guessed correctly that this young boy completely understood that his older brother was capable of such a murderous act, and he was struggling with whether to be shocked by this new truth or be proud of it.

Jedediah hesitated. The original purpose of coming to the Webster farm was to get his retribution—to kill the younger brother of the murderer to make up for the loss of his own younger brother. Even the Good Book condoned that type of vengeance. But the lack of resistance and his muted reactions were more effective than any physical defense Elijah could have mustered, and Jedediah suddenly understood that if he swung the pin mallet into the boy's skull as planned, he would be no better than a cowardly murderer himself. He eased his weight off slightly to come up with a new plan. He whispered harshly, "Listen carefully, boy. I'm going to exact my revenge upon you, and then I'm going to head down south and find your brother and kill him. I am going to ambush him just like I did you, and I will bleed him slowly and painfully. There's not a damn thing you can do about it neither. If you say anything to anyone, all you will do is indict your brother. And he'll be dead before you get any letter down to him to warn him. You see? That's your punishment, boy, knowing your brother is going to die and that you cannot do a damn thing about it. That, and by being hobbled."

The mallet flashed and struck Elijah flat on the forehead. The blow was meant to merely daze him, and he remained conscious as the man carefully positioned his right foot on a nearby pile of logs and swung the mallet onto his heavy leather boot. Elijah jerked erect and yowled in pain, and the gut-wrenching sound of snapping branches and breaking ice that the concussion had created left no doubt that all the bones in the boy's right ankle and foot had been broken with that one swing. After three more swings, there was nothing more than pulp contained within the boot.

Jedediah knew it was time to leave. If the boy's mother or anyone else in the house had heard his screaming, someone was sure to come out the kitchen door with a shotgun blazing. But he stopped and looked down at the barely conscious Elijah Webster on the ground. As he turned to walk away, the boy reached out and grabbed his leg. In a voice between a croak and whisper, he muttered, "My brother's killed more rebs than you could count on your fingers and toes, monster. And he'll take care of you, too.

You'll end up being nothing more than another notch on the side of his rifle."

As the boy passed out, his hand slipped off Jedediah's leg. The giant man gazed down with a look of admiration at the youth's strength, and he wished he could say something profound that fit the moment, but nothing came to mind. He made an unintelligible roar and started walking back toward town. He put the mallet back into the pocket of his parka and put his mittens on. If he walked fast, he'd have plenty of time to catch his train.

Chapter Fourteen

Zachary Webster vomited over the rail again. Like pistons in some kind of perverse machinery, the wave of heaving went down the line of the other men struggling with seasickness. The winter storm that had the New England coastline in its clutches and had delayed their journey by three days already now made the steamer crossing unbearable. Gale force winds whipped the ocean into swells taller than a man, and these tossed the vessel so violently that sleep was impossible. This trip marked only the second time that Webster had ever been on a ship in his life—the first having been the steamer trip down from Fall River in '61 on his inaugural trip south—and he did not have a seaman's stomach even under tranquil conditions. Being out on the rail at night during a storm was a wet and dangerous place to be, but it was much better than having to endure the building stench of vomit and the aroma of coal dust in the overheated cabins.

Webster followed the drift of a particularly large whitecap as it lumbered past the railing, nearly at eye level, and he hated himself for letting his body rebel against him. Throughout the action of the war, nothing had gotten to him like being on the water. As a sharpshooter, he had been ordered into the worst circumstances without any issues. He had entered dark shapeless spaces with no hesitation, climbed up into the top limbs of tall trees without fear, and he barely took notice anymore of the ever-present dead bodies, the excessive amounts of blood, the poisonous snakes, and all the ravenous bugs the war exposed him to. Yet being on a ship instantly made his stomach fight furiously to get out of his body! He resented the weakness the seasickness represented.

"Ah, boys, don't give up hope! This happens to many a man who works the seas!"

The line of soldiers turned to see who had just spoken. Their hair was sea-soaked and matted on their heads, framing ashen faces of sickened pallor. There, standing in the cover of the decks above was Lieutenant Wentworth. He had his hands clenched into fists and he was shaking them at the men. As if in defiance, a few men vomited again.

"As many of you probably know, my family is in the business of building ships in the town of Bath. As a child, I was expected to learn the ways of the sea to understand the needs of the captains and the sailors we were building vessels for. While you were all learning the trades of your fathers—tending the earth and harvesting crops, or the chopping of trees or the business side of whatever they do—my father decided that I should be put upon a ship to endure the worst the sea could dish out. I was sent out as a cabin boy on my first journey. Oh my, the bout of seasickness I endured on that trip was nearly endless! I was sick as a dog for seven straight days. I threw up so much, there was nothing left to come out, so I kept waiting for my stomach to jump out of my mouth and dance on the deck! Then the old salt of a captain gave me some remedies. I tried them and they worked. And now I'm going to tell you all what he told me to do."

The men looked at one another. One vomited suddenly, causing another tremor of heaving to course down the line. They looked back at the lieutenant with a glint of resentment in their eyes. They had been beyond annoyance with his first words of comfort, but he was clearly not seasick and seemed at ease on the water, so they wanted to hear more from him. He saw them eyeing him and paused dramatically. "The first thing he told me to do was get out of enclosed spaces and up on deck whenever I was feeling bad. The nose is one of our worst enemies out here. Smelling anything foul can make even the stoutest mariner queasy. You all have done the right thing coming out here to get away from the stench of those repugnant cabins!

"The second thing he recommended is harder to do on an ocean crossing or on a night passage like this, but you need to keep looking at the horizon. Staring at a fixed point helps your mind get the upper hand. Now, you are all on the wrong side of the ship to see any lights on the shore, so we should shift over to the other side. Let us all head back to the stern and go over to the starboard side."

None of the men moved because not one of them knew what *stern* or *starboard* meant, and they glanced at one another waiting for someone to be the first to either follow his order or ask the new lieutenant for an explanation. When he noticed their confusion, he motioned with his hands and said, "Come on, men, follow me!"

He started down the bucking and rolling deck. A few men, watching the lieutenant's drunken stagger of a walk, became nauseated again and vomited over the side. Still no one moved. The lieutenant turned around and saw the men frozen at the railing. He was astonished that they were not immediately following him, and an anger based in the fear of disrespect began to well up in him. "Men, if you won't follow me around to the other side of the ship to get some relief from this silly seasickness, what are we going to do when we get on the battlefield and I give you an order to follow me into a glorious battle? Now, come on, follow me, dammit!"

Webster and the other men finally understood that the lieutenant was *ordering* them to follow him, not *requesting* them to do so. They did not have his sea legs, so as he weaved efficiently down the deck with its bucking motion, they bounced helplessly between the bulkheads and the railing. Finally, they reached the other side of the ship and could see lights out in the darkness that resembled emanations from a pin-prick lantern. The lieutenant told them those lights were on land and were not moving. He forced them to stare at these and repeat to themselves, "I am not seasick, I am not seasick, I am not seasick."

Several of the men actually felt better, and the rest, although still nauseated, were not throwing up anymore. Then the lieutenant reached into his pocket and pulled out a shriveled root. He opened his pocket knife and began shaving it, cutting off slivers that had a pulpy citrine color. He handed a sliver to each man and encouraged them to eat. The men stared at the slices in their hands as if they were looking at leeches. The lieutenant hesitated, then hit himself in the head.

"None of you have ever seen ginger root before, have you? I knew there'd be a Chinaman on this boat somewhere, and I bought this ginger from him just now to help you men with your seasickness. Put that slice in your mouth. It's intensely spicy. Chew it, but don't swallow it. The juice will burn your mouth and send strong effervescences up your nose, but try to keep chewing it into a juicy pulp. It will calm your stomach. Here, let me show you."

The lieutenant popped his slice into his mouth and started to chew. After a few mastications, he blew out a loud breath. "Ooo-*ee*! That's some strong ginger! That's got a bite to it, for sure!"

The men did as they were told, but some spit it out as soon as it began to burn them. Webster had never tasted anything like it in his life. It felt like a miniature explosion in his mouth, and it produced a heat that made him exhale just as loudly as the lieutenant had. He mashed the ginger into a pulp and sucked the fiery juices down. He could feel these seemingly set fire to his stomach. He worried that such a caustic substance would inflame his already agitated belly, but he could feel the warmth extend throughout his body and calm it down. Then the lieutenant began to tell a story of being on a clipper ship in waves the size of houses, and soon the men were too engrossed with it to feel sick anymore. Between staring at the lights, repeating the declaration of being free of seasickness, chewing on the ginger, and listening to the stories of unbelievable sights, Webster felt almost normal again.

Lieutenant Wentworth smiled. "See, men? I told ya! It just takes some time to get used to it. With these remedies, you all could go and get a job on any ship in any ocean, I swear to you. As a matter of fact, after this war is over, if any of you are looking for employment, you should come out to San Francisco. When we're done kicking the Confederates around, I'm headed out there to run a shipping company for my family, and I'm going to be the boss, which means that I can hire all of you!"

Most of the men waved him off, but Webster didn't. He wasn't sure he ever wanted to work on a ship, but the thought of heading to a new land appealed to him. He was a veteran of enough battles to know not to make plans for the future, but he did sometimes wonder what he was going to do if he did survive the war. He knew for sure he could not go back to Augusta and his family, but maybe he would just head out west and see how he fared there.

Chapter Fifteen

Scarcely six months after one of the largest cavalry battles of the entire war, the Army of the Potomac converted the town of Brandy Station, Virginia, into their largest winter encampment. In the very center of this was the clapboard manor house of Farley Plantation that now served as the headquarters of the Union 6th Corps. This large, sixty-year-old building, with its fancy two-tiered portico entryway, had once been the headquarters of Confederate cavalry leader Jeb Stuart before the climactic battle of the previous June. It was rumored that Stuart and his men had left ugly messages scrawled into the wooden beams that mocked and belittled the Union and its soldiers, but General Sedgwick's staff had gone room by room and sanded these down until they could no longer be read. About two miles from this building, down the St. James Church Road and past the point where it merged with the Beverly Ford Road, was the all-important train depot. It was here that the line from Alexandria, some seventy miles to the northeast, brought train after train of supplies and men for the Army of the Potomac. The Union was amassing a huge force that, after quartering here for the winter, would push straight down into the heart of the Confederacy.

When Company D arrived at the Brandy Station train depot, they found it consisted of two train tracks and a single road sitting on top of a sea of mud. The endless flow of Union soldiers arriving daily to the encampment, coupled with the wet and inclement weather, meant that the ground was perpetually being churned into a thick and adhesive quagmire. Several corduroy roads of shaved logs made travel easier, but Company D discovered that these did not go very far, and the march to the area of their bivouac turned into an exhausting muddy slog. All of the fields surrounding

Brandy Station had been turned into camps for the different units of soldiers, and even though there were already fifty regiments of infantry and almost ten brigades of artillery living there now, the rumor was that more would arrive until the Army of the Potomac became one of the largest forces of the entire war.

Upon their arrival, the sharpshooters were ordered to set up temporary tents next to the other companies of their regiment. After spending a few days on guard duty of wagon trains and enduring picket duty around their encampment, the men from Maine would commence building their huts for their longer stay. Once these more permanent structures were in place, Company D would be officially in winter quarters until the weather cleared. They would join other units and participate in occasional raids on the rebels in the area, but mostly they would sit out the winter weather and wait for better climes for the upcoming campaign. Although the veteran soldiers of the company knew they should be happy to be free from the fighting, they equated winter quarters with a pervasive tedium that soaked into their bones and stained them with inactivity. But they'd already been through two such winters, and they all knew they would have to find ways to keep themselves from getting bored and listless.

After their quick supper around a large fire, Zachary Webster and Samuel Worthington went back to the virtual dryness of their tent. As they looked over at the new recruits who were not fortunate enough to get a tent, they smiled cruelly at the way these men were pitifully bundled up against the cold rain. With little protection from the elements, the greenhorns were going to have a rough night. As they were about to drift off to sleep, Samuel whispered to Webster, "So what do you really think of the new lieutenant?"

"He sure ain't like Lieutenant Butler."

"Naw, he talks a helluva lot more. He's just nervous, I reckon. Do you think he'll do all right once the guns start firing?"

"I dunno, for sure," Webster said. "He sure saved my bacon on that steamer. He had me over that seasickness right quick. But it's clear that although his family is highfalutin and all, he's not arrogant or too big for his britches. He doesn't treat us like we're his inferiors. Maybe because his family sent him off on those ships as a boy and he had to make a living in that world, he knows how to lead men without being a blowhard. Judging from his stories, he's definitely seen some amazing things on his trips! Have you heard him talk about those adventures at sea?"

"How could I not? The man has gone to almost every soldier in this company and talked with him. But come on, acknowledge the corn. What do you really think about Lieutenant Wentworth?"

Webster looked out at the darkness around the tent. "You know, the first time we raised hogs, Samuel, my pa took me with him when he went to buy the litter of piglets. Ah, daggone it, they were cute—all pink and little and flopping around as they played! Once we'd gotten them home and in the sty, most of them seemed to be scared of everything. If anyone got too close, they'd squeal and run away. But one of them was different than the rest. While the other animals would hang back until we'd left the pen, this one would nearly knock us out of the way to get to the slop. Matter of fact, the more we dumped in, the more the creature would devour it and wait anxiously for its next feeding. 'Cause of this, it grew far larger than the other ones. It was an impressively large hog, I can tell you. And I was sure proud of it! But I swear on the Bible, it had this odor coming off it that smelled fouler than the shit in the pen. I could not figure out what that smell was, but it ceased as soon as we slaughtered it."

He suddenly stopped talking. Because Samuel was the son of a quarryman and his family had never raised livestock, he wasn't sure what Webster's story was about, so the apparent parable had absolutely no meaning for him. He needed some clarification. "Are you saying that Lieutenant Wentworth is like a hog?"

Webster nodded solemnly. "Not a hog, per se, but *that* hog. The lieutenant's got the very same smell coming off him that that hog had. It ain't body odor; it's something much deeper than that. It's the smell of death itself. Some of our animals on the farm used to give it off, but I ain't sure I've ever smelled it coming off another living person before."

"Do my ears hear you correctly, Zachary Webster? Are you saying you think Lieutenant Wentworth is going to die?"

Webster's blue eyes somehow had a light all their own, and they shone in the darkness as he said, "As sure as I am that all fattening hogs must meet their destinies, Samuel."

Chapter Sixteen

The Augusta train station was bustling with activity when Jedediah Stiller arrived. The afternoon train to Portland was there, and preparations were being made to load it and send it on its way at the scheduled time. Although he knew none of the specific details about the route Zachary Webster and his company had taken, Jedediah felt some power in the fact that he was standing on the very spot they'd left from just a week earlier. And, as much as he wished he knew their exact destination so he could get down there quicker to find his brother's killer, he understood that was not the way this hunt would happen. He would work his way down south and start asking around to find exactly where the sharpshooter unit from Maine had gone. Once he found that out, he could get to Zachary Webster and kill him.

The service agents at the train station treated him like he was a leper when he bought his ticket, but he was accustomed to that. People always acted terrified of him when they first saw him. Even before he'd become a tattooed whaler and then the infamous hermit, his immense size had always put people on edge. Most were fearful, some were belligerent, but all seemed to give him extra space. He no longer held any resentment toward people for this treatment. Truth be told, he had begun to savor it. There was something invigorating about making people fearful, especially when it didn't have anything to do with what he did or did not do. It was a sign of instant respect, which stroked his pride enough to make him happy.

Jedediah was waiting to jump aboard the train when a staggering movement of humanity caught his peripheral vision. Like a predator who sees even the slightest activity in the woods, he swiveled quickly and watched as a drunken man shimmied toward the station. He didn't know exactly why, but he was curious enough to attempt to cut the man off from his intended objective. But the drunk, who was nearly incapacitated by his inebriation, seemed to sense the approach of a threat, and he sped up to get into the station before he could be overtaken. The man walked inside just seconds before Jedediah, but as soon as he was spotted by the ticket agent, he was instantly and scornfully reproached. "For Pete's sake, Vernon, I tole you already, we'll send someone out to your place as soon as Willie arrives! Go home and sleep this one off. I promise ya we'll let you know when he finally gets here. I really don't want to have to get the police on you again."

The drunken man mumbled something inappropriate and slanderous while moving his hand as if throwing an invisible object at the ticket agent, and then he spun around and headed back past Jedediah on his way out. The ticket agent definitely did not want to talk with the tattooed giant again, and he looked down at the counter so he would appear too busy to converse with him. Jedediah turned to follow the drunken man outside. He wasn't sure why, but he still felt it would be worth the effort to talk with him. It only took a few of his long strides to catch up with him.

"Well, he certainly wasn't very nice."

The drunk finally looked up and made eye contact with him. A pall of sobering fear went across the man's face as he did. Then he licked his lips tentatively. "Aw, I can't get no straight answers from 'em. When you hold all the power, you don't have to help out us commoners."

Jedediah nodded. "So I guess you're waiting on your...son?"

The man spit vehemently and nodded his head. "Aye, my son William is supposed to be coming back from the war. He got hisself all tore up in the victory at Rappahannock Station. Both his feet were blown off. Most soldiers with that kind of wound don't make it, but Willie's too damn stubborn to give up on anything. Just like his ol' man, that boy. But now I got to sit around here and just wait for somebody to tell me when he's coming back. And when he does, what am I gonna do then, huh? I mean, the boy ain't gonna be fit for working—he don't have no feet. What the hell will he do on the farm like that?"

Jedediah noticed that people were now boarding the train, and he felt the special urgency that comes from the possibility of being left behind. He had felt this many times when his ships were ready to leave port, and the tightening feeling now came back to him with a renewed freshness. But he wanted to see if this old man might be able to tell him anything that would help him find Zachary Webster. He shrugged. "Have you been here a while?"

"Yep, all this last week. I been here waiting for Willie through all this cold and through all these storms. I'm gonna stay here a-waitin' until my son comes home. Whenever I get chilled, I go over to the tavern to warm up and get some food and all. Then I wait and wait. And I have to put up with that little useless ticket agent—"

"Hey, I bet you've seen lots of soldiers heading back to the war, huh?"

The man nearly toppled over when he nodded. "Oh, hell yes! This place seems to be sending all of its young men down to take care of the rebs. Maine might be a little state, but we sure are doing more than our share to die or get wounded in this damned war!"

Jedediah glanced back at the train. Very few people were standing outside now, and he nearly broke into a run to board it. But he had one more question. "I've got a friend in Company D of the Second United States Sharpshooter Regiment. Did you see them head off the other day?"

"Aye, I saw them sharpshooters."

Jedediah nodded and waited for something more, but the old man didn't seem to want to continue. He tried to prompt him with, "How did you know they were sharpshooters?"

The man leaned in close. His breath reeked of whiskey and rotten teeth, and Jedediah held his neck stiffly to avoid the noxious smell when the old man whispered, "Them sharpshooters wear green uniforms. You can pick them out of a crowd of regular soldiers in parts like this, but I bet they're a sight harder to see in the green forests! Anyway, I talked to one of 'em whose family I know, and he tole me all about how they're gettin' back to the front. They have a helluva long journey down to Virginia. They go to Boston, Connecticut, New York, and then directly to Washington before heading back to the war! To me, it sounded like too much hurrying up to wait, but that's the life of a soldier these days, I guess. Until you get your feet shot off, that is."

Jedediah was about to turn and bound over to the train when the man grabbed his arm. "Now, my friend, would ya happen to have a little extra money to help an old man warm up just a little?"

Jedediah knew the man would do nothing but drink up his money in the tavern, but he'd been incredibly helpful. In fact, the information about Company D's travel plans probably saved him from having to risk his safety by asking strangers about possible routes and trains. As a matter of fact, with this knowledge about the specific steps of their journey, Jedediah now knew he could travel all the way to Washington before needing to ask for any information again, and that was definitely worth a meager piece of silver. He reached into a breast pocket and tossed a Seated Liberty silver half dollar into the air. The drunken old man was clearly surprised, but he reacted quickly and caught the coin before it landed on the snowy ground. He opened his hand to look at the coin in his palm, but when he lifted his head to offer a word of thanks, the giant was gone. The old man watched as the train pulled away, then he felt a chill go through him and he knew it was time to head over to the tavern to warm up again.

Chapter Seventeen

Catherine Brandford stared out her bedroom window and watched the dawning of the new morning. After the night of nocturnal upheaval she'd had, she was not well rested. Her sleep had been completely commandeered by an awful and repeating dream. In it, she was caught between two horned demons fighting one another. One was a brown fur-covered giant with blue whiskers. The other was smaller and forest-green in color. She couldn't see their faces, but she knew they were both evil. She wanted them to kill each other off and leave her alone, but they wouldn't allow her to be uninvolved in their conflict. No matter how much she begged and pleaded to remain a dispassionate bystander, an invisible force seemed to be pushing her to choose one over the other. When she finally helped the green demon kill the brown one in a vicious and gory battle, she'd awoken with a start. Unable to get back to sleep, she'd gone over to the chair by the window to watch the sunrise.

Jedediah Stiller's visit had completely upended her whole world. As soon as she heard his allegation that Zachary was Jonathan Stiller's killer, she knew it to be true. Any person who could coldly bash in the face of another soldier as he begged for his life was more than capable of murdering an innocent man on the streets of Augusta. Yet she also could tell that Jedediah was a creature well suited to killing in cold blood, and she had little doubt he was going to make good on his threat to pursue Zachary and kill him savagely in the name of justice. If two evil men so filled with hate were destined to kill each other, Catherine had to believe that God was pronouncing His judgment by letting them do so. After all, the world would be a much better place if neither man was allowed to hurt anyone ever again. Why should she get involved?

She brought her feet up onto the seat of the chair and hugged her legs because she knew the nightmare had given her the answer to that question. She couldn't just stand back and let it all happen without taking sides—she had to pick one of them. Perhaps the invisible force in the dream pushing her into the conflict was her conscience, or maybe it was God ensuring that His will would be done. It didn't matter what the source of the force was, it was now pushing her inexorably into the whole chaotic situation. She shook her head because she hated being such a powerless pawn. With this thought, she jumped up as though the wooden chair had suddenly become red hot. She wasn't an innocent bystander thrown into the fight between two evil men—she'd been the very source of the entire conflict! While her Zachary was away fighting in the war, she had become friendly with Jonathan Stiller. When he came over to cut wood for her father, she had made the lemonade and brought it out to him. He hadn't come up to the house to talk with her; she had been the initiator of their conversation. After all, she had so enjoyed the freshness of his attention and the novelty of being around someone new, she had never once tried to put on the brakes to the budding infatuation.

Why? It wasn't as if she'd fallen out of love with Zachary. Nothing he had done or not done had caused her feelings for him to fade, but she had to admit that courting a soldier who was far away and at risk of dying was exhausting. In her effort to protect herself from that inevitable heartbreak, she'd turned to Jonathan, who was present, safe, and very much alive. With him, she not only enjoyed the respite from having to worry all the time, she felt a new sense of hope in the fact that she could have a future that was not dominated by fears of death, and this was so novel these days, it had become intoxicating.

That being said, she'd never really been sure of what she and Jonathan actually had together. Sure, he was a good man—honest, hardworking, and he made her laugh—but she never fell completely in love with him. She enjoyed his attention and the thrill that came with that, but she had never once openly declared—not even to herself—that she was going to replace Zachary with him as her beau. Catherine had always assumed that her relationship with Jonathan was somewhere between a casual crush and a passing summer affair. She'd been greatly surprised to learn from Jedediah's rendition that his brother had actually given some thought to asking her to marry him! She had had no idea that his feelings for her went so deep, and she was pretty sure she would have said no to such a proposal.

When she'd first heard that Company D was coming home for a month-long furlough, she was actually very excited to see Zachary because she assumed their time together would erase any confusion she had from her interactions with Jonathan Stiller. But when they had their first visit together, it was clear that Zachary was a changed man, and she had even less clarity in the matter. She was desperate to rekindle their courtship, but he seemed to be pushing her away without knowing he was doing so, and she found herself frustrated and impatient with him. All she wanted was for Zachary to show more of his fire, but he didn't seem capable of that anymore. The innocent and open young man she'd fallen in love with was gone, and the new Zachary kept putting up a wall around himself anytime he was near her. And then, during their last visit, she had become so angry with his passivity and his acceptance of the rumors about Jonathan that she had snapped. If only he had fought for her like she asked...

She walked unsteadily to her bed. The cold wooden floorboards creaked with each step. She leaned heavily on the bedpost and hung her head. Suddenly, it was hard for her to breathe and her stomach balled up into a tight sphere within her. She had asked him to fight for her during their last visit! What if killing Jonathan had been the way this new Zachary showed that he was fighting for her? If this was true, she was the one who was single-handedly responsible for Jonathan Stiller's death!

She moaned loudly. If she was the one who had started the awful tryst, she couldn't step back and just let these murderous beasts fight it out—she needed to do something. But what could she do? For starters, she could head right over to the Websters' farm to tell them about her visit with Jedediah Stiller and warn them. Then she'd head to the Augusta Police and tell them everything. Everything.

Even if Jedediah was correct in his assessment that no one would get to Zachary before he did, Catherine knew she needed to finally start doing the right things to bring an end to this whole bloody affair. Clearly, up until this point, she'd done everything wrong. She could have chosen not to flirt with Jonathan in the first place; she could have been a good sweetheart to Zachary and written him more; she could have been more open with him during his time home; and she could have told Jedediah Stiller nothing when he'd confronted her in her parlor. Clearly, she'd failed in each of these decisions, and she was at ease with letting the Lord judge her for that, but she was not going to let herself fail again.

· · · · ·

By the time she had driven over to the Websters' home, the sun was hesitating ominously just above the treetops. Her father had offered only the slightest resistance to her leaving on this early morning trip; he seemed to sense his daughter's urgency and let her make her own way. After tying off the horse in the Websters' drive and hurrying to the front door, Catherine took her first notice of the other buggy in the dooryard. She wondered why there were visitors this early, but her mind was too awhirl with her own thoughts to ponder this deeply. She raised her hand to knock, but Mrs. Webster opened the door before she could do so.

"Oh, goodness, Catherine, how did you know?"

The woman's question totally flustered Catherine too much to speak. On the ride over, she'd prepared what she was going to say about Zachary's potential involvement in the murder of Jonathan Stiller and the vengeful older brother who was now on the hunt for him, but Mrs. Webster's passionate question made no sense in that internal dialogue. Catherine sputtered, then croaked, "Know what, Mrs. Webster?"

"About Elijah!" the woman replied with astonishment. She backed up and ushered Catherine into the house. A fire was burning in the fireplace and the oil lights were all lit. A man and a woman were seated on the sofa, and Catherine recognized them as Zachary's uncle and aunt, whom she had met several times. Both of them nodded toward her, but their faces were pale and tense. There was obviously something dire going on, and she turned back to Mrs. Webster to ask her for the details. But just then, Dr. Dixon came slowly down the stairs. He had the haggard look of a man who was wearied to the bone, and he carried a wooden medical case in his left hand. When he reached the two women standing at the foot of the stairs, he stopped and took his glasses off with his right hand.

Mrs. Webster held her hands together as if she was praying. "How is he, Doctor? Is he going to be all right?"

Dr. Dixon put his glasses back on and waited until Uncle Thomas and Aunt Clarice had joined them to hear what he was going to say. With his small audience now gathered, he sighed. "It isn't good. I had to take the foot. There weren't much left to it, but it had to come off nonetheless."

Mrs. Webster let out a short cry. She shook her head. "No, no, no! This cannot be happening!"

"I'm sorry, Mrs. Webster, but it was unavoidable. Elijah is starting to come out of the ether, and he needs to rest. He's lost a lot of blood, and even though he is young and strong, the next few hours will be crucial to see if he can survive this ordeal. My wife is tending to him right now while I go to my office to get a few more medical supplies. I will return as quickly as I can."

"Can I go up there, Doctor?" Mrs. Webster pleaded.

"Of course. Just let the boy rest. He needs his rest or he'll be lost."

She reached out and touched the doctor's arm. He smiled tentatively at her, then started to slide past and head to the door. He stopped suddenly and turned to beckon Uncle Thomas closer to him. The older man whispered so softly that Thomas had to lean in to hear him. "You need to go up and gather the wrapped bundle that my wife has and dispose of it somewhere. It contains what's left of the boy's foot and the bloody cloths from the surgery. I think it would be best if you take it all out of the room before the boy's mother sees any of it. Will you do that?"

Thomas nodded and showed the doctor out. He turned and walked past the women, saying under his breath, "The doctor asked me to take care of something before anyone else goes upstairs. So please stay here and wait for me to come back down."

The women watched as he plodded up the stairs, then Catherine put her hand on the old woman's arm. "Please, Mrs. Webster, tell me what's going on!"

"But I thought you knew!"

"No, ma'am, I just came over to talk to you about something else. What on earth has happened?"

"Elijah was attacked when he was on his way to the barn to check on a sick horse yesterday. He says a horrid monster came out of the shadows and smashed his foot with a hammer! I cannot, for the life of me, believe something like this could happen for no reason to such an innocent young boy!"

Catherine gasped, "Oh, how *horrible!*"

Mrs. Webster broke into tears. "I heard him scream, but didn't get out in time to see who attacked him. If it weren't for my brother coming by on his daily rounds to look in on us, Elijah would be dead. Thomas found me struggling to drag him back to the house. If he hadn't shown up when he did, we'd both be frozen to death out there! Oh, my goodness—can you imagine someone evil enough to do this?"

Catherine could, but she held her tongue. She hugged Mrs. Webster, saying, "Oh, I cannot believe this."

Mrs. Webster pulled back. "When I saw you at the door, I just thought you'd heard about Elijah and had come over to help. What did you want to talk to me about?"

But before Catherine could answer, Mrs. Webster staggered and looked like she would collapse. Catherine and Aunt Clarice caught her and supported her by her elbows, then guided her gently over to the sofa. Once she was seated, she broke down and sobbed. Seeing their exhaustion, Catherine asked, "Has anyone eaten or had any tea or coffee this morning? I could go in the kitchen and get some things started."

Aunt Clarice spoke quietly, "No, we haven't eaten or slept all night. It might do us all some good to get something warm in our bellies. It's going to be a long day."

"That is most kind," Mrs. Webster said between sobs, "but you don't need to bother yourself."

"No, Mrs. Webster, I need to do something useful. Let me fix some food—it's the least I can do."

Catherine headed into the kitchen. She worked to get the stove fire going from the embers, and she set out to get water for tea and coffee and cook breakfast. While she worked on this, she thought about what she needed to do next. Now that Jedediah Stiller had harmed Elijah Webster, everything was different, and she had to figure out a new plan. Her thoughts were interrupted by Aunt Clarice coming into the kitchen.

"Thomas just came down and reported that Elijah is starting to wake up, so Carrie has gone upstairs to be with him. I thought you might like some help in here. I sent Thomas out to milk the cow so we can have some fresh milk." The two women worked together in silence. They made coffee and boiled water for tea. Uncle Thomas came to the back door with a pail of milk, and Aunt Clarice set to making the biscuits. By the time they were in the oven, the kitchen was warm and aromatic. They were about to serve the breakfast when they were startled by Mrs. Webster standing in the doorway.

"Catherine, Elijah's awake and he wants to talk to you."

"To me?"

"To you."

Catherine wiped her hands on her apron and laid it on the counter before following Mrs. Webster out of the kitchen and up the stairs. When they entered the boy's room, the doctor's wife was wiping perspiration off his forehead. Mrs. Webster pointed to Catherine and said, "See, Elijah, I told you she was here."

The boy's face was white as a sheet and his eyes were dull and lifeless. When he tried to speak, Mrs. Dixon hushed him. But he was not to be deterred and whispered louder, "I need to talk with Catherine."

Mrs. Webster pointed at her again. "And here she is, Elijah."

"Naw, I need to talk...with her...alone, Ma."

Mrs. Dixon and Mrs. Webster exchanged glances and looked back at Catherine, who went toward the bed, saying, "Hello, Elijah. You can talk to me with these other ladies in the room, right?"

The boy feebly licked his lips. "You know I can't."

Catherine said, "You need to rest, Elijah. The doctor told us that you'll feel better if you do. We can talk later...when you're stronger."

The boy rolled his head on his pillow, creating a hollow in it. "No. Ma and Mrs. Dixon, please let me talk to Catherine alone for a moment. Just a short moment."

The two women looked at one another hesitantly, and as they walked past Catherine, their uncertain expressions betrayed their mixed emotions. After they closed the door softly behind them, Catherine slid closer to the boy and whispered, "A giant with tattoos on his face did this to you, didn't he?"

Elijah nodded. His voice was no more than a croak when he spoke again. "It was Jonathan Stiller's brother, Jedediah. He said he thought Zachary had killed his brother. Do you think that's true?"

"I think it is."

"Me, too." The boy's eyes grew larger. "He also said that you and Jonathan Stiller had fallen in love and were going to get married. Is that true?"

She shook her head. "No, that's not true, Elijah. The situation between me and Mr. Stiller was more complicated than I should have allowed, but I had not come to any such conclusion."

Elijah seemed to believe her, but when he spoke his voice was full of edges. "So you were romantic with Jonathan Stiller while my brother was down there fighting in the war?"

Catherine closed her eyes for a moment. When she opened them, she saw how badly the boy looked, so she took a washcloth from a basin by the head of the bed and wiped his sweaty forehead before answering him. "Nobody got too romantic, Elijah—you have to believe that—but I allowed the situation to go farther than I should have under the circumstances."

"Is that why my brother killed him?"

"Yes, I'm afraid so."

"Jedediah said he's going to find Zachary and kill him for what he's done. Do you think that's true, too?"

"Yes, I believe that to also be true."

The boy's gaze slid over to the window. "I ain't worried about that threat none. If the whole Confederate Army hasn't been able to kill Zachary, one man ain't gonna be able to neither. And I tole Jedediah Stiller that, too. My brother can handle himself."

Catherine continued to daub Elijah's forehead with the cool water. She got ready to say something soothing and reassuring, but the boy grabbed her wrist. "But *you* need to do something about this!" he pleaded. "You can't just sit back and let it happen."

Catherine gasped at the boy's choice of words. Then she said calmly, "I'm not exactly sure what I can do, Elijah. With Zachary back at the war getting ready to fight again, and Jedediah Stiller now on his way to find him, there's no way to stop either man. But I *am* going to tell the police the whole truth, and then let them do what they can."

Elijah tightened his grip on her with more strength than she would have expected from a person in his condition. "No, you can't do that! Nobody can know who did this to me!"

"But we have to tell them, Elijah! Then the police will go and find Jedediah before he gets to your brother."

"No, I don't want nobody to know! As soon as it gets out who did this to me and why, Zachary will be accused of murdering Jonathan Stiller. And I don't want that to happen to my brother. Or to my mother!"

"Well, as noble as that all is, Elijah, I don't think silence will help your brother any."

"But you can help him, Catherine. If you went down there and got word to him, he'd be ready for the monster's attack."

"But I can't—"

"You owe him that much!" the boy now yelled. "You owe him for what you've done to him! You owe him to at least try to do *something*, Catherine Brandford!"

Elijah's eyes had grown wild with delirium, and she could not free herself from his strangely strong grasp. She called out to the women outside the door, "Mrs. Dixon! Mrs. Webster! I need some help in here!"

The two women came into the room and over to the bed. When he saw them, Elijah let go and quieted down. Catherine hopped up and surrendered her place at the bedside to the onrushing women, and while they were busy tending to him, she slipped out of the room and down the stairs. She could see Aunt Clarice serving Uncle Thomas coffee and breakfast, so she grabbed her coat and silently left the house. She rushed to untie the horse, got in the buggy, and urged it forward. She had to get home and figure out what she was going to do to get the boy's haunting pleas out of her head.

Chapter Eighteen

Jedediah Stiller came out of the Boston & Maine train depot and scanned the snowy wasteland of Haymarket Square. The gas street lanterns barely lit the cobblestone plaza, yet he was able to see the imposing snowdrifts that the strong winter winds continued to shift and shape into frosty impediments to pedestrians. Very few people were out on the street in this weather at this time of night, and those that were did not wait long before getting into waiting hacks or heading down the dimly lit sidewalks to find protection from the elements. Jedediah looked back at the giant clock on the pediment of the huge depot and realized it was too late to even attempt traveling down to the Providence Railroad passenger depot near the bottom of the Commons. He would head there tomorrow morning after getting a good night's sleep. The giant man looked around again to get his bearings, and then, without hesitation, he started walking with the confidence of an imprinted memory.

He threaded his way through several deserted side streets, and crossed a couple of the larger thoroughfares before turning onto a smaller street that emptied into a small, open square. Jedediah knew none of the street names, but from his days as a whaler, he knew exactly where he was headed. In the middle of the block to his left was the familiar Mariners House. The way the four-story brick building stood shoulder to shoulder with the neighboring structures made it seem as if they all needed to huddle together to be united against the shadowy energy of the surrounding nighttime landscape. There were a number of active taverns and brothels nearby, and as the dark, faceless people scurried from one to the other, the opening and closing of doors allowed the sounds of screeching fiddles and unguarded laughter to escape into the cold and barren darkness outside. Jedediah licked his lips as he grinned at the familiarity of the scene, then quickly ducked into the doorway and entered the building.

As he approached the main desk, the older man standing behind it calmly looked up at Jedediah. He had a rectangular face with a very broad chin and his hair was neatly combed flat on top of his head, and although he seemed at peace, there was something offsetting in the power of his gaze as he waited to see what the new arrival wanted. He did not act surprised by either Jedediah's stature or his fierce appearance, and his facial expression remained impassive, as if he saw the likes of this personage more often than not. Finally, Jedediah broke the silence by saying, "Good evening, sir."

"Good evening."

"I am looking for a room for the night."

"I have one. Are you a mariner, sir?"

"I am a former whaler. I've stayed here before, many years ago. Tomorrow morn, I am to head down to the wharf to find my new ship."

The man pulled out a thick red leather-covered log book. "What is your name? And what was the name of the whaling ship you crewed for before?"

"Jedediah Stiller. I crewed on the *George & Susan*."

"Breakfast will be after morning services, Mr. Stiller," the desk clerk offered.

After paying, Jedediah headed up the stairs to his room on the third floor. He unlocked the door and put his seabag on the floor. He took off his heavy parka and sat down on the bed, but sprang up almost at once and paced the floor. He felt caged in this room, but he knew better than to allow himself to go back out into the "Black Sea" neighborhood, as there were too many temptations that could distract him from his primary mission. The news he had received in Portland about how the sharpshooters of Company D had been forced to wait three days in the barracks of Fort Preble in South Portland due to a locomotive boiler explosion reminded him that he was closer in his pursuit than he had originally thought. Instead of nearly a week-long head start, Zachary Webster was merely only a couple of days ahead of him. Given the inefficient travel the military was so renowned for and the difficult winter storm that New England had been dealing with,

Jedediah was now certain he was close to catching his brother's murderer, and he was like a tethered hound before a hunt.

A sudden soft rap on the door halted his thoughts and his pacing, and after a moment's hesitation, he made his way over to it and cautiously opened it. There, illuminated by a handheld candle, stood a stranger. The shadows seeped into the crags of his weathered face, and he grinned a kind smile. His bushy eyebrows and thick white sideburns were vaguely familiar to Jedediah, but he could not remember why.

"Sorry to bother you at this hour, Mr. Stiller, but I just happened to be sitting in the common area when I heard you give your name to the desk clerk. You may not remember me, but my name be George Blunt. I was the second mate aboard the *George & Susan*. I certainly remember *you*! No one made as big an impression as you did on the entire South Pacific whaling fleet, sir. I must say that you are still quite a legend there, my friend."

Jedediah's eyes opened wide with recognition. "I do remember you, Mr. Blunt. When I first saw you, your face looked familiar to me, but I could not place you. What is it you want of me tonight, sir?"

The man thrust his hand out. Jedediah looked down at it warily, then shook it. Blunt went on, "Ah, hearing your name again, sir, it made me reminisce about them good ol' days, and I be wondering if you would join me for a trip to a nearby tavern to talk about them over a mug of good rum."

"For what purpose, sir?"

"Ah, to catch up with one another. I'd treasure the chance to hear about your adventures and how you ended up back here in Boston. And I have news about some of the crew from that ship, including two I remember you being quite fond of—Benjamin Mason and Oliver Dexter. As a matter of truth, those two scoundrels are here in this very port at this very moment, and there's a good chance they may even be at one of the taverns near this establishment."

Although Jedediah knew it would be far more prudent to send this man on his way, he was too excited being so close to Zachary Webster to sleep. And, he had to acknowledge that he was thirsty for liquid spirits and the other outlets that only a tavern could provide. So he nodded his acceptance of Blunt's invitation. The man beamed with happiness. "Ah, excellent, Mr. Stiller. Let's make haste and see if we can catch those two rabble-rousers while they're sober enough to recognize you!"

Jedediah hefted his parka from the bed and went out into the hallway. He locked his door and turned to follow Blunt. He was over a head taller than the other man, yet, as they made their way down the stairs, the two men looked more like young boys sneaking out of the house for a night of mischief. When the stern man behind the desk saw them come down the stairs and prepare to leave the building, his voice boomed out, "You two gentlemen are not going out to imbibe, are you? We have very strict rules against that here at the Mariners House!"

Mr. Blunt turned and said, "Oh my goodness, no, kind sir. We're steadfast old friends, and we are just going to get a bite to eat and catch up on old stories. We will return within the hour, as sober as a judge."

They continued on their way without waiting for his response and walked quickly to the nearest tavern. When the wave of warmth from the coal stove, the smell of spilt beer, the aroma of the pipe tobacco, and the sodden sounds of illicit conversations hit them, Jedediah knew the evening was not going to end well for him. During those hard and violent years as a whaler, he had frequented similar institutions quite often to begin his nocturnal tempestuous affairs, and he now felt the same impulses and urges to do so again resurfacing.

The tavern was dimly lit, but Jedediah could see that the men who were seated at the long tables were mostly from the wharves. Several men in jaunty top hats wore their longshoreman hooks on their belts, while others wore the simple tunics of sailors. The men at the nearest table gave Mr. Blunt and Jedediah wary looks as they walked past with their cups of rum. They found two seats apart from the rest of the tavern's patrons, and they sat down. Just before they drank, Mr. Blunt pointed to the far corner of the room. "Hey, look there! I do believe that be Oliver Dexter right over yonder!"

Jedediah followed his companion's finger, but the man he was pointing at was clearly very old. Oliver Dexter had been Jedediah's age, so there was no way the old man was him. He shook his head. "You are either just plain mistaken or completely blind, Mr. Blunt."

Blunt laughed nervously. "Oh my! That's *not* him. My eyesight is certainly not as keen as it was when we were out whaling in the South

Pacific, eh? And speaking of that, here's to the South Pacific—where the whales are as bountiful as the beautiful Polynesian women!"

They clinked their tin cups together and drank. It had been quite some time since Jedediah had consumed any alcohol, and the familiar burn was joined by a sourness that surprised him. "Ach, this rum is bitter!"

"Have you not been drinking lately, my good man? This war has reduced us all to drinking and eating the putrid scraps left to us after the best is picked over for the war effort. All the good of everything goes right to them soldiers, while we are left with nothing but leather-like meat and bitter rum. We've all grown accustomed to drinking whatever is poured in our cups. I promise, after a few rounds of the stuff, you'll get used to the taste."

Jedediah felt the warmth of the rum working in his stomach. Bitter or not, the effect made him close his eyes and smile. He felt the drink put out certain fires within him and start a few new ones. He had missed this feeling, and he emptied the rest of his cup in one long slug to feel more of it.

Blunt smiled at him. "I will buy you another one, my thirsty friend, and then I want to hear what happened to you after I last saw you in Lahaina."

Jedediah noticed how the man's words echoed in his head, and he shook it gently to clear it out. He watched Blunt get the drinks at the bar and wave his hands over them like he was shooing flies away. The man turned and came back toward their table. A wave of fatigue suddenly hit Jedediah, and his eyelids felt so heavy he struggled to keep them up as Blunt set both cups on the table and sat down heavily in his chair.

"The last time I saw you, Mr. Stiller, was when the *George & Susan* was in the lovely harbor of Lahaina to pick up fresh water and supplies. Captain Cooper gave us all a night of shore leave, and you got into that fight with a man over a Hawaiian girl. Remember that?"

"I do, indeed, Mr. Blunt. How could I ever forget it? Captain Cooper was so anxious for me to meet that man from the *Resolution*, but I wanted nothing more than to be left alone. The captain wouldn't relent, and he herded me over to that strange warehouse. And when we got there, we could see what the bastard had done to that poor girl. No one seemed inclined to stop him from doing it again, so I took matters into my own hands."

"Oh, you certainly did. You beat him most soundly, Mr. Stiller. You know, after that man died, the captain had to pay a pretty price to the local authorities to assure your safe return to the boat. He did so, but you can imagine he felt doubly cheated when he discovered later that night that you had jumped ship. Of course, due to a mistake made by the other mates, your absence wasn't discovered until after we'd left port and were headed back out to sea. Do you know that we even turned around and came back to look for you? Of course you were long gone. I must say, Captain Cooper was quite displeased. He expected more loyalty from a man whose freedom he had just purchased."

Jedediah's eyelids were fluttering now, but they narrowed in anger enough to cause Blunt a momentary instance of discomfort. The big man slurred, "Captain Zephaniah Cooper never owned me, Mr. Blunt!"

"No, of course not, Mr. Stiller, I'm not trying to say he did. He just valued you greatly, that is all. He knew your prowess was unmatched by any other man in the fleet, and that only made your departure all the more devastating to him."

"Captain Zepheniah Cooper was a monster! After I rescued that girl, he sent me to the brig like some kind of prisoner! Down there in the bowels of the *George & Susan*, I came to the conclusion that I needed to get off that ship immediately. The salt air had gotten to the lock, so it didn't take much effort to crumble her. The men of the fo'c'sle were all sleeping off their drunken escapades and no one saw me gather my belongings and make my way off the ship."

"But why, Mr. Stiller? After the captain had just done what he did for you and for the value he placed upon you, why would you return his charity with that kind of disrespect?"

"Value? Charity? Captain Cooper was a cruel and ruthless man. Don't you remember how frequently he would order a crewman flogged? He went out of his way to make our lives unbearable. You know all this—you know I speak the truth. Before that night, I detested that man. But him condoning the rape of that Hawaiian girl in the warehouse sealed my hatred for him. He's lucky I never got the chance to meet him alone. He would have felt my ire."

"Oh, that may be all true, but it's history now. Where did you go after you left the ship, Mr. Stiller? I'm curious how you were able to vanish so quickly."

Jedediah's elbow slipped off the table, and he smiled foolishly at this. "That poor girl's family took me in. I made my way back to the warehouse to make sure she was okay, but she was no longer there. Several members of her family had gathered because they wanted justice for what had happened, and once they understood I was the one who had killed her attacker, they took me in and protected me. When anyone inquired about my whereabouts, they lied for me. I stayed with them for many months while they taught me their ways. I learned to love them as my family."

Blunt shook his head. "Incredible! What a tale! I swear by God, this is the last round I'm going to buy you, Mr. Stiller. But I want to hear about your time with the natives. Are they the ones that tattooed your chin and face?"

"No, that happened a little later with the Maori—"

"Oh, I want to hear that epic story, too, Mr. Stiller! But first I must get more rum for you, my friend. I will be right back."

Jedediah felt another wave of fatigue hit him. He was out of the practice of hard drinking, but his current inebriation surprised him. Two drinks seemed hardly enough to make him feel so drunk, but his fingertips were numbing and he felt as if his arms were made of lead. He could barely lift his hand to take the cup from Blunt when he returned to the table.

"Now, Mr. Stiller, let's drink to the opportunities this war provides us."

Blunt's words made no sense to Jedediah, and he leaned heavily on his elbow. "What opportunities could this war provide anyone?"

"Oh, you cannot believe the money that is out there for men like us, Mr. Stiller. Nowadays, if you have something that is desired, there is no limit to the amount someone will pay you for it. Oh, and this war desires so very, very much! Let's drink to that!"

Jedediah downed his drink. The burn was no longer there, but the bitterness had now built up an acidity capable of eating out his innards. When Jedediah looked around, nothing made sense. Blunt moved like some kind of mirage. One moment, he was directly in front of him, the next, he was tapping on his arm. The floor of the tavern seemed to suddenly lift up and the walls oscillated as the room began to spin. He looked for Blunt and found him talking to two men that Jedediah hadn't noticed come up to the table. When he started to ask who they were, his mouth refused to work.

Like heavy curtains being drawn across the windows, the edges of his vision began to darken. His head was getting so heavy, it tottered. He tried to move his hands, but they felt glued to the table. When he looked down at them, the world turned into a blackness that was sticky and thick like ink.

Chapter Nineteen

Even before he'd begun to fully regain consciousness, Jedediah Stiller knew he was onboard a ship. The smell of the sea, the rhythmic undulations of the floor, and the subtle groaning of the wooden beams were all the clues he needed. As he lay on his back and let his brain process what had happened to him, the way his stomach flip-flopped alerted him to the fact that he was going to be sick. He did not have the ability to stand up yet, so he merely turned his head and spewed bile onto the deck. He did this twice, and then he retched violently. Without moving his head, he opened his eyes. His vomit, which was now spreading like batter on a hot griddle from the motion of the sea, was threatening to wash back into his prone body, so he tried to move away from this foulness. A metal chain attached to a manacle around his ankle clanked and stopped him. When he looked up toward the end of the chain, he saw that a man wearing all black was standing over him with a wooden bucket in his hand. As he threw the cold ocean water down upon Jedediah, the man spoke in a voice like a snake's hissing. "Ah, Mr. Stiller, so kind of you to finally awaken. It's truly a pathetic sight to see you so encumbered after a night of imbibing. Tsk-tsk, drinking is indeed the device of the devil."

Jedediah furiously blinked his eyes to get the saltwater out so he could see his assailant. The voice was familiar, but his brain was not working well enough to gather his thoughts into recognition. When he finally could see clearly again, the man in black went over and put the bucket down near the wall and glared at him. He was a sizable man with large and powerful hands. He had thick sideburns which connected his full mustache with a trimmed beard, and his head was covered with jet-black hair that was neatly parted on the side. The man stared down at Jedediah, and his small, haunting eyes bored into him with malevolence. And although he was not typically intimidated by the glares of other men, this man made Jedediah uneasy. And this feeling triggered enough recognition that Jedediah gasped as he said, "Captain Zepheniah Cooper."

"I am wholly touched that you remember me, Mr. Stiller."

The events of the night before flooded back. Mr. Blunt. The tavern. The rum. Passing out after only three drinks. Now that he was waking up on a ship with Captain Cooper, he knew none of this was random. "Mr. Blunt did this?"

"Oh, he's a clever one. One of the best mates I've had during all of my days at sea, but he's found himself a real niche in that land-based business of his now. He does not like to be called a crimp, but he's clearly one of the best ones out there, I must say. You are not the first man he has supplied to me in this manner. Matter of fact, many of the ships leaving Boston these days carry someone who was shanghaied by Mr. Blunt."

"Mr. Blunt did this to me?"

"Aye, but that's not important now. You see, Mr. Blunt is also a bounty broker. Cleverly, he makes two impressive wages on each one of you dolts he brings to us captains."

Jedediah rubbed his head. "I don't understand what any of this has to do with me, Captain."

"I don't really have time to explain it to you, Mr. Stiller. After all, I do have a ship to command. But since you seem still in the dark, I will tell you just enough of what you need to know. The rest you will have to figure out on your own. Mr. Blunt knows that some of us captains have a need for extra assistance in filling our crews from time to time, so he lingers at the Mariners House to crimp them for us. He was there last night, waiting to ambush some dunderhead for me, when who should walk in but you! As soon as he heard your name again, the man realized he had the chance for a momentous payday. While we don't work directly together anymore, he was more than well aware of my desire to get my hands on you, Mr. Stiller, and you can imagine how excited he was to have you walk right into his clutches last night. He knew exactly how much I'd pay to have you sign on with me again."

"But I didn't sign anything!"

"Oh my, that Mr. Blunt has quite the system. He slips that tincture into the drinks. I don't even want to know what is in that devious medicine, for it can incapacitate a man with only a few drops. Now, you took more to subdue than anyone else he's ever shanghaied before—and believe me, he charges extra for that. Ah, but those are just more of the losses you are going to help me recoup while you are a crew member aboard the *Nipigon*!"

"But since I didn't sign anything, you cannot legally hold me."

"Pshaw—you certainly *did* sign the necessary papers! They now reside in the safe within my quarters, and they will not need to be molested unless you try to run away from me again. Then I will use them to have you legally hunted down for the reward."

"I did not sign any papers...at least not when I was sober, and you know that."

"Ah, you still don't understand how impressive Mr. Blunt's system for obtaining crew members is. It doesn't matter how he does it, but he gets all of his catches to sign the necessary papers as volunteers for service in the war effort. And because a signed document is a signed document no matter what the poor lout says was his condition when he did the signing, it is a completely legal contract in the eyes of the courts. That in and of itself makes for an ideal relationship between him and us captains. He makes his money by getting both a crimping fee and the bounty for the enlisting sailor, and we get a man who shows no permanent signs of abuse, and who is a legal member of our crew. The old way of using the copper pipe resulted in too many deaths or the loss of more than a few days of labor as the new sailors recovered from their knock on the noggin. But by using his magical tincture, the recruits need just a saltwater shower, a little rest, and then they're ready for working the deck. Oh, but not you. No, you are something a little different to me. So much more than just another warm body to crew my ship. I have real plans for you, Mr. Stiller!"

Jedediah started to shake his head fiercely, but it only made him dizzier. "I still don't understand. What could you possibly want from me, Captain Cooper?"

The man inhaled as he reared back like a cobra. "Ah, you still don't understand our relationship, do you, savage? I would've thought that moment of comprehension had already hit you, but maybe Mr. Blunt's tincture is stronger than I give it credit. I need to go back to the bridge, so I will leave you with those thoughts to ponder down here in your pen today. Maybe if you use your time wisely and do some deep thinking, you will grasp what we are to one another, Mr. Stiller. Before I go, however, let me give you a few clues to help you with this task. First off, why do you really think I bought you so many rounds of drinks whenever the *George & Susan* was in port?"

"You never did that—"

The captain put his finger to his lips. "Oh, I did, but you were just too drunk to realize where your endless drinks were coming from. And that leads right to my second clue: Why do you think I was always present whenever you became engaged in one of those horrific fights you were so prone to be a part of on the docks during those dark days? What possibly could a man like me gain from a member of my crew who was so consistently determined to get into violent fisticuffs with other whalers in foreign ports?"

"I still don't understand..."

"Now, I must take my leave—duty calls. But please do ponder on these questions some, and maybe when we have a chance to chat again in the future, you will have the slightest idea as to why I paid Mr. Blunt to procure your services again. Until then, Mr. Stiller."

The captain gave a mock salute and started toward the cabin door. Jedediah reached out to grab his boot and said fiercely, "You do not understand, Captain Cooper. I cannot stay on this ship. I'm in pursuit of the Union soldier who killed my only brother, Jonathan. I am close to catching him, but I must continue that pursuit! I must!"

Captain Cooper began to say something in quick rebuttal, but cocked his head in such a way as to indicate he'd just heard something intriguing. "You don't say, Mr. Stiller! Here I was, worried that you might've lost the fires that fueled your old fighting ways, and you now present me with proof that you still may have a sense of urgency within you after all. Hmm...perhaps there are enough of the same embers within you these days to start those flames anew. It is so helpful when the innate needs of others wholly intersect with your own, isn't it? Until later, savage."

The door opened enough to let Jedediah see that he was in the bowels of a steamship. When the door closed, he heard the captain lock a padlock outside. He closed his eyes to quiet the drums of pain blaring in his head. When he slowly opened them again, the light from the one small porthole illuminated the pool of his vomit on the deck. The captain's saltwater bath now diluted and dispersed it a little, but the sour aroma of it made him gag again, and he fought to crawl far enough away to not smell it anymore. The chain and manacle stopped him again, and he reached down to touch them. He pulled the chain taut and tugged mightily on it. The distinctive sound of the chain clapping against a metallic ring let him know he was chained to the rings that once would have secured livestock aboard the ship. With this realization, he understood the futility of his situation, so he closed his eyes and let himself fall into a deep sleep.

When Jedediah awoke, it was dark in the cabin and he knew that night had descended. He felt less groggy, so he crawled to the full extent that his chain would allow and felt around his enclosure as much as he could. He found his stuffed seabag, and he quickly ascertained that it had not been opened nor had the contents been molested. This struck him as foolish on the part of his abductors, and he smiled to himself in the darkened cabin. Although he didn't have a firearm inside the bag, there were several of his Hawaiian weapons and his bag of coins in it. When he caught a whiff of something nearby that smelled like food, he cautiously crawled toward it until he discovered the tray with a cold meal that had been placed inside his cell. Next to it was the wooden pail for him to piss and shit in. He searched around a little more, but found no bedding. He grimaced to himself because the coarseness of the wooden deck was beginning to hurt his hips.

He felt the individual links of the chain again. It felt similar to one of those used to secure the casks of whale oil on the ships of his past, and there was little doubt the chain was nearly new. These two factors meant that there was no chance he'd be able to break free. Indeed, a similar blind appraisal of his bindings revealed that any attempt to break or smash the pieces would end fruitlessly. All the metal components of his entrapment were new enough that the saltwater in the air hadn't begun to weaken them in the least, and he knew that escape was impossible at this point. He'd have to be patient and wait for a time in the hopefully not-so-distant future, but he wasn't sure he was capable of that.

The subtle movements of the ship began to lull him back into a familiar peacefulness, so he turned his thoughts to Captain Cooper's parting words. The resulting haziness from Mr. Blunt's potion had addled his brain enough to make him misunderstand the words that had been said, but now, as he regained some clarity, he struggled to understand what the captain had been inferring with his clues. His fights on the docks of the South Pacific had been both encouraged and witnessed by the captain, and he had paid Mr. Blunt a lot of money to shanghai him. As a matter of fact, the captain seemed downright giddy to have Jedediah back in his midst again. But why?

Then, in a flash of insight, Captain Cooper's words sparked a memory that Jedediah had long tried to keep buried within him, but now that reminiscence seemed intent to claw its way out of him. Once, after a night of drinking during shore leave in Honolulu, Jedediah had felt the omnipresent need to hurt someone again, and he had gone in search of a worthy opponent on the docks. Before he could find one, however, Captain Cooper and several of his mates had led him away from the potential fisticuff and toward the rear entrance of a nondescript building on the wharves. Inside, amidst the smoke of oil lamps and tobacco pipes, he found himself in a room full of benches that rose in a series of tiers around a boarded-open arena the size of a whaleboat. Men of all colors and creeds hurled shouts in various languages as they waved flapping paper money, shook golden coins in their hands like dice, and pointed and gestured wildly. It had taken his inebriated mind a moment to comprehend that they were in the midst of a dogfighting match.

In several languages, a man announced that the betting was now over and the much-anticipated fight was about to begin. Jedediah had never seen a dogfight before, and he was drunkenly intrigued enough to stay, though he'd regret that decision for the rest of his life. One dog was introduced, and it was a gigantic example of a noble breed. The announcer went on to say the owner had made a wager that his animal could take on and defeat three rivals, and that was the fight on tap. The other owner had three dogs chained up on the opposite side of the arena, and they were short muscular dogs that were whining to get into the fight. When the signal was finally given to release the animals, the owner of the three dogs only released two of them. The crowd seemed to understand something that Jedediah did not. He watched as the owner of the massive dog yelled frantically, but his complaints were drowned out by the frenetic agitation of the crowd.

The lone larger dog was attacked at once by the two smaller dogs, which coordinated their assaults to be simultaneously high and low. While one went for the adversary's front legs, the other sprang at its neck. As a veteran of his own inspired violence, Jedediah was not prone to squeamishness, but the noises, the yelps, the snarls, and the roar of the bloodthirsty crowd made his stomach tighten, and he looked away from it all for a moment. When he looked back, he saw that the tactic of the smaller dogs was working—one had lunged for the huge dog's throat and had it in its unbreakable bite, while the other continued to snap wildly at its front legs. The sound like a branch breaking and a bloodcurdling yelp of pain made it clear to the audience that the smaller dog had gotten hold of the bigger dog's front leg and broken it. The fur of the three beasts was covered in foamy slobber, and the two smaller dogs now seemed to pin the larger dog in a deathly embrace.

Then, in the blink of an eye, the large dog flipped the head of the lower attacker into its mouth and began to shake its head violently. This furious action snapped the neck of the smaller dervish, and the big dog then flung the lifeless carcass to the other end of the dirt arena. It struggled to dislodge the attacker latched onto its throat and the crowd cheered wildly, then Jedediah watched as the owner of the three dogs released the final animal to join the fray. Although the massive dog put up a fierce defense to this final charge, its wounds were too great for it to maneuver well enough to fend off the inevitable. And as the two smaller dogs took it down and killed it by ripping open its throat, and the crowd watched the beast's blood spill into the dirt, Jedediah understood the cold efficiency of the owner holding onto one dog until the larger opponent was too weak to defend itself.

The bettors were all in a frenzy, and the room erupted in a cacophony of curses and shouts, but Jedediah was so outraged by the killing of such a beautiful creature in such underhanded means that he rushed forward toward the ring. He never saw who intercepted him, but they must have used some kind of blackjack or leather sap on him because everything suddenly went black. He awoke back on the ship, and on the very next day, under orders of the captain, he was flogged in front of the entire crew. Afterward, he was told that he was never to interfere with another gambling event. His punishment was so severe because he had embarrassed the captain and the entire crew. He never went to another dogfighting match.

Now, Jedediah Stiller gasped. The enlightenment coming from the captain's comments was almost bright enough to illuminate the dark cabin. While he'd been a crewman on the *George & Susan*, he'd been willing to get into those fights on the docks, yet they were not just arbitrary events. No, they were arranged to provide gambling opportunities for the captains and crews of the other whalers. And if that was true, then Captain Cooper had probably made great profits off of Jedediah's victories. No wonder the man was so devastated when he'd jumped ship! It hadn't been only the loss of a capable crew member that had caused him pain—it was the loss of the betting revenue, too. And here he was, chained up in a cabin aboard a steamship like one of those beasts, waiting for the next fight. Jedediah groaned loudly and pounded the deck with his fist until his hand throbbed, for the truth of his current situation hurt him deeply. He was the captain's fighting dog once more.

Chapter Twenty

Joseph Brandford saw the note on the table and instantly recognized his daughter's handwriting. The silence of the house foretold the gist of the message on the folded paper, but he sat down heavily to read it anyway. He needed to know why his daughter would go off and leave him.

Dearest Father,

It is with a heart full of sorrow that I leave you without properly saying good-bye, but I could not take the chance of allowing you to talk me out of what I know in my heart I need to do. I have come to the unmistakable conclusion that I must play my part in helping out with the devastating war which continues to rage in this country. Seeing my beloved Zachary reminded me that every day, brave young men are lining up to throw themselves into the war's insatiable need for killing and maiming. While we in the North continue to enjoy our relatively carefree and peaceful lives, these noble patriots are willing to sacrifice everything for us, even though they are not getting the best medical care. This is unacceptable, Father. I am unable to stand by anymore and let these brave men continue to die from their wounds. I was conversing with Ardelia Adams the other day after church about this, and she made mention of the many women who are heading to New York City to join the U.S. Sanitary Commission to become war nurses. And that is exactly what I plan to do—travel down to New York and join the cause for giving our soldiers the best care I am capable of.

Please do not worry about me, Father. I will use caution throughout my travels, and I am assured that the Lord will watch out for my safety in this noble endeavor. I took the funds that I have been saving for a new dress as my traveling money, and I hope to be in New York as soon as the day after tomorrow. I hate to leave you alone on the farm, but I know you can take care of yourself. When I can, I will write to you and send you word from wherever I am. My love and a thousand kisses to you, my dearest father. Good-bye.

Your Loving Daughter,
Catherine

He read it again, and then refolded the paper and put it down gently on the wooden table. He gazed out the window at the small cemetery at the edge of the field. The deep snow had completely buried his wife's tombstone, but he stared straight at where it was and thought about how angry she would have been at him for letting their one and only daughter do such a crazy thing. He put his head in his hands for a moment, but then looked up defiantly. He struck the table with his fist and smiled. Catherine had been raised to be fiercely independent, and he smiled at the fact that his daughter would not sit around and wait for this world to correct itself; she was going out to do something to help it along. His smile broadened, and he let the negative emotions fly from his heart. He was proud of his daughter, and being sure of the purity of her intentions and confident of her abilities, he knew that the spirit of his dead wife would share his beliefs enough to feel the same pride.

But when he looked down at the note again, a wave of cold melancholy washed over him and caused a small tear to well up in the corner of his eye. He understood that the note was the only good-bye he'd ever get from his daughter Catherine, and although it was well written, it didn't suffice. There was so much more he wanted to say to her before his time was up in this world, and he wept with the certainty that he would never see his daughter again in his lifetime. And that made him sadder and more alone than he'd been since the death of his beloved wife.

Chapter Twenty-One

As the train rumbled toward Portland, Catherine tried to get Elijah Webster's delirious plea out of her head. But she knew he'd been absolutely correct—the only way to absolve herself from the sins she had committed was to intervene somehow between Jedediah and Zachary. If she didn't at least attempt to right her wrongs, her life would be forever tainted by the guilt she felt, and like some kind of consuming cancer in her soul, the rest of her life would become hollow and empty. It pained her to think of the difficulties that lay ahead for her father because of her departure, but she knew the decision to leave at once was the right one.

But now as the train carried her toward nothing but uncertainty, she found herself asking the question, *for what?* Or, more exactly, *for whom?* Before she went much farther, she needed to identify the real purpose of her trip. Was her goal to warn Zachary Webster? Or was it to stop Jedediah Stiller? Catherine knew that, although they seemed to be similar questions, their answers were not only quite different, but full of divergent implications as well. While it was obvious both men were horrible and cruel monsters and she still had half a mind to let them kill each other, the shrill voice of Elijah's pleas sliced through all of that. To truly accept responsibility for being the cause of it all meant that she could not sit back and let it happen. She needed to make a decision about who to save.

A sense of self-loathing suddenly made her feel nauseous. There was no way to forgive the fact that her own actions had led directly to the downfall of three men, maimed a young boy, and left at least three families with broken hearts. She fully understood that she was embarking on this outlandish trip in hopes of being given the chance to alleviate her own shame. Clearly, she was undertaking all of this to prove to herself that she was not also a horrific monster—that doing the right thing and stopping a killing in a world that was wallpapered with death these days was the only way to wash the blood from her own hands. The irony of it all made her laugh aloud to herself.

Now that she could admit she was the catalyst for the heinous events that had happened so far, and that that role made her as much of a guilty participant as both of the tormented men, she understood she still had to make one more confession—she was still in love with Zachary Webster. And while it was true his cold-blooded act of murder was vile proof of the depravity of his soul, it had been a crime of passion that she herself had asked him to do. Whereas Jedediah Stiller's lust for vengeance was based on a similar emotion, his crippling of an innocent boy was so filled with cruelty, it was indefensible. It was a difference of mere degrees, but it was enough to focus her feelings toward the two men. How she would get over her subtle fear of Zachary or how she would forgive him completely for murdering an innocent man was not as important as the realization that she wanted to save him and spend the rest of her life with him. Matters of the heart were never sane, but hers had spoken, and she knew what she needed to do.

Outside her window, the sun was setting, and Catherine understood the train would arrive in Portland in the evening—a fact that reflected just how poorly prepared she was for this trip. She had no way to find Zachary Webster and warn him, any more than she had the train schedules memorized. She had literally headed out the door and away from her home without any plan in place, and the foolishness of this now struck her as so funny, she laughed out loud again. Up until this point in her life, she'd always thought of herself as a woman of higher intelligence and gumption, and she knew it was now time to prove that in action during this trip. She would have to make the next decisions about her journey as soon as her feet touched the train platform in Portland, and despite the sheer madness of it all, she was suddenly brimming with self-confidence. With the choice made to save Zachary, she was spurred on with renewed urgency to get to him before that agent of retribution could, and she wished the train would move just a little faster.

Chapter Twenty-Two

A good night's sleep allowed Jedediah to completely rid his system of whatever poison Mr. Blunt had given him, and he awoke with a clear mind as the faint light of sunrise filtered into his cabin. He stood up without any dizziness and walked over to the porthole. A slight sea was gently rocking the ship, and on the far horizon, there was a razor-thin strip of the mainland illuminated by the rising sun. From this, Jedediah ascertained that his cabin was on the starboard side of the ship and they were currently headed south. Just what he could do with these fragments of deduction, he didn't know yet, but his brain was so starved for the facts about his circumstance, he smiled contentedly with even these two small pieces of the puzzle in place.

The door of his cabin suddenly swung open, and a large man with dark olive skin and greased black hair followed Captain Cooper inside. As the captain re-latched the door, he said in a voice that was slippery with evil, "See, Mr. Sinagra, I told you I had him in here!"

Jedediah started to say something, but the stranger squinted his brown eyes in anger as he pounced on him. After using his elbows to defend himself against his assailant's powerful punches, Jedediah finally shoved the man back and yelled, "Why is he attacking me?"

The man, whose large forearms and neck muscles strained the fabric of his shirt, was in such a pure rage that there was no way to reason with him. Just before the man began his next assault, however, Jedediah allowed his honed survival instincts to slip into place, and he took the stance of a man ready for a fight. That was when he noticed the smirk on the captain's face.

The sight of this made the reality of the situation become dazzlingly clear, and he came out of his combative crouch to stand fully erect. This move gave his attacker the opportunity to land a mighty blow to his midsection which took his breath away. The large man stepped back and rocked on his feet before saying, "*Se tu scopassi mia mamma, ti taglierei l'uccello e te lo ficcherei in bocca!*"

"My Italian might be a little rusty, Mr. Stiller, but I think he just said that he wants to cut your manhood off and shove it in your mouth."

Jedediah looked at the big Italian man, shook his head, and asked with a wheeze, "Why is he so infuriated with me?"

The captain's smirk grew more obvious. "Wouldn't *you* be a little angry to find out that the man who had raped your mother was traveling on this very boat?"

"You know I did no such thing!"

"Perhaps...but *he* doesn't. When I heard the news about his unfortunate mother being attacked recently in Boston and his personal anguish about it, it made sense to tell him that the evil perpetrator of this horrific act had been caught and was being transported on this steamship to the Fort Delaware prison. When I told him this, Mr. Sinagra wanted very much to meet you!"

"I know what you are doing, Captain Cooper, and I am not going to participate in your twisted sport. I'm not your cur for you to bait!"

The captain chuckled nastily. "I think you need to reevaluate your situation, Mr. Stiller. You see, Mr. Sinagra is very intent on killing you."

As if he'd understood the captain's remarks, the Italian came at Jedediah again. This time Jedediah brought his arms up to deflect the attack, but the man grappled onto him and tried to get his hands around his throat to choke him. Although his opponent was very strong, Jedediah knew he was stronger, and he held him at bay. Raising his voice, he implored, "I'm not who the captain says I am! I arrived in Boston only two nights ago and was brought aboard this boat against my will by a crimp!"

The man's face was twisted with rage, and it was obvious the English words had bounced off of him. He churned his legs and tried to drive Jedediah back. The two men grunted with exertion. Jedediah glanced at Captain Cooper, but the man was shaking his head in disappointment.

Seeing this, Jedediah snarled, "I'm not your fighting dog, Captain Cooper. I will not do what you want me to do."

"Then you will die, Mr. Stiller. Mr. Sinagra here has one thing on his mind—vengeance. He doesn't care about anything else. Your choice, though. I really don't care, one way or another."

Jedediah roared at the man, "*Il capitano è compreso! Io sono innocente! Non ho fatto male la tua madre!*"

Captain Cooper laughed. "Very good, Mr. Stiller! Even though your Italian was nearly flawless, he won't listen to you!"

Sinagra's eyes softened for a mere instant, then they hardened again. "*Il capitano detto fosse un male maligno, e che si tenta di mentire per me. Le mie orecchie sono chiuse per le bugie.*"

"I told you so, Mr. Stiller. Mr. Sinagra won't listen to your lies. He knows you are the devil!"

Jedediah's anger at the captain was building, and the hatred that had accumulated over his years on the whaler now smashed through the walls of containment that he'd put up during his later healing. In an explosion of power, he broke free from the Italian's grasp and pushed the man so hard that he crashed to the floor. When the man looked up, his angry expression was now laced with fear. He knew that the strength of the giant was clearly beyond his own, but he wouldn't stop until he had vengeance. He reached down into his tall leather boot, pulled out his folding knife, stood up quickly, and opened it. The knife was about eight inches in length, with a carved bone handle and a very slender, very sharp blade that was now locked into place.

"Uh-oh, Mr. Stiller," said the captain in a voice completely devoid of emotion. "I think things just went from bad to worse for you. Do you see what is in Mr. Sinagra's hand? That's an infamous Italian folding knife. From the way he's holding it, I think he's had some practice with it. I hate to say so, Mr. Stiller, but I think he's getting ready to fillet you like a flounder."

Jedediah backed up a little, tripped, and fell onto his butt. The captain laughed cruelly. "He's scared of you, Mr. Sinagra, and he's down on his ass. Kill him now!"

The large Italian man grinned crookedly and advanced with the spike-like blade leading the way. Jedediah stood and backed up two more paces.

Encouraged that the giant was afraid of the knife, Mr. Sinagra kept coming. When he thrust at the midsection of his opponent, Jedediah lunged with blinding speed and not only avoided the knife thrust, but wrapped a section of the chain—which he had gathered during his choreographed fall—around the wrist of the knife-wielding hand. In a motion that was quick and powerful, he broke the man's wrist. As the knife clattered to the floor, Jedediah whipped the chain loose, used it as a bludgeon, and shattered the man's jaw. The dazed Italian fell heavily to the floor. When he tried to stand, blood and broken teeth drained from his mouth, staining the wooden planks. Before he could rise, however, Jedediah wrapped the chain around his neck.

The captain looked on with amused eyes. Finally he said, "Well, what are you waiting for? You need to finish what you started, Mr. Stiller."

"I told you, I will not kill this man just to amuse you."

The captain clucked his tongue. "Have you lost your touch, Mr. Stiller?"

"Signor Sinagra, the captain has lied to you! Stop struggling and listen to me!"

"How wonderfully naïve, Mr. Stiller. Do you actually believe it will all end with you releasing him? Oh, I'm sure Mr. Sinagra will need some time for that wrist and that smashed jaw to heal, but he'll be just waiting for another shot at you. And in the meanwhile, the rest of the Italians in this crew will line up for their chance to get revenge upon the man who bested their comrade. You remember the loyalty that comes from being part of a crew, don't you? There will be a new adversary for you each day. Every single time this door opens, there will be another one you will have to fight for your life. Over and over. Their vengeance will become a fever that has no medicine. Man after man will take up arms against you, and I will not only encourage it, I'll help them get in here at all times of the day or night. How does that sound to you, Mr. Stiller?"

Jedediah looked the captain squarely in the eye. "Do you think you can scare me, Captain Cooper? Do you think I fear any man?"

The captain's eyes twinkled as he chuckled. "Ah, you're a very complex beast, Mr. Stiller. No, you do not fear any man. I'd even go so far as to say that you may have *lost* the ability to feel fear toward anything or anyone. However, you and I both know you do fear one thing these days—that you'll never get the chance for vengeance. You want to find and kill the murderer of your brother, do you not? Why be a prisoner in this cabin forced to fight for your life against daily waves of vengeful Italian crewmen? And all the while, the man who ended your brother's life will only get further and further away from you. How much distance will he put between you and him while you fight for your survival each and every day? But, like everything in life, Mr. Stiller, there's room for negotiation in this situation."

"What is it you want, Captain Cooper?"

The captain's eyes darkened. "First, I want you to kill this man."

The Italian understood enough to start thrashing. He was creating enough of a tumult that Jedediah knew he needed to be quieted. He began to put some force on the chain, lifting the man off the deck and pulling him up. The man continued to struggle, but the gagging and gurgling sounds of suffocation coming from his mouth signaled that he was about to lose consciousness.

"No, Mr. Stiller, I don't want you to just make him go to sleep. I want you to *kill* him! If you are too soft to do this, you'll never hear my proposal. And I can assure you that you *do* want to hear that. For it will not only give you a fighting chance to catch your brother's killer, it actually offers some assistance in the matter. And the truth is, you really have no other option. It's my proposal or this life of hell. That is the choice you have in front of you right now."

When Jedediah did not respond, the captain turned and headed toward the door. "I will inform the crew of your decision."

As the wave of hatred for the captain engulfed him, Jedediah effortlessly snapped Mr. Sinagra's neck with the chain. He laid the man's body down on the deck, and as the cabin filled with the stench of urine and feces, he stepped back from the corpse. The heavy tips of the man's leather boots kicked a hollow tattoo on the planks, but when that stopped the silence of the room was deafening.

The captain took a couple of steps forward to look at the dead man, but did not get too close to Jedediah. "Ah, I see you still have the blind rage to do what you need to do, Mr. Stiller. Very good. You will be glad to know that you passed the test I set for you today. You are not yet in true fighting shape, but you have the same animalistic fury and strength within you that made you the perfect savage fighter."

"What is your proposal, Captain Cooper?"

"I was particularly impressed that your Italian was so good. I had not expected that."

"Signor Durante was a good teacher."

"Ah, the old cook on the *George & Susan*. I should have known. His lessons have stuck with me, too, all these years. This skill continues to serve me well during these days of strife when the only qualified crew members I can find are Italian papist bastards! It pays to be fluent in their mother tongue to make sure they're not getting ready to stab me in the back, wouldn't you agree?"

Jedediah looked down at the dead man and grimaced. He spoke slowly, repeating his question. "What is your proposal, Captain Cooper?"

The captain drew in a deep breath before saying, "You will stay aboard the *Nipigon* for the next two months as my indentured servant, and you will fight whatever opponents are put in front of you."

"And why would I do that?"

"Because you not only want to avoid the Italian assassins who will come for you when they find out you killed their beloved countryman, but you also need to get off this boat to catch the killer of your brother. If you accept my proposal, I can assure you that both will happen."

"Idle promises."

"Oh, no; nothing idle about them, Mr. Stiller. If you agree to my terms, I am prepared to have poor Mr. Sinagra's body put into another hold and made to look like he hanged himself in the despair of knowing his poor old mother was raped while he was away at sea. He has been so dramatically despondent lately, no one will question his motives for this act. At the next port, I will also make contact with a Union spy I know and have him track the man you think killed your brother. Believe me, those spies have an uncanny ability to follow a scent to the source. If the man is a Union soldier, as you said, then he will undoubtedly be headed into winter quarters to wait for this infernal weather to break. If you give me a mere two months of service, savage, your brother's murderer will still be waiting for you, my spy will be able to find his exact whereabouts, and you'll be free to get your vengeance."

"You are bluffing!"

"No, Mr. Stiller, you have my word as a captain. If you promise to fight for the next two months and win each match, you will not only gain your freedom, you will know the exact location of your brother's killer and be close enough to get to him. To me, it seems you would be quite foolish not to accept this proposal."

"But you are a lying devil that cannot be trusted."

The captain frowned in mock dismay. "I am hurt by that heartless accusation, Mr. Stiller. Those are cruel words that should never be said between friends."

"We are not friends."

"Oh, well. I'm much more a man of honor than you give me credit for. And to prove that fact, be aware that I have had a legal contract written up which will render null and void the one you signed under Mr. Blunt's influence. It is in a safe in my quarters, and it states that you will be free to leave this ship the moment you have fulfilled this new contract with me. Win all the upcoming fights, and I will sign the document and give it to you when we drop you off at the docks while we are loading wares in Maryland or even Virginia. You will be legally free again. Do we have a deal?"

Jedediah pursed his lips. He could not trust the man in the least, but he also knew his promise of incessant violence from vengeful crew members was a sure thing, and he was not willing to have his chance to kill Zachary Webster ruined by the constant threat of attack by one of the late Mr. Sinagra's compatriots. He nodded slowly. "I agree to your terms, Captain Cooper, but I want to see the new contract with my own eyes."

"I wouldn't have it any other way. When I show it to you to prove it is real, you can tell me the name of the young man you are so intent on killing. That way, I can tell the spy as soon as we arrive in Providence tomorrow. I would shake your hand to seal the deal, Mr. Stiller, but I once saw you shatter a man's forearm with one hand in a fight. So you will have to excuse me if I decide to make this an orally agreed-upon deal."

The captain turned to leave the cabin, but before he shut the door he said quietly, "I will send a couple of men whom I trust to take that body out of here and arrange the hanging scene in another hold. I will also make sure some type of bedding is sent down here. I can't have you sleeping on the deck, curled up like some kind of dog, now can I?"

Chapter Twenty-Three

The bird-like movements, the gray jacket, the black bonnet, and her diminutive size made the elderly woman who flitted toward Catherine in the train depot resemble a tufted titmouse, but her somewhat cold avian appearance was offset by the warm and kind voice that came out when she cooed, "My goodness, young lady, please tell me you have somewhere secure to stay this evening."

The genuine concern in the woman's voice disarmed Catherine's initial impulse to lie to this stranger, so she said with a smile, "Well, ma'am, I'm on my way down to New York City to join the U.S. Sanitary Commission to become a nurse, and I was expecting to sleep at a nearby inn for the night. Would you happen to know of any within walking distance?"

"Oh my! That's what I was afraid of, my dear! The moment I spotted you, I knew you were a lost lamb in need of help. You do not need to settle for any unsafe lodging tonight. I have a warm bed and a private room at my own house for you. My carriage is out front, and you can be in front of a warm fire in a safe sanctuary quickly."

"Oh, no, ma'am. I could not be such an imposition on you! Please just point me in the direction of the nearest inn."

The woman looked at Catherine with eyes as clear and blue as mountain-stream water. "No, my dear, you must understand—I am doing God's work by offering a room to you for the night. My name is Mrs. Margaret Whitherby, and I belong to the Sherbrook Congregational Church here in Portland. Our minister, the Reverend Charles Watson, gave each of his parishioners the heavenly ordained mission of coming to the train stations of our evil city each and every night to protect the innocents we meet. As the menfolk are away fighting the war, the poor women of our society are left to be preyed upon by the wolves that circle in the depraved shadows. Poor little girls headed to the mills to find work and noble women like yourself headed to become nurses—you are all mere game for the likes of those villainous hordes! So, do not worry about being an imposition, for my invitation to you for a safe night in my own house is an act that I am not only happy to extend, but I find spiritually fulfilling."

Catherine wasn't sure what to do. The frigid wind outside the building was whispering bitter tales, and she looked around the empty terminal and realized that the woman's offer was better than fending for herself. She shook her head. "But I am not a Congregationalist, ma'am."

"You are a child of God, my dear. That's all that matters. Come on, we need to make haste to get to my house. It is nearby, but we must hurry."

"But the train to Boston—"

"Does not leave until ten in the morning, my dear. Come with me. I will have you back here in time to easily catch tomorrow morning's train."

Catherine was so charmed by the delicate features and soothing voice of the woman, she decided to accept the offer. She nodded assent, and the old woman smiled blissfully and beckoned for her to follow her out of the station. The cold air hit them viciously as soon as they stepped outdoors, but Mrs. Whitherby showed a surprising amount of spryness as she bounded over to the waiting carriage that was tied to a post near the station entrance. She motioned for Catherine to join her up on the bench seat, and then placed a woolen blanket across both of their laps before urging the horse on. The wheels clacked on the cobblestones as the horse pulled the carriage and its passengers up a steep hill. Soon they turned off onto a side street and approached a large brick house. As they neared the curb, Mrs. Whitherby announced, "See? That was not too long of a ride, now was it? This is my humble abode. Across the street, over there, is our church. It doesn't have a steeple yet, but we hope to construct one as soon as this terrible war is over."

A man came out of the shadows of the house and took the reins. "Oh, thank you, Geoffrey. Please take care to give the horse extra attention tonight. It's been standing in the cold too long. I do not want it to take on any illness."

The man nodded silently and let the women get out and walk to the front door of the house before leading the horse and carriage away. Catherine watched the man with some concern, and Mrs. Whitherby said, "Geoffrey is another member of the parish, and he takes care of my horse in a livery around the corner. The poor man lost his voice when his throat was slashed in a drunken mêlée down on the docks while he was in the evil grip of alcohol. He has learned from his mistakes, and is a good and sober Christian man nowadays."

The two women entered the house and were immediately warmed by the heat from a stove in the parlor. They were busy taking off their coats when Mrs. Whitherby turned and said, "I only found one lost soul tonight, Reverend Watson."

Catherine turned in surprise to see a tall man coming out of the shadows of a long hallway. He wore all black—his pants, his vest, and his long jacket were all as black as the feathers of a crow. There was a trace of white collar from his shirt, but the overpowering essence of the man as he approached them was of darkness. His graying beard was in the Donegal style, and he had a full head of hair that was neatly combed. He extended a hand as he neared, and said, "I am terribly sorry to have scared you, my child. My name is Reverend Charles Watson. I am the minister of the Sherbrook Congregational Church."

Catherine tentatively held out her hand and the man took it into his. She was startled by the softness and warmth of his skin, and although she was instantly on edge at the unannounced presence of a man in the house, she said a tad too quickly, "Oh, you did not scare me, Reverend. My name is Catherine Brandford, sir."

"I'm sorry, dear, did I forget to tell you that Reverend Watson lives in the carriage house behind mine? I do apologize for that oversight. He's become such a fixture in my life, I don't always take full notice of him."

"When I heard your carriage come up, I came over to the house to check on you, Mrs. Whitherby. I did not expect you to have company. I'm so glad you do, however, because it means we have the God-given opportunity to succor another innocent woman traveling alone in this world of evilness and discord."

Mrs. Whitherby shook her head mournfully. "Miss Catherine is traveling south to become a nurse for the U.S. Sanitary Commission. She wants to give comfort to those wounded and afflicted Union soldiers!"

"You don't say! That is so incredibly noble of you, my good young lady!"

"My beloved was killed in the war, and I learned that he died from unsatisfactory medical care. I can no longer sit by idly in the comfort of my own home and let those brave young men sacrifice themselves for us without doing something. I need to try to help, and becoming a nurse seems the best course."

From where this lie came from, Catherine didn't know. She was also unsure about the exact reason for telling such a falsehood. Maybe because the man and woman were strangers, and, although they seemed to be kind and sweet, she still felt the need to put up a self-protective front with them.

Reverend Watson smiled at Mrs. Whitherby. "Well, isn't this another moment of divine intervention in His plan for bringing the heavens down to this sin-filled planet of strife? This surely cannot be just a coincidence, it must be divine in nature. Don't you think so, Mrs. Whitherby?"

"I have not had a chance to talk to the child about our mission, Reverend Watson. We just met at the train depot, traveled through the frigid night, and, as you know, just entered the house. I thought such a conversation could wait until tomorrow morning."

"What conversation?" Catherine inquired.

The man's eyes gleamed with excitement as he replied, "We, too, are headed down south to lend our Christian hands to help heal the bloodbath that mankind has perpetrated on itself!"

Catherine looked uncertainly at Mrs. Whitherby, who was nodding with her eyes closed, and then at Reverend Watson, who looked ready to give a fire-and-brimstone sermon. She raised an eyebrow. "You and Mrs. Whitherby are headed down to the war?"

"Not just us, my dear child, the entire congregation of our church! The two of us are among the last to depart Portland. The rest of the participating parishioners left a few days ago to make preparations in Framingham, Massachusetts. They went to procure the necessary horses, wagons, and supplies for our trip. Mrs. Whitherby and I are departing tomorrow to join the rest of the flock. Once we are reunited, we plan to form an impressive wagon train that will proceed through the countryside of Massachusetts and Connecticut on its way to New York City. All the while, we hope to pick up new members for our mission from participating parishes along the way. By the time we board the U.S. Sanitary Commission steamer, *Endicott*, which will transport all of us, our wagons, and our supplies to Baltimore, we should be a small army of Christians headed to the front to give aid and succor to our fallen soldiers."

"Perhaps if Miss Catherine opts to travel with us on the train down to Boston tomorrow, we could talk more about it then, Reverend," Mrs. Whitherby said firmly.

"Ah, that would be wonderful! If we were traveling together, we would undoubtedly have much more time to talk about our plans. Now, you both look tired, my dear ladies. You should get some rest for our journey. Like Jesus the Christ said, 'Come unto me, all ye that labor and are heavy laden, and I will give you rest.'"

"Indeed, Reverend. We will see you in the morning. After I show Miss Catherine to her bedroom, I plan to retire myself. She may not need much sleep, but an old woman like myself must prepare for the rigors of what awaits us in every step. God bless and good evening, sir."

Reverend Watson bowed to Mrs. Whitherby, then to Catherine. He pivoted and walked back down the hallway and into the shadows of the house. They heard the sounds of a door being gently shut, and Mrs. Whitherby closed her eyes. "Ah, the good Lord did not make many men like Reverend Watson. You will be hard-pressed to find another man cut from such fabric, my dear young lady."

Without waiting for a reply, Mrs. Whitherby took up a candle and went around the parlor snuffing out the lamps. The darkness of the night crept into the house, curling around the corners and slithering down the hallways as she did this. Catherine followed the woman closely as she climbed the stairs and entered a small bedroom that was cold and lifeless as an empty tomb. Here she used her candle to light the lamp beside the large wood-framed bed that occupied most of the room. The window was clouded with hoarfrost, but Catherine saw that the bed appeared quite cozy with the multiple down comforters on it. She also noticed that the bedroom had its own keyed lock, and she felt safer knowing she could lock herself in for the night.

As she took in her surroundings, her hostess said, "I do hope you will have a comfortable night. There is a chamber pot beneath your bed to save you the trip to the outhouse. I know this room gets cold, but the comforters should allow you to be warm while you sleep."

"Oh, thank you, Mrs. Whitherby. I am most grateful for your hospitality!"

The woman clucked her tongue as though remembering something. "Oh, I do want to apologize if it seemed the Reverend and I were trying to take away any of your freedoms by inviting you to travel with us tomorrow. We are so protective of young women traveling alone, I think we just assumed that if you're on the same train, we could ride together and you could enjoy the safety in numbers. I do hope you will do that, but please do not think our offer was an effort to infringe upon your own independence! I can assure you we did not intend to do that, my dear."

"Oh, no, neither of you made me feel that way, Mrs. Whitherby. I agree with you both. I think it makes sense to travel together—if there's room on the train car, of course."

"I will wake thee in time for breakfast, my dear Miss Catherine."

"Good night, Mrs. Whitherby."

"God bless and good night, dear." Mrs. Whitherby closed the door behind her, and Catherine listened to her walk down the hallway and go into her own bedroom before she turned the key. The bolt fought her at first, but then it went into place with a gentle *thunk*. She hoped Mrs. Whitherby hadn't heard her do this, or wouldn't be too offended by it if she had, but she assumed the woman would want her guest to feel secure.

As she got undressed and slipped between the cold layers of the comforters, Catherine thought about how her quiet life had been shattered completely in a flurry of horrifying events, and how her whole existence now seemed like a haphazardly wobbling top. To be entering the bed of a complete stranger who would soon become her traveling companion on a mission so uncertain and so reckless only seemed to reflect the current condition of her life. As she hugged her arms to her chest to hold the heat in, she said a prayer for her continued safety, and hoped it would not fall on deaf ears.

Chapter Twenty-Four

When Mrs. Whitherby knocked on the bedroom door the next morning, the sun had not yet fully risen and the darkness outside the window looked menacing. Catherine awoke as soon as she heard the woman's kind words of greeting, and she hopped out of bed and got dressed. By the time she came down the stairs, there was a mug of tea and a bowl of porridge for her at the table. As she sat down to eat, she announced, "You have a lovely home, Mrs. Whitherby!"

The elderly woman nodded and glanced around the room. "Whatever material comfort I have these days is completely due to my dear departed husband, Alfred, God rest his soul. He made enough money in his business ventures to leave me in such a commodious house. After the good Lord chose to take him from me so early, I must say I was lost for quite some while. Then Reverend Watson came into my life and we found that we had much in common in our beliefs and faith. He has helped me find the righteous path again."

Catherine said, "Does it make you somewhat sad to leave all of this behind while you go on your church's mission?"

Mrs. Whitherby stopped what she was doing. "Of course. But if the commandments of God for his people were always easy to follow, we would not go off course so often, would we, dear? But I know that this house and our beloved church are just edifices. We can rebuild them. But we cannot rebuild the young men who are dying from their mistreatment at the hospitals. What we are all headed off to do is so much more important for the work of God than securing and maintaining buildings. Plus, I know that

Geoffrey will take care of this dwelling and its contents the best that he can."

"What needs to be done before we have to leave for the train? I can help you with those tasks."

A loving smile spread across Mrs. Whitherby's face as she said, "You must be an angel sent from the Lord! I found myself wondering how I would get everything done before it was time for us to depart. I mean, Reverend Watson has already made the carriage house ready for a long-term absence, but I'm on my own in preparing this big house. He'd like to help me, of course, but he's busy securing the church and seeing to last-minute details. We will see him at the train depot."

The two women ate their breakfast and drank their tea, then set to work getting the house ready for their departure. As they spread white sheets over the furniture to keep the dust off, they worked silently except for the older woman's continuous humming of hymns. Catherine had the warm, sentimental memory of herself as a young girl helping her grandmother clean her house, and she was momentarily filled with gratitude that she'd had the good fortune to find a protective guiding angel. And because Mrs. Whitherby, Reverend Watson, and Catherine were headed off on the same train, she didn't worry about staying on schedule while she helped with these homely chores.

· · · · ·

Geoffrey drove them to the train station, but due to the amount of baggage Mrs. Whitherby brought, he was forced to make another trip alone to gather up the rest of the woman's possessions. Even so, they arrived at the depot earlier than was necessary. Reverend Watson was already there, and he helped them into the station and purchased the tickets. When it came time to board, the three of them moved as if they were a family unit. They found plenty of seats in a car that was not yet full, and arranged themselves so that Mrs. Whitherby and Catherine could sit next to one another while facing Reverend Watson. They settled in and got comfortable, and before too long, the train began to huff its way out of the station and head south. They sat in silence as they watched the city of Portland fade from view behind them.

Reverend Watson spoke quietly. "I do want to apologize, Miss Catherine, if I came across as overeager last night about your joining us on this trip. I'm no longer a young man, but I still find myself utterly amazed whenever the Lord's mysterious workings are revealed to us enough to see the mechanics of His wisdom. I think your appearance in our lives is such evidence, and I will accept no acknowledgment other than you were sent to us by Him. There is no rational explanation for your arriving when you did and with such a similar pathway as ours. But I do ask for your forgiveness if my assumption that you would join us caused you any discomfort."

"No, Reverend Watson, there's no need for apology," Mrs. Whitherby said with a kind shake of her head. "Miss Catherine and I talked about this last night, and she knows that neither of us meant any harm with the enthusiasm of our invitation."

"That's right, Reverend. It turns out I am benefitting from meeting you two, as well. I am grateful for the company to Boston."

Mrs. Whitherby patted Catherine's arm lovingly. "Yes, she was a real dear and helped me get the house ready. I don't know what I would have done without her."

The minister put his elbow on his knee and leaned toward them with interest. "Now that we have some time, Miss Catherine, please tell us a little about yourself. We know next to nothing about you."

The man's expression was one of such kindness, she shrugged off any annoyance at the seeming invasion of her privacy. Instead, she began to talk about growing up in Augusta on her family's farm. When she got to the part about her mother's death, both Reverend Watson and Mrs. Whitherby gently comforted her and encouraged her to go on with her tale. They even offered their own stories of sadness from the early deaths of Mr. Whitherby and Mrs. Watson. Catherine found them to be earnest listeners, and she talked more than she had been prepared to, as she became more comfortable with them.

"And tell us more about this beloved whose death caused you to want to become a nurse," Reverend Watson said with a nod.

Catherine hated to keep enhancing her original lie, but she now effortlessly spun a tale that included some of the facts Zachary had stated in his letters about Gettysburg. In her new rendition, he'd been wounded by a bullet in the leg and had died from the resulting infection in the nearly barbaric conditions of a field hospital. Then, using the smattering of information she'd gleaned from her conversation with Ardelia Adams at church, she weaved together a story about writing to the U.S. Sanitary Commission and arranging to train as a nurse in New York City as soon as she could arrive there.

The mention of Zachary's senseless death from the conditions of the field hospital caused Reverend Watson to begin an impassioned oration on the horrors of the war and of man's foolhardiness. He spoke eloquently on the matter, and his eyes flashed with indignation. But when Mrs. Whitherby noticed some fellow travelers in the train car taking notice of his loud discourse, she soothingly reminded him that his sermons should be given from the sanctity of the pulpit and in front of a completely assenting audience of his congregation. He followed her eyes and nodded in agreement, then resumed in a calmer voice, "I must say He is working in ways I never imagined possible, Miss Catherine. I believe the good Lord has brought us together to make this world a better place. I think this"—he paused as he motioned with his hands to indicate he was speaking about the three of them—"could become a relationship that benefits all of its members and all of humanity!"

Catherine was feeling comfortable enough with her two travel companions to giggle at the air of self-importance the reverend had just attached to their train trip together. She shrugged her shoulders and said, "Well, I do think we make good traveling companions."

Reverend Watson looked at Mrs. Whitherby and nodded vigorously. "Oh, yes! Of course that is true. But there's so much more we can offer one another!"

"How so, Reverend Watson?" Catherine asked, tilting her head with uncertainty.

"During the summer of this last year, our congregation—not to mention all the residents of Portland—had two back-to-back exposures to the ugliness of this war. And although our lives were turned upside down by the savagery, I now see these two events as the seeds for the good we are doing today. First, our peaceful city was invaded by Confederate pirates who commandeered a ship and had a gunfight right outside our very own harbor. Shortly after that, the atrocious Battle of Gettysburg that took your Zachary was fought. Our newspapers were clogged with the long lists of the dead and wounded from Maine. And there were many familiar names on those lists, I can tell you that. Those two events got the congregation talking about doing more to help pacify this troubled world we all live in. That was when the good Lord sent us one of His brightest angels, Miss Sarah Westlake."

When he suddenly stopped talking and frowned, Mrs. Whitherby continued the tale. She relayed how, during one of their regular nights at the train station helping young women make it safely on their travels, Mrs. Whitherby and the reverend had encountered Sarah Westlake, a nurse of the U.S. Sanitary Commission, who had come to do an inspection of the medical facilities at Fort Preble in South Portland. Due to some ineptitude of military leadership at the fort and perhaps a dose of misogyny, the young woman had not been sent a wagon for transport, and thus had been left stranded and alone at the train depot. With little prompting, the young nursed had accepted their offer of a safe bed for the night, and the three of them had talked until the wee hours of the next morning. They discussed the awful medical conditions in many of the Union field hospitals, and the immense need for qualified nurses and supplies to care for the flood of casualties. Reverend Watson was so inspired by her tales, he called for a church meeting the very next day. The entire congregation showed up and heard her retell the horrific details and describe the overwhelming needs. Every single parishioner was so moved by what they had heard, they immediately implored her to tell them how they could help.

Reverend Watson began to speak again in a warm, warbling voice about how Sarah Westlake had understood that she was on the precipice of something even greater than just the medical care of a few soldiers. She saw their congregation, wholly committed to the cause, as the start of a virtual army of nurses. According to her plan, the members of the congregation she trained would then be able to go on and become trainers themselves. The impact of such an approach would have untold benefits for the betterment of the lives of countless Union soldiers, so she penned a letter to the U.S. Sanitary Commission to ask for supplies and funds to begin instructing the entire congregation to become nurses. Even without a reply back, she set about educating the parishioners on how to become highly qualified medical assistants.

While she lived with Mrs. Whitherby in the very room in which Catherine had just slept, she instructed them in the use of anesthesia, proper bandaging of wounds, the simple stitching techniques used in battlefield hospitals, the needs of patient care, and even some rudimentary surgical procedures. Her patience seemed to be unlimited and her skills great, and the men and women under her tutelage practiced repeatedly until Miss Westlake was confident that each and every member of the church could serve as a qualified and proficient nurse in any medical facility.

Reverend Watson paused and gazed out the window of the train car. After a moment or two of silence, he went on to describe Miss Sarah Westlake as one of the most compassionate, caring, and thoughtful people he'd ever met. His voice broke as he described the love his parishioners had for her and her tireless efforts with them. The accolades continued for some time, but his voice became shakier until it was hoarse with emotion, "She was like a daughter to me! Even though my dear wife and I always wished the Almighty had blessed us with a child like her, He had different plans for us..."

His voice trailed off and his hand moved up to wipe a tear from his eye. He took several deep breaths, but didn't continue. Mrs. Whitherby put her hand on Catherine's forearm and said in a hollow whisper, "One night, she went alone to pick up some supplies at the train station without informing either of us. We still don't know why she would have done that, but Sarah, God bless her soul, was an independent spirit, and I suppose she just wanted to get the supplies without troubling anyone. She didn't come home that night, and she wasn't seen alive again. Her battered body was found behind a building in a squalid area of Portland a few days later. The police reported that heinous things had been done to her, but no suspects were ever brought to justice."

Mrs. Whitherby stopped talking and Catherine gasped. "Oh, how awful! What a tragedy!"

Then the three sat in silence for several long moments as the wheels click-clacked and the car rocked to and fro with the rhythmic cadence.

Finally, Reverend Watson turned to look directly at Catherine. "Her untimely death became an act of martyrdom. As soon as my congregation heard the horrendous news of her murder, they immediately agreed that we could not let such an angel die in vain. We all pledged ourselves to God that very afternoon for the mission we are now undertaking. We know we can never bring Miss Sarah Westlake back from the peaceable kingdom she now shares with our heavenly Father, but due to the death of that amazing young woman we signed a covenant with God to do whatever is necessary to help heal wounded Union soldiers."

He went on to describe the Herculean efforts the congregation had undertaken after pledging itself to the mission. They submitted endless paperwork to enlist themselves in the cause of the U.S. Sanitary Commission. They raised funds and donated their own money to procure medical supplies, wagons, and horses. They began a tireless letter-writing campaign to parishes along the route to New York City asking for additional volunteers. And as each of these tasks was taken on and successfully completed by the inspired congregation, the goal of leading a Christian medical corps to the war became more and more of a reality. Although there were many naysayers at every step, their unfettered devotion to accomplishing their goal was so great that there was no obstacle too big or too daunting. The reverend concluded with, "Just the very presence of Mrs. Whitherby and myself on this train bespeaks the depth of our devotion!"

Catherine was nearly hypnotized by the story. All the details, the twists and turns, and the emotional retelling had completely captivated her. Now, as she looked out the window and saw they were approaching the city of Boston, she was shocked to realize that the absorbing tale had made their lengthy journey so much shorter. She shook her head in amazement. "I cannot believe my eyes! Look! We are about to enter the city of Boston. Listening to your story, Reverend Watson and Mrs. Whitherby, has made time absolutely fly by."

Reverend Watson glanced at the urban scenery outside and then looked intently at Mrs. Whitherby. There was an almost imperceptible nod between the two before he leaned forward and said to Catherine, "Then I should make my offer before we arrive at the station. Come with us, Catherine Brandford! Come with Mrs. Whitherby and me and the rest of our congregation, and we will train you to be a nurse better than even the U.S. Sanitary Commission could possibly do. We've learned the lessons taught by our beloved Sarah so well, I am certain that our capacity to train others is far superior to what you might get in New York City. Come with us as we travel the countryside, ministering to the poor masses and adding to our army of Christian nurses!"

Catherine was taken aback by the offer. Looking down, she saw that Mrs. Whitherby's tiny hand was now clutched around her wrist. She shook her head and found her voice. "Oh, Reverend Watson, Mrs. Whitherby, I cannot go with you. I must continue on to New York as I had planned."

"But Miss Catherine, we are all headed to the same place. Our path might be more irregular and a little slower than just taking the train to New York City, but the good we can do in the name of God Almighty, our Father, will make it all much more worthwhile!"

Catherine shook her head emphatically. "I'm sorry, I really am. I have so thoroughly enjoyed my travels with both of you, and I'm most grateful for your hospitality and your generosity, but I need to be in New York as soon as possible. I cannot come with you and your parishioners on your mission. I cannot claim any kind of divine inspiration behind me, but I am most determined to get to the U.S. Sanitary Commission to commence my training as quickly as I can."

Mrs. Whitherby released Catherine's wrist and sat back and sighed. "We understand, my dear. We just hoped you would give the offer some thought before you quickly dismissed it. Our plan is to enter New York on Palm Sunday, a mere twenty days from today. If you come with us on our journey, you'll be a qualified and trained nurse by the time we enter the city. But if you continue on by yourself, dear, there's no guarantee you will even receive the necessary training from the Sanitary Commission by that date. Surely you can see the benefits of traveling within a protective and nurturing family of people over the dangers of continuing alone."

"Oh, I do, Mrs. Whitherby, I do. It's just that I have a fire burning within me to get to the front as quickly as I can."

"But that's just it, my child, the armies of the Confederacy and the Union find themselves now awaiting weather decent enough to resume the slaughter. There is no real front for you to go to now. And, as Mrs.

Whitherby just said, staying with us actually is a guaranteed quicker access to superior nursing training. Please, give our offer some thought before you make a final decision."

"I am sorry, but my mind is made up. I am overwhelmingly grateful for your kindness, but I feel compelled to keep heading on my way."

Mrs. Whitherby clucked her tongue. "You are a grown woman, Miss Catherine Brandford, and you must decide things for yourself. You are neither my blood nor my relation, and that being so, I must relinquish my great desire to coerce you into staying safe and traveling with us."

Catherine smiled at her and patted the elderly woman's hand. Mrs. Whitherby managed a weak smile in return, but when Catherine turned to look at Reverend Watson, his eyes were squinted with a smoldering anger. He shook his head and hissed, "'He, that being often reproved hardeneth his neck, shall suddenly be destroyed, and that without remedy.'"

Chapter Twenty-Five

Jedediah watched through his porthole as the *Nipigon* docked at the wharves of Providence, Rhode Island. When he lost his view as the steamship nestled against the wooden trusses, he turned to face the door of the cabin to wait for what he knew was coming. After an uncomfortably long delay, Captain Cooper finally unlocked the door and walked in with another man in tow. In the captain's hand, a military Colt revolver glistened in the sunlight. He gestured with this for Jedediah to back up against the wall. The rat-like mate named Mr. Spencer came around and cautiously bent down to release the lock on the manacle around Jedediah's ankle. With this task completed, he slid furtively back to his protected position behind the captain, which made Jedediah chuckle at the man's fear as he took one deliberate step away from the wall. Captain Cooper raised his revolver to stop him. He sneered, "Well, Mr. Stiller, are you ready?"

"We'll see, Captain Cooper. We'll see."

The captain tilted his head and said tonelessly, "Not to sound like some Union general wind-boxes, but it's either victory or death for you today. Do not forget that."

The captain put the revolver in the large pocket of his coat and sidled around until the tip of the barrel touched Jedediah's back through the cloth. "Like we talked about earlier, Mr. Stiller, it don't do you no good to make unnecessary movements or attract too much attention, right?"

"I will be on my best behavior; you have my word on that."

"I have this gun on that, Mr. Stiller. Slow and deliberate. Mr. Spencer will take the lead and make our way for us, but you will follow close to him, but not too close. Do you understand, Mr. Stiller?"

"I do."

"You are to walk when we walk, stop when we stop. Unless you're addressed directly, you're not to talk to anyone! Understood?"

"Aye, aye, Captain," Jedediah replied flatly.

Such dramatics were unnecessary. Jedediah had no intention of risking getting shot in an escape attempt, especially since he had absolutely no idea about the layout of the ship. He'd been able to piece together some clues about his situation, but he knew he was too unprepared to even consider an escape. He also knew that Captain Cooper was far too anxious on this first trip out, and any kind of unexpected movement might cause him to pull the trigger.

"I'll behave, Captain. You just make sure you don't shoot me by accident."

"Just keep walking and shut your mouth, savage."

The three men walked through the doorway and into a long passageway. It was Jedediah's first time outside his enclosure, and he inhaled sharply and enjoyed the momentary freedom. Although they could hear the din of the hustle and bustle of the crew and the continuous shouting from the wharf, the three men encountered no one as they made their way. When they reached an open freight door, Mr. Spencer stopped the procession and reconnoitered a small gangplank that led to the shore. When he was satisfied that none of the crew or the longshoremen would see their departure, he motioned for them to continue. The trestle was nothing more than a few rough pieces of lumber, and Jedediah looked down between them at the sheen on the dirty harbor water below.

The captain nodded at a man who seemed to be supervising the actions of the crew from afar and said quietly, "It looks like Mr. Johnson has everything in order. I know they've already begun to load the crates of carbines from the Burnside Rifle Company. That should take a few hours. Then they can start to work on loading them uniforms from Atlantic Delaine Mill. 'Course, they're having to labor a bit harder, seeing that they've been a little shorthanded since you dispatched one of my best crew members, Mr. Stiller."

Jedediah did not acknowledge the captain's attempt at dark humor, but kept walking with his shoulders hunched forward and his head down like a condemned prisoner being led to the gallows. There was a relative thaw happening in the Providence weather, and although the temperature was hovering just above freezing, the much-needed respite from the frigid temperatures of this particularly vicious winter gave the air a brief feeling of rebirth usually reserved for spring. For Jedediah, the sunlight on his face and the foul creosote smells of the wharves made him grin. Freedom was something he'd taken for granted since jumping ship from the *George & Susan*, and he swore he would not allow himself to become so complacent about such an important thing after he was far away from Captain Cooper and the *Nipigon*.

Their little procession continued among the buildings of the wharves. At last, Mr. Spencer headed toward a particularly nondescript door, and Jedediah looked around for people or wagons that would indicate a fight was being held within, but there weren't any. They entered the building. It felt chillier inside than outside, as if the space was purposefully holding onto the cold. They went through a series of anonymous doors until they came to a central room that had gas torches illuminating a plank-lined arena surrounded by terraced benches. A crowd of nearly a hundred men watched their entrance, and an eerie silence hung in the room like smoke. The space was heated by a large coal stove, which blazed red from the flames within. Due to this, the room was uncomfortably hot.

As the three men walked toward the opening into the arena, Captain Cooper said with an evil chortle, "Isn't it ironic that this space was originally built for auctioning livestock, Mr. Stiller?"

Jedediah ignored him and studied his surroundings. He saw that all of the men in the room wore clothes that reflected the fact they probably came from some kind of money. Mr. Spencer peeled off from their group just before they entered the arena, apparently to seek out the bookmakers, and Jedediah shook his head as the little man pulled a large wad of paper money out of his pocket and waved it around with authority.

Captain Cooper took his hand out of his coat pocket and gestured at several men he seemed familiar with. As they walked over the sawdust-covered floor to the area designated as Jedediah's corner, the captain ordered, "Take that ridiculous jacket off and strip off any undershirts you have on, savage."

Jedediah did as he was told, and a swell of enthusiasm spread through the audience. With the sheer size of his upper body muscles and the vivid geometric shapes and lines of the tattoos that almost completely covered his back and chest visible, men who wanted to change their bets or add onto them now yelled with an urgency that shook the rafters.

In the opposite corner of the arena was Jedediah's opponent—a massive red-haired man who was also naked to the waist. By the way he held his torso erect, arms low and elbows close to his waist, Jedediah discerned that the man was an accomplished boxer of some skill. As he watched him throw a few practice punches and move fluidly on his feet, Jedediah growled. Captain Cooper whispered, "His name is Seamus O'Hara, and he's the reigning bare-knuckle boxer of this fair city. He is going to be a much tougher nut to crack than Mr. Sinagra, that's for damn sure! If you hesitate like you did with that Italian, O'Hara will pummel you into a pulp."

A shrill whistle from the head bookmaker to a man who was leaning against the planks signaled that the fight was about to begin. Both fighters and their handlers were motioned into the center of the ring, where Captain Cooper hissed into Jedediah's ear, "Remember, Mr. Stiller, the only way to fulfill your contract and leave my service alive is for you to win all your fights. Any fouls or losses will not be tolerated. Do I make myself clear?"

Jedediah nodded so subtly it appeared he was just looking up. In the center of the ring, Captain Cooper announced to the gathered group, "I assume this fight is being run under London Rules."

The other manager snorted with contempt. "What? I hope you left your hoop skirts outside the ring, *ma'am*. No more mamby-pamby questions, Captain Cooper!"

The appointed referee shook his head with shared contempt at the captain's question before saying brusquely, "We fight today, gentlemen, until only one man is left standing."

Captain Cooper turned to O'Hara's handler. "I really thought Mayor Knight might make an appearance, Mr. Doyle."

"Ah, he had other things to do, Captain Cooper. Maybe next time, if there is a next time."

"All right, gentlemen," the referee said, pointing dramatically to the exit of the arena, "we have a fight to put on today."

Jedediah, the giant red-haired boxer, and their handlers returned to their corners. Before leaving to take a seat in the stands, Captain Cooper whispered hoarsely, "Make sure you stay within the rules the referee just made clear."

Jedediah watched where he went to sit down, and he stared contemptuously at him. The tension inside the space increased as the referee looked around and then yelled, "Fight!"

The two men came out and circled one another. Jedediah was not about to rush too quickly into the range of the big man's powerful punches, and the boxer continued to move his arms like pistons and step gingerly around the ring. The crowd shouted encouragement and curses at the two fighters, which prompted O'Hara to come up quickly and land two blows to Jedediah's face. Not only were they two of the fastest punches he'd ever seen, each one was like being struck with a metal boom, and he was dazed by their power. He lunged at O'Hara, but the man neatly and efficiently sidestepped his advance. As Jedediah passed him, the boxer tattooed him with two more fast but less powerful jabs. The crowd hollered and jeered at the exchange. Jedediah recovered and made two more lunges, but each time the result was the same.

He could feel the skin around his eyes tightening with swelling from the blows, and he was woozy. He glared at his opponent, and the man was smiling at him with a combination of confidence and contempt. It was clear from his expression that he knew he was a superior fighter and it was just a matter of time before he finished Jedediah off. He even gestured with his head, inviting Jedediah to make another lunge at him.

Jedediah was about to, but then he hesitated because he fully understood one of the biggest problems he was facing. In all of those fights on the wharves during his whaling days, it was his blind rage that had fueled him. He'd won every battle because none of his opponents could match the level of his pure anger. Whenever he looked at who he was fighting, he saw them as the same agents of death who had robbed him of his loved ones, and with that mindset, he felt wholly justified in maiming or killing them. By the time he jumped ship in Hawaii, however, the fuel for that rage had been nearly used up. Then, during his time with the strange

Polynesian people who adopted him as a member of their families, those flames had been completely extinguished. And when this healing was completed, he knew it was time to return home to Augusta.

Those hateful flames of rage had definitely been rekindled by the murder of Jonathan, but he knew that they burned solely for Zachary Webster. Try as he might, Jedediah couldn't muster enough murderous intent toward the red-haired boxer who was now outfighting him. He attempted to pretend his opponent was Zachary Webster, but it didn't work. After pacifying that monstrous side of himself over the years, he now needed to find some way of tapping into it again to win this fight and keep alive the chance to get vengeance for his brother.

Just the thought of never catching up to Zachary Webster gave him a healthy enough wave of ardor to jolt him out of his momentary complacency, and he charged at the boxer again with his powerful legs pushing him forward. As soon as O'Hara saw Jedediah coming toward him, however, he pivoted gracefully on his feet and avoided the awkward assault while landing two more solid punches to the side of his opponent's head. As Jedediah stumbled and almost fell, he saw the trace of a patronizing smile on the man's lips.

The crowd began to sense that the fight was already decided, and they shouted curses and insults at the outmatched fighter and at Captain Cooper for wasting their money. In the midst of this, Jedediah's eyes locked onto the captain's. The man's expression was so completely devoid of emotion, it was impossible to tell if he was feeling anything at all. This angered Jedediah more than he was prepared to acknowledge, and he roared with frustration at his opponent—which only added fuel to the spectators' fiery taunts. But when he regained his calm, he found the new source for his rage—Captain Cooper. The unfathomable anger he held toward the man would have to serve as the surrogate for the murderous intentions he held for Zachary Webster, and once he'd accepted this fact, the veil of mindless fury descended on him. He knew that if he could figure out how to outfight the talented boxer, his newly rediscovered rage would help him win the fight.

Just as he was about to charge, he glanced up at the captain again. Something the man had said before leaving the ring was snaking its way into his consciousness, but he couldn't exactly pin it down. While he was distracted, O'Hara made a charge of his own and landed a series of painfully strong blows to Jedediah's body and face that made him fall onto his back. The last punch had broken his nose, and when he stood up, blood dripped down over his lips and into his mouth. The starkness of the pain made Jedediah suddenly remember the captain's exact wording, and he instantly understood what he had to do. He put his hand to the bridge of his nose and crushed the cartilage back into shape again, which caused some in the crowd to react like they'd smelled something foul. The confident smirk on O'Hara's face had grown too heavy to hold, but now, as he watched his opponent fix his own nose, an altogether different look came over him.

Eyes gleaming with pain and fury, Jedediah slowly advanced on his opponent. The man continued to move about like a boxer, and he was ill-prepared for the giant's leap at his midsection. The two men fell to the sawdust floor in a grappling heap. In this tight position, Jedediah unleashed a series of harsh rabbit punches. When O'Hara tried desperately to grab hold of his opponent's arms, he quickly found that the giant was much stronger than he had realized. Jedediah overpowered the man and savagely bit down on his ear. There was a strange guttural roar as Jedediah stood up with most of the man's bloody ear in his mouth, dangling like the fatty gristle of a cheap steak. As the crowd loudly voiced their shock, he dramatically chewed it up and swallowed it.

O'Hara jumped up with his hand covering the wound. Blood flowed down the side of his neck and onto his chest. He looked around and said in a thick Irish brogue, "The bastard just fuckin' bit me!"

Before anyone could react, Jedediah tackled him again. His legs churned as he lifted the big man off the ground and drove him backward with bone-crushing force against the planks of the ring. O'Hara was slow to get up, but Jedediah was not, and he sent a powerful uppercut into the man's face while he was still bent over. The blow obliterated the man's nose, leaving it a bloody pulp. O'Hara's eyes suddenly went white with fear and he awkwardly tried to get to his feet. Before he could, Jedediah kneed the man in the head. The blow was so loud and brutal, the crowd became as silent as a church congregation because they all knew the fight was now over. The crushing tackle against the planks, the smashing uppercut to the face, and the powerful knee to the head would have killed the average man. That the Irishman could even attempt to stand again was a miracle. Now it was a matter of just how much punishment the tattooed giant would be allowed to apply to O'Hara before the fight was stopped.

Jedediah permitted his opponent to stand up, but the man was so unstable on his feet that he had to lean against the planking to remain erect. And he was unable to defend himself against the next punch to his head. The force of this blow flipped him over the wall and out of the ring. Nearby spectators scurried away to avoid the fighter's body, but still tried to urge him to get back into the fight. They didn't want to touch him, though, since both fighters were now coated with sweat, blood, and sawdust in a foul smear. The referee instructed Jedediah to get back while he helped O'Hara stand up and return to the ring. The man could barely stand on his own—he was all done—but the referee led him back into the enclosure to end the fight.

Jedediah scanned the crowd. When he made eye contact with the captain this time, the man's emotionless expression had been replaced with a grin that was somewhere between a malicious smirk and a victorious smile. He mouthed the words, *Good dog.*

O'Hara was as good as out on his feet, so when Jedediah unleashed the next roundhouse punch at his head, the blow twisted the Irishman's body around and threw him to the ground. With his opponent lying face-down on the floor, Jedediah put his arm around the man's throat and yanked him to his feet. The ease with which the tattooed giant was now handling the muscular boxer as if he was nothing but a light sack of grain silenced the crowd as they waited to see what would happen next. The wounded pugilist writhed desperately in Jedediah's strangling grip, but he could not break his hold. Soon his feet were no longer touching the ground, and he began to succumb and go still. With victory literally within his grasp, Jedediah looked up at the captain to watch his expression when he snapped this man's neck. But this time, Captain Cooper mouthed, *That's enough.*

There was something in his eyes that made Jedediah obey the command, and he dropped O'Hara to the ground. Although unconscious, the Irishman's elbows locked and kept him propped up on all fours. Jedediah frowned and hit him with a downward punch that many of the spectators later described as a wooden axe handle hitting a melon. The man's body flattened, and he lay prone in the sawdust, barely breathing.

Jedediah moved to his corner to start putting his clothes back on. That he'd just beaten a man nearly to death in front of a large group of spectators did not seem to register with the giant, and he appeared to be getting dressed to head out to church.

Although the crowd was a seasoned bare-knuckle-fighting audience, they seemed too stunned by the overt violence they'd just witnessed to react fully. Captain Cooper and Mr. Spencer took advantage of this confusion and hurried from their seats to the bookmaker to collect their winnings before moving into the arena to gather Jedediah. The captain gestured with his hand in the coat pocket to remind Jedediah that the gun was still pointed at him, and he shook his head and grumbled, "That was ugly, Mr. Stiller. It took you too long to figure out that you couldn't outfight the man, and then too short a time to dispatch him in your savage manner. It is good you didn't kill him, however. We have far too many venues to go to in the next two months to have them all spooked out of producing a fighter to challenge you. Hopefully, O'Hara will survive until the *Nipigon* has cleared the docks and is halfway to New York. If he doesn't, news like that travels faster than the wind, and we could find ourselves on the outside looking in. That would not be good for any of us, Mr. Stiller."

"Captain Cooper, first you tell me I can't lose. And now you're telling me I can't win. Make up your damn mind!"

The captain waggled the revolver in his pocket menacingly. "Let's just get out of here before this crowd decides to get nasty about the outcome. We can talk about the details of your life and death onboard the boat. Move along, savage."

They worked their way out of the ring and headed back the way they had come in. As they neared the exit door of the room, a meaty hand slapped down on Captain Cooper's shoulder. "Hold on there! That was not the type of fight that me or my fighter were expecting. I cannot feel but a little lied to. The mayor is not going to be pleased with it neither."

Captain Cooper's reaction to the surprise attack was to spin around wildly and nearly pull the trigger of the revolver in his pocket, but upon seeing it was only a disgruntled Mr. Doyle, his hand eased up enough to come out and lift the man's hand from his shoulder. As he did this, his face spread into a greasy sneer.

"Ah, Mr. Doyle, your fighter put up one helluva fight. I thought he had the thing won there for a few minutes, but that's how these fights go, isn't it? One minute, you're the king; the next, you're the pauper!"

"Ain't no one in this place laughing now, Captain Cooper. Like I said, the mayor is going to be told about this, and I'm sure he will not be pleased one bit."

The captain thrust his index finger into the man's chest. "Well, that might be very true, Mr. Doyle. I know that if my fighter was being mopped up off the floor, I'd be a bit displeased, too. Just remind the mayor, and yourself while you're at it, that the next time the opponent's manager inquires if the fight will be fought under London Rules and you mock him and his masculinity, you just might need to take him more seriously. If you had done that this time, your man would have wiped the arena floor with my savage. But since you didn't and chose to ridicule me instead, well...you see what my fighter did to yours. Now, if you will excuse us, we have a boat to catch. Until next time."

Mr. Doyle growled, then shook his head. "After this debacle, Captain Cooper, I doubt there will be a next time."

The captain grinned knowingly. "Ah, there will be. I'd wager money on that, Mr. Doyle."

Chapter Twenty-Six

Catherine promised to stay with Mrs. Whitherby while Reverend Watson went to make arrangements for their next leg of travel to Framingham, and the two women waited in an uneasy silence. The three had not really conversed since the issuing of her refusal to travel with them any farther, and Catherine could tell that, although the reverend was merely disappointed, Mrs. Whitherby was more than a bit angry about it. The bird-like sharpness of the woman was now overly apparent as her head turned, bobbed, and refocused quickly like a nervous songbird. And no matter how much she scanned her surroundings defensively, she refused to make eye contact with Catherine.

When the reverend came back, he did so with a uniformed man. He seemed excited and awkward with enthusiasm. "Please tell these ladies, my good kind sir, what you just told me."

The man was clearly annoyed at being dragged over to talk to the two women, and he sighed dramatically before saying, "The three of you need to take a hack to the Boston & Lowell railroad depot over at the foot of Billerica. There you can all catch the train to Framingham."

Catherine spoke up. "But sir, I'm headed to New York City."

The man said, "Yes, ma'am, but as I already told the reverend, trains don't leave for that city from this here depot. To get to New York, you have to go to Park Square, where you catch the Boston & Providence. But you don't want to do that, not today."

"Why don't I want to do that today?"

"There was a small accident on the B & P line earlier that's jammed up the tracks between here and Providence. There's no telling when the route will be cleared. It could take a few days or even a little longer. So you would be better served to catch the Boston & Worcester train with these fine folks at the B & L depot. That is a short-turn train to Framingham, where you can wait for the train to Worcester. From there, you could catch the next Providence & Worcester train. It is a little out of your way, but you have a better chance of getting to New York quicker if you go that way."

"What is a short-turn train?"

The man rolled his eyes and sighed loudly. "It's a train that doesn't go to the full extent of its line, but stops short and turns around to come back to its starting place. This allows people to travel into Boston from some of the surrounding towns with more frequency. Like I said, once you get to Framingham, ma'am, you'll be able to catch the next train to Worcester."

The reverend lifted his finger triumphantly. "You see? By traveling on with us, Miss Catherine, you are assured of continuing your journey to New York City. So I have taken the liberty of hiring a hack to take the three of us to the depot that this good man has advised us to go to. What do you say?"

Catherine looked at Mrs. Whitherby, and she was smiling at her again. The situation seemed to be unwinnable. If she refused and tried to keep going as she had planned, she wouldn't make it any farther south on the train for several days. But if she went on to Framingham with these two people, she would. However, she wondered if Mrs. Whitherby and Reverend Watson would allow her to get on the train to Worcester without another scene of unsightly debate and argument. Although it did not seem likely, traveling with them was the only way to insure she would get where she wanted to go. Certainly, being stranded alone in Boston did not strike Catherine as the best choice, so she nodded with her eyes closed and said, "All right, let's go to Framingham."

Throughout the hack ride, the buying of tickets, and the boarding of the train, Reverend Watson and Mrs. Whitherby were reanimated. Catherine had to smile at their childlike joy about the beginning of their journey, but she kept waiting for them to reopen the argument about the merits of her continuing on with their congregation. But they didn't. Not once. Instead, they talked excitedly about the new nursing techniques Sarah Westlake had shown them—how to administer medicines and anesthesia, how to wrap wounds with bandages, and how to feel for a person's heartbeat on their wrist. Their voices were patient and kind, and she let them instruct her with the knowledge they seemed so eager to share. Just like their conversation had made the trip to Boston seem so much shorter, the enthusiastic and earnest medical instruction made time pass so quickly that they were all surprised when the train slowed and came to a stop at the Framingham depot.

Reverend Watson said with a chuckle, "Well, I, for one, certainly see why they call it a short-turn train!"

A man was there to meet Mrs. Whitherby and the reverend, and he stood with his hat crushed up in his hands in anticipation. He greeted both of them with a hearty embrace, and bowed when he was introduced as Mr. Mallory to Catherine. He was overjoyed to announce that he and Mr. Morton had been able to procure everything as instructed, and he reported that two beautiful new Moses ambulances were outside the depot awaiting them—one loaded with the bandages and tools, the other with the medicines and chemicals, especially the ether and chloroform. Upon hearing this news, Reverend Watson clapped the man on the shoulder in a congratulatory gesture and told him to take the ambulance with Mr. Morton and head back to the gathering point at the First Baptist Church. He explained that Mrs. Whitherby and he wanted to show Catherine the other ambulance and the supplies before insuring she was settled and safe for her train to Worcester.

Outside the depot, Mr. Mallory put Mrs. Whitherby's trunk and bags into the rear of one of the two nearly identical wagons. He bowed to the women and then walked with the reverend over to the other ambulance. Mr. Morton was already in the passenger seat, and he waved his hat at them. With a peal of laughter, the two men drove off.

Reverend Watson returned to the two ladies smiling ecstatically. "Ah, those gentlemen have done such good work while down here! I tell you, we'll be ready to head out tomorrow on our trip!"

Catherine waited for them to renew their invitation at this point, but neither of them seemed inclined to do so. Instead, Mrs. Whitherby raised her arms and said, "Blessed be the name of the Lord from this time forth and forevermore."

The reverend nodded solemnly. "Well, Miss Catherine, before we leave you here to await your train to Worcester, my dear, why don't you take a look at our beautiful new Moses ambulance? Up front, you can see that it is being pulled by two beautiful and powerful creatures. Those two ebony giants are Percherons donated to the cause by a local true believer! The Army may want to slide them out and put in their own team of horses for a more fleet speed if they need this ambulance during a battle, but these two majestic steeds have enough power to pull us on our journey.

"Mrs. Whitherby and I will be seated there on the bench while I drive. See how the wheels are smaller up front? They make the ride smoother and give us better steerage. Now, you probably noticed that the other Moses ambulance Mr. Mallory and Mr. Morton were driving had open windows along the sides to allow for good ventilation. Well, for this one, we wanted to be able to shut out the elements better than that, so we asked for solid panels. These all come out easily and can be replaced with canvas. But for the trip down south, this wagon will be shut up tightly. Mrs. Whitherby, why don't you show Miss Catherine the storage underneath while I hop aboard and make sure those two men stored everything safely?"

The elderly woman smiled and took Catherine by the arm, guiding her to several smaller kegs bound by iron staves to the bottom of the wagon. She knocked on these and the dull response revealed their emptiness. "See? This is where we can store all the water we need for our medical station to have drinking and washing water. The areas around the battlefields won't always have clean water, so we'll have to bring our own."

While Catherine looked down at the oaken casks, Mrs. Whitherby pointed out the hooks that hung from the bottom of the wagon like metallic icicles. She spoke with great pride as she explained that these would all be full of pots and pans when they were nearer to the battlefields, thereby providing an endless supply of cookware to feed their patients. She then pointed up to the rolled canvas at the edge of the top of the ambulance. "Do you see that? Those canvas rolls unfurl and make a tent that completely surrounds the whole vehicle. When we need to care for the sick and wounded, we'll just unharness the horses, set the brake, and set up the tent and stake it down. The ambulance becomes an instant hospital!"

Just then, the reverend came down the steps on the back of the wagon.

"Those men are saints! Everything is stored perfectly and safely. And they put folding cots in there for us to sleep on. I took the liberty of moving one of those surgical sets out so you can show it to Miss Catherine before we take her back into the depot."

Mrs. Whitherby spryly climbed the steps and exclaimed loudly, "Oh, this is even lovelier than I expected! There is plenty of room to move six soldiers away from the battlefield!"

Catherine came up and stood in the doorway. There, on the floor of the wagon, was a new wooden box. When it was opened, there was an amputation saw, scissors, and small handheld sawing blades in the red-velvet-lined lid. In the bottom part of the box, a set of surgical knives and a tourniquet with a brass screw and red straps were nestled in their places. The blades were all shiny with newness and glinted in the midday light. She leaned over to see the tools more closely, but she never saw the cloth laden with chloroform until it covered her nose and mouth. Her surprised gasp only caused her to inhale the sweet-smelling vapors more quickly, and then the odor grew sour as the edge of her vision became fuzzy...and then everything went dark.

Chapter Twenty-Seven

Jedediah was sitting on his cot in the cabin when the captain suddenly came in, smoking a pipe and looking concerned. "Ahoy, Mr. Stiller."

"Captain Cooper."

"Oh, don't get up on my account, sir," the captain said sarcastically.

Jedediah looked up at him with steely eyes, but remained seated. The captain chuckled to himself and leaned against the wall near the door. "Mr. Spencer reports that you did not fare too badly from the blows that that giant Paddy mackerel-snapper landed on you in Providence."

"I'll survive."

"Oh, I have no doubt of that, Mr. Stiller! If there's one quality you continue to amaze me with, it's your ability to do that. No, I did not come here to see if you would survive—that's clearly something as ingrained in you as your savagery. I am here to make sure that you will be physically sound enough for the next fight when we get to New York tomorrow."

"I will."

The captain nodded and puffed on his pipe. "Good, good. Then I can assume we'll be assured of another victory."

"If all the fights are like the last one, I'll have to get used to a different brand of opponents than the ones I fought on the wharves during the whaling days. Plus, *I'm* different these days."

"You mean too sober, right? That can be remedied, Mr. Stiller. I noticed a lack of your usual aggression in Providence. For a moment there, I worried that you had become some kind of gelding. I even considered for a minute or two that you were not as much of a savage anymore. Then you bit off the man's ear and ate it, and I realized that you're still the same old monster you've always been."

"Savage. Monster. Dog. You certainly use the lowest of words to describe me, Captain Cooper. I would take offense, but I know you're right down there with me. You like to think of yourself as better than me, but we both know that's not true. You may stand up on the bridge, but you and I are cut from the same cloth, Captain, aren't we now?"

Captain Cooper clucked his tongue. "Hardly, savage. You and I have nothing in common."

"Yet here we are, intertwined again, eh?"

"I thought I had made our relationship completely clear, Mr. Stiller, in our previous conversations. Maybe O'Hara hit you harder on the head than you know. Let's be clear, once and for all—you are the animal and I am the master. There can be no more similarities than that. We are not cut from the same cloth, because we're such completely different creatures, you and I. You will fight for me successfully for the next two months because you want to pursue and kill the man who murdered your brother. I want you to fight successfully for the next two months because I need the added income. See? One of those desires is driven by the brimstone of hell, whilst the other is from the heavenly desire to better oneself."

"If I had never touched your skin, Captain Cooper, I would assume it to be cool and dry like the scales of a poisonous serpent. You certainly have the forked tongue to fit that description. That being said, however, something you just said does remind me of a question I have been mulling over down here in my solitary cabin."

"Oh? And what would that be, Mr. Stiller?"

"Why two months?"

"You mean, other than the fact that we have a contract stating our service agreement lasts two months?"

"Yes. When you first uttered that time frame, I thought it had been pulled out of your hat. But you keep making reference to it. Why?"

"I do not need to tell you everything, now do I?"

"No. Just a curious sod am I. Maybe I'll inquire with Mr. Spencer next time he comes down here."

"Oh, he would not know the real reason. As captain of this ship, it is for me alone to determine what my crew needs to know. Mr. Spencer does not need to know any of this."

"Of what?"

The captain inhaled. "Ah, Mr. Stiller! I will try to explain this in such a simple way that even you will understand it. First of all, have you given any consideration as to why you have found me in my current situation? The last time you saw me, I was a successful whaling ship captain in the Pacific Ocean. Did you never wonder how I came to be the captain of a battered Great Lakes steamer on these ridiculous coastal hopscotch cruises?"

Jedediah shook his head, saying, "I've heard that whaling was slowing down, so I assumed you had no choice in the matter."

The captain snorted. "I always have a choice, my good man! Always. The owners of the *George & Susan* saw the writing on the wall, so to speak, and they asked me to come talk to them and give my opinion on the future of whaling from the viewpoint of an experienced sea captain. I explained how we were seeing fewer of the leviathans out there and had to travel farther for any financial gain from whaling. So when they told me they were watching the imminent rise of kerosene which could replace whale oil as a source of lamplight, we all had to concede that, without a doubt, there would be no real future for the whaling fleet. The only option we could agree on was to keep sailing their ships until there were no more whales or the entire fleet rotted and sank, whichever came first."

The captain took several large puffs on his pipe and exhaled the smoke toward the ceiling of the cabin. "Well, I can tell you none of that was attractive to me. I weren't going to be the captain on no ship filled with desperate men to work them hard until the vessel came apart at the seams and sank. I may have had an inflated idea of my self-worth, but I knew that was not my destiny, Mr. Stiller! Now, when this orgy of crazed killing started, I saw a way to make a huge profit from the war. It struck me that, if the conflict lasted longer than a few weeks, as some were suggesting, the Union Army was going to need transportation on the seas in an unprecedented way. I gathered the owners together and made my pitch—if they bought a fleet of fairly well-maintained steamships that had been plying the Great Lakes, they'd have their hands on vessels untouched by the corrosive qualities of the ocean, yet designed to take on rougher waters, and for cheap prices. Vessels like that could be quickly outfitted as cargo carriers for coastal trade and chartered to the United States federal government for huge profits. In those early days, the Union was in a panic because they were completely unprepared to supply the war effort.

"Like me, the owners immediately saw the potential for making quick money! They gave me the cash backing to head out and find one such suitable vessel to purchase. And I found the *Nipigon*. She was a freighter and ferryboat on Lake Ontario, where the storms almost rival the ferocity of the ones on the Atlantic. Not only was the ship clearly designed to take a heavy sea, she was in good enough shape to need only a minor overhaul before putting her into service. I bought her for a paltry sum and immediately chartered her to the U.S. Army Quartermaster Department. To show their gratitude for my leadership in the project, the owners gave me a stake in the new transportation company created to pull off this endeavor. The only catch was they demanded that I be the captain of this vessel.

"Now, I must admit, I was more than a little irked with the role I was forced to play in the enterprise. After all, I had thought I'd worked my way up from the wheelhouse to the headquarters. But then the contracts started rolling in, Mr. Stiller, and I became a big fan of this war. A big fan. In those early days, the need for transport of troops, supplies, prisoners, and weaponry was so great, it was common for us to get five hundred and fifty dollars a day! And since the powers that be were too distracted by other things that needed their attention, it was far too easy to take their money. So we steamed this old gal along at five knots and made the usual day-and-a-half trip from Boston to New York in closer to three days. We cruised around slowly and charged the government outrageous sums, and no one seemed to notice! In less than a couple of months, we had already recouped the purchase price of the *Nipigon*, and after that, all the money we took in was lining our pockets faster than we could count it!

"Unfortunately, as soon as the government noticed our good fortune, they wanted to curtail our success. The days of unlimited charges and slow cruising speeds were gone, and we were left to negotiate charter prices at lower rates and told to double our speed between ports. Our profits went down, but they remained high enough to make the whole venture somewhat worthwhile. Then my business partners and I got wind that the end was near. With the war inevitably winding down and more competition from similar boat brokers, the teat that was the boon for transport ships will go completely dry very soon. These owners are barons of industry, so they know when the time is ripe for getting out before being pulled down. For them, it's just moving money from one side of the board to the other. But for me, the investment is more personal. So, when the end of this profitable business does come, I risk being left standing out in the cold and rain. And I will not let that happen."

Jedediah snorted contemptuously. "Don't tell me—a new round of reduced chartering fees will be announced in two months!"

"Aye. No one knows for sure how low they will be, but whatever they are, they'll be too low to make the money we are accustomed to making."

"So the owners plan to sell this ship and get out of the racket before then, eh? Leaving you without a job, Captain Cooper?"

"Ah, see what I mean, Mr. Stiller? You are sharper than one would assume from your rough exterior. Yes, in about two months or so, the *Nipigon* will most likely be sold to new owners who are satisfied with making less profit. The crew will be paid less, the tension aboard the ship will continue to mount, and either the vessel will be destroyed by an act of violence or it will burst apart at the seams from within. Either way, I want to be very far away from her when that happens."

"And meanwhile, you and the owners will make a healthy amount of money by betting on me in these unlawful fights?"

"Bah, don't think so small, Mr. Stiller! All the money this vessel makes is shared with the owners. The harder I work and the more dangerous the job becomes, what with evading Confederate gunships and mines and torpedoes, the less I see. Our smaller profits are divvied up after expenses and we each get our small portion of the crumbs."

"Ah, but your 'ownership' of me is not something your business partners know about, is it? Any money you win at these fights goes directly into your own pockets. And you don't have any real expenses since you ain't exactly paying me, even though I'm legally a crew member. You have my signed document stating so in your safe. And you feed me food that is purchased for the crew anyway. There's no expense for you."

"See? You understand it all, Mr. Stiller. If you keep winning the fights, I get to keep all the spoils, and at the end of our two-month agreement, I'll be rich enough to head out West and buy into a shipping company of my very own. I've grown tired of my place in the pecking order here on the Atlantic coast, and I want a new start where I can jump up a few rungs and be away from the helm, and just collect the profits from other men who are sailing for me. As soon as the owners decide to sell this scow, I plan on taking my family out to San Francisco to start a new life."

Jedediah stood up from his cot, and the captain shot him an anxious look.

"Then you must think that the Fates smiled on you when they brought the two of us back together, eh?"

"Oh, you have no idea, Mr. Stiller! Just the booty from that first fight was more than enough to erase what I paid Mr. Blunt to get you, and still left me with a healthy profit. From this point on, the rest of the money you win for me is a bonus. We're scheduled to be in a port every three to four days, so you can figure it out, Mr. Stiller. In the next two months alone, you may get the chance to fight twenty times! If each fight pays like the first, I will need a crate to carry all the money you're going to win for me!"

Jedediah almost laughed. "I don't see how you'll be able to keep my presence a secret for that much time, Captain."

"Ah, but it's not a complete secret. As you saw, the officers of the ship are profiting from you too, Mr. Stiller, as I am allowing them to wager on you with their own money, and that has been very good for crew morale, let me tell you! It also assures me that they will not ruin the flow of profits by tattling on me."

"But the regular crew doesn't get a piece, am I right?"

"Pshaw, they're nothing but animals, and after all, chattel does not deserve a chance to profit from the hard work of others."

Jedediah shook his head. "You know, the more I think about it, Captain, even snakes would be embarrassed to be compared to the likes of you."

"Hmm, you may be right there, Mr. Stiller. But, speaking of the crew, they're the real reason I came down to talk to you today. They're getting a little too curious about the padlock on the door of this empty cabin. The tragic apparent self-immolation of Mr. Sinagra seemed only to inflame their conspiratorial beliefs, and I shudder to think what they would do if they found out that you're living alone in this lap of luxury while they're all confined to the squalor of the cramped crew quarters. So, to disperse their curiosity and tension, while you and I are taking care of our business in New York, the crew is going to load this cabin full of hospital supplies. Mr. Johnson will make sure to hide your cot and pack the room leaving enough space for you to move around. After we sneak you back in, you can begin a regimen of moving crates around to regain some of the fighting strength that seemed so noticeably lacking in the last fight. We'll have to move you out when we reach Baltimore so the crew can unload it, of course, but that shouldn't be too hard."

"And where will we be headed after Baltimore?"

The captain inhaled sharply and said, "Oh, you don't need to worry yourself with that, you mindless savage! You let me steer the ship wherever I choose, all right? You just concentrate on winning those fights. And remember, if you win them all, you're a free man again in two months!"

Chapter Twenty-Eight

When Catherine awoke, she was bound and gagged upon a cot in the Moses ambulance. The side panels were all secured tightly and the rear door was shut, so the only light coming in squeezed around a loose sheet of canvas separating the driving bench from the main compartment of the wagon. She tried to pull her hands free from the bonds, but they were too tight. She began to thrash about, but there was no slack, so she stopped and listened. Due to her struggling, the only sound she could hear was the pounding of her own heart.

Once this quieted down, she could discern voices coming from outside, and it soon became clear that Reverend Watson was bringing a large group closer to the ambulance. She heard him say loudly, "This, my flock, is the ambulance that Mrs. Whitherby and I will be sharing for the journey. I wanted you all to see it and to know why we intend to keep it further away than the other wagons of our procession. You see, we have chosen to store all the chloroform, ether, alcohols, and other hazardous chemicals we'll be using in our hospitals in this ambulance because we think it is wiser to concentrate all those dangers in one vehicle. Since these substances can so easily catch fire and explode, we will keep this wagon isolated from the rest of the group at all times. I'm also going to ask each and every one of you to stay some distance from it, for all it would take is one mere accidental spark to blow us all up."

There was a murmur of understanding from the group. When nothing but silence followed, Catherine took the opportunity to thrash and moan as much as her restraints would allow. She could not do much more than writhe and make a weak cooing sound, but by the way Reverend Watson began to loudly intone a spontaneous prayer, she knew she'd made enough noise for someone to hear her. She tried to get louder, but the prayer's volume drowned her out.

"Dear Lord Christ Our Savior, give us the guidance to find our way on this journey so that we never lose sight of Your intended path for us. Make our hearts open to the lessons we will be confronted with. Quiet the doubts raging within us to allow us to do Your will. Purify us, Dear Lord, so that we might be worthy to complete the tasks You have sent us to do on this mission. Give us the capabilities to minister to the sick, tend the wounded, and help make Your world a better place. In Your name, Oh Lord, we pray with open hearts and souls. Amen."

The crowd dispersed and Catherine waited for what would come next. The rear door of the wagon sprang open and blinding daylight poured in. Two black figures entered and stood next to her cot. She stopped struggling and waited for her eyes to recover from the change in light so she could see who they were. The taller figure bent over her, while the shorter figure seemed to be fiddling with the supplies on the shelves, opening boxes and clinking metallic objects against glass. Of course, it was Reverend Watson and Mrs. Whitherby. As Catherine's eyes darted from the sinister smile on the man's face to the activities of the elderly woman behind him, her fear caused her breathing to form a stout wheeze as it came out quickly over and around the gag in her mouth.

"Oh, Catherine, you cannot be such a naughty creature and make so much noise when my congregation comes near this wagon! Why couldn't you have just accepted our offer to travel freely with our group like a good girl? If you had done that, none of this would have been necessary. You would not be tied up and you would not require the medicine Mrs. Whitherby is preparing for you right now. You could have been one of the flock, and we would all have had the time to let the growing affection we feel toward one another develop naturally. But no, you had to spit in the face of our kind offer. And this is the consequence of that decision. You have no one to blame but yourself, Catherine Brandford," Reverend Watson concluded with an eerie look of devotion on his face.

Catherine frantically tried to look past him to see what Mrs. Whitherby was doing, but the reverend bent down and put his hands on her cheeks. When she tried to resist his touch, he roughly grabbed the sides of her face with his strong fingers and forced her to look into his eyes, which were black and intense. "You have no one to blame but yourself. For everything that is going to happen to you, you are at fault. If you'd only been as well-behaved a young woman as Sarah Westlake, you could have avoided all this roughness. It could have been postponed. As it is..."—and here he moved his hand down to the juncture of her neck and shoulders, where he gripped her hard enough to make her wince—"you'll have to endure the harshness you brought upon yourself."

He smiled and his thumbs pushed down into the base of her throat and made her choke. She thrashed to get a breath, but he released the pressure and kept moving his hands down her body. As they came to her breasts, his fingers clenched hard. The pain of his grasp made her buck on the cot, but the man's sinister smile did not change. He released his hold, but his fingers retracted from her chest slowly until they found her nipples through the fabric of her bodice. As he began pinching them harder and harder, he hissed, "And you are going to be punished for your insolence, my dear angel. Punished again and again to bring you closer to God."

She closed her eyes to fight the excruciating pain and screamed into her gag, but when she looked again at him, the man's eyes had rolled up into their lids as if in ecstasy. When he began to move his hands back and forth, Catherine nearly lost consciousness. But then she heard the sound of Mrs. Whitherby striking the minister's arm as she hissed, "Charles! This is not the time for any of that! Stop it now!"

He released his grip and stood up, looking down at the elderly woman sheepishly. "I'm sorry. I lost my control for a moment."

"You still need to help people prepare for our departure tomorrow morning, and you cannot do any of that with the member of your manhood straining against your pants like that! Get yourself back under control, for goodness sake! I will administer this medicine to keep her quiet until we have the uninterrupted time to enjoy her like we want to tonight. But now is not the time."

"Quite right. I will go and tend to the flock, Mrs. Whitherby."

Catherine was so focused on him, she didn't feel the woman grab her left arm and stick her with the hypodermic needle. But she felt the burn as Mrs. Whitherby pushed the plunger in, and her veins flushed with the chemical. She was powerless to pull her arm away from the hag's grip and found herself becoming dizzy as the needle was extracted.

Mrs. Whitherby reached over and caressed her forehead. "Go to Morpheus, my dear. That morphine injection will ensure that you stay quiet and do not attract any more unwanted attention. Because you are so strong-willed, I fear you may need a nearly constant dosage to keep you in the right frame of mind. I am not sure we have enough for the entire trip, but like Reverend Watson said, you have no one to blame for any of this except yourself. And, as the Good Book says, 'Pride goeth before destruction, and a haughty spirit before a fall.'"

Catherine tried to move her head away from the woman's gnarled touch, but she was quickly losing consciousness, slipping toward slumber with the thin-skinned hands firmly planted upon her forehead. Through the narcotic haze, the old woman looked like the Angel of Death bending down to bite her on the lip.

Chapter Twenty-Nine

Zachary Webster, Samuel Worthington, and Jacob Robinson made their way directly to the provost marshal with Captain Small's orders. This piece of paper authorized them to begin hunting in the forest between their camp and the Rapidan River. They were looking for a band of Confederate skirmishers who had been harassing the Union scouting parties which were mapping the area for the upcoming campaign. After several guides and scouts were killed by a hidden rebel sniper, Union skirmishers had been sent out to find him. Unfortunately, their efforts had been unsuccessful. So the captain had ordered these three members of Company D to engage this Confederate unit and kill their marksman. Because direct approaches hadn't worked, he hoped these more clandestine methods would result in the death of a reb sharpshooter, the disruption of the enemy skirmishers, and the gain of some useful intelligence through the capture of prisoners.

Although spring was trying to break the bonds of the harsh winter, the Virginia woods were still under its influence. Several sunny and warm days of thawing had melted most of the snow on the ground and allowed small patches of snowdrops to spring up, but the trees and shrubs were still leafless. The overall bleakness of the forest meant that the sharpshooters' gray overcoats not only helped them stay warm in the damp and dismal surroundings, but let them blend in with the drab scenery. And since the plan called for the three men to split up and use the camouflage of the underbrush to move slowly and undetected during their search, there was an urgency in their steps as they cleared the camp and dissolved into the forest to begin their hunt.

Webster was thrilled to finally be out of the cramped space and away from the foul odors of the log huts of their winter quarters. For the first time since returning from Maine, his heart pumped vigorously and his senses were keen again. And, as he watched the two other sharpshooters spread out, he felt the swell of bloodlust return to him. The three soldiers were all veterans of this type of operation and very adept at working like a pack of wolves to force their opponent into making a fatal mistake, and he felt assured of success.

The reports from the ambushes were all similar—each time the Union scouts had encountered this unit of reb skirmishers, they were lured into the enemy sharpshooter's range by the most vulgar insults from a loud and brash officer, and the results had been lethal. The three men of Company D, using their own ambushing experience, had predicted that the next location for the skirmishers' attack would be farther up the road, and with this destination in mind, they fanned out and made their way separately and stealthily. When they reached the site, they would set up in different vantage points for the best shots. But their success depended on the ability to find the rebel skirmishers while avoiding detection and then extrapolating the location of their sharpshooter before he was able to shoot. The three men knew they were going to need a great deal of restraint to wait for the precise moment to make their assault. But they were confident that they all had more than enough of these qualities to be successful.

The first day proved to be fruitless. When the setting sun caused the shadows to grow and consume the terrain, Webster found a secure space in a dense pocket of hemlocks near a spring to bivouac for the night. The evergreens seemed to hold the cold, and the snow on the ground was flecked with brown needles. When he bent down to drink from the spring, the water in the small pool was so cold it burned his lips. As the darkness of night began to saturate the air, he stayed vigilant, sitting with his back against one of the monumental trees. His ears were able to pick up the merest sounds—the skittering of nearby voles and mice and the haunting sounds of distant owls. As he let himself drift into a half-awake catnap, he hoped the next day would prove to be more worthwhile.

• • • • •

When he awoke with the rising sun, there was frost on his overcoat, but he didn't bother to wipe the ice crystals off before setting out to stalk silently through the woods. After several hours of this, he came to a rise in the forest floor that provided a natural overlook of the spot on the road where they thought the next attack would take place. He found a secluded spot under a large tree and took up position there. From where he was, he had a great view of the road and the surrounding forest, and he carefully looked through his scope to scan for any targets.

Out of the corner of his eye, he caught the movement of three men as they made their way down the road. Because they did not wear Union uniforms and appeared quite youthful, they looked like teenage boys walking to the store rather than Union scouts. Webster was impressed with their courage in the face of such a dangerous situation, but he had to wonder if they minded being used as bait. Since it was part of the soldier's role in warfare to accept the fact that one might be used as a lure or a diversion whenever the situation called for it, he knew the men didn't have a choice in the matter. And as he sighted through the scope and watched for potential ambushers, he had to wonder whether he and the other two sharpshooters were the hunters or the hunted in this operation. He smiled at the irony of this juxtaposition and the true nature of their current existence.

As the scouts passed, it appeared they were going to do so unscathed. But then Webster caught sight of the butternut-colored uniforms of Confederate skirmishers through his scope as they began to move from their hiding places and take up position for an ambush. Webster fought his initial urge to fire on them and hoped the two other sharpshooters would also hold off. Since the reb sharpshooter was the real target of this action, and not the skirmishers, Captain Small had been clear when he said that, even if they had to watch a bloody ambush take place, they were to wait as long as possible and find the location of the enemy gunman before taking him out. From their continued silence, Webster figured his fellow sharpshooters were following those orders.

He scanned the woods methodically. If there were skirmishers there, the sharpshooter had to be hidden within range of them. He couldn't see anything on his first pass, and he hoped that one of the other men had a bead on the shooter—but he doubted it because there hadn't been any shots from them yet. He panned back and watched the movements of the men closer to the road. He wished the skirmishers would start their attack so that he and Samuel and Jacob could finally see the puff of smoke from Johnny Reb's Enfield and have the man in their sights, but no rifles had been fired yet. Webster slowed his breathing as he prepared for the inevitable ambush.

When it came, the attack triggered a series of events that spread out from the center like the fractures on a broken mirror in random, yet interlocked, pathways. The Confederate skirmishers waited until the scouts had passed them, and then one of them had the audacity to yell, "We got you now, you Yankee cocksuckers!"

With the first volley of the ambush, one scout went down immediately. The other two found cover and returned fire with their revolvers. They fired furiously, but not wildly, and it was clear that in spite of their youthful appearance, these men were battle-tested fighters. Webster admired their discipline in the face of an attack in which they were so outnumbered. However, the reb sharpshooter would not betray his location by taking a shot at the scouts, so as Webster frantically scanned in front of him to locate the enemy, he had to wonder why the reb gunman was waiting. Meanwhile, the skirmishers, emboldened by their initial success, seemed content to keep attacking the scouts.

A thunderous volley of gunfire suddenly came from the road. Startled, Webster jerked his rifle toward the noise. A Union company of riflemen had silently taken up position and put the Confederate skirmishers in a crossfire situation between them and the two well-defended scouts. And as the unit laid down a round of withering fire that seemed to overwhelm the skirmishers, the Union captain stood up to bravely lead his company's charge. As soon as he saw this, Webster knew the reb sharpshooter now had his target, and he resumed his scan of the forest to find him before the man could accomplish his task. But the clouds of gun smoke, the yelling, and the general chaos of the gunfight made it hard to focus on any one target.

The concussion overhead was as stunning as a clap of thunder on a cloudless spring day. When the Union captain's head exploded in a shower of pink mist and the lifeless body fell like a plank of wood, Webster instantly knew that the Confederate sharpshooter was up in one of the nearby trees. He started to roll to get a shot off, but saw a puff of smoke come from a position lower down the hill. This caused an explosion on the tree above him which showered him with chunks of bark. When no body dropped from the sky, he knew the shot had missed, and he got ready to take aim. But the Union company of riflemen, reacting to the death of their captain and the smoke from the gunfire coming from the woods, now swung their guns wildly to counter the perceived attack. As they sent a thick screen of lead down below Webster's position, he hoped to God that, whichever member of his unit was down there—either Samuel or Jacob—they had enough protection to avoid this murderous volley.

Without hesitation, Webster now spun onto his back with his rifle pointed almost straight up. There, about twelve feet above him, was the Confederate sharpshooter hiding behind the trunk of a large pine tree next to the one that Webster was positioned behind. The reb had found a perfect shooter's platform in the crotch of branches that afforded him a clear view of the roadway, yet kept him completely out of sight. Webster aimed and fired. His bullet hit the man just below the rib cage, and it ripped his lungs and shredded his heart on its way out through his shoulder. He fell like a sodden carpet to the floor of the forest. Webster quickly crawled over to the lifeless body and took shelter behind the shooter's tree just as complete pandemonium broke out and he was pinned down by the barrage from the Union riflemen, the scouts, and the Confederate skirmishers.

When the gunfire let up a bit, Webster figured the rebel force was retreating from the battle, and he knew they were probably headed back to their lines with the satisfaction of just winning a clear victory. For not only had they forced the Union to play its hand and send an entire company to back up the scouting unit, but their sharpshooter had succeeded in taking out a captain as well. The Union scouts, seeming confident that the firefight was over, made their way cautiously back to join the riflemen. Webster realized he would have to wait—again—to see what this combined force would do next. If it went on the offensive to root out the perceived threats from the ambushing skirmishers, it could certainly cause more trouble for him and his fellow sharpshooters.

But the Union soldiers began to skedaddle back up the road in the direction they'd come from, leaving their dead captain and several others, including the dead scout, where they lay. This undignified retreat made Webster shake his head a little with shame, though he knew it made the situation much easier. He waited until they were far enough away before looking over the body of the dead reb for what he could take from it. There wasn't much—just some letters and photos of a wife and children and a nice pocket watch—and he took these and put them in his overcoat before scrambling down the hillside to the spot where the first shot had come from. As he approached, he made the sounds of an owl, Company D's signal to avoid being shot by their own men. When he received an owl call back, he knew it was safe to proceed. However, when he saw Jacob Robinson bent over a lifeless form on the ground, he knew Samuel had been killed.

Robinson whispered, "We've got to get out of here!"

Samuel had been hit multiple times, and Webster closed his eyes and clenched his jaw with emotion at the sight of his dead friend. Every muscle in his back seemed to tense, and he stood as stiff as a scarecrow. His response was so unexpected, Robinson reached over and grabbed his wrist. But when Webster opened his eyes again, there was such intense anger in them that Jacob Robinson regretted being so close to him. An uncomfortable silence engulfed them, but then the other sharpshooter barked, "We need to get out of here before them rebs come back!"

"I ain't leaving Samuel here."

"He's dead."

"I ain't leaving him here."

"Well, we can't carry him back to camp, and we can't take the time to bury him neither! I'm telling ya, them rebel skirmishers are gonna bring reinforcements here right soon. If not them, then the Union forces are gonna come back and scour these woods. We need to skedaddle *now!*"

They didn't speak again for a moment, and the telltale sounds of birds resuming their songs indicated that the forest was recovering from a battle. Webster looked around and said calmly, "Head back to camp, Jacob. Tell Captain Small we got the rebel sharpshooter bastard and that I chose to spend more time out here to gather intelligence and do further damage to the enemy."

"You know the captain'll have my hide if I tell him that!"

"Then lie to him. Tell him you saw Samuel dead and you couldn't find me, so you assumed I was dead, too. Then remind him that it was better for you to come back than get captured. He won't be upset with that report."

"Just come back to camp with me now, Zachary. Samuel would want ya to, you know that. He'd want ya to be able to fight another battle with Comp'ny D. C'mon back to camp with me."

When Webster looked over at him, Jacob Robinson saw a darkness descend over his comrade and he knew it was better to just leave him to do what he needed. Robinson turned away and said, "Ya don't have much time. Git back soon as ya can."

Webster nodded, and then watched as the man left him. He looked down at his dead friend and fought with his emotions. Over the course of the last three years, he had witnessed enough to accept that death was an integral part of this war. Yet now that his tentmate was a corpse on the ground in front of him, he felt an uncontrollable rage start to bubble up from the darkest places in his soul. He scooped up the lifeless body and draped it over his shoulder, and with his rifle in the other hand, he scrambled back up the hill to the tree where the dead rebel sharpshooter lay. He knew just what he was going to do, and the inhumane, sinister nature of it was not repugnant to him in any way. As a matter of fact, as he commenced the tasks necessary for setting his trap, his face broke into a sharp and hateful shard of a smile.

Chapter Thirty

The fight in the warehouse in New York City was similar to the one in Providence, except for the fact that the audience was far larger, the fighting arena was much more developed, and the bookmakers exuded a new air of professionalism. As a matter of fact, the fight felt less like something underground and unlawful and more like a semiprivate event attended by the city's well-to-do businessmen, local politicians, policemen, and even a couple of Union generals.

Jedediah's opponent this time was an Englishman, and he looked like a gigantic bulldog. Everything on the man was thick. His rounded head had little hair on top of it, but his nose, eyebrows, and cheeks were all thickened by the battles he'd fought. His jaw was square and looked like it could sledge posts into rocky soil, and the man's neck, chest, and shoulders were muscular and broad. Each of his fists was the size of a smoked ham hock, and the skin on them was toughened like leather. As Jedediah crossed into the ring, the man gazed at him with the confident and nonchalant look of a proven veteran of battle.

Once the fight started, it was clear that, while this man was not as fast as the Irishman in Providence, he was even more powerful and skilled in fisticuffs. Jedediah quickly learned that his punches were devastating. After the man's first solid blow broke his nose again and knocked a couple of teeth loose, he understood that he needed a more selective approach than he'd used in the first fight. To tackle his opponent the way he had in Providence would be fatal against this fighter, so he held back to wait for the best opportunity to rush the man. But when he got his chance, it was like hitting a brick building, and the man's stout posture and strong legs made knocking him down seem impossible. While Jedediah futilely tried to tackle him, the powerful boxer landed two vicious body blows that made his vision flash white.

While Jedediah recovered from the Englishman's attack, he found his rage quickly. This opponent not only had the speed to outfight him, but the power to humble him, and the anger from this started to burn within his body. Jedediah tried to punch the man, but his jabs merely glanced off his skull as if it was made of iron. When he started aiming his blows at the man's body, they didn't seem to do any real damage there either. The bulldog swung a wild roundhouse that could have killed a man, but Jedediah moved quicker than seemed possible for a man of his size. As his opponent's massive fist sailed past his face, he saw his window of opportunity, grabbed the man around the chest, and began wrestling with him. The two men were physically equals, and they pushed and pulled in a deadly embrace as each tried for the advantage with their strong and agile limbs. Finally, Jedediah powered his hands up to the man's face and gouged out his right eye.

The crowd roared to life as they saw this. The Englishman reacted with a shocked and prolonged roar and fumbled with the dangling ivory orb. But Jedediah didn't hesitate. He tackled him, lifted the man off his feet, and crushed him against the boards of the arena. With his stunned opponent pinned against the low wall, Jedediah pushed his head back so his neck connected with the top edge of the boards. Then he brought his right hand down in a savage blow that unceremoniously snapped the man's neck. Jedediah backed up and let the lifeless body slide to the floor before heading back to his corner to get dressed. The crowd raucously celebrated the end of the short but vicious fight.

This time, the captain and Mr. Spencer took their time collecting their winnings before coming into the ring to fetch Jedediah. Despite the outcome of the fight, they seemed far more at ease than they had in Providence. As the crowd continued to buzz with excitement at what they'd just witnessed, the captain gave his fighter small pats on the shoulder in congratulations and even accepted offers of praise from some of the spectators.

Jedediah was mildly surprised by this, and as they walked out of the arena, he asked, "I thought you were gonna be upset at me for killing that man, Captain Cooper, but you seem happy. Why is that?"

The captain stopped and turned toward his fighter. "This environment is more suited to that kind of outcome. This city not only has more of a stomach for just that level of violence, but an appetite for it. You're a big hit here, but just know that everything's going to change from this moment on. Now that you've done what you've done, we won't get too many pugilists as future opponents. We will need to be ready for the wave of rough-and-tumble fighters who will eagerly volunteer for the chance to challenge you. You'll just have to be prepared to face men who are less boxers and more brawlers—but I don't think that'll be a problem for you, do you, Mr. Stiller?"

Jedediah shook his head. "Naw, that just makes it easier for me to win."

Captain Cooper nodded, but added, "Hmm, maybe. But keep in mind that from now on, you're going to meet more of your own kind—savages. Any semblance of fighting with rules will be gone, and you'll be faced with fighting just to survive. Again, you're an expert at that, so I'm not worried."

•   •   •   •   •

The captain's prophecy did not come true right away. In the next fight, in Philadelphia, the fighter was another trained pugilist, but Jedediah made quick work of him nonetheless. The fight did not end with the death of his opponent, but it was clear the man would never walk without a cane afterward. The captain seemed to relish the cruelty that Jedediah had dealt out and the shock from the stunned audience as they left the arena. Because the fight was over so quickly, the three men had time to wander about the city while the crew finished unloading the cannons and rifles, the woolen material for uniforms, and the hospital supplies from the *Nipigon*. When the crew began to take on the foodstuffs for Fort Monroe, the three came aboard undetected, and Mr. Spencer and Captain Cooper escorted Jedediah back to his cabin without incident.

At the door, the captain said coolly, "Well, Mr. Stiller, you've certainly earned yourself some rest. We sail to collect a different kind of cargo this evening, and so there will be no more fights for the next four or five days. Make the most of the rest, but do not allow yourself to grow soft. Mark my words, the fights will get much tougher from this point on, and you will be sorely tested by your opponents. You've bested three highly skilled fighters, but the hellions coming your way might just be the creatures that haunt your nightmares. You cannot afford to let your guard down."

"Don't worry yourself, Captain Cooper, I'd never do that."

"Oh, I know, I know, Mr. Stiller. Your desire to get revenge on your brother's killer is the flame that burns deep inside you. I can see the desperation as you fight, and you've done a wonderful job tapping into that fire to fuel you. I warn you now, though, you're going to need an endless supply of that fuel to survive the rest of the fights."

Jedediah opened his mouth to reply, but the captain had already left the cabin and locked the door. He sat down heavily on his cot and shook his head. He felt confident that someday he would get his revenge on Zachary Webster, but he wondered if he'd ever have a chance to get even with Captain Cooper. The very thought of crushing the man's throat in his hand made him smile as he sat alone in his empty cabin and listened to the familiar sounds of the ship.

Chapter Thirty-One

Zachary Webster waited in the crotch of that pine tree for a night and most of another day before he heard the sounds of a small group of men approaching tentatively below him. He hadn't slept, but his mind was crystal-clear. He grinned evilly in anticipation of the shock those rebs were going to have when they came upon the scene at the base of the tree, and he was prepared to kill them all.

It was only a matter of moments before he heard one of them cry, "What the hell is this? Aw, Lord in the heavens! I can't believe what them godless Yankees done now!"

Webster could tell the other men were joining the first, and that they were letting their disbelief steal their caution. He listened carefully to figure out how many were there and counted the angry voices of six different men. Then another new voice said, "I tole y'all, these Yankees are nothin' but heartless cocksuckers! What else can ya call a class of evil creature that'd lower itself even further by pullin' down the pants of a dead man, bendin' him over a tree, and shovin' his own rifle up his arse like this?"

When Webster cautiously peered around and down the trunk and saw the seven men around the posed body of the dead sharpshooter, foolishly grouped too closely together as they gawked at the spectacle, he knew he had them where he wanted. He slowly aimed at the two men standing closest to each other and pulled the trigger. With such a downward trajectory, the bullet traveled through both of their bodies. Before the other men had a chance to react, Webster threw himself down on them. He broke his fall by smashing the stock of his rifle onto the top of another man's head and shattering it like a ceramic bowl. He jumped back up with his bowie knife in one hand and the reb revolver in the other, and in a move that seemed like a flowing dance, he thrust the knife under the rib cage of one man as he fired the revolver into the neck of another. One of the two men still standing swung his gun up at him in panic, but Webster dove out of the way just as the gun went off. He landed right at the butt of the rifle sticking out of the dead Confederate sharpshooter, so he pulled it out, aimed it at this nearest soldier, and fired. With a look of surprise, the young boy fell backward with a bloody wound in his chest. Fleetingly, Webster realized that taking the time to load and cock the Enfield before shoving it up the dead man's ass certainly had proved worthwhile.

"What manner of devil are you?" the sole survivor now asked, looking around at the carnage in obvious shock. He dropped his revolver and slowly raised his arms in surrender.

Webster picked up his own revolver, aimed it at the man's heart, and said coldly, "The kind that's bringing you in as my prisoner, reb."

He grabbed the man's arms and quickly bound his wrists behind his back with a leather belt. He jabbed him with the revolver and hissed, "If you move in any way that I don't like, reb, you'll be dead in a single heartbeat."

Webster prodded his prisoner over to the thicket where he'd hidden Samuel's body. With a wary eye on the rebel officer, he gathered up his rifle and hefted his friend's lifeless body onto his shoulder.

After they'd walked a short distance, the Confederate officer seemed to come back to his senses and said, "Aw, no, my Yankee friend, you ain't gonna try to carry that body all the way, are ya? You know the rest of my troops are right on our heels, don't ya? You won't be able to make your way through this forest like this."

"You shut up, reb! Don't you worry your pretty little head about me. I'm fine. Just keep your mouth shut and your feet moving. Plus, who said anything about us trying to weave through these trees? Naw, we're headed down to the road and try that route."

"All right, you Yank devil—it'll be your own funeral! Once we're down on that road, you'll be out in the open enough for my men to get a shot at ya."

"You got an uppity mouth on you, reb! Just keep walking. You know we're far more likely to run into Union soldiers coming this way to clean out this forest of you vermin. If I can keep them from shooting both of us, we might just make it all the way to camp before dinner."

They came down the hillside and onto the road. They could hear shouts behind them and then a few random shots, but they were able to move along without having to dodge for cover.

"Yeah, I must admit you put on quite a display back there, Yank. Very impressive, indeed. Never seen such a murderous lout in my whole life."

"Keep talking, reb, and you might shorten that whole life to just a couple more minutes."

The muddy road made walking difficult, but Webster poked the barrel of the revolver into the prisoner's back to urge him on. The man picked up his pace but continued his diatribe as he plodded along.

"What I don't understand, Yank, is why men like you continue to fight and die for these niggers. It don't seem like a noble cause to sacrifice yourself or your friends to, does it?"

"Just keep walking," Webster growled.

"I mean, that man you're carrying on your shoulder—seems to me you care very much about him. How could you not, if you're willing to tote him miles to give him a proper burial, right? But he died in vain, didn't he, Yank? He died for nothing. He gave his life for nothing more'n to give them black bastards their freedom."

"I'm not going to waste my time and energy debating such stuff with you now, reb. Maybe I can come over to the prison you're gonna be in and we can talk freely about it later."

"Don't it bother you that all this killing and dying is for nothing but a bunch of smelly niggers?"

"Shut up and keep moving, reb. I ain't fighting for no black men, I'm fighting to keep the Union together."

"Hmm, so you're one of good ol' Abe's stepchildren, huh? You're shedding your blood to reunite our glorious nation. You do know it ain't gonna mean nothing in the end, right? Even if the all-powerful Union is able to force us to come back into the fold and you do give them niggers their freedom, it won't change a damn thing, right?"

"I said, shut up and keep walking, reb. It's tiresome just listening to you."

"I mean, look at the two of us. Who do you figure is better off at the moment? I gotta say it's me. I might be headed to some Yankee prison camp, but from what I've heard from men who've either been paroled or escaped back to our lines, them places ain't that bad. There's a roof over your head and enough food to eat. I figure if I can stay healthy, I actually have a good chance to survive till the end of this war. But you, my friend, you're much more likely to die when the next Yankee offensive begins."

"Your logic seems flawed, reb. We're winning this war and you know it."

"Yessir, sho' nuf, y'all may be winning the war, but our leaders value the lives of their soldiers much more than your barbaric generals. Grant and his cronies seem willing to sacrifice you men until the ground runs red with your blood. Why? 'Cause they know that if they lose a few thousand of you, there's more and more waiting to line up and die for the cause."

"This here war will be over before too long, reb."

This comment made the prisoner smile snidely. "Oh, sure, it could be over within a year or two, at most. But where will you be then, my friend? Will you be buried next to that man you're carrying on your shoulder? Or will you be an anonymous corpse on some battlefield that pops up whenever it rains too much and says, '*Boo*'? And, even if you're lucky and live through this whole thing, will your life really be better off with us rebels defeated and them niggers running around free? I doubt it. Matter of fact, Yank, I think if you do survive this whole ordeal—and I'd say the odds are surely stacked against you on that one—you ain't gonna be able to get no job 'cause all the niggers are gonna take all of 'em from you white men. When that happens, Yank, why don't you come back down here and find me, and I'll let you work on my tobacco farm. What do you say?"

Webster scoffed, but didn't utter a reply.

After a short silence, the prisoner spoke again. "Your silence tells me I may be making more than a little sense to you."

"Naw, it means I'm sick of listening to your jabber. Don't you ever shut up?"

"Not me, Yank. I've surely got the gift of gab. But you know what I'm saying makes some sense, don't ya? I can tell you been pondering these very same things lately. You're starting to wonder why you keep fighting this war. And you wanna know when the killing and dying will end."

"What I wanna know is when your breath for talking will end. I got no control over the end of the war, so I don't worry about it none."

"That's just it! Maybe you need to, Yank. Your friend there *did* die in vain. If you don't think so, ask yourself what his death accomplished in this battle. Nothing. Not in the big picture. The Union lost an officer, the Confederacy lost an officer, the Union lost a sharpshooter, and the Confederacy lost one helluva sharpshooter. But if you play any chess, you know that pawn-for-pawn trades are acceptable when they don't impact the outcome. Truth is, your friend's death and my capture are nothing to help this war end any sooner. Don't you see? It's all meaningless. That must bother you some, Yank, don't it?"

Webster had no chance to answer before they ran right into a patrol of Vermont sharpshooters from Company F of the 1st United States Sharpshooters. After the initial tension of the encounter was diffused by clearing up his identity and his unit, the company's captain came forward demanding to know what a lone sharpshooter was doing on the road with a dead man over his shoulder and a captured rebel in his charge. Once this explanation was given, the prisoner was transferred to their custody and a wagon was procured to carry Samuel Worthington's body back to camp. For all of his bluster and talkativeness during their walk on the road, the Confederate officer now went sullen and walked away silently with his guards, neither glancing back nor acknowledging Webster's presence again.

As he was escorted back to his company's section of the camp, Webster noticed there was a pall of despair over everyone he saw. When he asked the Vermonters, they coughed and acted uncomfortable before reporting that an accident had occurred the day before at the Brandy Station rail yard. When he pressed them for details, they would only say that a train's boiler had exploded while it was being unloaded and the violent blast had killed several men. But they got very tight-lipped after saying that much, and the group walked on in silence the rest of the way.

When he entered Captain Small's tent, he was surprised to see a very pale Lieutenant Wentworth sitting in the captain's chair. Webster walked up to the desk and glanced around with a confused expression. The lieutenant exhaled loudly and rapped his knuckles on the desk before saying, "You'll have to excuse me, Mr. Webster, if I don't get up to greet you with much enthusiasm today. You've returned in the midst of some upheaval, as I'm sure you've heard, so there are some overriding questions and concerns that must be attended to first before any pleasantries can commence from our reunion...I'm assuming you have a copy of Captain Small's original orders?"

Webster reached into the pocket of his overcoat and found the befouled paper. He brought it out, unfolded it, and handed it to the lieutenant. The ink of the original dispatch was smeared with mud and blood, and it was hard to read. While the man struggled to decipher the smudged script, Webster said softly, "Sorry, Lieutenant, but no one has told me about the upheaval you speak about. The men who brought me here talked about a train explosion, but they would not elaborate on anything more than that, sir."

Wentworth looked up from the note. "Indeed, a train boiler exploded and killed many men yesterday. As the Fates would have it, Captain Small and several members of our own company were there on routine guard duty when it happened, and the captain and two other of our soldiers were killed in the blast."

There was silence as Webster allowed the news to soak in. He looked away and gazed at the corner of the tent. The lieutenant caught this subtle gesture and said, "He was a very good man, that Captain Small. He will be sorely missed by all of us and by the Union Army. I am assuming his role within the company for the time being, pending some decisions in the matter from Headquarters."

"I see."

"So, that's why this is an especially complicated time for you to come back from some kind of operation that neither I nor any other commander in this entire camp knew anything about. Apparently, Captain Small thought it best to ignore the regular chain of command and not notify anyone that three of our men were out hunting a unit of skirmishers and their sharpshooter. Mr. Robinson returned with some details, but he lacked the official paper to complete the picture. He did report that you all killed the sharpshooter and helped end an ambush set by those skirmishers. However, he also indicated that Samuel Worthington died and you were missing. So while your return does add some crucial details, Mr. Webster, it also creates some tough questions for me."

"Yes, sir."

The lieutenant waited for him to say more, but he remained stone-faced. The official orders were barely decipherable, but there was enough legible print to indicate that Captain Small had indeed issued orders for a sharpshooter team comprised of Webster, Worthington, and Robinson to search out and kill the Confederate sharpshooter responsible for several deaths. Why exactly the captain had chosen to keep the action secret would go to the grave with him, and the lieutenant shook his head at the task before him of cleaning up a mess that only got uglier with each new detail.

"You can confirm that Samuel Worthington was killed?"

"Yes, sir."

"You saw this with your own eyes, Mr. Webster?"

"Yes, sir. I did not see the outright killing, but I brought his body back with me."

There was an uncomfortable silence as the lieutenant tried to picture how that task had been accomplished. He rapped his knuckles on the desk again. "Mr. Robinson came back the day before yesterday. What were you doing during this time?"

"Waiting for the skirmishers to come back for the body of their sharpshooter."

"And did they?"

"Yes, sir."

"What happened then, Mr. Webster?"

Webster cocked his head and looked at the man as if he had just spoken a foreign language. He sucked in some breath. "I attacked them."

"To what end?"

"To kill the enemy."

"To kill the enemy, *sir.*"

"Yes, sir."

There was something in the air that made Webster lift his head a little and sniff around like a primal beast before saying, "I attacked them, killed them, captured their officer, and brought him back to camp."

The lieutenant could not contain his shock. "You brought a captured Confederate officer to this camp? Where is he now, Mr. Webster?"

"The boys of Company F of the First U.S.S.S. took him away, sir."

The lieutenant rapped the table again; it was a nervous habit he sincerely wished he could break. "I'm not sure that the death of a Confederate sharpshooter for a Union sharpshooter is a fair trade, are you?"

"Samuel Worthington was a very good man, sir, and a very good soldier."

"Yes, he was. And it's too bad the Confederate sharpshooter killed him."

"It weren't him, sir."

"Pardon me? I thought you said you didn't see the killing of Mr. Worthington."

"That's right, sir. But I know the reb sharpshooter only fired once and killed a captain of the Union force that came to ambush the Confederate skirmishers. I shot the reb sharpshooter after that, so I know it weren't him who killed Samuel, sir."

The lieutenant shuffled some papers on the desk in front of him and found what he was looking for. "That's right. Mr. Robinson said the Confederate skirmishers ambushed a scouting party, but their attack was thwarted by the actions of an unknown company. I'm still trying to ascertain which unit that was and why they were out on that road, but I guess they had more right to be there than you three did, Mr. Webster."

"Yes, sir."

"Are you suggesting the Confederate skirmishers killed Mr. Worthington?"

"It is possible, sir. The lead was flying pretty heavy. But I cannot be sure which bullets were coming from the reb skirmishers and which were coming from the Union troops."

The lieutenant looked up sharply and his eyes bored into Webster. "Are you aware you are insinuating that Mr. Worthington was killed by friendly forces? Do you realize just how grave a charge that is, Mr. Webster?"

"I am doing nothing of the sort, sir. I am merely reporting that I know for a fact the Confederate sharpshooter did not get a shot off at any of us. So he could not have been the cause of the man's death. Samuel was shot by someone else, be it the reb skirmishers, the scouts, or the Union infantry unit. All three forces were involved in the firefight."

The lieutenant stood up abruptly and paced behind his desk. "Oh, this is a muddy mess indeed, Mr. Webster! As if it weren't enough for me to be thrust into the role of leadership due to such a freak accident, I now find myself having to unfurl the fronds of this confusing situation. There's only one person who could rightly do this, and he's now dead. But that's the way of these wars, is it not? So, even though there are still far more facts that need to be gathered from this matter, whether they be from the unit that engaged the skirmishers on the road or from the captured Confederate officer in custody, as acting captain of this unit, I must make a decision regarding appropriate treatment for you.

"So, Mr. Webster, it is my opinion that you were following orders up until the time you decided to remain behind and ambush those skirmishers. At that moment, I believe you were acting above and beyond the scope of the original orders given to you by Captain Small. I need a little time to assess whether I think you need to face any discipline for those decisions and actions. But the whole situation is made much cloudier due to the death of Captain Small. There's no doubt in my mind that he exceeded the range of his authority by giving you men these orders in the first place, but the man is dead and I am wholly unwilling to besmirch his reputation with even a hint of concern. But clearly, his lack of proper communication put several groups of Union soldiers in a compromising situation that resulted in the death of a sharpshooter."

"Yes, sir."

The lieutenant stopped pacing and looked hard at Webster. The man seemed to be neither rattled nor upset by what he was hearing. As a matter of fact, it was hard to see if he had any interest at all in what was being said. Wentworth hoped it was purely due to the fatigue that the man had to be feeling and not something darker. He sat down heavily. "Mr. Webster, you are to confine yourself to your hut for the time being, and you are not to discuss the events of the last few days with anyone unless it is someone I identify as acceptable. Do I make myself clear?"

"Yes, sir."

"There is far too much ugliness with this whole incident to dig too deeply at this moment. We need to preserve morale at any cost, and that means the details of this sordid occurrence need to be deemphasized. I'm in no way inferring that such breaches of duty can just be swept under the carpet, but there are times when protecting and preserving the state of an army is more important than getting to the bottom of the truth. It is my belief that, rather than stir things up with an investigation that will only unhinge everything we've built so far, we need to sit on this one until its impact fades. That being said, you need to be taken out of the spotlight for a time, and you must do your part not to exacerbate the situation. Sergeant Amberson will escort you to your hut. Good day, Mr. Webster."

Chapter Thirty-Two

Jedediah did not know that the *Nipigon* was transporting Confederate soldiers until he heard their lamentations coming from the cabin next to his. He had tried to look out the porthole to see what was happening while the ship was stopped, but whatever cargo was being brought aboard was loaded on the port side, and nothing but open water was visible to him. When he heard the shuffling of feet and the clinking of chains in the passageway outside his door, he guessed that prisoners were being brought on the ship, but had no idea about the specifics.

Captain Cooper clearly enjoyed keeping him in the dark about their destinations, but Jedediah was still able to piece together the handful of clues he could gather from his porthole view and from their conversations together. He correctly guessed that they were at the mouth of the Chesapeake Bay. The *Nipigon* had apparently been heading southerly at eight knots for twenty-four hours, which gave him a rough idea of their geographic location. Also, the continued absence of concern over potential threats from the Confederate Navy indicated that they were still close to friendly waters.

But later, from holes in the cabin walls that were left when some pipes had been removed a long time ago, he heard the unmistakable voices of men with thick southern accents. The sounds of pacing and several tough rebukes from outside his cabin door told Jedediah there was now a detachment of Union guards in the passageway watching the prisoners during the voyage. His curiosity got the better of him, so he whispered through the hole in the cabin wall, "Psst, hullo there?"

There was muttering and shuffling as men on the other side of the wall moved to find the source of the voice. After a moment of uncertainty, they whispered back, "Hullo there, yourself. Are you also a prisoner of war?"

Jedediah chuckled, "No, I am not."

There was a collective inhalation from the other side. "You sound like a Yankee!"

"That's true. I was born and bred in the state of Maine."

"Are you a soldier or a guard?"

"Neither. I'm a prisoner, just like all of you."

There was more mumbling as the men interpreted his comment. "Pshaw! If you're a Yankee, you must be some kind of common criminal."

"More like an unwilling passenger."

The men were abuzz as they tried to figure out why he was being held prisoner on the same vessel they were. When there was a momentary pause in their conversations, Jedediah asked, "Where do you all hail from?"

This caused a heated debate, and Jedediah could hear them arguing about whether they should tell him anything. One man said loudly enough for all to hear that he thought this might be a Yankee trap to get them to give up some kind of secret, and he went so far as to say it must be an intelligence-gathering ploy to lull the captive men into dispensing vital information.

"I was just curious, that's all. You don't have to talk to me if you don't want to."

After another brief discussion, the man closest to the hole whispered, "We're all Confederate officers being transported from Fort Monroe to the Yankee prison at Fort Delaware."

"You don't say."

Another voice hoarsely whispered through the hole in the wall, "Well, mister, you've got all of us real piqued over here. We can't figure you out none. You're a Yankee, but you ain't a spy, a criminal, nor a sympathizer. It just don't make sense to any of us why you're a prisoner on this-here boat, since you haven't tole us no real reason why you're here."

"I am the captain's fighting dog," Jedediah said quietly. When there was no reaction, he began to tell his story. He told them about his whaling days with Captain Cooper and Mr. Blunt. Then he told them about Jonathan's murder and being shanghaied in Boston and the fights he'd been a participant in during the trip down the coast. When he was done, the initial response was a shrill whistle. Finally, the voice on the other side of the hole said, "We thought *we* was in bad shape, but you're in a much worse place than us, partner."

"How you figure that?"

"'Cause all we have to do is sit tight in that prison and don't die from illness. We all know we'll either be paroled back to the South at some point or traded for some Yankee officers later on. But no matter what, we ain't gonna be asked to kill or risk gettin' ourselves killed by nobody for quite some time. You, on the other hand, you ain't got no choice in the matter."

Another voice suddenly spoke up. "You given any thought to escapin'?"

Jedediah shrugged even though the men couldn't see him. "'Course I have. But without knowing where I am or the layout of this ship, it would be suicide."

"I know you are not a supporter of the Cause, but since we are all prisoners on this-here ship, we could work together to get our freedom. We all took notice of our surrounds as we were loaded onboard. There's almost ninety of us, so we've got the guards and the crew outnumbered! What do you say?"

"But those guards do have the guns. And I can't think of a way to get the upper hand on them. Plus, even if we were able to get out of the cabins, what then?"

"Pshaw! I'm sure we've got some men in here who could steer a boat. Hell, couldn't *you* do it, for that matter? You must've learned how to navigate a ship while you was on that whaler."

Jedediah was about to answer when the doors of both his and the prisoners' cabins crashed open simultaneously. His reflexes instantly took over, and he was on his feet and away from the hole when the captain came in with his revolver drawn. As he pointed it at Jedediah's chest, he could hear the guards threatening violence against the prisoners on the other side of the wall. The captain sneered, "And what the hell do you think you're doing?"

After using his eyes and arms to pantomime that he had been sitting on his cot, Jedediah said, "Was just about to fall asleep before you came bursting in here, Captain!"

"You're lying! The guards heard those rebel prisoners talk about escaping. They came and got me."

"I don't know what they thought was happening, but I did not even know there were prisoners onboard until you just said so. I was only trying to get the rest that you urged me to get so I will be fit for the next fight."

The woolen blanket on Jedediah's cot was shoved to the side and the straw mattress looked like he'd been lying on it, so Captain Cooper shook his head dubiously and uncocked his revolver. "Aye, Mr. Stiller. You *should* be getting some rest. But I have given clear orders to those guards to load their rifles and be prepared to shoot anyone who even appears to be *thinking* of talking on my ship! Those fleabag rebel prisoners have to spend a grand total of fifteen hours onboard the *Nipigon*, and they have just reserved the right to do so in silence—with no more talking of any kind. Same with you."

He turned on his heel, left the cabin, and locked the door behind him. Jedediah sat down heavily on his cot. He knew better than trying to speak again to the prisoners. Now that the guards and the captain were aware the conversations had taken place and their attention was heightened, this lot of men were a lost cause as allies for an escape attempt on this trip. But he was sure the *Nipigon* would be back to Fort Monroe sometime in the future to pick up more prisoners, and the seeds for planning his escape were now sown in his head.

Chapter Thirty-Three

Catherine Brandford's life became a phantasmagoria of the most unimaginable horrors. The morphine that was injected into her veins daily kept her trapped in an amorphous consciousness that was a mixture of whirling delirium and fleetingly sharp moments of incomplete sobriety. The lightless environment of her incarceration combined with her drug-induced state to create a kind of timeless dreamworld. And because there were no points of reference that could be completely identified as true, she had no way to discern where reality started or ended and no concept of the passage of time. Everything was so distorted that her dreams, her waking moments, and her life became nothing more than a continuous cycle of outlandish scenes overlapping one another. With each passing day of forced addiction, her brain grew more addled, and she was nearly convinced that this was the way she had always lived and the way she was doomed to live for all eternity. So, in an attempt to preserve herself, she acknowledged that resistance of any kind, emotional or physical, would cause her more damage than good, and she let her psyche snuggle down into the warmth that came through accepting her new world and her repulsive role in it.

Her semiconscious dreamlike state provided Catherine some protection, too. The visible scars—needle marks on her arms, lash marks on her lower back and buttocks, bite marks on her breasts, and burns on her rib cage and inner thighs, as well as those covered by her undergarments—would be lifelong evidence of the heinous acts inflicted upon her during her captivity, but the visions that plagued her were too surreal for her mind to accept. As the boundary between reality and hallucination continued to be a thin and permeable membrane for her, Catherine took some solace in the fact that the repugnant images in her head of Reverend Watson and Mrs. Whitherby doing unspeakable things to one another and to her inside that wagon were as likely to be unreal as they were to be real. And to keep any shred of sanity, she was all too willing to let her mind protect her in the face of such uncertainty. After all, it was far easier to find a haven in doubt than to bear the slings and arrows of the truth. She wanted to survive, and she knew that if she allowed her brain to acknowledge what was really happening to her, she would find a way to slit her wrists.

Still, she was haunted by a swirling vortex of nightmarish images. And there was no escape from them. If she closed her eyes, she saw them projected on the insides of her eyelids, and if she opened her eyes, she saw them happening to her. There was Mrs. Whitherby, digging at her own crotch like she was scratching at poison ivy, while Reverend Watson violently thrust himself inside Catherine as he recited verses of the Twenty-Third Psalm. Or she saw the elderly woman acting like some kind of little monkey, clapping her hands and cackling at the pain the man was inflicting with his leather flogger, his cigar, or his fingers as the old woman knelt down and ate from the fruit that hung between his legs. Or the two of them taking turns cruelly humiliating Catherine as the interior of the wagon rang with peels of evil laughter that were gradually overwhelmed by the tormentors' own sickeningly contented gasps and moans of pleasure.

Catherine was exhausted by the struggle to keep herself inside her own body. Sometime during these horrendous experiences, her mind let her believe she could float to the ceiling of the ambulance and see everything that was being done to her as though it were happening to someone else. She saw herself being forced to take the old man's member into her own mouth until his seed dripped from her chin. She saw herself tied to her cot and various agents of torture applied to her until her tears mixed with the saliva on her face. And she saw Mrs. Whitherby and Reverend Watson tenderly feed her from a ceramic bowl with a wooden spoon before they prayed over her. And then she saw herself pinned down on the cot by the weight of the minister as he pushed himself into her again, her splayed legs like the broken wings of a great bird, and the slaps on his bare buttocks being applied by the old woman's skeletal hand with the perfect rhythmic accuracy of a fine pocket watch.

Again. Again. Again.

Chapter Thirty-Four

After the work gang of black slaves loaded the kegs of gunpowder on the DuPont Company wharf in Wilmington, Delaware, the atmosphere onboard the *Nipigon* had an almost palpable tension that ran through the timbers to the very keel of the vessel. This was due in part to the fact that the new hazardous load had just turned the ship into a floating bomb. But there was also something unspoken and unseen building up to become as explosive as the cargo. It may have been triggered by the dangers of this run or the cruel behaviors of Captain Cooper, but something far more combustible was at the very core of the floating community on the *Nipigon*, and the return to New York proved to be a turning point. Actually, those crew members who were still alive six months later could point to that routine unloading and reloading of the ship in that city as the singular beginning of the end.

Jedediah was smuggled off the ship as the crew gingerly unloaded the gunpowder, and went with Mr. Spencer and Captain Cooper to the very same warehouse where he'd killed the Englishman. The surroundings and the arena were familiar, but as soon as he entered the ring, it became startlingly clear that the captain's prophecy had come true. Standing in his corner of the ring was a large man wearing a black leather mask that covered his head and protected his nose, ears, and eyes. He was bare above the waist, and his upper body was covered with so many pink and jagged scars that it looked like a map. On his forearms, the broken glass that spangled his leather armguards sparkled in the lamplight. The man was not bobbing and practicing his swings like a boxer but was shuffling from foot to foot in anticipation of the fight.

As soon as he saw his opponent, Jedediah groaned involuntarily. He did not feel fear from either the masked man or the possibility of his own defeat, but he knew this fight was going to cost him in ways the others had not. When Captain Cooper heard his reaction, his eyes snapped to the man's handler with a steely stare. In a low voice, he said to Jedediah, "Well, well. They were much quicker in their response to your reputation than I had anticipated."

The fight's outcome was never in question. Unlike the previous contests with the pugilists, Jedediah was in control of this battle from the moment the referee started it. If there was one thing he knew how to do, it was to defeat this type of opponent. He did so with a frighteningly methodical approach that ended with the man's head facing a hundred and eighty degrees from its natural inclination. But Jedediah's wounds from the fight—the deep cuts on his cheeks, chest, and arms that bled too freely—would need stitching onboard the ship. Even as he struggled to put his clothing on while the material soaked up his blood, he shook his head with the realization that these kinds of victories were far too costly to take even an iota of satisfaction from, and he looked at Mr. Spencer and Captain Cooper with dark and brooding eyes.

Just before they cleared the arena, a man approached them. From the way the captain's body stiffened, it was clear that this portly and well-dressed man was someone of great importance. He looked over at Jedediah and flashed a crocodile grin. "Very impressive, Captain Cooper. Very impressive. That man your savage just treated like a roaster chicken was a highly regarded fighter in these parts. To see him...uh, dispatched so quickly was quite unusual. And I find myself envying another, and I am not the type of man who likes to feel that emotion. Ever."

Captain Cooper shrugged. He looked at Jedediah. "He is, without a doubt, a unique prospect."

"How much?"

"Excuse me?"

"Oh, come on, Cooper. Do not pretend you don't know what is happening here. How much do you want for your fighter?"

If the captain was surprised, his eyes did not show it. He shook his head. "Oh, I am very sorry, sir. He is not for sale."

"Everything in this world is for sale, Captain Cooper, you know that. How much for your fighter?"

"No, I'm sorry, sir, he's not for sale. That is the truth. I will not sell him for any amount of money."

The man chuckled. "As the captain and part owner of that scow you are overcharging the federal government with, you cannot be a total fool to believe that the money you're now raking in will continue to flow with the same volume. You must see your reality on the horizon. Just your involvement with these events and betting money on this man tells me that you know the end for your business is at hand. I could make you a wealthy man, Captain Cooper, a very, very wealthy man. You sell this fighter to me, and you could be making a hefty profit that even keeping him won't pay you."

"No, sir. As I said, he is not for sale."

"I'm losing my patience with you, Captain! I never figured you for a man who would let foolish sentimental values get in the way of his love of money. You'll be a very rich man if you accept my offer here today, sir. Don't waste this opportunity."

"Good day, sir. As I have said repeatedly, my fighter is not for sale. Not today, nor any day. Thank you."

"Next time, there will be two of those fighters waiting for him!"

"The more the merrier, sir. I've witnessed this man best four foes at one time. I can honestly say that nothing *you* threaten me with will scare me into selling my fighter to you."

"They will be wearing more than just glass-covered armguards next time. I can promise you that the fighters you'll be facing in the future will be armed with even more tormenting and torturous implements."

"Arm them to the teeth, my good sir! This beast here can take on anything."

The man raised his brows in surprise. "Ah, I see what's going on here." His fleshy head turned to speak directly to Jedediah. "But do you?"

Jedediah had been listening without appearing to do so, but he now looked at the pompous man with chagrin. The man sighed heavily. "He wants to use you up. For some reason, he wants your opponents to shred you to pieces. He cares not whether you live or die. As a matter of fact, I think he seeks the latter. Any sane man who cared one ounce about his fighter would give strong consideration to my offer. But he's not, and I now know why—this man wants to see the red of your blood spilled in an arena more than he wants to see the color of money in his fist. You need to think about whether you want to leave this world as some kind of disposable trash or as a glorified and honored fighter!"

"He does not need to think at all, sir. He only needs to fight and win. Good day!"

The man seemed genuinely disappointed as the captain turned away and herded his little procession out of the arena.

•   •   •   •   •

Back at the *Nipigon*, the event they had so far avoided finally occurred. As they got to the gangplank to board the ship, they encountered one of the regular crew members. He was a skinny man who moved with ferret-like energy, and he scurried across the wooden planks, almost bumping into the three men at the end. He initially gasped at nearly touching the captain and his mate, but his eyes were drawn to the bloodied and tattooed face of Jedediah, and he cowered in fear. "*E' vero! Il diavolo vive di questa barca!*"

The captain and Mr. Spencer seemed too overwhelmed by the implications of this chance meeting to respond, but Jedediah said gently, "*Eh, è fatto.*"

The man hurried away and ran off to the other crew members, who were still carrying cargo aboard the ship. They could hear his birdlike chirpings, and the captain shut his eyes and exhaled loudly. "Well, I would say that our little secret is now out. It appears we will need to take care of a few things, Mr. Spencer."

"Aye, Captain."

•   •   •   •   •

When the ship docked again in Providence, the captain and mate made a much more concerted effort to hide their departure from the ship while the crew was working. Their anxiety was obvious, almost palpable, and Mr.

Spencer made them wait until he was certain the path was clear before they hustled back to the now familiar warehouse.

There, however, they encountered an unpleasant armed guard at the doorway who informed them that there would be no fight today. When Captain Cooper asked if there were *any* fights happening, the man shook his head and said roughly, "None for your fighter!"

When the captain tried to walk past him on the pretense of talking to one of the fight organizers, the guard slowly reached for the revolver in his belt. The captain grimaced. There was no need for a violent conflict in this situation, so he turned the procession around and headed silently back to the ship.

During their trek back to the *Nipigon*, both the captain and Mr. Spencer seemed edgier than usual, as if they were expecting some kind of trouble. They were so distracted when they put Jedediah back in his cabin, they left him alone without so much as a glance as they walked out and locked the door.

For his part, Jedediah was grateful there had been no fight. He needed the rest. Even the steam up to Providence had not allowed enough healing from the vicious fight in New York, and every time he lifted his arms, it felt as if all of Mr. Spencer's crude stitching would pop open. The captain stayed away, so he did not know the next destination or the schedule for the upcoming ports of call, but Jedediah secretly hoped he'd have another week before the next fight.

He did not get his wish. They quickly returned to New York, and Jedediah had to fight two men who were armed. They had straight razors in their boots, and they pulled the blades out early and bloodied Jedediah deeply before he was able to subdue them both and use their own weapons on them. Before the fight could be stopped and the rampaging tattooed giant brought under control, he had neatly sliced off both men's ears and noses, and the sawdust on the arena floor was challenged to soak up the volume of blood that had been spilled.

Afterward, back on the ship, Mr. Spencer set about stitching the new deep lacerations from the razor-wielding dervishes and resewing the previous wounds that had popped their stitches. To Jedediah's surprise, Spencer openly questioned the captain on the continuing impact of these types of battles on their fighter. When there was no audible response, he was even brash enough to wonder aloud if Jedediah could take much more punishment like that of the last two fights. But when Captain Cooper's dark eyes flashed and held his with an unflinching cruelty and determination, the mate had to look away. When the captain walked off without a word, both Jedediah and Mr. Spencer completely understood that the mate was never to question him about the fighter again.

Jedediah's last fight for the captain took place in Philadelphia. Although it was not the armed blood sport of a New York fight, the opponent was such a skilled pugilist, he punished Jedediah with well-placed blows to his stitched wounds whenever possible. He pummeled Jedediah thoroughly before being overwhelmed by a ferocious physical assault that left him unconscious and with two broken arms.

Later, as Jedediah waited in his cabin for Mr. Spencer to come and restitch him, he became concerned by the appearance of blood in both his sputum and his urine in the piss bucket. A bleeding exterior was one thing, but he now had evidence that there was damage deep inside of him as well. And he knew that these kinds of wounds were much more serious than even the most ghastly lacerations on the skin. He stared into the bucket with consternation and hoped he wouldn't have to fight again any time soon. If he did, he risked getting further injured on the inside, and he knew he could die.

So when the captain came down to his cabin and flippantly announced that he wouldn't have another fight for nearly a week, Jedediah was relieved. During this announcement, the captain also let slip that the delay was due to the fact that they were headed to Fort Monroe again. With no fight to endure and the prospect of another load of Confederate prisoners to conspire with, Jedediah suddenly found something that overwhelmed the coppery aftertaste in his mouth—the taste of freedom.

Chapter Thirty-Five

While Catherine swam the opiate-induced stream of consciousness from one grotesque and unbelievable scene to another, her life had existed in a self-contained and protective flow of numbness. But then, without warning, that current carried her right into the sharp coral reefs of reality, which ripped at her clothing and lacerated her skin. New shudders of pain pulsed through her system, and her sodden brain slowly began to comprehend that her blissful swim was coming to a painful end. The watery covering over the lenses of her eyes became dark and as thick as stew, then drained away to reveal a world that was strangely stark and quiet.

She found herself in a nondescript bedroom with an unknown and faceless woman who gently comforted her. The smells of her surroundings and the textures of the helping hands upon her were so different, she came to the conclusion that they did not belong to those barbaric creatures who had taken such pleasure in torturing her. At first, she fought the meaning of this, but then her body gradually relaxed into acceptance.

But no matter how much peace was now seeping back into her world, she was possessed by waves of intense anger that forced verbal insults to pour out of her like volcanic eruptions. And as she thrashed about during these moments of severe distress, she felt new bindings grind into the flesh of her wrists and ankles. Her ravings became so monumental that she seemed to be vomiting up a hateful black goo from the very inner cavities of her soul. She thrashed and she shouted, but the response to her outbursts was always comforting words and loving, tender touches. As confusing as this was, it confirmed that whoever was taking care of her now was immune to her toxic words, screaming, and vile effluents. Even though she was incapable, she tried desperately to control herself to show the gratitude she was feeling inside.

But she was as unable to curtail her fits of anger and cursing as she was to calm the feverish shivering that racked her body as viciously as if she were lying in a snowdrift.

And through all of it, the kindness in the voice was unwavering. It lovingly repeated over and over, "You're safe now, Catherine. You have nothing to fear anymore. You are safe."

As her dreamlike images hardened into more complete and caustic memories, Catherine began to resign herself to the fact that she had just survived a hellacious lifetime of atrocities. The horribleness of this made her want to resist the seemingly naïve messages of the soothing voice. Then, one day, her body grew tired of resisting, and she finally surrendered to a slumber that was both peaceful and serene. When she awoke, she could see the face of her caretaker clearly, and she looked into the older woman's cool blue eyes and smiled weakly at her. The woman smiled back and cooed, "Ah, you're back amongst the living, Miss Catherine. You are a strong creature, my dear. Your recovery would have killed many a young man physically bigger and stronger than you."

She wanted to reply, but the peacefulness that the woman's comment caused made her fall into another slumber. When she awoke the next time, the bindings on her wrists and ankles were gone, and she was tucked into the clean-smelling covers of the bed in a manner that reminded her of the way her mother had sealed her in for sleep every night when she was a small girl. She looked around the room and saw the same elderly woman smiling back at her.

"Hello, Catherine, my name is Mrs. Ketchum, and you are safe in my house in New York City. We do not need to talk about any of the details of your experience right now, but you should know that you were rescued from two godless monsters who addicted you to morphine as part of your tortured imprisonment. The wretched anguish you have been experiencing, my dear, has been a monumental fight against that. I am told by those who are qualified in this field that the worst is over for you now, so please find comfort so you can fully heal."

Catherine's brain could not yet process everything the woman had said, but her voice was so strong and the bedroom so protective that she felt, for the first time in recent memory, safe. And this new feeling was enough to keep her from fighting the urge to fall asleep again.

As Mrs. Ketchum watched the young woman's eyelids flutter and then close, she knew that this restful sleep marked the beginning of the transformation from tortured victim to convalescing patient, and she felt a warm sense of optimism finally push its way into her awareness. She looked out the curtained window, closed her eyes, and inhaled deeply. When she opened her eyes again, she went to the bed and gently touched the young woman's forehead. Now that she was confident enough that Catherine had turned the most challenging corner of her recovery, she felt she could leave her alone to attend to the myriad of responsibilities she had allowed to pile up when she'd chosen to nurse this young woman back to health. She was careful not to close the door completely as she left, leaving it ajar just a finger's width.

·　·　·　·　·

When Catherine awoke the next time, she knew she was alone, but that fact did not scare her. She sat up and scanned her newfound sanctuary. Although the furniture and decorations of the room were utilitarian and sparse, everything had such a quiet quality that she knew she was in a household of some wealth. Nothing seemed opulent, just well-made. The bed was certainly sturdy and comfortable, and she was content to remain ensconced in it. She looked over at the window, and it was open slightly to let fresh air into the room. It was curtained, but intense sunlight poured through the lace and onto the floor. Under normal circumstances, Catherine would have wanted to get right out of bed and explore a new place in the warm embrace of springtime, but the security of the bed was too comforting to leave, and she was content to just listen to the continuous sounds of wagons, horse-drawn streetcars, and people outside.

Mrs. Ketchum had said that she was in New York City. She had said other things as well, but Catherine struggled to organize them all into a meaningful explanation of how she had ended up here in this bedroom. Her inability to remember completely filled her with questions she needed to ask the older woman when she came back. The distortion of her narcotic-based imprisonment continued to intertwine her memories and taint her dreams, and Catherine felt the mounting frustration of trying to build something solid from substances that were too fluid to hold shape.

There was a little silver bell on the bedside table, and Catherine remembered the older woman had said it was for her to signal with if she needed anything. She did not want to ring it, but she did so now because she could no longer stand not to have the answers she sought. When an unknown young woman came in, Catherine recoiled. The woman saw her reaction and talked very fast with a thick Irish brogue. "Ah, Mrs. Ketchum has had to go to a meetin' this afternoon. She's a rather important lady in the war effort, don't ya know. But she told me to come up here whenever ya rang that bell. I know we haven't been properly introduced and that I startled ya by comin' in right now, and I do humbly apologize 'bout that! My name is Bridget Cullwick, and I'm one o' Mrs. Ketchum's house servants, ma'am."

Bridget seemed almost as unsettled as she was, so Catherine croaked weakly, "It's nice to meet you. I'm Catherine, Catherine Brandford."

"Yes, ma'am, Mrs. Ketchum said that were your name."

Catherine turned away and gazed out the window. She had been fully expecting to see Mrs. Ketchum and ask her the questions, and now that her fear of this stranger was abating, she couldn't stop the disappointment from showing on her face.

Bridget noticed this and said, "Did ya need somethin', Miss Catherine?"

Catherine started to shake her head, but then asked boldly, "Do you know how I got here, Bridget?"

"Yes, ma'am, I do."

"Oh, please tell me! I need to know!"

"Ah, Mrs. Ketchum said to wait till she got home to say anythin' to ya 'bout that."

"Please, Bridget! How did I end up here in this bed? The last memories I have are too dark to even mention, and I just don't understand how I went from being in Hell to being in Heaven like this. I have no idea how that happened, but I've been lying in this bed trying to figure it all out, and it's driving me crazy. More than anything else, Bridget, I need to be sure this is not part of the nightmare—that I'm not still dreaming. I need to know if I'm truly saved."

Bridget stole a glance over her shoulder and clucked her tongue loudly. She moved forward toward the bed and said, "Ah, I don't know all them details or nothin', Miss Catherine, but apparently them bad people took ya into the mountains o' northern New Jersey. I don't know why they did that, but they did. While you were there, the wild people of that area discovered ya and decided to rescue ya. Again, ma'am, I don't know all them details, but somehow they got ya away from them monsters. As luck would have it, a woman of those people used to be a trusted maid of Mrs. Ketchum who'd gone back to live with 'er clan up there. Once ya were rescued, that woman thought it best to bring ya here for Mrs. Ketchum to heal, and that's what they did."

"Where are they? Can I thank them?"

"No, ma'am. They ain't too comfortable here in the world outside their mountains, so they dropped ya off with Mrs. Ketchum and skittered right back home. Mrs. Ketchum, bein' a patron and a nurse with the U.S. Sanitary Commission, took ya right in and got ya cleaned up and under a doctor's care. Gettin' ya healed weren't too perty neither! You went through some awful violent moments—fits o' swearin' and yellin' that woulda made a sailor blush—tossin' and turnin' so bad we had t' tie ya to the bed. You screamed about the most horrifyin' things my ears ever heard! But then ya got quiet and peaceful, and here ya are."

"Then this is real. I'm really here, Bridget?"

The young woman moved forward and pinched Catherine's arm gently. It wasn't terribly painful, but she responded by saying, "Ow!"

"Sorry, m'lady, but that's how I figger out when I'm awake or asleep sometimes. See? You ain't dreamin' none."

Catherine gasped. "So I'm truly awake and I'm really here in this bedroom in Mrs. Ketchum's house in New York City. This is all real! But what about the visions I see in my head? Can they all be real, too? They are too horrible..."

"Please, Miss Catherine, I swore t' Mrs. Ketchum I wouldn't tell ya nothin' that would hurt ya in any way. If she finds out that I've gone and told ya too much, she'll be right cross with me."

The panic in the young woman's voice helped disperse the dark images that had begun to gather, and Catherine put out her hand. "Oh, Bridget, I'm so grateful you told me some scraps about my rescue. It will help me sleep better—and I won't tell Mrs. Ketchum about any of it, I swear."

The smile on Bridget's face was so genuine, it warmed Catherine's heart. As she watched her leave the bedroom to continue her duties in the house, she digested all of the new information. She was saved! She was not dreaming this, it was real. Somehow she had been put through the worst conceivable situations, but had been rescued. She knew that such divine gifts could not be squandered, and she resolved to make a new commitment to living her life in a way that reflected her gratitude. She needed to repay this world that had thought enough of her to save her from the miseries of her captivity.

That evening when Mrs. Ketchum came to the bedroom, the older woman's usually bright face was grim. "Bridget just admitted what she did today. I'm so angry, I could chew nails!"

Catherine reached out to her and said, "Oh, please don't be mad at her, Mrs. Ketchum! I begged her to tell me what she knew so that I could feel like my feet were in reality again. It's hard to explain, but apparently morphine does such a good job of dislodging the anchors that hold us firmly to the truth, I find myself struggling to figure out what is real and what is not. If I cannot accept that this room and you are real, I'm doomed to keep waiting for the next horrifying scene to drown me with evil. Such waiting can only cause a person to go insane. So please, I beseech you, don't hold any anger toward Bridget! By telling me the scant details of how I got here, she gave me the peace to accept that, for whatever reason, I was rescued, and I'm wholly determined to cherish that fact and build on my good fortune."

Mrs. Ketchum's kind expression returned, and she smiled. "I see. Here I was, trying to protect you at all costs when you actually needed a little dose of reality to begin the healing process. Well, the one thing you've shown me so far is that you're a helluva lot stronger than you look. Hmm..."

She paused to pull over a wooden chair that was nestled against the wall near the washstand and sat down. "I guess that, without stirring you up too much, you need to hear more of the details of your rescue to help you fully understand your current situation. I'm not sure what exactly Bridget told you, but yes, you were brought to me by the people of a former beloved maid of mine by the name of Elsa Van Dunk. She worked for me for over a decade, but she ultimately felt the pull to rejoin her family in the mountains of New Jersey. I was as sad saying good-bye to her as I would have been saying farewell to my own sister, I can tell you that!"

"Bridget mentioned some kind of wild mountain people up there."

The older woman rolled her eyes. "That's a bit of an exaggeration. Although the people of that region *are* a bit of a mystery, there are several cruel and untrue stories that swirl around them. Truth is, no one knows the whole story about these people, and since they keep to themselves and stay away from civilization, they remain the subject of idle speculation. The best theory Elsa could offer was that their Dutch ancestors found themselves on the wrong side after the Revolutionary War and sequestered themselves in that remote location to avoid retribution from the victorious colonists. But over the years, they've welcomed many other people who have also been persecuted or felt unwanted. Supposedly, even some of the West Indian mistresses of the Hessian troops found a home there. Their accepting attitudes encouraged escaping slaves, gypsies, and the last members of a few ancient Indian tribes to find a haven there as well, and the group expanded. Because of this mixture and the way they keep to themselves, the local people don't like or trust them. They spread rumors about their mental instability and suggest that the population is full of inbreeds. They even refer to them as 'Jacks 'n' Whites'!"

"Jacks?"

"'Tis a racist and cruel way to refer to runaway slaves. So the name has its roots in anger and a petty nastiness that I find unsavory. I refuse to call them 'Jackson Whites' the way many people do."

"Did my rescuers tell you much about where and how they found me?"

Mrs. Ketchum pursed her lips. "Hmm...like I said, they keep to themselves and don't like to talk too much. All they would say was that a minister and an old white-haired woman came to them in a fancy wagon on the pretense that they needed more morphine to take to the war and had heard that the local medicine woman had a surplus of it."

"Reverend Watson and Mrs. Whitherby!" Catherine hissed vehemently. "My last solid memory is of them kidnapping me in Framingham, Massachusetts. I met them in Portland and traveled with them there. They told me they were part of a wagon train of Christians headed to the war with the Sanitary Commission. They lured me into their ambulance and covered my face with a cloth soaked in chloroform. After that, everything becomes a horrible nightmare..."

When she started to weep, Mrs. Ketchum continued forcefully, "I am part of the Sanitary Commission myself, Catherine, and I will inquire about them tomorrow and see if any of their claims were true. Anyway, according to your rescuers, those two were odd enough to arouse their suspicion, so they set about finding out what was really going on in that wagon. Their curiosity led them to you. They instantly saw your plight and intervened on your behalf. I guess, in the course of their actions to rescue you, the contents of the wagon caught fire and exploded in a most impressive scene of destruction! The wagon and those two monsters were burned to ashes."

Through her tears, Catherine said, "So they're dead?"

The older woman closed her eyes for a moment. "Yes, they both died in the flames. You need to put your mind at ease now. Those two vile abominations will never hurt you again. Their souls are back in the fires of Hell for all eternity."

"Oh, thank God!"

"But we need to be careful not to extol the behavior of your rescuers too much, because even though their actions were noble, their curiosity and vengeful nature would only feed the image of them as being feeble-minded savages."

"I understand, Mrs. Ketchum. I'm eternally grateful to them for whatever they did. I just wish I could let them know that."

"I have sent a note to Elsa about your recovery. I'm sure they will be most happy to hear about it, since they took such an interest in your well-being, my dear. "

"I just want them to know how grateful I am."

"They will. Now that you are safe and fully recovering—"

When the young woman inhaled sharply and looked away, Mrs. Ketchum waited to see what had caused this reaction. Finally, Catherine said very quietly, "I'm not sure I can ever fully recover, Mrs. Ketchum. I'm still haunted by what they did to me. I keep reliving the horrors. If I have to keep seeing those horrendous scenes for the rest of my life—"

The older woman put her finger on Catherine's lips. "You know, I once knew a woman who lived through a terribly shocking event. She discovered her husband hanging from the ceiling in the spare bedroom of their home. She'd had no warning of his sadness, and the discovery of his body opened her up to the very core. After his funeral, she came back to the empty house, took the key to that room, and locked it tight without so much as a glance inside. If there was anything in there of value, she wanted nothing to do with it anymore. And to this day, she has never opened it up again. She won't even talk about it, and she's trained herself not to think about it either. The person who buys her house after she dies will be the first to enter that room since she turned the key in the lock.

"And that is exactly what I think you should do with those horrible memories, my dear. You should leave them in that space in your mind, turn the key, and lock them up there forever. You don't need to torture yourself or those around you by going through the torment again and again. Lock them up! Lock them up and throw the key away so you'll forget. You should never speak about it again!"

Catherine knew that shutting off a room in a house was far easier than sealing off a section of her mind, but she attempted to do it now. She closed her eyes, but the horrifying images returned and played on the backs of her eyelids. When her face tightened, Mrs. Ketchum yelled, "Lock them up, dear! Don't look at those images! Don't attempt to understand them. It will only torment you. Lock them up! The only way you will survive is if you do that, my dear. Lock them up!"

Chapter Thirty-Six

As the *Nipigon* steamed south, Jedediah began to work on loosening the bracket on the wall of the cabin. He quietly gathered up the loose links of his chain, and with slow and steady pressure, he applied his full strength to it without making any noise. He knew he didn't have much time before they reached their destination, and he kept his focus on the task. By the time the ship stopped to load the prisoners at Fort Monroe, Jedediah was sure he had worked the bracket so loose that, with one strong yank, he could pull it free from the wall. With this task complete, he went to his cot and tried to rest while the prisoners were brought aboard. His mind was awash with the details of plans and contingencies, and he lay awake and stared at the ceiling.

When the ship started heading north, Jedediah waited to make sure the conditions were identical to the first time. He listened carefully to ascertain whether the next cabin was indeed loaded with Confederate soldiers and whether there were guards in the passageway on patrol. Once he was satisfied with these facts, he whispered into the hole in the wall, "Hullo, there. I need to speak to the highest-ranking officer."

After some shuffling on the other side, a hoarse whisper came back. "Hullo, yourself. My name is Lieutenant Henry Anderson of the Confederate States of America blockade runner, *Ella and Anna*. To whom do I have the pleasure of talking today?"

Jedediah pushed closer to the hole and tried not to let his urgency get the best of him. "Mr. Anderson, we don't have much time, so please listen carefully to everything I have to say before you respond. I know you're going to need a heaping load of trust to do what I am going to ask you to do, but I hope I can win that trust in the next few minutes."

When nothing but silence followed, he continued. In an abbreviated manner, he told the major about his situation, about the last batch of Confederate prisoners, the soldiers and the captain's response to their conversing through the same hole, and about his plans for escape. At the end of his diatribe, he handed Mr. Sinagra's folding knife through the hole. The knife disappeared, and the voice said, "All right, Yank, we're with you. But may God have mercy on your soul if you're lying to us."

Jedediah went to the wall and heaved the bracket out with one silent pull. Then he started whispering the bogus escape plans loudly enough for the guards outside to hear. As similar divulges came from the Confederate prisoners in their cell as well, Jedediah heard shouts and scuffling out in the passageway as the captain prepared the assault on the prisoners' cabins. When his door banged open and the captain blindly flew into the space with his revolver extended before him, Jedediah brought his chains down onto the man's wrist, snapping it like a twig and sending his weapon to the deck with a heavy thud. An upward thrust with the chains caught the captain under the chin and knocked him out cold, and he fell lifelessly to the floor of the cabin. Without hesitation, Jedediah picked up the revolver, popped into the passageway, and fired the gun at the ceiling. The echoes of the concussion were deafening in the narrow space, and he roared, "Surrender your arms at once and we won't kill you!"

When the smoke from the revolver shot cleared, he could see several young men in Union uniforms paralyzed with terror. He snatched away their rifles before the Confederate prisoners streamed out of their cabin and swarmed over those men who had not put down their guns. The men made way for another man who walked purposefully toward him saying, "Mr. Jedediah Stiller, I presume. Lieutenant Henry Anderson of the CSA Navy. It's a pleasure."

Jedediah's appearance seemed to intimidate both sides of the conflict. His overall size was startling to take in, but the combination of the facial tattoos, bruises, and stitches only made him more monstrous.

He looked around and said, "Lieutenant, you are the military man in this situation, so I defer to you to order your men to take control of this ship. I only ask that they not harm the members of the crew—both the common men and the officers. They are mostly innocent men living under the same tyranny of the captain, and they don't deserve to be killed."

The Confederate naval officer stiffened and said, "What do you take me for, Mr. Stiller? A godless savage?"

Jedediah scoffed at the man's apparent jest, then grew serious. "I am going to take the master of this ship, Captain Zepheniah Cooper, to receive the punishment I think he deserves for his misdeeds and indiscretions. This may stain the actions of you and your men, and I hope that is acceptable to you."

Anderson looked at him and seemed to contemplate something, then he nodded. "We must move with more haste if we are going to take control of this vessel. Do what you think is right with Captain Cooper, and we will convene for a final conversation up in the wheelhouse later, when the dust settles."

"Aye, Lieutenant. And I do need to trade this revolver for the folding knife I handed over."

There was a pregnant silence that was finally broken by the hoots of some of the Confederate prisoners as they turned to spread through the ship. After Anderson handed the knife back to Jedediah with a wry smile, the giant man went to retrieve the unconscious captain from inside the cabin.

When Jedediah entered the boiler room with Captain Cooper's body draped over his shoulder, he found most of the Italian crew huddled there in fear. He let the captain's body fall unceremoniously to the floor and then looked at the men in front of him with an expression devoid of emotion. He placed the folding knife on the floor and kicked it toward them. They were startled by this action, but they quickly recognized Mr. Sinagra's knife. The crewman who'd seen Jedediah in New York started chattering in Italian to the other crew members, and they looked at him with growing fear.

When the man was done talking, Jedediah spoke to them in broken Italian to explain what he could. As he told them about being forced to fight Mr. Sinagra and the lie that the captain had told the man to incite him, their eyes narrowed into angry blades of vengeance. He then assured them that the Confederate leader of the mutiny had guaranteed their safe return if they would help the ship sail close to a southern port. All the men nodded or shrugged, acknowledging that they really had no choice. Seeing this, Jedediah concluded with his own shrug, "*A mali estremi, estremi rimedi.*"

The captain, who had just regained consciousness, tried to raise his head to see where he was. He was still groggy, and his eyes wallowed with pain and uncertainty. When he tried to speak, his shattered jaw wouldn't work and everything was garbled.

Jedediah looked down at him without pity. "I think you're going to find it harder to spread your lies this time with your forked tongue not working properly, Captain. I'm going to leave you here with these *paisanos* and let them give you the care you deserve." He bowed slightly and said, "Until we meet again, Captain Cooper."

The captain reached out to grab Jedediah's leg, but he stepped away too quickly and the man swiped at nothing but air. Then he started mumbling garbled pleas for mercy, but Jedediah shook his head and said, "Not this time, devil. You are all theirs! *Egli è tutto vostro!*"

The captain's blood-curdling scream only ended as the door to the boiler room clanked shut. Outside, several of the Confederate prisoners looked at Jedediah with trepidation, but he gestured at the door and said, "The crew agrees to keep the boilers stoked for your journey as long as you don't bother them or hurt them."

The men relaxed then and led him up to the *Nipigon*'s wheelhouse, where Lieutenant Anderson was commanding the man at the wheel to turn the ship around. He smiled at Jedediah. "It turns out that not one member of this Yankee crew is overly concerned with our present need to take this ship to Norfolk so we can get back home. As a matter of fact, they all seem more than content to let us sail her there. After we disembark, I give you my word that the crew will be allowed to bring this vessel safely back to Union-controlled waters. What do you have in mind for yourself, Mr. Stiller?"

Jedediah stared out the windows at the rising sun. "Where are we, Lieutenant?"

"From the length of time we've been steaming and the presumed destination, I would venture a guess that we are currently off the coast of Delaware. I haven't had a chance to look at these charts, and I'm unfamiliar with that lighthouse off our port side, but I'm assuming we are a little more than halfway up the Bay of Delaware. Wherever we are, we need to get this old gal turned around and headed south at full steam in advance of any pursuit."

Jedediah nodded and then added, "I need to take one of the lifeboats."

Anderson stared at him for a moment. He pursed his lips and said slowly, "You realize that's going to make it harder for us on the other end, sir."

"I know that, Lieutenant. But I need to get off this ship and get back to what I was doing before Captain Cooper kidnapped me. I cannot ask you to drop me off somewhere, nor do I want to find myself where you all are headed. So the only solution I can see for this dilemma is to get in a lifeboat and row myself to shore."

"We are quite a few miles offshore, Mr. Stiller."

"Yes, sir, we are."

"You do realize that we cannot slow down for you to do this? I cannot risk our own flight to drop you comfortably in the water. It's going to be one helluva rocky ride to get that lifeboat in the water at this speed, you know that, right? There's no guarantee you won't overturn the moment the boat hits the water, and as uncivilized as it is to say, we can't come back for you if you do!"

"I understand all of that."

Anderson nodded briskly. "All right, then. I will have a few of my men help get a lifeboat ready for you. I must say that I wish you would choose to come with us. We need more men like you."

"My heart is committed to my own cause, Mr. Anderson. But, if it is any consolation, that does include killing a Union soldier in the near future."

"Well, Mr. Stiller, I pity that poor bastard. Good luck to you, sir."

"And to you and the rest of your men."

Jedediah went back to his cabin and got his seabag before walking to the lifeboat on the deck behind the starboard paddlewheel. With the boat's boilers fully stoked and the vessel speeding along now, the water was churned into a froth. With no second thoughts, Jedediah hopped into the boat and let the Confederate crew swing him out on the davits and cut the lines with axes. The small boat dropped toward the water, thumped its stern on the side of the vessel, and had its bow driven into the wake. Jedediah pitched forward onto the deck, but the little vessel popped up like a cork and spun away from the departing steamboat. He regained his seat and waved at the crewmen, who returned the gesture with a resounding huzzah.

He had fallen awkwardly against the seats, which had hurt him even further, but without hesitation, he grabbed the bucket at his feet and started bailing the ice-cold water the little boat had taken on in its awkward launch. Once it was nearly empty, he put down the bucket and lifted the long oars into the oarlocks and started to row. Pulling back made the stitches on his ribs and the injuries inside of him rebel painfully, and he closed his eyes as he fought the urge to vomit. He wanted to wait for the feeling to pass, but he knew he did not have that luxury, so he began rowing mechanically. When he looked over his shoulder at the lighthouse on the coast, it looked very, very far away.

The *Nipigon* continued to speed away spewing black smoke, and Jedediah had mixed emotions as he watched it go. His survival was much more uncertain alone and vulnerable in a small lifeboat in the open waters, but he was free. The sudden memory of Captain Cooper's little-girl shriek as the Italian crew members descended upon him made him smile to himself, and he realized that, now that he had his vengeance upon Captain Cooper, it was time to hear Zachary Webster plead for *his* life. He knew there would be unnamable difficulties ahead on his arduous journey into the unknown, and his desire to feel the greater sense of reward from watching his brother's murderer die a slow death would be the fuel he needed to make it through them.

Chapter Thirty-Seven

The lifeboat was far too heavy for one man to row easily, so Jedediah had to use every muscle as he powered the cumbersome craft toward the lighthouse on the distant shore. The pain was intense, and he gritted his teeth to keep it at bay. He could feel the subtle popping of his stitches from the strain, and the continued wounding of organs deep within his body. From time to time, he glanced over his shoulder to gauge the progress he was making, but it seemed so ponderously slow, he stopped doing this altogether. Instead, he chose to stare at his feet and concentrate on just keeping his arms in motion to make the time go faster.

The *Nipigon* was no longer visible, and he found himself imagining the fate that had befallen Captain Cooper. Seeing the fury so clear on the faces of the Italian crewmen in the boiler room, Jedediah assumed the man was quite literally in pieces right now. But he'd learned the hard way never to discount Cooper's chances of weathering any ordeal. Although he doubted it would happen, he had a lingering sense of dread that the two men would somehow meet again, and if they did, Jedediah just hoped he would see the man coming this time.

In this particular moment, however, whether the captain was alive or dead mattered not a lick to his survival. The most compelling task he was faced with was how to get this wallowing bitch of a boat to the shore and start making up for all the time he'd lost. The Confederate lieutenant had identified the coastland as Delaware, but Jedediah had no idea where exactly he was going to land. It didn't really matter, since wherever he came ashore, he was definitely closer to Zachary Webster than he'd been in

Boston. If Captain Cooper had been correct in forecasting that the Union Army was still in winter quarters, Jedediah knew he still had some time to catch up to his prey before the fighting started. And although this was the slightest of consolations, he took it as good enough news to keep rowing.

When he sneaked another look at the lighthouse a little later, its proximity was surprising. The structure itself was not very imposing. It was nothing more than a large white farmhouse with what looked like an extra tall chimney rising above the roof. This structure contained the lanthorn and gallery of the lighthouse, but there was no discernible light coming from it at this hour. Jedediah stopped rowing to stare at it for a moment, and he hoped no one was up there looking out at him. When he started up again, the pain in both his hands made him wince. Each one was well blistered from gripping the wooden oars, and the searing sting of them made him cough and spit over the gunwale. His phlegm was as pink as the inside of a tropical fruit, and he knew that was a very troubling sign, but he disregarded it and focused on keeping the oars moving. He dipped them, took a bite, and pulled back with his whole upper body. And even though he'd been able to help power whaleboats after wounded leviathans in his whaling days, he now wondered if he possessed enough strength to take this craft all the way to shore.

After what felt like the entire day, he finally heard the sound of waves breaking. The lighthouse, which had been the sole landmark for which he'd aimed since leaving the ship, now worried him with its closeness. If there was a keeper and his family, their presence could be a hindrance when it came to landing unnoticed and continuing on his journey without alerting the authorities. So Jedediah began to steer his craft toward the mouth of a river that fed into the sea just north of the lighthouse. If the keeper was as vigilant as he was supposed to be, Jedediah's progress had probably been watched through a spyglass for the entire row-in, and he might even be hailed as he passed by. If luck was with him and he could get ashore without being seen, he had a chance for an unchallenged escape. Since no one was aware of the *Nipigon*'s fate yet, he still had the benefit of complete anonymity. If he could get far away from prying eyes and away from this damn lifeboat, he could just blend into the scenery and vanish from sight.

The river was almost a hundred yards wide, but there was very little current to fight against on the incoming tide. However, whenever the tide turned and the river started to flow out again, upstream passage would become much harder. Jedediah couldn't control that, so he concentrated on rowing and surveying his surroundings. The land around the river was a flat and apparently endless salt marsh that spread out as far as his eyes could see. There was a measure of comfort in the knowledge that there weren't likely to be many people around these parts, but it also meant he had to stay longer with the boat, since traveling by water would be much easier than trudging by foot through the marshy terrain. The river snaked around in a series of random turns. Jedediah exhaled a breath of relief that he'd seen no one. But when he did this, his ribs and insides hurt enough to make him close his eyes and stop rowing. He was tired, battered, hungry, and thirsty, so the momentary respite felt good. But the current quickly began to slow the forward progress of the boat, and he knew he needed to get upriver several more leagues before he could even consider stopping to rest. He began to row slowly again. He was no longer dangerously exposed on the open water, but he had to reach one of those distant clumps of trees on the horizon so that he could ditch the lifeboat.

When a sudden breeze made him shiver, he foresaw what was happening to him. As his shivering grew in magnitude and his head ached, he realized he needed to find a protected spot to stop when the fever hit him with its full force. But everywhere he looked, he saw inaccessible areas of thick mud and wildly sprouted reeds. He went past several smaller creeks and streams that fed into the river, but there were no good landings. His arms moved the oars feebly, and he hoped he could hold off what now seemed inevitable. When his teeth started chattering and his shirt was moist and sticky on his skin, he felt the first pangs of anxiety. He was prepared for the delirium about to commence, but he was desperate to beach the boat before that happened. If he lost consciousness in the middle of the river, it would gently sweep him back to the open water, and he knew that a drifting lifeboat usually attracted the most unwanted attention. It would be the cruelest of defeats to be discovered unconscious in that way.

After the river's path made a large oxbow, he spotted an open and relatively flat beach of mud at the mouth of another larger tributary, and he steered the boat toward it. As his vision blurred, he tried to build up a ramming speed to beach the boat, but he was no longer strong enough to do so effectively. Nevertheless, when the vessel ran up onto the slimy bank and lurched to a stop, Jedediah was thrown off the bench and landed painfully in the bottom of the boat. He lay there, helpless to get up, and let the shallow water in the bilge wash over his skin and cool his fever. He was aware that it was raging out of control now, but he was surprised when his view of the sky and the tree branches overhead began to distort as though etched in quicksilver, and the songs of shorebirds became eerie and haunting. Everything started to go dark, but before the veil dropped completely, he saw two distinct shadows move toward him. These apparitions gained definition until he could make out two interested brown faces gazing down at him. He smiled at them and said in the warm Hawaiian language that he was home, and then the veil descended.

•   •   •   •   •

The nightmares that followed were some of the worst Jedediah had ever endured. The visions were not only upsetting, they seemed hell-bent on punishing him as much as possible. The image of his dead child being picked at by crows in the graveyard in Augusta were replaced by ones of his wife whoring herself to Mr. Blunt on the street near the Mariners House in Boston. Suddenly, it was as if he was one of the dogs feasting on his dead brother Jonathan near the warehouse in Augusta, and he saw himself gnawing on a large femur bone in the snow. There were scenes of flames so realistic he felt the heat on his skin, and other moments when it felt like he was being held under water. Captain Cooper, with a supporting army of leather-masked fighters, chased him with an open shackle, and he yelled and tried to run, but his feet felt like they were bound with rope. He felt their straight razors cut into him, and he shrieked in pain and spoke in tongues.

The horrendous images eventually stopped and the darkness became like black velvet draped over his face. He felt a renewed calmness that allowed him to breathe easier. When he was finally able to open his eyes, he looked around and took stock of his surroundings. He was lying atop a crudely built wood-framed cot, and the entire space smelled of smoke and fertile earth. The dwelling he was in was not made of stone or wood, but was a wattle-and-daub mixture of mud and dried reeds. There was enough sunlight coming in through the large doorframe to see that the space consisted of one central room based around a rough stone hearth and chimney. A brown-skinned young woman was working by the small wood fire there, and he tried not to alert her that he was awake. He looked around again and began to assess his situation.

The young woman was humming to herself, and it seemed to be a familiar hymn or a sea ballad, and Jedediah found himself oddly relaxed by it. When he lowered his head back down, he let out a small involuntary groan. The woman's head spun around. "Aw, Lawd, you're awake! Lie still, sir. I'll go get Ezra."

She ran out, and Jedediah could hear her going off in the distance, and then he heard two sets of footfalls coming back toward the hut. He wanted to sit up to face whoever this Ezra was, but when he tried to move his hands, he found himself tethered to the wooden bench he lay upon. He pulled harder on the hemp ropes, but they were strong and well tied. He started to thrash, but this hurt too much, so he stopped and tried to calm himself.

The expressions on the faces of the older man and the young woman betrayed their fear. After an awkward moment in which no one spoke, the old man bent toward Jedediah and said soothingly, "My name's Ezra and this-here's my daughter Miryam. I do humbly apologize for tyin' ya to that-there cot, suh, but you was thrashin' and yellin' so bad with delirium, I felt the need for them restraints. I'll cut them ropes off your wrists now, if that's all right with you."

Jedediah nodded and said with a pained voice, "That would be greatly appreciated."

"Now, ya hafta understand that we, of all people, hated to do anything that could be thought of as being imprisonin' to ya, suh. But you were so violent from your fever, I thought it best to make sure ya stayed put. Safer for all of us, you understand. I didn't mean no harm, though."

"Of course. I would've done the same thing."

The man undid the knots and backed up quickly, a hint of fear still in his eyes. He took up position in front of his daughter and said, "We don't tend to get too many visitors here, so you can imagine how startlin' it was to discover you in that boat on the shore. When we seen you were in such bad shape, we lugged ya back here to heal ya, suh. When the tremors of the fever dreams hit ya, there was nothin' left to the 'magination about the acts of violence you were seein' and the evilness that was comin' for ya."

Jedediah sat up painfully and rubbed the raw areas on his wrists where the rope had been. His head hurt so badly that he was nauseous. He sat there with his eyes closed and tried to gather himself. Finally, he said, "I'm grateful to you both for saving me. My name is Jedediah. Jedediah Stiller."

"Nice to meet ya, suh."

"How long was I out?"

"Near three whole days."

"Three days! Where's that lifeboat you found me in?"

Ezra looked back at Miryam and she shook her head.

"I'm sorry, suh, but I sunk it."

"You sunk it?"

"Yes, suh. I saw the manacle 'round your ankle and the chain still on it, and I figgered you was some kind of escaped prisoner or somethin'. The boat was too big for us to use around these parts, and even too big to hide in the brush. And seein' a deserted craft, be it floatin' or beached, woulda been the most tellin' sign to anybody who might be comin' after you, so once I took out the wood for your bed, I figgered it best to just sink it and let the river swallow the evidence. Me and Miryam don't need no undue attention comin' our way neither."

Jedediah's head was still throbbing, but as he gazed at the two dark-skinned people standing in front of him, he suddenly grasped their situation. "Are you escaped slaves?"

Father and daughter exchanged panicked glances, then Ezra nodded vigorously. "Yes, suh. That's the truth. We didn't hurt no one in our escape, nor did we do anything violent to get away from our owners, but when the Lord gave us the opportunity, we took it. We escaped into this-here salt marsh and been livin' out here for the last couple years undisturbed. You're the first white person to see us in a long, long time."

Jedediah ran his hand through his hair. "Huh. Well, you did the right thing to sink that damn lifeboat, Ezra. I'd have to say that our plights are far more similar than you'd ever guess. First of all, I'm not an escaped criminal from a jail. I swear to that fact. But I was imprisoned as a fighting slave for an evil man. I was escaping from him when you found me."

Miryam took a step forward. "See, Papa, I tole ya them wounds on him was from fightin' and the fever were from somethin' wrong on the inside of him."

Jedediah looked into her brown eyes and found a disarming sense of compassion there.

"Yes, I had some bleeding going on inside me. I guess that's why the fever came on."

Miryam reached out and touched his forehead. Her hand felt warm and soft, and Jedediah closed his eyes at her act of tenderness. She nodded her head approvingly. "He's cool as a cucumber now, Papa. I'd venture a guess that the fever's done with him."

"Then I need to get going," Jedediah said as he prepared to get off the cot.

Ezra and Miryam remained silent. Finally, the older man cleared his throat. "It ain't none of my business, Jedediah, but I surely don't think you're in any shape for travelin' right now."

"But I have to, Ezra. I cannot thank you enough for taking care of me for three whole days, but I need to move on." When he swung his legs over the side of the bed, he noticed that the shackle on his ankle was missing.

The old man said quietly, "I took the liberty of removin' that manacle, suh. No man deserves to be shackled!"

Jedediah smiled. "Thank you, Ezra. Thank you, Miryam. I cannot express my gratefulness to either of you for saving me."

Ezra shook his head. "Like I said, Jedediah, it ain't none of my business, but I think you should stay with us a few more days to gather your strength. Just cuz you ain't got no fever don't mean you're ready to take on what lies ahead of ya. Why race off? Do ya think people are huntin' ya right now?"

The worry lines and wrinkles on Ezra's face were the map to a hard life of slavery, abuse, and hardship. But there was kindness in that face too, and Jedediah said, "I doubt it, Ezra. I was a captive on a ship that was commandeered by Confederate prisoners, and I'm not sure whether anyone knows about that event yet."

"So there's a good chance no one's lookin' for you?"

"I wouldn't think so. I was worried that the lighthouse keeper might have watched me rowing in, but no one came out to speak to me as I went past. If he didn't see me, I didn't see anyone else who did."

Miryam smiled and said, "That lighthouse keeper's name is Mr. Fitzpatrick, and he's notorious for bein' too far in the bottle by the noontime to see anythin' too clearly!"

"Well, then, I'm pretty sure I made it here without anyone else knowing."

"Good. If no one's pursuin' ya and no one knows you're out here, you're safe. Why run away when you ain't ready? Stay with Miryam and me and rest up to let your innards heal, Mr. Jedediah. As soon as you're really able, you can go on."

"There's something I need to do, and I cannot rest until I do it."

"But you ain't in no shape to do nothin'! Even if you was to get up and leave right now, what could ya do in your current state? You can barely stand or walk. What chance would ya have of gettin' very far like that? If you was to rest up here for a few days, you'd be much better."

Jedediah shook his head firmly. "No, Ezra. I need to at least *try* to keep going."

Ezra cleared his throat and said, "Jus' like I was talkin' about with your boat, suh, we don't need no undue attention. If ya head off and get captured in the next town cuz you're too weak to make a good escape, then peoples are gonna be askin' some questions 'bout how ya made it through this-here marsh, and then they'll come lookin' for us. It would be to our benefit, too, suh, if you was to rest up and make a proper escape when you're fully able."

Jedediah looked into their imploring eyes, thought about the pain that came with every little movement, and knew that the man's assessment of the situation was correct. If he pushed on and had another feverish attack somewhere else, he would become easy pickings for someone to capture him—and that would be costly for all of them. But he didn't want to give Zachary Webster any more time to escape, so he started to stand up from the cot.

Miryam reached down and grabbed his arm. "Please, Mr. Jedediah, don't rush off. You nearly died! If it weren't for some herbs and tinctures that Ezra had for these kinds of wounds, I fear you'd already be dead. There ain't no reason to drive yourself to an early grave! What would that accomplish?"

He wanted to protest, but the woman's expression and touch were enough to convince him to stay. And Jedediah Stiller understood that these two runaway slaves in this Delaware salt marsh had some kind of instant connection with his heart that was unnervingly strong, and he needed to see for himself just how deep it actually went. He relaxed his body, lifted his legs back onto the bed, sighed loudly, and lay back. "All right, I'll stay until I'm healed enough to leave. But as soon as I can, I'm gonna help out around here some. I can't just take advantage of you. And as soon as I'm in a better shape, I'll be leaving to continue what I need to do."

Ezra took Miryam's hand and they grinned contentedly at Jedediah. When Ezra spoke, his voice was as soft as sun-drenched leather. "You rest up as long as you need. As the Good Book says, Jedediah, 'Blessed be God, even the Father of our Lord Jesus Christ, the Father of mercies, and the God of all comfort; Who comforteth us in all our tribulation, that we may be able to comfort them which are in any trouble, by the comfort wherewith we ourselves are comforted of God.'"

Chapter Thirty-Eight

Zachary Webster was confined to quarters for over a week. Being trapped inside the log hut was punishment enough for him, but the lieutenant's orders calling for none of the other soldiers to talk to him proved to be just as punitive. Although far from being a social creature, he hated being uninformed about the actions of other members of his company even more than he detested his own idleness. By the time the sergeant retrieved him and brought him back to talk to the lieutenant, there was a barely contained energy in his steps from the anticipation of the extra duties that might be assigned to complete his punishment. Any activity would be better than the slothful and hopeless existence he'd just endured in the hut.

The lieutenant's face looked different, and it took Webster a moment to realize that he had shaved off his beard. He seemed far younger than he actually was, yet there was a tightness to his expression now. He returned Webster's salute with a warm, "Good day, Mr. Webster."

"Good day, Lieutenant Wentworth."

"Um, it is Captain Wentworth, now, Mr. Webster. In the face of Captain Small's death, I was promoted to lead Company D during this next offensive. With about a month to prepare for it, the powers that be thought it best if the transfer of leadership happened seamlessly and quickly."

"Congratulations, sir."

Captain Wentworth arched his eyebrows at Webster's politeness. "Well, thank you very much, Mr. Webster. As I said during the last time we conversed, Captain Small's death was a great loss to the Union Army and he will be sorely missed by all of us. I can only hope to attempt to fill his shoes."

"Yes, sir."

"So, over this last week, Mr. Webster, I was given the unenviable task of reviewing Captain Small's leadership of Company D during his service as your captain. I've come to some conclusions that I know are not going to be altogether popular with you men, but I have acknowledgment from my superiors that they are nonetheless correct. It is my opinion that using you sharpshooters as some type of guerrilla warriors was a reckless and dangerous approach. I think that giving men—even veteran sharpshooters like yourself—such unchecked freedom and secrecy that their goals and targets are withheld even from other nearby Union units can only lead to more unfortunate situations such as we saw during the last action you were involved in. The death of Samuel Worthington must be taken as an example of why we need to utilize the skills of the men of Company D in a far more restrained and responsible manner. Therefore, I have been ordered, and I intend to carry this out to the best of my abilities, to train and prepare this unit to participate in the actions of the newly structured Army of the Potomac and to become an integral component of the force, not an unbounded fringe wing of it.

"Sometime in the next few weeks, we will break down these winter quarters and move closer to the camps of the units in II Corps that we will be supporting in the next offensive. There will be no more independent actions for you or the rest of this company. From now on, your sharpshooting skills will be employed for the common good, and we will train you all as part of the regular corps.

"I think that sums it up, Mr. Webster. You may go back to your hut and talk to others, but I'd advise you to stay clear of the events that led up to the death of Samuel Worthington. You and the other sharpshooters are permitted to move freely, but you are all to stay here in camp and not venture outside its boundaries. If you disregard this order, sir, I will ask the provost marshals to use lethal measures to stop you. Do you understand everything I have said here today, Mr. Webster?"

"Yes."

Captain Wentworth's eyebrows shot up in surprise. Webster noticed, straightened up and said, "Yes, sir."

"Good day, Mr. Webster."

•   •   •   •   •

The ensuing transitional period of inactivity at Brandy Station was the most torturous of the entire winter encampment. As the weather improved and talk about the next offensive was on every man's tongue, being forced to wait around frayed the patience of the whole company. The men became more and more desperate to find ways to smash through the boredom, and Webster was disappointed to learn that he'd missed both the mule races, which had provided some good betting opportunities, and the shooting contest between the different sharpshooter regiments during his confinement.

Apparently, General Alexander Hays, commander of the newly formed 2nd Brigade in II Corps, had come to camp questioning the value of the sharpshooter regiments. A contest was called between the best marksmen from some of his regular troops and chosen members from the two sharpshooter regiments in camp to settle the matter, once and for all. Although the marksmen were highly skilled, after witnessing the extraordinary shooting of the men in green tunics, General Hays became a vocal true believer.

While he listened to his cabin-mates talk about the joys of changing a general's mind, Webster could not help but notice the new presence of a deep-seated melancholy taking hold of him from the captain's words. General Hays might have become an advocate of the sharpshooters in *his* brigade, but who was going to do that for Company D? Were they truly fated to be nothing but glorified fodder to buffer the regular infantry like the captain said? These questions rolled and boiled within him, and he felt sickened because he knew the answers.

When the order to break camp finally came, the men jumped into action with a nervous excitement that released weeks of pent-up frustration. In record time, they broke down their huts, assembled their packs, and prepared for the march to the new camp where they would set up their tents again and start training with the other units of the new brigade. The men of Company D were more than happy to be replacing their winter monotony with the newness of joining this brigade, which would be led by none other than Brigadier General J.H. Hobart Ward, a decorated hero from the Battle of Gettysburg. And even though the men from Indiana, New York, and Pennsylvania all seemed like good fellows, the sharpshooters of Company D were particularly looking forward to being near the 3rd Maine Infantry again, since many of them came from the same towns of their home state. They all knew their lives would once again be filled with unending duties and drilling when they got to the new camp, but the chance to talk to other men with similar accents about home and some shared landmarks and activities enlivened their steps.

With Samuel Worthington gone, Webster was assigned to share a tent with Monroe Washburn. As it turned out, Washburn's tentmate, Charles Pratt, had been killed in the train explosion. Captain Wentworth had initially figured he would pair each with a new recruit, but upon further thought, he had changed his mind. His concern was that the initial excitement a new recruit might feel at being paired with a notorious battle-tested member of the company would soon morph into a strange uneasiness akin to slumbering near a feral predator. On the other hand, the two grizzled and hardened veterans, having fought side by side, knew one another well enough to have developed a mutual understanding of the indelible scars—both physical and emotional—that the war had heaped upon them. As it turned out, the two new tentmates established a comfortable relationship almost immediately.

The Army of the Potomac was in an uneasy state of change. After President Lincoln named General Ulysses S. Grant as the general-in-chief of the Armies of the United States in early March, the War Department ordered the old I and III Corps to amalgamate into the II, V, and VI Corps of the new reorganized army. This caused strong resistance among the veteran soldiers who had fought with those units for almost two years. The fact that these men were so close to their reenlistment dates gave them the confidence and courage to demonstrate their discontent. This included sewing their new spade badges of the II Corps onto the seats of their pants while grudgingly holding onto their old diamond insignias. At first, this was viewed with concern by the leadership, but soon the discord came to be seen as helping the Union's cause. After the long, harsh winter, the Army of the

Potomac was angry enough to want to fight—with one another, with the new leadership, and most importantly, with Lee's Army of Northern Virginia. And, in its current state, the force was as well-fed, well-supplied, and ready for action as any Union Army had been during the three years of the war.

The massive force began training for hours each day, and an unprecedented number of reviews were called for, including a parade before none other than General Grant himself to show their readiness. And as the sea of blue and green uniforms moved in unison in a nearly constant state of preparation, the military efficiency required to organize such an immense force was put into place. Soldiers were taught to recognize the identifying shapes and colors of the emblems of the various corps. The trefoils, diamonds, triangles, Maltese crosses, and crosses of the 2nd, 3rd, 4th, 5th, and 6th Corps, and the red, white, blue, and green that distinguished the four divisions within each of those corps had to be memorized to maintain some kind of order in the midst of the chaos of future battlefields. These badges were immediately attached to their kepis or over the left breast of their uniforms, and as the numbers continued to swell, it became common to hear the various units described in conversation as the White Diamonds, the Red Crosses, or the Blue Shamrocks rather than their specific state regimental names.

Zachary Webster watched it all with a sense of detachment. Even though he could see that the Union Army was becoming more powerful by the day, he found himself having more doubts about their chances for success. It was easy to see that Captain Wentworth was keeping the reins tight upon him and the other sharpshooters through the constant drilling, but he could not shake the feeling that their reserved role would not only reduce their effectiveness for the rest of the war, it would make the men of the whole company expendable. Perhaps the death of his father, the strange furlough home, the loss of his beloved Catherine, the murder of Jonathan Stiller, the gruesome deaths of Samuel and Captain Small, the rantings of the Confederate officer, and his punishment after the action against the rebel skirmishers were taking a toll on him, for he found himself much less certain of what he was doing in this war.

Before, he'd never needed much incentive to follow the orders that

Captain Small dispensed. But now he felt such a lack of satisfaction in the commands that Captain Wentworth was issuing on the parade grounds that he even allowed himself to wonder if he'd made a horrible mistake in reenlisting. He was well aware that doubt created a weakness that could not be replaced with strength. That kind of uncertainty needed to be cut out like a cancer—but he couldn't see how that would be possible under the new command of Captain Wentworth.

Chapter Thirty-Nine

During the first two weeks that Jedediah spent with the escaped slaves in the great marshland, he allowed himself to recuperate. He slumbered deeply like a child, even during the day. Whenever he awoke from these naps and lay on his bed in a groggy, semiconscious state, he smelled the aromas from the cooking area and heard the sing-song humming of Miryam, and he felt content.

Both Miryam and Ezra had quickly developed a sense of trust with the giant tattooed stranger in their home, and part of this was due to his overt weakness. For although he was clearly a man capable of great physical strength, in his current state of recovery he was more like a gigantic infant in need of nurturing, and they tiptoed around his cot when he slept, taking turns tenderly touching his head as if he were a cherished younger member of the family.

As Jedediah's need to rest ebbed and the desire to get up and walk around grew stronger, Miryam allowed him further mobility, but she continued to control the extent of his activities. She wouldn't allow him to do anything she perceived as injurious in any way, and whenever he argued the matter with her, she only had to hold up a finger of defiance to stop the debate. He marveled at her strength, and he grinned foolishly whenever he backed down to her authority. And as he helped her with the chores around the hut, the literal distance between them seemed to melt away until they were working side by side, their hands and bodies occasionally touching as they kneaded the bread or cleaned the game for supper. Jedediah's male pride, somewhat wounded because he was only good for the perceived womanly duties of cooking and cleaning, seemed to be healed as well, by the balm of being so close to this special young woman.

Although Miryam seemed willing to trust Jedediah, he noticed that she was very protective of her own story. All his attempts to learn more about his hosts were rebuffed with warm silence or a gentle deflection into more banal topics. However, eventually, their conversations deepened organically with the mildness of the springtime weather and the abundance of animals that supplied their food. Because Delaware was a northern state that continued to reject President Lincoln's Emancipation Proclamation, Miryam and Ezra were unable to travel into the nearby towns to trade, barter, or sell anything for fear they would be captured and returned as slaves. As a result, they'd become self-sufficient.

When they'd first entered the marshland, they were far from ready for life there, and they'd nearly starved to death. It had been their good fortune to run into a hermit who claimed to be one of the last members of the Nanticoke. Not only did that specific tribe have a uniquely accepting stance toward runaway slaves, but the man had lovingly taught Ezra and Miryam the ways of his people, passing along the skills necessary to survive off the land.

Whenever Miryam talked about the hermit, her eyes filled with tears. She made a point of saying that he'd not only saved their lives, he'd become a dear member of their tiny family until his death. She pointed out that their survival was due entirely to his lessons—the food they ate, the hut they lived in, the dishes and utensils they carved themselves, and the techniques and tools of hunting, trapping, and fishing were all evidence of the age-old skills the man had passed down to them.

Even the faith in the spirits the Nanticoke people believed in was given to them. They'd mixed the native peoples' spirituality with the Christian beliefs they'd adopted as slaves and the ancestral tenets of the African heritage so woven into their souls. According to Miryam, they wholeheartedly believed that their own fragile lives were so completely dependent upon the water, the earth, the plants, and the animals to survive, they needed to keep the spirits happy in order to keep themselves alive. So they enthusiastically made special offerings to Manito, the giver of good fortune, and they tried to appease Okee, the powerful evil spirit, too.

They strove to make Manito happy enough to let them live in his salt marsh and Okee content enough to keep the white man away.

When those first two weeks of recuperation were complete, Ezra reached out to Jedediah to help him with the fishing and hunting. The simultaneous spring migrations of the waterfowl and the shorebirds, the waves of fish coming in from the ocean to spawn, and the reawakening of the land animals all marked a boon of plenty that was crucial to their tenuous feast-or-famine existence in the marsh. Ezra was putting all of his time and energy into successful days and nights of hunting and trapping, and Jedediah could help with that immensely. As the older man feverishly worked to get his snares, weirs, and traps ready, he also crafted a bow, a quiver of arrows, and a spear for Jedediah to hunt with. Once these were done, the two men headed out together in the dugout canoe.

For the next few days, they went about with the unspoken tension of two strangers. They were stiff and reserved with each other, and as a result, their teamwork suffered. The tasks and efforts in their trapping, hunting, and paddling required an intimacy that could only come from the vulnerable condition of dependency, and their relationship had not yet reached that level. So when the older man asked a question that had been bothering him, he did so in a way that did not reveal how much power the answer held for him.

As Jedediah worked at the task of setting the stakes back for a fish weir, Ezra shrugged his shoulders and said, "Jedediah, what exactly *were* ya on that ship you escaped from?"

The specificity of his question caught Jedediah off guard, but he took his time to explain how he had been shanghaied by Mr. Blunt in Boston and put aboard the *Nipigon* for the sole purpose of fighting to make money for the captain. His graphic details of the gruesome combat made Ezra whistle and shake his head in disbelief, but something in the man's eyes showed that he needed to hear more. It took a moment for Jedediah to understand what that was, but then he remembered that when he'd originally described his plight to Miryam and Ezra, he'd used the word *slave*. That was not a term to be uttered lightly with two escaped slaves, and the older man was quietly challenging Jedediah about it now. Being an imprisoned man was a far cry from being another man's possession, and Jedediah comprehended the importance Ezra put on that distinction, so he spoke in a hushed tone.

"After a fight in New York City, a man offered to buy me. Even though Captain Cooper declined his offer, it was understood—by both the captain and me—that I was his property to sell or not sell. Up until then, I thought I was a free man being forced to fight for the captain. But after that, I knew I belonged to him—I knew then that I was his slave."

This admission broke down the last barrier between the two men, and with it gone, Ezra began to share the details of his own troubled life. He'd been born on a plantation in Louisiana and then sold away from his family and his home to a cruel and unsuccessful farmer in Virginia, who immediately married him to one of his choicest Negresses to "produce litters of strong slaves." After a few years of relative happiness, Ezra watched as his progeny was sold like farm animals to other plantations to raise much-needed funds for the master. First, his sons and daughters were sold as chattel, and then his wife was sold away to pay off some outstanding debts. And finally, he was sold, too. He went off to a kinder master in Delaware, and Ezra thanked God for saving him from the cruelties he'd experienced, but he never fully recovered from losing his family. Over time, however, he fell in love with Miryam's mother, who was also a slave on this new farm, and he'd been allowed to marry her. Miryam was the youngest of the three children they had birthed together. And for a while, their lives were peaceful enough to afford them a deeper emotion that nearly resembled happiness.

When the landowner unexpectedly died, the man's children swooped in to take over the farm's affairs. They had a different view on the management of the farm and its slaves, and they set about to correct the perceived weaknesses of their father. Their first act was to sell Ezra's two young sons to increase revenue. However, seeing her children sold away from her literally broke his wife's heart, and she died. Once her body was buried in the slave cemetery on the farm, the new owners declared that they were going to sell off Miryam next. Ezra could not allow that to happen, and he knew he needed to do something quickly.

The old man paused for a moment and looked up at the low clouds scraping the treetops. The sounds of the salt marsh seemed to amplify and dominate the sudden silence. He coughed and looked back at the river. "I swear to you on the Bible, Jedediah, I did not set the fire, but I truly believe God was lookin' out for us. On the very night that we was prepared to escape into the darkness, flames hit the main house and spread all through the farm. In their haste to put out the blazes that were threatenin' the important buildin's, them white men fightin' the fire musta forgot about us poor slaves in our sheds. Our area went up like tinder. Amidst all the confusion, me an' Miryam runned away into the woods. I know we shoulda helped out, but I weren't gonna allow them white men to sell no more of my life away. We run an' run till we come to this-here salt marsh an' met the Nanticoke man I know my daughter's tole ya 'bout."

Jedediah said with concern, "So do you think anyone's still looking for you two?"

Ezra shrugged. "By all accounts I've heard, folks believe that me and Miryam both died in that fire. There was so much destruction, they didn't look too close for us afterward. The farm was gone, so nobody was too concerned 'bout losin' two expendable Negroes like us. But we know there's always slave catchers and bounty hunters lookin' to make quick cash from catchin' runaways, so we stick close to the most deserted parts of the marsh, an' we don't never venture too close to the white people no more."

Now that their relationship had moved to a new level of intimacy, Ezra began to treat Jedediah like a son as he instructed him in the ways of their survival. Instead of just setting up the snares, he taught him how to catch beaver, muskrat, fox, otter, mink, opossum, and woodchuck. Jedediah marveled at the way the old man used sticks, trees, rocks, and leather thongs to make ingenious and effective spring-pole snares and stone deadfalls that provided food on a daily basis. As they visited the different trapping sites, they almost never came away empty-handed. And after the day's gathering filled the bottom of the canoe with the carcasses of animals that supplied them with meat, bait, bones, and pelts, the old man's spirits were lifted so high, he quietly sang songs that praised God's bounty. Some days, they would have to make several trips with the canoe loaded to capacity from their hunt, and Miryam would take the cleaned meat right to the small smoking huts and the pelts to the drying racks.

As young boys, Jonathan and Jedediah Stiller had spent many days in the Maine woods trapping and hunting, so Jedediah was a capable learner when it came to those skills. But becoming proficient with a bow and arrow was far more challenging. He just wasn't able to handle them well enough to hit his targets, and Ezra frequently put him to shame by sneaking up on an unsuspecting flock of northern pintails, American black ducks, or green-winged teals and showering them with lethal arrows. The old man tried to be humble as he picked up the lifeless bodies by their feet and carried them to the canoe, but he was barely able to hide his triumphant smile. Jedediah's failure at duplicating Ezra's success turned his tattooed face crimson with frustration.

His ability to use a hunting spear, however, was another story. Between his prowess as a harpooner on the whaling ships and the way his adopted Polynesian family had taught him to effectively wield such a weapon in battle and in the hunt, he could hurl the spear with shocking velocity and deadly results. His success in spearing white-tailed deer, muskrat, Canada geese, snow geese, and marsh rabbits made up for any of his deficiencies with the bow and arrow. Ezra was in awe at the way Jedediah threw so fast and true that he was even able to spear striped bass, alewives, and shad at some of their weirs. His skills were so great with a spear that the old man ventured to ask about his previous experiences, and when he heard Jedediah's vaunted tales of hunting whales and other men in faraway lands, he began to look at him with greater respect.

In the frenetic atmosphere of reaping the sudden richness of spring, Jedediah was too busy and too happy to be preoccupied with the passage of time. He enjoyed the daily excursions with Ezra, and he particularly looked forward to the times when Miryam joined them. As they used bait to catch white perch and catfish in the depths of the rivers or gathered mussels, oysters, and crabs closer to the ocean, he often found himself looking at her and offering to help her more than she really needed. His body felt healthy and strong again, and the direct sun of the springtime warmed him in ways that he had not felt in a very long time. When he caught himself ogling at Miryam's womanly shape under her dress as she bent to gather clams in the mud, or tried to glimpse her nubile breasts as they hung free in her blouse when she leaned over the hearth to prepare dinner, he felt ashamed. He hadn't allowed himself such lustful urges since the death of his wife, and he had the sour feeling that he was betraying her. Then he came to the awkward realization that he was falling in love with Miryam. And it utterly confused him.

Ezra and Miryam had no such confusion. They had completely accepted Jedediah as a permanent member of their family, and they acted as if it were only a matter of time before Jedediah and Miryam became a couple. The old man shamelessly sought out ways to leave them alone together, and the young woman seemed eager for those opportunities as well. One night, after what had become their daily routine of sharing stories around the fire before bed, Ezra suddenly stood up and declared that he wanted to head out on a nighttime hunt. When Jedediah asked if he wanted help, the old man looked at him incredulously and waved him off before walking wordlessly into the darkness of the salt marsh. Miryam watched her father's departure, then went over to her bed and undressed. Jedediah hesitated momentarily because he was so shocked by the transparency of the old man's plan and the complete compliance of the young woman, but he knew he wanted the same thing.

When Ezra returned the next morning with a handful of ducks for cleaning, the three people were unified in the understanding that Miryam and Jedediah were now wedded. There was no awkwardness in this sudden change, and they openly discussed the need to build another hut so the old man could sleep through the night without interruptions. It surprised Jedediah how quickly and easily their relationships had changed from hosts and guest to members of the same family, but he relished the joy that the reopening of the barricaded areas of his heart gave him as he realized for the first time that he now had a wife and a father again. He wasn't completely sure how it had happened, but his life was suddenly whole once more.

Chapter Forty

Even though it was clear she was improving with each passing day, Mrs. Ketchum continued to handle Catherine as gently as if she were made of porcelain. Although she resisted trying to imagine the unspeakable horrors the young woman had experienced in the back of that ambulance with those two monsters, the older woman thought about it more than she wanted to admit. She could not comprehend how anyone could endure such a thing, and so, to her way of thinking, Catherine was severely broken—she just hadn't realized it yet. It was Mrs. Ketchum's plan to allow Catherine the time to heal sufficiently enough so that she could travel back to Maine and be reunited with her father. But since she fully expected the young woman to collapse at any moment, she was overly cautious not to do anything that might cause such a breakdown to happen in her house.

That all changed on a particularly sunny morning when Catherine came downstairs fully dressed and with a recent newspaper in her hands. There was not an ounce of timidity or fear in the young woman's expression as she walked directly to the expansive wooden dining table at which Mrs. Ketchum sat and nearly threw the copy of *The New York Times* next to the woman's breakfast. She put her hands on her hips and said forcefully, "I want to become a Sanitary Commission nurse!"

Mrs. Ketchum looked down at the headlines about the upcoming U.S. Sanitary Commission's Metropolitan Fair. She was pleased by the way the reporter had stressed the inhumane conditions of many of the Union field hospitals and the need for proper medical supplies and staff, but since she was still too protective of Catherine, she said, "But, my dear, do you *really* think you are ready for that kind of exposure to such horrors?"

"I am. I truly am, Mrs. Ketchum."

"After going through what you went through, do you really think—?"

"As you so wisely advised, Mrs. Ketchum, I've locked all of that up and thrown away the key. It's as if it never happened. I started this whole journey with my mind set on becoming a nurse, and now I'm more than ready to continue on with that goal."

Catherine's defiant voice echoed in the dining room, and the older woman clucked her tongue and shook her head. "Do you have any idea about the true horrors our soldiers are facing, my dear? Their blood is being spilled every day, and our men are left maimed and dead. Do you really want to face that in your fragile state?"

Fiery anger welled up inside Catherine and triggered something else she'd suppressed with all the other toxic experiences of her journey. She hadn't forgotten about Zachary Webster and why she was chasing after him, but the recent calamitous events that had befallen her had eclipsed everything else. Now that she was free from those sinister elements, the memories of her prior life were released like spring water and began to seep to the surface. "Yes," she said vehemently. "I do know what the war is doing to our men, Mrs. Ketchum—it is killing them! And I know this from personal experience!"

Then she related the whole tale of Zachary Webster without pause and without censor. Sometime during the story, she sat down in one of the chairs next to Mrs. Ketchum, who was completely captivated by the revelations. When she finally finished, Catherine was surprised by the intensity of the older woman's gaze.

After a brief silence, Mrs. Ketchum drew in her breath and said, "Well, that certainly changes everything, doesn't it?"

Not fully understanding what she meant by that, Catherine slowly nodded her head.

Mrs. Ketchum laid her linen napkin beside her bowl. "And you're sure you love this man?"

"Yes, ma'am, I do."

"Even though he is a cold-blooded murderer?"

This stark statement made Catherine gasp slightly, but she responded calmly, "He wasn't born a murderer, Mrs. Ketchum; he was made into one by this horrible war."

"Yet you still want to save him?"

"Yes, I do."

"By becoming a nurse?"

"Yes. I want to save other soldiers, and I want to save my Zachary."

Mrs. Ketchum tilted her head. "But which is it, my dear? Do you want to save this one man, or do you want to become a nurse and save other soldiers? They may not be simultaneously possible."

"I know you're going to call me a naïve little girl, but I think I can do both. I want to help other soldiers by training to be a nurse, but by doing that I can also be close enough to find Zachary, and save him."

"And what if he's already dead, dear? What if you go down there and see the worst of what we humans can do to one another on the battlefield, but you never find your Zachary. Do you think you can live with that?"

"But don't you see, Mrs. Ketchum? Maybe that's why this plan of becoming a nurse makes perfect sense! I know you've been thinking that I will go back to Maine as soon as I am able, but that was never my plan. I need to continue on my original path. But if I were to do that and just walk out of this house without training or experience, I'd become nothing more than a lost soul wandering through this devastated world, and in my despair and hopelessness, I can see myself becoming as broken as you now think I am. But if I become a nurse, I will have a real purpose helping others heal while I look for Zachary. If my search for him is, indeed, in vain—if I never find him or discover he is already dead—well, I will still have my patients. I won't be lost or purposeless because of them."

Mrs. Ketchum looked deep into Catherine's eyes. They were brilliant with strength and resolve, and she understood that she had completely misjudged this young woman at her table. The extent of her brokenness was still debatable, but the power and toughness within her were nearly inconceivable.

The older woman stood up. "Well, Miss Catherine Brandford, if this is what you truly want, I'll make arrangements for it to happen. I know the people to talk to, and I think I have just enough pull to help you through some of the difficulties that might ensnare other women wanting to volunteer. I do have one request, however."

"What is that, Mrs. Ketchum?"

"I insist that, while you are in training, you reside here in my house."

"Oh, but I don't want to burden you, ma'am."

"Nonsense!" the woman cried. "I insist! You're such an amazing creature, young lady, I think you would be doing me a favor by staying and letting me bask in some of your light."

"Yes, ma'am, if you insist."

"You're damn right I do!"

Mrs. Ketchum spent the next week doing as she had promised. Although she ran into more obstacles than she had expected, she persevered. Catherine's young age and orphan-like status made many of the men who organized the recruitment and training of nurses for the Union Army hesitate and try to stall, but Mrs. Ketchum was neither swayed nor bypassed in her pursuit. She skillfully set out on a campaign that reached several levels of the process simultaneously and even pitted some of the male leaders against each other. Personal friendships with Dorothea Dix and Dr. Elizabeth Blackwell gave her the leverage she needed to finally get Catherine enrolled in the month-long training program at Bellevue Hospital, starting immediately after the Sanitary Commission's Metropolitan Fair. Though the fight was thoroughly exhausting, Mrs. Ketchum was invigorated by her victory, and she found herself smiling more often than she thought was possible after telling Catherine the good news.

This period of waiting proved to be essential for Catherine to prepare herself emotionally. The internal debate still raging inside her about the motives and goals of her current path required a little more time hammering and forming to fit them into shape, and she used her time alone in the bedroom to do just that. By the time Mrs. Ketchum told her the good news, she had come to a healthy self-understanding of what she was striving for. Her primary goal was still to help Zachary Webster, but she would become a nurse as a means to start her greater mission in life of helping the world to heal itself. Within this, there was the required proper arrangement of love, compassion, and purpose, so she felt well prepared to take on the untold tests that lay before her.

• • • • •

While Mrs. Ketchum and Catherine walked down the crowded aisles of the Metropolitan Fair, the older woman asked quickly, "What unit is Zachary Webster in?"

"He's in Company D of the Second United States Sharpshooters."

"Do you know what corps his unit has fought with in previous battles?"

Catherine shook her head and shrugged. "Why?"

Mrs. Ketchum gazed down at a massive iron plowshare displayed in front of them and responded without looking at Catherine. "Because you're going to need to know *that* before you head off and start searching for one man in the Union Army, my dear. I can begin to inquire about that information, and perhaps by the time you finish your training, we'll know exactly where he is."

Several days later, when the two women were riding together in the carriage, on the way to Bellevue Hospital for Catherine's training to begin, it was clear their relationship had become similar to that of a mother and daughter, and they easily surrendered to the implications of that connection. And though they threw themselves into their separate daily pursuits, the two women looked forward to sharing the events of their days over a large dinner together each night. During these meals, Catherine would listen intently as Mrs. Ketchum spoke with unfettered optimism even when the sometimes harsh realities of bureaucracy within the U.S. Sanitary Commission seeped into her stories. And Mrs. Ketchum had strong words of encouragement whenever Catherine's morale dipped lower due to the day's inanity at the hospital. Usually this resulted from the constant belittling the male doctors and trainers hurled upon the women volunteers, but sometimes the silliness of bandaging and rebandaging the strangers drafted into service as models made Catherine wonder if she was being adequately prepared for the difficult tasks the nurses would have to take on while serving in field hospitals or Union Army convalescent facilities. She was constantly reminded by Mrs. Ketchum that although it appeared as if the other volunteers were being coddled, it was because they all had not been as tempered by life as Catherine had.

Mrs. Ketchum took an active role in several aspects of the training. She decreed that Catherine would practice bandaging on her every night before bedtime, and they spent hours in this endeavor. Whenever mistakes were made, Mrs. Ketchum kindly but quickly corrected them, and then made her do it all over again. Catherine even received lessons on topics that weren't covered at the hospital. The amputation of limbs was referred to quite frequently but never taught to the nursing trainees. At home, however, the older woman was determined that Catherine should know the skills necessary for that procedure, and she repeatedly schooled her on the particular techniques and needs until she felt confident the girl could be of real assistance in such a surgery. The fact was, they were a perfect team. Mrs. Ketchum was a knowledgeable and intense instructor, and Catherine was a dedicated and curious student. After only a few weeks, it was quite clear that the nightly extra practice was paying off. Catherine's heightened skills and toughened personality made her stand well above the rest of the volunteers, which ingratiated her with her instructors and created an envious environment with her peers.

One Saturday afternoon, Mrs. Ketchum surprised Catherine by announcing that they were going to the hospital to observe a surgery on a poor horseman who had been mangled in a freak carriage accident. Because the man was scheduled to have his infected leg amputated, the experience was seen to be very beneficial to witness firsthand. On the ride over to Bellevue, Catherine was able to settle the butterflies in her stomach by merely glancing over at the calm and serene Mrs. Ketchum beside her. Once in the seats of the gallery above the patient, she worried that the event was going to be too horrific for her to withstand, but she was shocked to discover that the odor of the wound and the guttural sounds of the patient did not affect her negatively. In fact, neither the copious amounts of blood from the procedure nor the noise of the bone saw quickly cutting through the man's femur made her queasy in the least. However, the familiar smell of the ether and chloroform reminded her too much of her abduction in Framingham, and she momentarily felt the urge to flee the room. When Mrs. Ketchum noted her agitation, she thought at first it was due to sensitivity to the bloody scene on the operating table, but quickly understood that it was not the gore but the awful memories being brought back, and she immediately proffered her hand. Catherine looked down at it on her lap and seized it firmly in her own.

On another morning, Mrs. Ketchum took Catherine over to the Sisters of Charity's St. Vincent's Hospital to spend the day there as a visiting nurse. As Catherine was about to get out of the carriage and walk into the imposing brick building, the older woman took hold of her arm and implored her to pay particular attention to the care given to the patients by the nuns of the hospital. Even though her day would be overly full of assisting in changing soiled bedsheets and other mundane tasks, Mrs. Ketchum stressed the importance of watching the nuns. Once the carriage pulled away and left her standing there, Catherine turned and headed through the doors of the hospital with the confident stride of a seasoned nurse.

At the end of that day, during dinner, Mrs. Ketchum asked quickly, "What did you notice today?"

Catherine was completely spent. The ceaseless pace of the nuns, the examples of utter destitution all around, and the pervasive smell of human feces that had seeped into and stained her nasal passages and clothes had taken every ounce of energy she had inside her. She hesitated a moment to find a few words to describe just how unspeakable what she'd witnessed had been, but she did not have the energy or resources to do so.

When Mrs. Ketchum noticed her silence she clarified her question. "Don't dwell on the ugliness, Catherine. Focus on the care that was being given. What did you see the nuns doing? What did you notice about them?"

Catherine finally found the three words that described the tireless caregivers: "Compassion, fortitude, and efficiency."

Mrs. Ketchum clapped her hands together. "That's my girl! You must remember that, no matter how awful your world becomes as a nurse, dear. It is your job to disregard your own revulsions to administer care as compassionately and completely as you can. As an Army nurse, you will encounter much, much worse than you saw today, and you must use the image of those nuns as examples of how you should hold yourself on the job. Do not fall prey to your own weaknesses; rise above and conquer them!"

Before the month-long training was up, Catherine received a letter from a surgeon by the name of Thomas A. McParlin. He was Medical Director for the Army of the Potomac, and his letter was straightforward and to the point. Catherine Brandford had been heartily recommended by her instructors at Bellevue Hospital's nursing program, and he was assigning her to the medical corps of the II Corps in the new Army of the Potomac. She was to arrange immediately for transport to Washington City, where she would be united with other newly recruited doctors and nurses as they prepared for the upcoming spring action down in Virginia.

Catherine looked up with a confused expression after reading the letter three times. She handed it to Mrs. Ketchum, but the woman barely scanned it before saying, "Oh, that is wonderful news, my dear! We need to get you ready to go to Washington!"

"You had something to do with this, didn't you?" Catherine said with a smirk.

The elder woman shrugged. "I may have pulled some strings, that's true. But you've earned everything you've gotten by working so hard and becoming an outstanding nurse. I can tell you that I did not have to persuade anyone at Bellevue to recommend you, for they were all more than effusive with their praise. I just needed to do some digging to find out where your sharpshooter and his company are now. When I was told they are part of the II Corps, the rest was easy. Dr. McParlin is overwhelmed with the need to find enough qualified nurses to administer care to the tidal wave of wounded expected from the next stages of this bloody war, so he was more than eager to have your services and your skills, my dear. You will have to work in some very challenging and dangerous conditions, Catherine, and I fear you may be tested as much or even more than your previous ordeal, but you will be as close as you can get to the battlefield on which your beloved is fighting."

In her bedroom, Catherine packed her clothes in silence. Because her rescuers had not been able to save her possessions before the ambulance caught fire and exploded, she had arrived in New York with nothing. Mrs. Ketchum had quietly built up a small wardrobe for her of suitable dresses and other garments, and as she carefully folded these and put them into her new carpetbag, she fought the feelings of self-doubt at the thought of leaving the older woman. She was comfortable and happy with her adopted mother, and she wasn't sure if she really wanted to leave at all. In all likelihood, Jedediah Stiller had made his way to the front by now and he and Zachary had already settled their differences. If so, they were probably both dead. Or imprisoned. If that was true, she didn't need to leave the safety of this luxurious mansion in New York City and the tender care of someone whom she loved and cherished.

It only took her a moment to banish those thoughts. She was a nurse now, and as such, she had a job to do that was bigger than herself, Mrs. Ketchum, Zachary, or Jedediah Stiller. Becoming a nurse had not just been a means to an end, but a true calling. She had shown a real aptitude for the profession, and her nursing skills were needed to take care of Union soldiers. Whether Zachary Webster was alive or dead or she was comfortable and happy in Mrs. Ketchum's presence did not matter anymore—she was in pursuit of something higher than her personal desires.

The ferry ride across the Hudson River to the train station in Jersey City was windswept and cold. The two women stood at the rail and watched the frantic activity of other ships in the harbor. Catherine noticed small tears sliding down Mrs. Ketchum's cheek, and she tenderly wiped them off with her gloved finger.

Mrs. Ketchum said, "I'm terribly sorry about this dreadful show of emotion, my dear, but I'm just realizing that I will likely never see you again. And that does so break my heart! You and I have only known each other for a relatively short time, but I feel as close to you as I have ever felt to another human being. The Lord did not deem me lucky enough to have my own daughter, but He certainly gave me an extraordinary opportunity to feel what that is like when He sent you to me! It's making me as weepy as an old hen."

"I feel the same toward you, Mrs. Ketchum. I can never repay you for what you've done for me. You have, quite literally, saved me. Maybe I will come back this way again afterward..."

"Pshaw! Don't be naïve, Catherine! After this war, you are destined to head off in a new direction and create a new life. That is the way it should be. All I ask, if I may be so bold as to request something of this nature, is that you write me whenever you can. Tell me the trials and tribulations you face, and then tell me that you are safe and happy. Is that too much to ask?"

Catherine put her hand on the woman's shoulder and looked into her eyes. "I will write you as frequently as I possibly can, Mum."

Chapter Forty-One

Had Ezra and Miryam not possessed the rich and complex tapestry of spiritual beliefs from their combined cultures, they would not have been able to see the true message of Jedediah's dream so clearly, and they wouldn't have understood that he needed to follow its direction.

The dream, although troubling, was not a nightmare. It began with a vision of the sunrise over the salt marsh. The intense colors of the dawning sun on the reeds were warming, and the pure and simple sounds of the songbirds were calming. Near the spot where he'd first been discovered in the lifeboat, Jedediah saw the image of his wife and child standing before him. They looked peaceful and happy as they smiled at him. He knew they were dead, and he didn't try to reach out for them. They waved and turned to head into the reeds, but their path was blocked by a wall of flame and a pack of mangy, starving dogs. When his wife and child turned back to look at him, it was clear they were unable to get past these obstacles. Then the dream restarted again. After the fourth time, Jedediah awoke.

As they ate their breakfast, he told Ezra and Miryam the details of the dream. Without saying anything, Miryam looked at her father and reached out for him. The older man responded by taking her hands into his. Then he hugged her, and she started to cry.

Jedediah was befuddled by their reaction, so he asked respectfully, "Do you two care to include me in this moment of sadness?"

Ezra disengaged from his daughter and sighed. "We know what that vision is tryin' to say to you, and it makes us despair, Jedediah."

"It's just a dream, Ezra."

"No, it is much more powerful than just a dream. It's tellin' ya that ya need to leave us an' finish the task ya started."

"You must leave, Jedediah," Miryam responded with a sniffle.

He looked from one to the other and said, "You two are daft if you think I'm gonna leave just because of a bad dream."

"It'd be a transgression of the worst kind if you ignored the clear message of such a vision, Jedediah. Think about what it showed ya. Your wife and child are happy with ya bein' in this salt marsh with us, but they cannot truly go to their restin' place as long as you hold onto vengeful feelins' 'bout the murderer of your brother. Miryam and me took notice when ya retole us about his killin', that it was them dogs gnawin' upon his body that upset ya the most. The meanin' of them animals bein' in your dream is real clear."

Jedediah glanced at Miryam. "But I'm happy here with you two. I gave up my vengeful ideas when I became Miryam's husband. I want to stay here and live with you."

Wiping her eyes, Miryam said, "But your soul needs to have its vengeance before you can move on. If you don't get it, you won't be able to let go of your past, and you'll never be truly happy here with us."

"But I *am* happy! The serenity I've felt while living here with you has healed whatever was broken inside me. Now I can see that my future lies here, with both of you."

Miryam reached over and touched his face. She traced the tattoo markings with her finger and a tear dripped from her chin. "Oh husband, I *do* want you to stay, but the dream's message is clear—your wife and child cannot get no rest until you finally purge the flames of vengeance and the awful memories. You can't be selfish now with your own happiness. You must do this for them as much as for yourself."

"But I want to stay."

Ezra stood up. "We ain't goin' nowhere, Jedediah. This is our home an' we'll be livin' here till there be no more breath in our bodies. You must follow the instructions of this dream, an' we'll be right here whenever ya're able to come back. You've helped us store up more food than we'll need, an' now that the first wave of birds is over, it's the perfect time to head off and continue your journey. "

Jedediah shook his head. "That's just it! It's pointless for me to keep chasing that man. He went back to the war, and I have no way of getting to him."

"The dream is tellin' ya that ya gotta try."

"It's only a stupid dream!" Jedediah said in frustration.

Miryam gasped slightly and then said, "Dreams are the way the spirit world makes contact with us and tells us what we should do, Jedediah. To ignore such a clear message would be to spit in the face of those spirits. Do that, and they stop wanting to help you. They'll leave you to die alone."

"But I don't want to go!"

Then Ezra spoke. "But the spirits want ya to, Jedediah, an' you must do as they say. So tonight I'll paddle you as close as I dare to the road. From there, you can find your way into the town of Smyrna. There's a train station there, and you can head north to Wilmington. Then ya catch another train south to Washin'ton."

Jedediah was startled by Ezra's knowledge of the railroads, but he had grown accustomed to the old man surprising him. He responded sharply, "Even if I make it that far, then what?"

"What was your 'riginal plan?"

Jedediah shrugged. "Just ask around about the soldiers in the green tunics. But I don't think that will get me where I need to go. Not anymore. It's been too long for anyone to remember seeing some sharpshooters from Maine come through on their way back to the front."

They had moved outside as they talked, and now Ezra turned the canoe over and wrestled it toward the water. "There's a man I know might be able to help in Washin'ton."

"Who?"

"Name of Wilbur Johnson. He's the servant man in a famous brothel there. He's got connections, an' I would venture to guess that if ya ask ol' Wilbur to help out with this, he'd be able to. Or know someone who could."

"Hmm, Ezra, and how exactly do you know someone who works at a brothel in Washington?"

Ezra chuckled. "It ain't what your mind's thinking, Jedediah, that's fo' sho'! My master once took me on a trip to Washin'ton when he had to take care of some legal business down there. He ended up at the brothel, and while I waited 'round for him to finish up in the house, I met Wilbur. Turns out he ain't just a servant—he helps runaway slaves get north to freedom. He was a man of most amazin' abilities, an' I think he can help you, too."

"How can you be so sure he's still there?"

"Cuz he ain't never gonna be without a job in that line of work, an' he's in the right place to keep helpin' folks!"

The three of them spent the day out on the marsh. The snares were less full and the fish were more fickle, but they were able to scrape together enough to make the day worthwhile. They didn't talk about Jedediah's departure again, but there was a pall of sadness over them. Jedediah wished he'd never told them about the silly dream in the first place. He spent the entire day trying to explain that he was willing to ignore the supposed message, but Ezra and Miryam were immovable on the subject. In fact, they made it clear that they were expelling him forcefully whether he accepted the urgency of the message or not.

After supper, Ezra came up with an excuse to head out into the marsh again, and left the young couple alone for the last time. They made love and clung to each other, but by the time Ezra came back, Jedediah was dressed and had his seabag ready. While Miryam stood at the doorway of the hut, the two men pushed the canoe into the water, climbed in, and began to paddle away. They watched the woman wave frantically and tearfully until they went around a bend in the river and no longer could see her anymore.

Dusk faded into darkness, yet Ezra seemed to navigate with ease through the confusing and shifting labyrinth of the marsh. They traveled in complete silence, and Jedediah understood the risks that Ezra was taking by paddling him this close to civilization and the dangers that Miryam faced being alone at the hut, and there was enough fear coming from both men that they could smell it in the cool nighttime air.

When they came to a wooden trestle over the river, Ezra steered the canoe toward the bank. As the bow gently grated into the shore, he whispered, "If ya climb up to that road and walk it north to the first road ya come to an' turn left, you'll be in town by sunrise if ya keep a quickened pace. This is the most dangerous part of your trip, Jedediah, as the peoples 'round here are uneasy 'bout nighttime trav'lers. Avoid meetin' up with any of 'em, and just slip into town as quiet as ya can."

Jedediah nodded.

"Good luck, son. Come back to us soon."

They shook hands and Jedediah got out of the canoe. He watched the vessel and its occupant become entirely engulfed by the darkness before he climbed up the embankment. At the edge of the road, he listened for any sounds, and when he heard nothing, he started walking. His strides grew longer as his pace became more purposeful, and he didn't look back at the river again. He needed to be at the train station by dawn.

Chapter Forty-Two

Like some kind of nocturnal phantasm, Jedediah loped along the road through the night in the direction Ezra had indicated. He heard the familiar nighttime sounds on either side of the dirt roadway, but he saw neither creature nor person along the way. As he walked on through mounting fatigue, he mulled over the latest confusing events of his life. Ezra and Miryam's conviction that he must heed the dream was startling in its purity and strength. There'd been no debate, no dissent, and no way to deny the power that the message held for them, and he now felt the familiar pangs of shame that he'd experienced when his Augusta family had closed their doors to him in his youth. But this time, the expulsion was so different. While his blood family wouldn't allow him to be himself, his new family was throwing him out to heal himself with the fulfillment of his bloodlust. And this juxtaposition of values thoroughly confounded Jedediah.

The small town of Smyrna was just awakening when he strode quietly through its lifeless streets and headed toward the train station. When the ticket agents came to work that morning, they were surprised to see such a distinctive-looking stranger lining up to buy a ticket to Wilmington, but they couldn't argue against taking his money, even if he did appear to be some kind of beast. After he made his purchase, Jedediah felt self-conscious and awkward as he tried to avoid attention by retreating to the shadows of the trees around the station. When the train arrived, his heart quickened with excitement, but when the call to board finally came, he forced himself to walk toward it as steadily and confidently as the other travelers.

The ride to Wilmington was uneventful, but saturated with tension.

Because the train was not very full of passengers, there was no way for Jedediah to hide. Even though he kept to himself, it was obvious the other occupants had taken notice of him. However, as he feigned sleep and covered his tattoos with the felt hat Ezra had given him, they eventually forgot he was there. And once the train reached the city of Wilmington and he saw the thick crowds waiting by the tracks under the protective overhang of the train depot, Jedediah knew he could lose himself in them and regain some anonymity.

He boarded the Philadelphia, Wilmington & Baltimore Railroad train headed south, and there were so many people around him that he felt relaxed enough to slumber all the way to Baltimore. He awoke when the train came to a complete stop at the President Street station. No one in his car moved, and he was unsure whether he was supposed to detrain here or not. As it turned out, their delay was scheduled, and Jedediah was glad he had waited and watched the other passengers instead of panicking.

A longstanding city ordinance prohibited locomotives from passing through the city, so each train car had to be uncoupled from the inbound train and pulled slowly by horses down President Street and along Pratt Street to Camden Station, where it would be attached to a B&O locomotive for the final leg of its journey to Washington. And as his car now crept by the busy warehouses and docks of the harbor, Jedediah observed the frantic activities of the longshoremen and bustling stevedores with interest. But the vividly unpleasant memories of his shanghaiing in Boston made him turn away from the window and sit back with the mild sense of dread.

The train from Baltimore pulled into the B&O Depot in Washington late in the afternoon. Jedediah had to navigate through confusing torrents of humanity, as the station was completely packed with people—Union soldiers, politicians, and travelers—and the noise was deafening as he made his way out to New Jersey Avenue. He scanned the bland rural openness of the town with uninspired eyes, but when he saw the gigantic white Capitol looming two blocks up the hill from the train depot, he was stunned by its stark and luminous power. The newly completed pearl-white dome was tinted orange-red by the dusky sunlight, and it almost looked soft and warm as it sat atop the alabaster base. His eyes returned to his immediate surroundings as somberly dressed pedestrians, noisy black carriages, and utilitarian horsecars made their way along the dusty and manure-dappled roads and walkways. Overlooking them all, the stoic marble Capitol sat like a Grecian temple atop the hill.

He had never been to Washington City, and he had no idea where the brothel he searched for was located. As a seamen, he'd become comfortable with finding his way around unknown cities. But this time things were so different, he wasn't sure how to proceed. Asking about the location of a popular brothel wasn't the type of question he could pose to just any passing stranger. Clearly, he should ask a man, but if he picked the wrong one and offended him, it could result in the local police being notified—something he wanted to avoid at all costs. But the uncertainty of knowing how to tell which passerby would not be offended made him pause and let several potential targets pass by him. He was worried that if the crowds got too thin, the chances of running into the wrong person would be greater.

When he saw a group of black men loading freight into a wagon on C Street, he knew he would ask them. There was a good chance they might know the location of the brothel, and if they were offended by his question, they were probably less likely to notify the authorities. So he moved closer to them. He tried not to startle them, but they began acting wary as soon as he was close enough for them to notice him. When he said hello in a quiet voice and they looked at him, they seemed ready to run away in pure panic. They were uncomfortable with any white stranger speaking directly to them, but it was almost more than they could handle to have one that looked like this tattooed giant. When they heard his question, however, knowing smiles appeared on their faces—but faded as they became suspicious that this man might try to trick them and get them in trouble.

Jedediah hoped that their hesitation would not lead to a stony silence, so he decided to mention Wilbur Johnson's name. Unfortunately, this tactic backfired, and the resulting hostile looks from the men let him know that protecting Wilbur was of paramount importance to them.

"An' what you want with Wilbur?" one man asked, suddenly emboldened.

The question immediately turned the tables on the encounter. Now it was Jedediah who had to be careful not to be duped into indicting himself in something illegal, and his own hesitation aroused their curiosity. When it looked as if he was finally going to speak, they crowded in a little closer to hear his reply. He shrugged. "I'm trying to find someone fighting in the Union Army, and a friend of Wilbur's recommended I talk with him to see if he knows a way to sneak down to Virginia."

Their eyes grew large. Another man asked dramatically, "*What*? You *want* to sneak down to Dixie? You ain't no spy, are ya?"

Jedediah quickly decided that the best tactic to defuse such an explosive topic was to quickly and succinctly tell the story of pursuing his brother's killer and meeting Ezra and Miryam. When he finished, the men were uncomfortable with the truth he'd just told, and they shuffled their feet and looked at the one man who seemed to be the leader of the group. He shook his head and said softly, "If you can wait till we're done here, you can ride on the back of our wagon and we'll drop you off on our way past."

One of the other men grabbed this man's shoulder and hissed, "But what if he's a spy?"

The leader looked at each of the men in turn and then shook his head at them. "Naw. If the Confed'racy is so clever as to send a man as outlandish as this one and have him tell a story about killin' a Union soldier who murdered his brother to get a couple of niggers to implicate themselves, then I'll give 'em more credit than I ever have. Don't you worry; if he's somethin' he ain't, Wilbur'll be sure able to tell."

The men went back to work, but Jedediah could tell they were not at all comfortable with the deal that had just been brokered. They continued to be wary of his very presence near them, and they watched him with vigilant eyes. When they were done loading the wagon, they signaled for him to hop aboard. He did so, but the way no one spoke to him made him feel like a pariah in their midst. The wagon slowly made its way along New Jersey Avenue and around the horseshoe in front of the Capitol before heading up Maryland toward a bridge that spanned the City Canal. As the wagon clattered across the narrow bridge, someone in the group said, "At the end of the next block, hop off as we go by. You'll find Miss Annie's house of business 'tween this-here street and Maine Avenue. If you're lookin' for love, ya go in the front door. But if you're looking for Wilbur, ya go to the back."

Jedediah did as he was told and watched as the wagon continued to clip-clop down the street. No one in the crew turned to observe his departure, so he walked on toward the sidewalk that led to a house that appeared to have a lot of activity inside. He found the gate to the back door of the big brick building. He looked around to be sure no one could see him, then he opened the gate and continued up to the house. When he knocked on the door, an elderly black man with snow-white hair answered it. He was obviously surprised by the appearance of the man in front of him, but he smiled formally and said, "Sorry, suh, but I think you wants to go to the front door to find what you're looking for!"

Jedediah shook his head and smiled back. "No, sir. Ezra up in Delaware said that I needed to come to the back door if I wanted to talk with Wilbur Johnson."

The man's countenance completely changed, and he was instantly transformed from the subservient black "butler" to a man who was much more powerful and in control. He looked Jedediah up and down and said, "You don't say? Hmm...ol' Ezra mentioned me to you, huh? You better come inside. All you can do out here is attract the kind of attention that you and I definitely do not want."

Wilbur pointed to a small chair by the doorway where Jedediah could wait while he returned to his duties for a time. The cooks and servants in the kitchen stared at the tattooed white man sitting there as if he was a wild animal, and they whispered hushed comments and warnings about him.

When Wilbur finally came back, Jedediah told him his whole story. The older man whistled softly. "That tale sure does have some sand to it! A brother's murder and vengeance sought, enslaving sea captains, living with runaways, and even marrying a black woman! I don't think I've ever heard a story with such grit in my life, suh. And I'm not sure exactly how I feel about the whole thing neither. But that being said, Mr. Jedediah, I remember Ezra, and if he thinks enough of you to let you marry his daughter and give you my name, I guess I should at least *try* to give you some help. I can't think how I can be of any real assistance, though, 'cause my job is usually with getting people up north, not down to the south!"

Jedediah nodded. "I know. But I just can't go down to Virginia and wander around aimlessly as I search out this man in the midst of the war. If I had a way to find out where he is and get there, I could be done with this business. Ezra suggested you because you seem to have your finger on the heartbeat of this city."

The old man chuckled. "That I do. That I do. The men who come in our front door are the men who run this city, this nation, and, more to the point, this whole damn war. We get Union generals in here who love nothing more than telling the girls about the next offensives and their divisions and brigades. Us niggers and whores usually know more about the war than the newspapers or even the congressmen. I wouldn't be surprised if we could get the information you need by just prompting some of the girls to ask the whereabouts of the different units. Is there anything about the man's company that might stand out but not sound too specific and arouse suspicion?"

"Yes, they're sharpshooters, they wear green uniforms, and they're from Maine. I don't think there are many green-uniformed troops from Maine out there."

"Good, good. I will try to get a couple of the girls to get their johns talking about that topic this very night!"

"But getting the information could take a long time, Wilbur. I can't wait around for weeks to get to this man. I'm close, but the more he gets into the war, the harder it will be to get to him."

Wilbur shook his head. "Naw, Mr. Jedediah, I might have an answer for you by tomorrow morning. If you know the soldier was headed back to Virginia, I'd bet he's somewhere near to Brandy Station. Lately, we've had a bunch of Union Army men come through the house spouting off about the big offensive that's about to start down there. More than one of these men has boasted that the army they're amassing will be poised and ready to make their way straight toward Richmond. If your man is there, we just need to get a specific brigade or division or corps that his unit is in so you won't be wasting your time looking for him. I'll give you some food and a place to sleep for the night, and we'll see what information we can get for you. I know it's hard to be patient, suh, but that's what you need to be right now."

"Thank you, Wilbur. I would be dead in the water without your help."

"Isn't that the craziest thing? Here you are, a white man needing a black man's help to kill another white man and then go back to a salt marsh to live with some runaway slaves! Ha! That's sho' funny, isn't it? And you need me 'cause you're dead in the water... hmm...dead. You're dead...in the water. Hey, I suddenly got me an idea, Mr. Jedediah. But you can't sit on this tiny ol' chair all night. You stick out here, and somebody is gonna take notice and start asking questions. I need you to take this plate of food to the shed out there in the yard. Find a space inside and rest. I just had a plan pop into my head, and I think I may know a way for you to get yourself to where you need to go. You're just gonna have to trust me."

Jedediah had no other choice, so he accepted the plate of food Wilbur thrust into his hands and went out to the small brick shed without protest. Inside, he sat on the floor, ate the food, and even let himself doze. The sounds from the house were loud, and the careless laughter or the popping sound of a champagne cork roused him from a deep sleep several times. Each time, he would sit up and remember where he was. He felt uncomfortable to be trapped in the shed and he dearly missed both Miryam and Ezra, but he was convinced that Wilbur would be able to help him find Zachary Webster. Once he'd killed the man, he'd be able to return home to the salt marsh. And that happy thought made him grin as he fell back to sleep.

Chapter Forty-Three

By the time Catherine reached the B&O Depot in Washington City, it was well after sunset. She was greeted on the platform by Mrs. Geraldine Stanwyck, an older woman who worked at the U.S. Sanitary Commission headquarters and a good friend of Mrs. Ketchum. After exchanging brief pleasantries, Mrs. Stanwyck chirped that they needed to hurry off to her house for a quick bite of supper and a good night of sleep before Catherine began the rest of her trip.

Catherine's hands tightened on the handle of her bag when she recognized the similarities of this encounter to the nefarious meeting of Mrs. Whitherby in Portland. In her mounting anxiety, she even scanned around for a route of escape. But then she breathed deeply and calmed herself down. She trusted Mrs. Ketchum enough to believe that she would never expose her to a similar experience, and that meant she had no reason for this level of concern.

Oblivious to Catherine's discomfort, Mrs. Stanwyck hustled her out to her carriage like a mother hen ushering her chicks out into the yard.

The nighttime carriage ride did not reveal much about the capital city or her host. The majesty of Washington remained hidden within the darkness, and the gas streetlamps were not able to dispel it enough to see any further than the streets. As for Mrs. Stanwyck, she neither asked about Catherine's life nor spoke about herself during the ride. She chatted only about the hectic schedule that awaited Catherine over the next couple of days and the need for her to be rested to take on the ordeals that lay ahead.

Upon arriving at the house, Catherine was given a quick bite to eat and sent to bed with the warning that their day would start before sunrise. She was too excited to fall asleep right away, as her mind was too jumbled with thoughts about her future. But eventually the darkness of her room and the comfortable bed lulled her to sleep.

As promised, she was awoken before dawn and given a rushed breakfast. With the sun only tickling the eastern skyline, the two women sped to the U.S. Sanitary Commission headquarters building on F Street by carriage. They needed to pick up the paperwork that Catherine needed to join the small group of surgeons, stewards, and nurses who were gathering on the grounds of Georgetown College. From there they would take a fleet of new ambulances to Brandy Station and join the medical staff of the II Corps field hospital. With these papers in hand, they headed quickly through the city to the college campus.

The fresh light of the new morning and the deserted streets made Washington seem like some kind of slumbering behemoth. Catherine knew it was only a matter of hours before it would awaken and resume its energetic wartime hum, and she secretly wished she could stay longer to see that happen. However, she also knew that the real purpose of her time here was not as an idle traveler, but as a nurse headed right to the battlefield.

Upon arriving at the gathering site, Catherine was surprised to see six new Moses ambulances parked outside one of the college buildings. The sight of the same type of vehicles in which she had endured unspeakable horrors at the hands of Reverend Watson and Mrs. Whitherby unnerved her enough to force her to look away quickly, and she pressed her chin into her shoulder. As before, Mrs. Stanwyck noticed none of Catherine's reactions, and she quickly introduced her to the other women of the volunteer nurses group, handed her paperwork to the commanding medical officer, then said a hasty good-bye and hustled away. Although slightly perturbed by the woman's brusqueness, Catherine understood that Mrs. Stanwyck had far too many important tasks to accomplish to take the time for any kind of sentimentality. And as Catherine watched the older woman walk away, her eyes focused on the horizon and her chin jutted ever so slightly like the prow of an icebreaker, she thought about how an army of women like Mrs. Stanwyck could probably win this war single-handedly, if given the chance. Another young nurse started talking to her, and this shifted her attention back to her new companions.

By the time the medical recruits arrived at the Brandy Station train depot later that day, they were already exhausted from their arduous trip. The crudeness of the train yard did nothing to lift their spirits, but that all changed when they saw what was actually taking place in the vicinity. As the new ambulances rumbled over the local corduroy roads, the stewards, nurses, and doctors were astounded at the scope of the operation they were traveling through. Brandy Station had the population of a very large city, and the countryside around it pulsed with masses of soldiers marching, training, and preparing. An endless blue sea of uniforms created a startling visual display, and it ebbed and flowed around white tents arranged in the neat straight lines of the various military camps. Not only was there ceaseless activity at these camps, but the roadways between them were clogged with mule teams pulling wagons of supplies at a frantic pace.

There was something ominous about all this activity, and the omnipresent hum in the air indicated that something important was about to commence. Any fatigue the new volunteers felt from their journey evaporated as they dove into the turmoil of Brandy Station and began their perilous duty. The group now found themselves in the middle of a place with an infectious bustle that none of them had ever experienced before.

When the ambulances finally arrived at the current II Corps field hospital, which consisted of a small camp of log cabins with white canvas tops, the new medical staff found that the place was so caught up in the whirlwind of preparations, no one had time to take notice of their appearance. When their presence was finally acknowledged, they were ordered to their differing tasks without ceremony. Some were sent to take care of the sick and injured soldiers who had been deemed able to recover before the offensive began, while others were put to work processing those who probably would not recover and were being sent back by train to hospitals in Washington. Even as these tasks were being completed, the very buildings of the field hospital were dismantled and the essential medicines and equipment transferred to the fleet of waiting wagons and the newly arrived ambulances.

When Catherine finally was able to lie down on her cot in the nurses' tent that night, well after midnight, it was the first time she had stopped moving the entire day. In the relative peace of the moment, she started to grasp the true magnitude of her current situation. Not only was she in the same camp as Zachary Webster, she was actually closer to him than she'd been while he was on furlough in Maine. But in the darkness of the tent and with the strange sounds of a military camp outside, she wrestled with the hard truth that while she was probably close enough to touch him, it was going to be almost impossible to find him. Between fulfilling her duties and familiarizing herself with the field hospital's practices, she would not have a single spare moment to search for Zachary. She laughed at herself for having the foolhardiness to believe that finding a soldier in Company D of the 2nd United States Sharpshooters was going to be like finding someone at a church picnic. It was abundantly clear that Brandy Station wasn't really one place after all, but a series of camps stretched far and wide over the surrounding area, and finding just one man in such an expanse was likely to be harder than finding a needle in a haystack.

Even so, Catherine now finally took the time to congratulate herself. She had endured horrific experiences to get to this place, but she'd made it through those to arrive at the very camp she needed to be in! And while she would not give the harrowing ordeal or her kidnappers any credit whatsoever in this accomplishment, she had to acknowledge that the resulting relationship with Mrs. Ketchum had been instrumental to both her training as a nurse and her placement in the same Union Army corps as her Zachary. If she'd been spared all of those terrors, where would she be now? Not here, that was certain.

When she'd begun her journey, she was nothing more than a little girl walking around in a world whose size and complexity she wasn't even capable of imagining. How utterly ridiculous she'd been to think she could navigate such a difficult journey alone! It was Mrs. Ketchum's influence that had gotten her here, and she would never have met that kind and determined woman if she hadn't endured...

Her brain abruptly shut down that train of thought. Those wounds were still far too raw, and as Mrs. Ketchum had said, the door to them needed to stay locked for the rest of her life. She turned that key now and thought instead about the reality and purpose of her new pathway.

She was a trained Union Army nurse who was about to be ordered into the midst of another clash in the war. And with that new designation came an entirely different true north on her moral compass. She knew her primary duty was now ministering to the injured men of this war, and not attending to her own selfish needs. But that created its own conflict. If she was at another camp and far away from the man she sought to save, she knew she'd throw herself into her nursing and let the Fates decide the outcome of the conflict between Zachary Webster and Jedediah Stiller. But now that she was so close, she knew she couldn't just stop looking for him.

As her breathing became deeper and she started to fall asleep, she let herself accept the fact that if she was going to save Zachary Webster at all, she would probably do so inside the field hospital or out on the battlefield as a nurse.

Chapter Forty-Four

When the shed door sprang open, Jedediah bolted upright to fend off the invader. The fearsomeness of his defensive pose frightened Wilbur so much, he lifted his arms to shield his face. After his heartbeat steadied, the elderly man said in a hushed but urgent tone, "Hurry up, Mr. Jedediah, we need to move. If you want to find this man you seek, you got to get going this very minute."

"Wait—you know where he is? How can I get to him?"

Wilbur waved his arms. "No, suh, we don't have no time for this conversation now! You got to get yourself going so's I can take you over to Uptown before I go to work!"

Jedediah grabbed his seabag and followed the man out to the waiting wagon. He jumped in beside Wilbur just as the man cracked the reins and got the horses moving. They traveled in silence until Wilbur started to talk without looking at his passenger.

"Last night, a gentleman from the War Department took great relish in spilling his loins and then his guts with one of the girls. He couldn't stop talking about the upcoming offensive General Grant is about to put forth from Brandy Station to win this war. When prompted by a few subtle questions, he even mentioned something about the placement of the troops with the green uniforms. Turns out there are two regiments of them sharpshooters there, and they're both assigned to General Hancock's II Corps, so finding the specific man you seek ain't gonna be that hard."

Jedediah was shocked but happy with this news. "I cannot believe you were able to get that information so quickly! Now I just need to figure out a way to get to him."

Wilbur kept staring straight ahead and replied, "That's where my plan comes in, Mr. Jedediah."

"Your plan?"

"Yessuh. You see, some men who are members of my church told me recently that they're being conscripted as a burial detail. They're fixing to leave today and head down to the very offensive that that buffoon spoke of so openly last night. The Union Army's trying to learn from their mistakes in the earlier battles of this war. As it happens, the presence of unburied bodies littering the battlefields has been a major point of embarrassment for them. So in this next offensive, they're sending gravediggers to follow the army and properly bury the dead. 'Course, they ain't expecting no niggers could do it without a couple of white leaders, so them burial teams've all got white *massahs* running 'em."

Wilbur went silent and vehemently spit a great wad of phlegm down at the road. He shook his head. "The reason these men talked to me after church was 'cause they're all skittish as steers at the slaughterhouse. They ain't got no problem with burying the corpses—they've all lived with that kind of death since they was born, and even more since becoming runaways—but the fact that they're headed right back down to the lands of their captivity with an untrustworthy white man as their leader has them jumpy, to say the least. This man is so underhanded and mean, they're all sure as anything he's gonna try to sell 'em back to the southerners the first chance he gets to make some extra money."

Jedediah nodded knowingly. After all, if Captain Cooper had taken the offer in New York, Jedediah's fate would have been very different. That experience had taught him that a slave lacks even the God-given power to determine his own destiny, and the sour recollection of his own powerlessness continued to cause occasional unease even though he was a free man again.

He spoke softly, but his tone was strong. "And you think that if I joined this group, I could not only get transportation to where I need to be, I could make sure this man doesn't do any of that?"

Wilbur's head did not move and his expression did not change, but he spoke firmly. "When these men first approached me, I didn't think I could help them, and that caused me great distress. But something you said last night reminded me about them, and I saw how we all could help one another. If you were to ask the son of a bitch leading this burial unit about joining, you being white and all, he might let ya come along. Especially if you don't talk none about the money aspect of it. If he thinks you'll help out just to get a ride down there, or that you'll take a nigger's wage to make the gravediggin' lighter, he might just take you on. And if he does, you got a ride all the way, right to where ya needs to be. 'Course, there ain't no guarantee that the man'll agree to any of this, but it don't hurt to ask, right?"

"I can be somewhat persuasive when I need to be, Wilbur."

The black man glanced at Jedediah and nodded. His skin tingled with the implications of the giant's last comment, and he momentarily wondered if making a deal with Satan left an indelible stain on your own soul.

They drove to the end of Maine Avenue and then turned onto Seventh Street, and ahead of them lay the bridge that crossed the Washington City Canal. The smell of sewage drifted around them on the morning breeze.

The appearance on their left of a reddish-brown sandstone castle caught Jedediah's attention, and he said, "Wilbur, what on earth is that?"

The black man scowled. "Don't ask me, Mr. Jedediah. I don't know nothin' about these buildings. They got nothin' to do with me or my life. What I know is Miss Annie's house and the Negro neighborhood near the old Contraband Camp and Hospital called Uptown, which is where we're headed. I can tell you about the railroad depots and yards and the wharves on the river 'cause I've taken many a runaway to them places to send them northward, but I can't tell you about these-here buildings 'cause they're full of white men who have nothin' to do with me."

"I understand, Wilbur. I was just surprised to see a castle here, that's all."

Wilbur sighed loudly and said, "I'm tole it's some kind of museum, but I ain't been inside it. I don't know if black people can even go in. But I do know that the hands of slaves helped to build it, that's for sure. But then again, that's true about most of the buildings hereabouts in our fair capital city. Even the precious Capitol building that President Lincoln stood in front of with his hand on a Bible was built by slaves. That don't seem to bother folks in these parts. Ya know, I'm told this war is supposed to be about stopping slavery, but this-here city and most of this country was built by slavery. That don't seem right, does it?"

Jedediah stared around with interest, and Wilbur continued, "This big building on the right and them long skinny white buildings next to it are the Columbia Armory and Hospital. We get lots of men from there over at Miss Annie's house. But we also get quite a few men from all over this town—from the castle, from the Capitol, from the gov'ment buildings all in front of us. Hell, all the men in Washington City seem to come to her house at one time or another!"

As they approached the canal, Jedediah could see the massive stub of the unfinished Washington Monument beyond the castle. The fresh morning light gave the buildings of this area a softer appearance, and he gazed at his surroundings with childlike awe. The downtown area was a mix of open spaces, townhouses, and huge temple-like buildings. They passed a large brick market that was starting to come alive as vendors and buyers took up their stations for the day's transactions.

In front of them, other imposing structures stood like quiet and powerful sentries, but Jedediah now knew better than to ask Wilbur what they were. It was too early in the morning for much activity, and the quietness of the neighborhoods made Jedediah feel more secure. Up ahead, the houses got smaller and more spread out as the wagon rumbled toward the outskirts of the city.

He looked over at Wilbur and felt emboldened enough to address the question that had been bothering him. "Wilbur?"

"Yessuh?"

"I don't mean to be rude by asking this, but I'm wondering why you're helping me. I mean, most people wouldn't be as accepting of what I need to do. So why are you doing it?"

The older man chuckled. His face wrinkled when he smiled, and the dawn's illumination found its way into the creases and lightened his countenance. "Ya know, Mr. Jedediah, I was just asking myself that very same question. It ain't my place to give out forgiveness or permission to any man, white or black. I'm a simple ol' nigger, but I sees life as the complicated thread that it is. I ain't thrilled to be helping in the death of a Union soldier, but if he done what you said, he's got comin' whatever you're bringin'. I ain't gonna bore you with my own tales, but I will say I've had the need for vengeance once or twice in my life. And whenever that's gone beggin', it weren't no feeling I savored none. Your bein' sent here by ol' Ezra helped your case in my eyes, but let me say this: my purpose in helping you ain't purely for you to get your vengeance. It's also about havin' you help some of my people. As I said, life can be most complicated."

They rode in silence the rest of the way. The well-built brick houses of the city neighborhoods petered out, and in their stead were buildings constructed with scavenged materials and more rudimentary architectural skills. They could hear and smell the chickens and hogs behind the crude plank fences and could see the woodsmoke spiraling up from the chimneys. The street became a rough dirt road, and the wagon pitched and tossed on the uneven surface. Up ahead, a simple building sided with the choicest wooden planks and topped by a modest country steeple was the site of a gathering crowd around a large covered wagon. On its canvas side was a crudely painted emblem—a black crow holding shovels in its claws—and even from afar, the emblem stood out stark and ominous.

Wilbur slowed the wagon and stopped next to a hitching post of rough-hewn logs. He leaned toward Jedediah and said in a low voice, "I'll go find the men and tell 'em about our plan while you head over to that ugly white man at the reins of that mule team and ask him for your ride. His name is Thorton Blagan."

Without waiting for a reply, Wilbur jumped down, wrapped the reins, and skittered off into the crowd. Jedediah watched him go and knew that was the only sendoff he would get from the man. He climbed down with his seabag in hand and meandered over to the covered wagon. The man sitting there on the driver's bench had greasy hair that was plastered to his skull from wearing a hat. Oily curls hid his large ears. His nose was bulbous and framed by purplish veins that betrayed a lifetime of drinking. His waxy eyes were sunken behind heavy lids, and when he turned to take in Jedediah's approach, they were crossed like a Siamese cat's. His long face ended in a broad stubbled chin. He had his arms folded across his chest, and his body was scrunched in a defensive posture that bespoke his annoyance and scorn at the people gathered around him.

He spat a stream of tobacco juice onto the ground and asked

menacingly, "And what do *you* want?"

Jedediah advanced until he was standing right next to the wagon seat. He narrowed his eyes and said tightly, "I was wondering if I could join your unit."

Now that the stranger was so close and his size and tattoos were clearly exhibited, the driver showed a glimmer of fear. But when he answered, his voice was confident. "Naw, don't need no more help. And the sooner these sorry niggers get done crying and going on like this, the sooner we can get going."

He stopped talking as if the matter was closed, but Jedediah was determined. "I'm pretty strong and I could make your work easier."

The man looked at him sharply and shook his head. "Naw, we don't need no more help. Got all the niggers we need—six of 'em."

"Well, Thorton," a weak voice said from the shadows inside the wagon, "don't be too quick to discount the man's offer."

Another white man came forward and poked his head out of the shadows. His hair looked too big for his head, and the way his eyes wandered vacantly and his mouth never closed seemed to indicate he was mentally deficient. As he hitched closer to Blagan's shoulder, alcohol fumes drifted out of the wagon toward Jedediah.

"I said, we don't need no more help, Tom! Why don't you just shut up and sleep off this last bender like we agreed."

"I'm just saying, Thorton, that many hands make labors light. Maybe you shouldn't refuse this big man's offer. That's all."

"You're getting as uppity as one of these niggers!" the driver hissed angrily. "I said no, Tom. I ain't asking you to engage me in any more conversation on the matter. The man asked me to join this unit, and I said no. I'm the leader, so that's the end of the story. No need for further talking. Just lay down back there and sleep it off."

As the drunken man lowered himself back inside the canvas covering, the surly Thorton Blagan looked at Jedediah with steady eyes and a blank expression. When Jedediah didn't immediately respond, the man shrugged and went back to staring into space with his arms crossed.

"Well, maybe you can help me out by just giving me a ride to Alexandria, then."

Blagan turned back to him as if surprised that he was still there. "I ain't no type of hack. I said no. And that's that. Go away if you don't want no trouble."

Jedediah grasped the side of the wagon and pulled it down to him, bringing the man closer, and his voice was cold and emotionless. "I can tell you one thing, Thorton, you do not want any trouble from me. You could let me ride in the back of your wagon and it wouldn't cost you a thing. Just a little ride with your unit to Alexandria—that's all I'm asking for."

Impressed by the giant's display of strength, Blagan unfolded his arms and jerked his thumb toward the back. The oversized oiled-canvas coat he wore made a rasping sound.

"All right, mister, I don't want no trouble. If you wanna ride in the back with them niggers to Alexandria, that's fine by me. But that's as far as you're going, you got that?"

Jedediah released his grip on the wagon but kept his scathing gaze on Blagan for a few more seconds. Then he gave a slight nod and walked around to the back of the wagon, threw his bag in, and clambered up. When he looked out at the crowd, all eyes were on him and their expressions were uneasy. He hoped Wilbur had found the gravediggers and spoken with them. And thinking about the old man again made Jedediah glance toward the spot where his wagon had been parked, but it was already gone.

"All right, you goddamn niggers!" Blagan bellowed as he donned his black wide-brimmed hat. "These dead Union soldiers ain't gonna come to us for burying. We got one helluva long way to go to do our jobs. If you ain't too busy crying and pawing over each other, get in the damn wagon and let's get going!"

Jedediah helped the men with their bedrolls as they climbed in. Quick introductions were made, but the men's eyes were glued to their crying and waving family members as the wagon pulled away and left them behind. The mule team moved with the noisy jangle of brass halter buckles and clopping hooves, and when they turned a corner and the men could no longer see the crowd, they all settled into their own spaces, closed their eyes, and appeared to sleep. The drunken white man slumbered in the front of the wagon, and his loud snoring added a certain rhythm to the other sounds of their progress. He had far more room than he needed, but none of the black men wanted to be too close to him, and they crammed into their tiny spaces without debate or comment.

As they made their way back toward the city, Jedediah could not dismiss the feeling that this whole plan was greatly flawed. He knew Thorton Blagan would betray him at some point, and he needed to be prepared for that moment.

Washington was now awake with frenetic activity, and Jedediah marveled at what looked like a kind of orderly chaos. When they slowed to a stop and the driver began speaking loudly to someone, Jedediah tensed for a possible confrontation. However, the conversation was merely an easy exchange between Blagan and a soldier checking for proper paperwork so they could join the wagon train to the front. The sound of paper being handed back was followed by the meek order that they were to take their place with the other supply wagons and wait to cross the Long Bridge later that afternoon.

The wagon moved suddenly, traveled a short distance, and stopped again. Jedediah poked his head out and saw that there were dozens of such vehicles in the open space at the base of the Washington Monument. All of them had different emblems painted on the canvas tops or wooden sides, and they were informally grouped according to these. Jedediah sat back down and listened to the sounds of the men and animals that would comprise the supply train.

"Hey, friend, you still plan to go with us all the way to Alexandria?"

Jedediah looked to the front of the wagon and saw the driver turned around on the bench and facing him. Without making eye contact, the black gravediggers watched the conversation closely.

Jedediah cleared his throat. "Yep."

Blagan rubbed the stubble on his chin with long, dirty fingers. "Uh-huh. Sure, sure, that's fine. Just don't expect me to feed you. These niggers know I ain't gonna be feeding them no more than I have to, and you shouldn't expect any different."

"I don't expect anything from you. Like I said, I'm just along for the ride. But if you were to let me go with you all the way to the war, I could make your life easier."

"Uh-huh. Well, we'll see about that," the driver said flatly before turning his back on the men in the wagon. Jedediah didn't like Blagan's tone. As Wilbur had warned, he was a conniving and shifty one, and Jedediah tilted his head thoughtfully as he weighed his options.

When he looked around at the gravediggers, they all seemed to want him to say something but were too afraid to ask anything themselves. When Jedediah finally spoke, he did so without addressing anyone in particular. "I'm assuming Wilbur talked to you all about me."

The men glanced nervously at the sleeping man in their midst, but he was still snoring soundly so they nodded furtively.

One of the men whispered, "He tole us you might be able to stop him from sellin' us back into slavery."

"I can't promise too much, but I will try. But you're gonna have to trust me more than you might feel comfortable with. Are you all ready to do that?"

The men indicated agreement and sat silently waiting for Jedediah to say something more. But before he could, someone outside started talking to the driver. The voice was so nasal it sounded like a foghorn.

"Say there, friend, you wanna head with me and some of the other drivers over to Wilkerson Tavern? It's on the other side of the canal over yonder. We ain't gonna be moving till they put them planks back on the bridge, so why should we sit in this hot sun and just wait around for the Army to get its head out of its ass?"

Blagan hesitated. "Well, I am right thirsty and a drink sounds mighty fine indeed. Tell you what, my good man, let me get things in order here, and I'll join you there."

The other drivers walked off and he turned to the men in back. He looked down at the sleeping drunk and made a face. "Mr. Buck is in charge while I go to get us some supplies. I'll be back in plenty of time to continue on. Do not leave this-here wagon for any reason if you don't want a world of trouble! You all hear me?"

"Oh, yessuh!" the six gravediggers answered in unison.

"Excuse me—sir?"

The driver looked at Jedediah with agitation. "What?"

"Well, it seems to me this might be an excellent opportunity for me to repay your kindness for letting me ride with your unit."

"How's that?"

"It'd be my pleasure to go with you to the tavern and buy you a drink or two. Seems the least I could do for your generosity. What say you?"

The man looked sideways and licked his lips. "Aye, that would be a most civilized thing to do, indeed. Sure, why don't you come along, and we can drink to the success of this outing we're all on."

Jedediah went to the back gate of the wagon and jumped out. Six black faces looked out at him with imploring eyes, and he calmly said, "I'm leaving all of my belongings with you. Will you make sure they're taken care of till I get back?"

The gravediggers sat up straighter, for there was something in the giant man's voice that made their hearts race. When he grinned warmly at them, they relaxed a little and prepared themselves for the heat of the midday sun that would soon make the enclosed space uncomfortably warm.

When Jedediah came back a couple of hours later, alone and wearing Blagan's coat and hat, they all knew what had happened. And as the giant climbed right up to the seat of the wagon and took the reins in his hand, they sat in the sweltering heat and prayed for forgiveness for their involvement in whatever dark and sinister event had just taken place.

As the sun began to settle in the western sky, there was a loud call for the supply train to begin moving out toward the Long Bridge. The most essential supplies were at the front of the line, and many of them were already crossing the Potomac River when Jedediah's wagon started forward. The fact that the gravediggers were at the very end of the procession surprised no one. On orders from a sweaty, heavyset Union soldier, Jedediah flicked the reins and the mules joined the stream of animals and wagons on the move to Virginia and the battlefront.

The supply train plodded along until they all gathered again near the Orange & Alexandria Railroad yard. With surprising efficiency, the teams of mules and horses were unharnessed and loaded into special railcars, while the wagons were wheeled onto flatcars and cinched down for transport. The drivers and men boarded the passenger cars, and as soon as one train was completely loaded, it departed for Brandy Station. Once it cleared the rail yard, another empty train was positioned for loading. There were so many wagons, the process continued late into the night.

While they waited their turn to get on the train, the gravediggers found themselves in an area a half mile from the rail yard. They set about building cooking fires and getting a meal and coffee in them before it was their time to depart. Another Union soldier came around to check the paperwork again, so Jedediah showed him the greasy folded papers as he identified himself as Mr. Thorton Blagan. The six gravediggers' faces tightened with fear as they listened to the exchange, but as soon as the paperwork passed the test and the soldier moved on, they grinned wryly as they ate their food.

When the drunken man finally awoke, Jedediah went to talk with him alone in the back of the wagon. They spoke in such hushed tones that none of the other men could hear them, but when Tom Buck came back to the fires, he was more pale than usual. It was instantly evident that he had wholly accepted Jedediah as the new leader of the unit. No one was sure of his exact connection to the real driver, but he seemed neither saddened by the implied demise of the man nor overly concerned with the new counterfeit one. And for someone who had just slept off an alcoholic bender, he had a surprisingly large appetite for supper.

When the gravedigger wagons were finally loaded onto a train, only the white men were offered space in the passenger car for the ride to Brandy Station, while the black men were told to stay in the wagons. While most of the leaders of the other burial details went to their cars, Jedediah and Mr. Buck chose to stay with their men, and they all curled up like slumbering dogs to attempt to sleep during the train ride.

All but Jedediah. He sat alone on the driving bench and watched the embers from the locomotive's smokestack flow past their vulnerable canvas top like a meteor shower. The wind was blowing on his face and the nighttime woods were an impenetrable black wall on both sides as the train steamed along, and he stared into this darkness as though looking for portents of his future. In his solitude, Jedediah was intensely thoughtful, and he was surprised to realize that all of his thoughts were about Miryam and Ezra. Now that he was finally headed to the exact location for his act of vengeance, he could not shake his melancholic mood. And while he acknowledged an inkling of anticipation about being so close to a hard-won goal, he had to admit that his emotions were dominated by something he had not felt in a very, very long time. He was homesick.

Chapter Forty-Five

When the order to break camp was finally issued, the countryside around Brandy Station exploded into an endless tumult. The area took on a dreamlike quality as giant bonfires burned throughout the nights to allow the preparations to proceed unhindered by darkness, and the sounds of dismantling the massive camp were loud and continuous. Shouting men, creaking caisson axles, the constant snapping sounds of whips on oxen and mule teams, the hoofbeats of steeds bringing messages to and from headquarters, the shouts of sergeants organizing and assembling their fighting units, and the whistles and shrieks of a continuous stream of trains to and from Alexandria fed the growing excitement and anticipation until it almost reached a boiling point.

The men of Company D took down their tents and awaited further orders. The sharpshooters were ready for imminent action, but the awkward eagerness of the new recruits betrayed their greenness, and the veterans watched them with smirks on their faces. When the massive fires were finally extinguished and the shadows of darkness grew longer and swallowed everyone and everything, a silence descended upon the camp that heralded the successful dismantling and the official waiting period for the upcoming march. The men became as impatient and twitchy as wild horses, and some of them scratched at themselves with anticipation or had involuntary guttural upheavals. Their packs were filled with three days' rations, their cartridge boxes were full, and their bayonets were in place. The soldiers were laden and ready for battle.

The men of II Corps brimmed with confidence. They were under the command of General Winfield Hancock, and he was considered one of the best Union generals the country had. He had gained the nickname "Superb" during his successes in the Peninsula Campaign of '62, and his name was thrown around as one of the heroes of the Battle of Gettysburg. The soldiers had the utmost respect for the man because even though he had been gravely wounded during that battle, he'd refused to be taken to a hospital for medical care until he was sure the victory was complete. The fact that he was still in considerable pain from those wounds only enhanced their dedication to him.

General Hancock's four division commanders—General Francis C. Barlow, General John Gibbon, General Gershom Mott, and General David B. Birney—were also held in the highest regard as being among the most capable. These leaders, all of whom had been wounded during the war, had shown a fearlessness and hardiness that was thoroughly admired by their troops. With the force completely rested and supplied, the leadership up the ranks as solid as it had ever been, and the new overall aggressiveness of General Grant at the very top, the troops were sanguine about the outcome of the impending battle.

When Zachary Webster heard some of the men boasting about the guaranteed success of the offensive, he shook his head and spat angrily on the ground before moving away from them. His demonstration caught the eye of many of the veterans in the company because it was another example of a new darkness that had settled on the man. Usually, he'd been steely and emotionless before a battle, so seeing him publicly exhibit such raw emotion unnerved them, and they kept their distance from him.

Just before midnight, the order was finally given to move out, and the men formed ranks and began to march. Under the celestial lights of a starry sky, the massive force headed out like some kind of gigantic sea creature unfurling its tentacles. The network of dirt roads came alive with the sounds of shuffling feet and muffled coughs as the men trekked past the dark and formless forests. Although it was nearly impossible for such a large group to make its way silently, the soldiers did their best to stay quiet and prepare themselves for an extended nighttime march. Each man was keenly aware that the success of the offensive hinged on their ability to silently position the force in the lap of the Confederacy, and they struggled to move out as quietly as they could.

By the time the sun rose above the treetops, the men of Company D had marched through the town of Richardsville and were on their way to the Rapidan River. The seemingly endless line of marching troops stretched as far as the eye could see, and the flood of the blue uniforms of the soldiers and the smattering of the green tunics of the sharpshooters created a river of humanity flowing down the road.

The men had marched silently through the night, but now some of them began to sing with the happiness that came with the dawn, but Webster neither joined in the singing nor joked and joshed with his fellow sharpshooters. Instead he struggled with the beginnings of a new emotion about the impending battle—it wasn't fear, as such, but a gnawing sense of dread. Given Captain Wentworth's comments on the new use of the sharpshooters, and the way they'd been training with the regular infantry, he expected the worst for himself and his fellow soldiers. It seemed obvious to him that whenever the sharpshooters were allowed to break away from the ranks and act as snipers, they not only inflicted more casualties, but captured more enemy soldiers as well. However, the record showed that the opposite was also true. Whenever they were put into the battle lines in a traditional manner, they had suffered very high casualties. Because of this, it was clear to him that the sharpshooters were in for the worst during the upcoming action. This thought brought a caustic and sour sensation to rise from the pit of his stomach, and though he tried to keep it down as they marched, it kept springing up and made it hard for him to breathe.

At Ely's Ford on the Rapidan, the troops of II Corps came to a bottleneck as the force squeezed down to cross the narrow wooden pontoon bridge the engineers had erected. The coolness of the dawn had evaporated, and the heat of the day had started to build. The heavy packs, the marching, and the day's lethal temperature had begun to take their toll on the spirits of the men, and they waited impatiently for the chance to fill their canteens with river water. As Company D finally crossed, they were unnerved by the noises the anchoring ropes made under the strain of the river's spring flow and the great weight of the army's combined mass. The level of the walkway rose and fell with the buoyancy of the burdened pontoons, and the men— both hardened veterans and green recruits—quickened their pace with anxiety, fearing that if they fell into the water, they would drown because of their loaded backpacks and their own inability to swim.

From the river, they continued to a field just past Chancellorsville, where they were ordered to stop and make camp. As each company began to pitch their tents in their allotted areas, they realized that the site was the exact location of the well-known battle of the previous year. Not only was there still debris and other salvageable mementos from that battle on the ground, several partially exposed shallow graves could be seen nearby. Upon closer examination of these, the bones of the dead soldiers appeared to have been exposed either by the harsh winter or by the actions of starving animals. While many veterans averted their eyes from these scenes and talked reverently, some particularly irreverent men actually gathered a few of the skulls and positioned them in a ghastly pile to point out the horrible head injuries from bullet, bayonet, or sabre. Several veterans were outraged and barked furiously, "Have some respect!"

•　　•　　•　　•　　•

The exhaustion from their grueling twenty-five-mile march made it easy for most of the men to fall asleep despite the intense midday heat, and they slumbered heavily through the afternoon. When the cooking fires were started at sunset, the men emerged from their tents with bleary eyes and their skin and uniforms chalked white with the road dust of the march. As they gathered around the fires, the conversations took on the quiet whispers of intimate discussions about unspeakable topics. The new recruits listened carefully as the veterans described the ghastly evidence from the previous battle as an ominous harbinger of the fight that lay ahead, and the reverence in their voices spooked these younger men. And while some made jokes about camping out in graveyards, their laughter was brittle with tension. Most sat with their shoulders hunched protectively and sucked on their pipes with an intensity reserved for the most thoughtful of times.

The overall sinking of morale was reported to Captain Wentworth, and although he was extraordinarily busy with preparations for the coming battle, he decided it was worth the effort to walk around his company's fires to show his presence and uplift the men's spirits. As he made his way down the straight lanes between the tents and found the congregations of soldiers around the fires, the men stood and stiffened appropriately to his approach. After dispensing his usual encouragement to the men, he felt he'd been able to lighten their mood.

All but Zachary Webster. While he stood and gave his attention to the captain's speech, the man's countenance just wasn't right. And as the captain was about to turn and continue on his rounds, the thought crossed his mind that it was better to lance a boil than leave it to fester, and he came back to their fire.

"Excuse me, Mr. Webster. I cannot help but notice that you are particularly reserved tonight. I am expecting all of the veterans to be leaders for the less experienced soldiers, so I would love to hear what brave wisdom you want to share with them."

Webster was startled by the individual attention, and when he saw that the other men were looking at him uncomfortably, he returned the captain's gaze with eyes tight with anger. He knew Captain Wentworth was not only challenging his loyalty in public, but putting him in his place. For if he were to respond that he had serious doubts and fears about the way the sharpshooters were going to be used in the upcoming battle, he would be deemed either a coward or a rabble-rouser. And if he said anything else, it would be nothing but an obvious lie.

Webster cleared his throat as he chose his words. "We're sure to whip them, sir. We're sharpshooters, and we can shoot better and kill better than any other soldiers in the Union Army, and we've proven that each and every time we have been given the chance to do so, sir."

Captain Wentworth nodded but grimaced slightly. The man's reply was good, but there was enough of a subtle jab in it to be taken as a mild form of insubordination. However, since it had been said aloud in front of the other men, there was no way now to question his true intentions. So the captain addressed the entire group. "You will all be crucial to the success of this campaign!"

With that, Captain Wentworth turned and continued on his way. The men around the fire sat silently for a moment to let him get some distance from them, and then they began to whisper among themselves. Finally, a new recruit by the name of Wyatt Morse got up and took a step forward. "Come on, Mr. Webster, what do you really think about the upcoming battle? You've been sitting over there like a hidden ember, smoldering quietly without burning anyone. What do you truly think we're in for?"

Some of the men whistled at the boy's audacity, but Webster shook his head and grinned slightly. Morse had been next to him whenever the company drilled recently, and the young man's confidence had impressed him. He sighed heavily and said, "As you know, we fought here last spring. What we discovered is that this whole region is a god-awful place."

There were a few nods and more whistles. The fire crackled loudly and startled them all. Then the new recruit spoke up again. "How so, Mr. Webster?"

Webster chuckled at his persistence. "Well, you noticed the woods surrounding this place as we marched in here today, didn't you?"

The young man shrugged nonchalantly. "Sure, but woods are woods."

"Naw, these are special. They're so thick, it's damn near impossible to even walk through 'em. But since they ain't got a lot of roads crossing 'em, you've *got* to walk through 'em. And if you have the misfortune of having to fight in 'em, you cannot see the enemy until they're right on top of you. With the trees and bramble so tight like that, the cavalry and artillery can't support us soldiers when we really need it. So it just comes down to you and the enemy in the middle of that tangled mess."

"Sure, but the rebs have to fight in these same woods, don't they?"

"Oh, yes, that's quite true. But for reasons that are still foreign to me, this appears to be familiar territory for many of them. They know this land so much better than any of us. Last year, them rebs had an uncanny ability to turn the hidden ravines and low-lying swamps that lurk in them damn thickets into ideal ambush sites. We kept stumbling on whole lines of entrenched reb infantry hidden in these places, ready to let 'er rip."

"And you think that's what awaits us tomorrow?"

"Yes. If it worked once, why wouldn't they try it a second time? But that's not the worst of it. Just look at how these fires are raging tonight. It's been a dry spring down here and these forests are tinderboxes ready to light up with the merest spark! All it will take is a bit of gunfire and everything'll become like hellfire. It happened during last year's dance, and I can still hear the screams of the wounded as they burned alive in the wildfires which scorched the battlefields. I just hope to God we can march ourselves past this region before the real fighting starts."

There were knowing nods and worried mumblings among the men. The new recruits shuddered at the news, and the silence of despair settled upon them. Webster hated himself for stating these truths to mere boys who were ill-prepared to take it, and he realized he did not want to be the agent of doubt in their hearts as they entered this campaign. So he shrugged with exaggerated nonchalance and tried to sound convincing when he said, "But we're sharpshooters and we're specially trained for just this type of battle. We always use our surroundings to our advantage and we take care of each other. We're gonna all come out of this fine, but I pity the regular Blue Coats in this one."

His comment caused several of the men around the fire to smile, but this only made it instantly obvious who were the new recruits and who were the hardened veterans. For the battle-tested men knew better than to buy the optimistic fluff that Webster had just spun. The truth was this place in which they were going to be fighting for their lives very shortly was as bad as he'd said and worse, and those men who'd fought amid the suffocating trees and underbrush before now clenched their jaws and closed their eyes as they imagined the horrors they would face if they had to battle there again. Some of the recruits saw this, and their smiles slowly fell away as a new and even heavier silence descended on the group. And as the endless calls of the whip-poor-wills haunted them, they knew in their hearts that they might not survive this action.

Chapter Forty-Six

Buglers woke the camp at sunrise, and after a quick breakfast of hardtack and coffee, the order was issued to break camp and form into units for another day's march. The dawn sun was already warming, and it was clear the day was going to be extraordinarily hot for early spring. By the time II Corps resumed its march southward on Furnace Road, perspiration was already cascading down the men's faces and off their chins onto their tunics. The sharpshooters were ordered into the forest to protect the flanks of the marching columns, and as they dissolved into the thickets, Webster looked back and watched the countless soldiers' shiny bayonets shimmer in the stark sunshine like the quills of a porcupine. And he was suddenly aware that the thunderous creaking of boot steps had drowned out the sounds of the birds.

After a short trek through the treacherous copse, one of the new recruits blurted out to no one in particular, "Good Lord! You weren't kidding none about these damn woods! They're too thick to walk through, let alone fight in. How in hell will we know when the enemy's attacking us?"

"When you smell their breath," another man replied dryly.

Some newer recruits nearby laughed out loud at his comment, but after seeing the complete absence of smiles on the other faces, they all grew serious and intent on what was in front of them.

The all-encompassing forest seemed to contain and amplify the day's heat, and the men struggled with it and with the difficulty of moving through such a tangled space with their rifles and heavy packs. When they heard the distant rumbles of sudden artillery fire and the angry snap of rifle shots off to the west, the reaction ran through the ranks like a wave, both in the ones attempting to traverse the tangled brambles and in the ones on the open road. The sharpshooters became like excited hounds approaching their prey, while the marching soldiers found a renewed urgency in their steps from the realization they would soon be seeing action once more.

When the columns arrived at the Piney Branch Church and turned onto Cartharpin Road, their progress was unexpectedly halted. The massive marching force was sharing the road with countless messengers on horseback, who rode to and from headquarters to distribute orders and pass observations to the commanders. Various supply wagons for those units which had already engaged the enemy had plugged the congested area, and a traffic jam had ensued. Chaos reigned for the moment as the commanders, their voices pitched higher with a hint of fear, issued confusing and mistaken orders.

The more experienced soldiers in the column remained standing in place but shifted uncomfortably at being stopped and exposed on the open road. Only the sight of General Winfield Hancock himself riding ahead to untangle the congestion gave the men some solace, and soon they started marching again, but in a completely different direction. Instead of heading south, away from the sounds of the battle, they now headed north up the Brock Road and right toward it. Due to this redirection, the units who were at the intersection, especially those brigades of General Hays and General Ward, were now the head of the phalanx as the column set out on its new path to the fighting.

The sharpshooters continued in their flanking role for the procession. Many of them were fighting exhaustion from the effort needed to navigate through the tangled saplings. Despite their fatigue, however, the likelihood of running into the enemy propelled them forward. And as they continued to hear the staccato of gunfire in front of them, they could tell the conflict was much more than just a brief exchange between skirmishers—they were headed right into the midst of a fierce and widespread battle. But the veteran sharpshooters, having done this more times than they could count, let the adrenaline push them excitedly onward, for they knew what to expect. Those men who had never been in a battle before, on the other hand, were wide-eyed and pale with the fear that worked its way up from their groins.

When the troops arrived at the junction of Brock Road and Orange Plank Road, General Hancock ordered Hay's brigade and Ward's brigade to immediately start constructing earthworks on the south side of the intersection. Next to them and across the Orange Plank Road, three brigades of General John Sedgewick's VI Corps, who'd come down from the north to form the upper line of the attack, were already entrenched. These men signaled to these new arrivals that they were glad for their presence, and then resumed what they were doing. Mott's brigade came up to the intersection and began to fortify themselves along the roadside next to Ward's men. As the soldiers furiously started to chop down small trees, move logs, and dig dirt to fill in between the logs, the sharpshooters took up a position to provide support. But Captain Wentworth charged over and yelled at his men, "No, no, no! All soldiers are required to help with the construction of these defensive stands, even you! Everyone must do so immediately!"

The sharpshooters reluctantly turned to their new assignment, and Webster clenched his jaw in frustration. He was certain that if Captain Small were still alive and in command, the unit would've been sent out as skirmishers to seek out the enemy and hit them while the rest of the force prepared itself for the larger assault. But clearly that wasn't the role of the sharpshooters in this battle, and Webster threw his energies into the construction of the defensive structures. Their very lives would probably depend upon the strength of these sheltering earthworks before this battle was over. But as he labored at this task, he could not ignore the return of the sickening feeling that this new role for the sharpshooters was going to cost him and the rest of the men of the 2nd U.S.S.S. quite dearly.

In the midst of II Corps' construction activity, the three brigades from Sedgewick's VI Corps were ordered to leave their defensive bulwarks and head right into the thickets as the first move of the offensive. The sharpshooters watched as some familiar faces from Colonel Lewis Grant's Vermont Brigade went forward and vanished into the tree line. A nervous silence settled onto the area as the sounds of the big force could no longer be heard and the men of II Corps listened for what would happen next. A sudden explosion of musket fire from within the trees indicated that those men had just walked into an ambush. And as several stray bullets whizzed through the foliage and pattered into the earthworks and surrounding trees, several terrified retreating soldiers burst from the woods and beelined it back to the safety of their trenches.

Captain Wentworth began barking orders for the men of Company D to form a skirmishing line and head into the forest to support the men of Grant's brigade. They left all their packs behind and quickly advanced. As they pressed forward, the new recruits added to the general tension by asking childish questions and acting frightened. When the thickness of the vegetation and the noise and smoke from the rifle fire made vocal commands ineffective, bugle commands were issued to prevent confusion. The sharpshooters cautiously made their way toward the unseen enemy half expecting to stumble into their own ambush, but none came. When they discovered a small stream, they descended the embankment and stooped to fill their canteens. They were all parched and knew that another opportunity at drinking water would probably not occur again during the battle. But as they went about this task, a hidden rebel force opened fire on them from the top of the next rise. Webster and the rest of the sharpshooters scattered for cover behind trees and ground clutter. When the bugler issued the order to fire at will, they responded immediately.

Webster found himself pinned down behind two saplings that provided only scant protection, but he continued firing his rifle with precision at the enemy soldiers, who were overshooting their marks because of their position on higher ground. The air was filled with the insect-like sounds of flying lead and the *thunking* noises as these missiles hit the trunks of the trees. Foliage cut by the stray firing fell like gigantic green snowflakes onto the chaotic scene on the forest floor. Although they were the victims of a well-planned ambush, the sharpshooters' withering return fire backed the rebel force down from its high ground and away from the fray. The sharpshooters instinctively began to move forward to pursue them, but Captain Wentworth, his sword drawn dramatically, barked, "Company D, hold your line!"

Webster shot the captain a furious look of disbelief at this order, but he held his position and continued to fire only at presented targets. The regular regiments of Ward's brigade streamed past their position and pursued the retreating enemy force further into the depths of the woods. As they watched wave after wave of soldiers push past their location, several sharpshooters attempted to join them, but were ordered back to immediately start building a new set of defensive breastworks in the middle of the forest. The men, their adrenaline flowing from the skirmish, turned their agitated energy to the hasty construction of a rudimentary entrenchment among the roots and fallen trees, but they were unable to do so without looking up often to see whatever they could of the battle.

For the rest of the afternoon, the sharpshooters supported Ward's regiments from their rough earthworks among the trees. They lay behind this protection with their rifles aimed, but the sounds of the gunfire were far in front of them. Thoroughly frustrated, Webster fought with the invisible negativity within him. He was disgusted with having to hold this ridiculous line in the middle of the forest and miss the real action. As he watched the stretcher bearers head past them with crates of ammunition on their empty stretchers and return a little later with the bodies of the wounded on them, his bitterness began to consume him.

The men around him noticed his darkened state, and they secretly pitied whoever he was going to unleash his wrath upon when the sharpshooters were finally allowed to fight again.

Chapter Forty-Seven

As Catherine helped another ambulance unload its cargo of broken bodies, she glanced over at the surgery tents and the growing piles of amputated limbs behind them. The field hospital of II Corps wasn't fully set up as yet on the Carpenter Farm, a couple of miles from the battlefields, and now that the ambulances choked the road with their grotesque loads, the medical staff was struggling to keep up.

Nothing in her training had prepared her for the devastation of the wounds she was witnessing or the sheer volume of casualties. She shook her head and laughed bitterly at the relative calm of the surgery rooms she and Mrs. Ketchum had visited in New York City and how there'd been a couple of doctors for each patient. Here in the open expanse of the farm, littered with the bodies of wounded men gasping and moaning with pain in the hot midday sun, she understood how purely futile her present duties truly were.

As part of the team of doctors, stewards, and nurses whose responsibility it was to meet the arriving ambulances and discern which men needed immediate surgery, which ones could survive the wait for delayed treatment, and which men could not be saved, Catherine was grimly aware that their field hospital was overwhelmed. While the doctors made all the fateful decisions and pronouncements, the stewards carried the wounded to areas of their designation. The nurses, meanwhile, struggled to get water and comfort to those who most needed these small mercies. But there were already too many to manage, and most of the wounded men continued to call out for them and grab for the hems of their dresses as they bustled past. Many soldiers called out the names of the loved ones waiting for them at home.

Catherine expected to see Zachary Webster on one of the incoming stretchers, but it hadn't happened yet. She was still in shock from the flurry of events over the last few days. They had followed closely behind the marching column of II Corps from Brandy Station, over the Rapidan River, and into Chancellorsville. After a sleepless night of preparations, the medical caravan left the shadows of the force and headed to the farm where the scouts had recommended putting up the field hospital. Though she knew she had probably been close enough to actually touch Zachary at times during the last few days, she'd been so busy that she might as well have been on the other side of the world! Now that the hospital was awash with waves of the wounded, she no longer had the luxury of thinking about him and his whereabouts.

Catherine was an excellent nurse—despite the shortcomings of her training. She remained calm and unflappable no matter how chaotic the processing of the wounded became, and although her heart had broken a little when she watched her first patient die in front of her, she was able to balance her melancholy with the compassion she needed to dispense care to those still alive. Mrs. Ketchum's advice about remembering the nuns in the hospital stuck with her, and even though the odious smells of fear and death and piss and shit wafted through the farm like smoke, she found herself unaffected by it. The task at hand was so momentous, she couldn't dwell on anything that was not crucial to her duties.

As she walked between the rows in the section of the wounded, one red-haired man with a thick New York accent grabbed her dress as she went past. She tenderly tried to touch his hand and asked him gently to release her, but his grip was steely strong. He looked up at her with imploring eyes. "Are you an angel? Am I dying? Oh God, I don't want to die!"

She knelt down to soothe the man, but his hand let go of her dress and caught her by the wrist with surprising speed and strength. "Or are you an evil witch? Which is it? I asked you a question, woman, answer me!"

Catherine was uncomfortable with the man's restraining of her, and she answered with more shrillness in her voice than she wanted. "You're slightly wounded, sir. You're not going to die. You've been shot in battle, but the doctor has looked at you and said you're going to recover."

"You lie!" The man's eyes grew large and he moved his lips in an agitated way. "When I saw that hideous giant and his bunch of niggers carry me out of the woods and put me on a wagon with a black crow on its side, I knew. I knew! If that ain't all a pronouncement of death, I surely don't know what is! And you must be that devil's slave if you can lie so straight to a dying man!"

A wave of pain made the man loosen his grip and Catherine was able to pull away. She stood over the man and said firmly, "But I am not lying, sir. You're going to be fine. You must be having some kind of visions due to your wounds and this horrible heat. Drink this water."

As she tilted a canteen toward his mouth, he snarled at her, "You probably poisoned it, you witch! You are in cahoots with that devil with the tattoos all over his face. You two are conspiring to send me down to the fires of Hell, aren't you?"

A *"giant" with a tattooed face...?* Catherine leaned closer and whispered, "Were these tattoos like swirls of smoke on his chin and cheeks?"

"Of course they were! You know what your cohort looks like! Evil vines of tattoos growing up the giant's face like the blackness of his soul reaching out and up from his black heart. And then he put me in a wagon with the very mark of Death upon it! Oh God, I'm going to die! I'm going to die in this godforsaken land and you're sending my soul to the fires of Hell!"

A steward hurrying past yelled, "Miss Brandford! The doctors in the surgery tent have requested you there. They asked for you by name, so you must go immediately."

She nodded at him and looked down again at the wounded soldier. He was now shaking his head and crying quietly. She wanted to comfort him, but she had to go—no time for any of that. But as she made her way, she thought about the fact that Jedediah Stiller was now at the battlefield, too. This meant she would not have the opportunity to get to Zachary first and warn him, and she clenched her hands together and prayed that the rebels would kill him quickly before the awful giant could exact his revenge upon him.

Chapter Forty-Eight

Jedediah watched Mr. Buck drive off with another load of wounded soldiers in the gravediggers' wagon and felt the growing frustration that this new role his unit now found themselves in was not only keeping him from tracking down Zachary Webster, but was continuing to grow and engulf their every movement. After the maddeningly slow days of the support-wagon procession and the perpetual stopping and starting as they crossed the pontoon bridge over the Rapidan, he'd been completely surprised by the almost immediate conscription of his gravediggers and their wagon into emergency ambulance duty. They'd only just reached the open field with the other gravediggers to await their orders to begin burying the dead when a pockmarked Union soldier approached and asked to see their paperwork. He informed Jedediah that the battle they heard in the distance was already overwhelming the available ambulance corps, and he was thence ordered to take his wagon and crew down the Orange Turnpike toward Brock Road to help transport the wounded to the II Corps field hospital.

The truth was Jedediah was both frustrated and conflicted by his current situation. While he understood that his dispatching of the wretched Mr. Blagan in the alley next to the tavern meant he'd assumed command of the burial detail and that his role also included the continued protection of his black gravediggers, he struggled with the fact that he could no longer abandon them whenever he wanted. The cost of his decision had been that his personal mission of revenge on Zachary Webster had been replaced by this new duty to these men. If he were to leave them in order to look for Webster, and they were resold into slavery, he knew he would not be able to live with himself.

Yet here he was, agonizingly close to the man he sought! Somewhere on this very battlefield, if he was still alive! All Jedediah had to do was ask some of the wounded soldiers for the location of the company of Maine sharpshooters and he'd know exactly where to go. And once he knew that, he could find the man and accomplish his mission. After all, the chaos of the battlefield would be the perfect place for him to slip in close to Webster, kill him, and slip out again undetected. But he could not do that if it meant he had to leave his men unprotected and vulnerable.

So, when they'd first arrived at the area where the Union soldiers hunkered behind the earthworks on Brock Road, and his burial unit was swept into the service of resupplying the troops and transporting the wounded, he'd made his decisions based on what would be best for his men, not for himself. He did not trust Mr. Buck to look out for them, so Jedediah knew he had to stay with them through the maelstrom at the front. They would transport the wounded and dying to the safety of the entrenched road, then send Buck on alone to take the wounded to the hospital in the wagon.

Now, as they hustled unarmed into the tangle of the thicket amid the fire-and-brimstone sounds and smells of muzzle fire, he had to laugh at the inanity of the moment. He was no soldier, but even he could see this was no land to be fighting in. The woods were so dense, there was no way to tell who was who and where anything was located. The place itself seemed devilishly designed to confuse and disorient anyone foolish enough to venture into it, and he now realized the dangers that he and his men faced—they would either get hit by one of the stray shots that filled the air like rain or wander right into an attacking wave of rebel soldiers. This last possibility would be the most ghastly for the former slaves, but if any of them were thinking about it, they certainly didn't show it. The gravediggers seemed possessed with an uncanny drive to rescue wounded Union soldiers, as they fearlessly and tirelessly worked to find them and carry them out to the waiting ambulances.

With the six men of his crew carrying three stretchers loaded up with ammunition, Jedediah took to toting two wooden crates of rifle cartridges under his arms. As soon as the party located the next pocket of wounded, they shed their ammunition onto the ground to be picked up later by some of the supporting troops, and gathered up the wounded to take them back to safety. With constant muzzle blasts coming from every direction, the seven of them worked with manic haste. Once the injured were on the stretchers, they headed back the way they had come. Maneuvering the wounded men through the tangled underbrush was difficult and time-consuming, and the gravediggers' bodies glistened with sweat, their faces stained with fatigue.

On one such trip with a load of wounded, Jedediah saw a flash of green on one of the stretchers and hustled over to see who it was. There lay a young boy in a green tunic, his right arm flopping as if it were boneless. Jedediah said passionately, "Ho, you're a sharpshooter!"

The boy, grimacing with pain from the jostling of the stretcher, gazed up at the tattooed giant who was leaning down to speak to him, and his eyes went wide with fear. In a trembling voice, he said, "Aye, I was. I think my sharpshooting days are done now."

Jedediah looked at the boy's mangled limb and nodded solemnly. "Where you from, son? I hail from Maine. I have many friends from my hometown in Company D, and I'm hoping they're all safe."

The boy took a moment to answer. "I'm from Burlington, Vermont. I was in Company F."

"You don't say. So, is Company D nearby?"

"They were just down the line from us." Then his face blanched and he went silent.

The black gravediggers were clearly interested in the conversation, and Jedediah knew he'd risk too much exposure if he asked the boy any more questions, so he let the stretcher bearers go on ahead of him. Turning briefly toward the constant sounds of the fight taking place in the enveloping forest, his eyes strained to see the invisible. Zachary Webster was right here—somewhere in this very jungle of trees and scrub! After all this time and so much effort, he was close enough to touch the man who had killed his brother.

The sounds of his men struggling around an obstacle brought him back from his thoughts, and he hurried to catch up to them. He knew his crew would most likely be recovering the wounded well into the night, and he only hoped that his path would eventually cross that of Company D. If so, he'd finally get his chance to kill Zachary Webster.

Chapter Forty-Nine

While most of the men of Company D rested, Webster was too busy listening to the sounds of the night to sleep. The day's intense fighting had ceased with sunset, but now the movement of men and wagons and the random caterwauling of the wounded penetrated the darkness. The blackness of his mood rivaled that of the nighttime woods. The events of the day only seemed to put a cap on the feelings he'd been having for quite some time, and he sat ruminating upon it all now. Being used as nothing more than general infantry troops seemed to him to be an unforgivable squandering of the sharpshooters' skills, and the asinine behavior of Captain Wentworth made him furious.

Before the furlough, he'd never had a reason to question the leadership—he just did whatever Captain Small told him to do. But since coming back to the war, he'd found himself increasingly filled with uncertainty. The new role of Company D and the new command of Captain Wentworth were two things that were allowing the saturating feelings of self-doubt to overwhelm him. He had to wonder what he was doing in this Virginia forest, huddling behind crude breastworks, and waiting for the orders that would make them targets, not soldiers.

The leafy canopy was too thick for him to see individual stars, but he did catch keyhole-sized snippets of the nighttime sky. It looked like a cloudless evening, and he assumed the stars were visible to anyone out in the open. He wondered what those stars saw when they looked down on this battlefield. Could they see him penned, far from the action, with the rest of these soldiers that the new leadership now seemed to think as common as mud? That the sharpshooters of the 2nd U.S.S.S would end the first day of the battle providing support for the ass-end of the force made him work hard to swallow the bile that rose in the back of his throat. He hoped the next day would present opportunities for him and his company to show their true skills. He'd been in enough battles to know that he and the other men were an inconsequential piece to a gigantic puzzle, but he also knew in his heart that, if allowed to do what they did best, they'd be able to kill some rebs, and that's all he could ask for these days.

After a brief snooze, Webster awoke with a start. He looked up toward the sky again and found it was starting to lighten with the promise of dawn. He wanted a cup of coffee to start the day, so he built a small fire and started boiling the water. Other men began to awaken and join him. They had not had a chance to drink their coffee or eat a quick breakfast before the officers nearby started barking orders. Captain Wentworth appeared suddenly, bellowing excited commands for the men to prepare for battle. Something about him seemed different, and it took a moment for Webster to discern what it was. The combination of the captain's new bravado and the thickness of his voice and movements were familiar enough to him— he'd seen many a man act the same way after a night of drinking alcohol. The realization that the captain was drunk made Webster angry.

The sharpshooters gathered up their arms and headed deeper into the woods. When they passed several regiments of Ward's brigade who were encamped behind their own breastworks and shallow trenches, the men of Company D understood that they would be leading this day's offensive. For some, this caused constricting pangs of fear, but for Webster, it unlocked the desire to finally kill someone that had festered throughout the impotent first day. He was honed, primed, and ready to do this, and his smile was cutting and sinister as he made his way forward.

When they finally came upon the Confederate pickets and began to exchange gunfire, there was not much resistance. After firing off a few rounds intended to stop the Union force, the rebel soldiers skedaddled. But before anyone could celebrate this false victory, several veterans reminded the men aloud that the pickets merely did what was asked of them—slow the advance and then retreat to warn the rest of the rebel force at the main line. The true tribulations still lay ahead of them.

Captain Wentworth yelled out, "All right, Company D, close ranks and form a tight fighting line!"

Several of the men, including Webster, looked at the captain in shock. Using that tactic in such a thick and inhospitable area was surely condemning many of the soldiers to death, and the veterans struggled to understand the apparent disregard of this fact by their leader. When they saw the massive line of the rest of II Corps forming behind them, they knew they were to be the very tip on the spearhead. Before the sharpshooters could process the ramifications of this, the bugles sounded for the entire force to charge the Confederate lines, and with a loud shout the men moved as quickly as the heavy brush would allow.

As Webster charged forward, his eyes made out the rebel position ahead, and he raised his rifle and started shooting at the best available targets.

Captain Wentworth worked his way over to him and shrilly shouted, "Don't take too much time to aim, men, just fire, fire, fire!"

Union muskets went off like thunder rolling through the forest. The noise was overwhelming, and the smoke blinding. The rebels answered the shots, and their bullets whizzed through the air. Most clipped off leaves or thunked into tree trunks, but some made the sickening sound of lead hitting a human body. Men all along the line began to fall, including many of the sharpshooters, but the next couple of Union volleys clearly broke the enemy's line in places. Confederate resistance seemed to diffuse instantly, which caused the soldiers around Company D to cheer and fire with greater enthusiasm.

The Union attack slowly moved forward for the next hour. Any gaps that developed in the enemy's line were like open doors that the men poured through, and they fought their way toward the retreating forces. As they fired at the fleeing men, Wyatt Morse leaned toward Webster and said with a smile, "You made it sound like we'd be living through Hell on earth in this battle, Mr. Webster, but this is easy going!"

Webster shook his head as he watched the young man work his way forward and continue firing his rifle. He had a premonition of impending danger, so he scampered over to a protective stand of trees and carefully aimed his rifle. Suddenly, Morse jumped backward and fell lifelessly to the ground, the victim of a Confederate bullet. A new intense round of muzzle firings were followed by a bloodcurdling wave of rebel yells. Webster looked over at another veteran sharpshooter nearby and yelled, "Reinforcements!"

The other man nodded and continued to fire his rifle. The volume of gunfire from the Confederate position seemed to increase, then it doubled, and then it quadrupled. The woods became a scene of complete carnage. The hail of incoming bullets hit anything that was standing open and exposed, and the sharpshooters dove for cover to return fire. Cannons could be heard booming from the north, and the sharpshooters were grateful they did not have to contend with those destructive forces in such a cramped and unprotected battle line.

When the men of the 2nd U.S.S.S. had exhausted their ammunition, the order was given to fall back and resupply. They worked their way slowly to the rear of the action, and set about filling their cartridge boxes with "forty dead men." They quietly assessed who was missing and prepared for the next round of fighting. There was no time to mourn their losses, as the sounds of the battle seemed to intensify. Once rearmed, the men of Company D were ready and eager to return to the action, but Captain Wentworth seemed to lose some of his fire and he hesitated with his order to get back into the fight. Webster and several other veterans noted the impact their captain's indecisiveness had on the men, so they took it upon themselves to rally the unit to rejoin the attack without a formal command from their leader.

For the next few hours, the scene was unlike anything that even the most battle-seasoned men had experienced before. While it was clear the rebel positions were reinforced and strengthened enough to launch a series of counterattacks, the Union soldiers held their ground with an equally furious defense. The smoke of the rifles and the density of the undergrowth of the forest made visibility so uncertain, unreal specters swooped in and swirled around them with impunity. Bullets continued to shriek through the air, small trees were severed by shot, and soldiers along the line fell with sickening regularity. The sharpshooters, their rifles almost too hot to hold from the constant firing, kept pouring shots into the Confederate line with abandon.

Then, before noon, just as it seemed the battle would develop into some kind of stalemate, several "White Diamonds" from Mott's brigade ran in full panic from the southern part of the line toward the sharpshooters of Company D. When someone asked what they were doing, one of the men responded in a shriek, "We're in full retreat! I ain't seen nothing like it—out of nowhere, a bunch of ghostly rebels showed up out of thin air, and they outflanked us in McAllister's brigade. It weren't just a few neither, and there's more and more of 'em flowing out of that unfinished rail bed and slicing their way across our lines! We gotta get the hell outta here!"

They quickly headed off into the dense vegetation. There was no time to contemplate their news or their departure, as the enemy bullets were continuing to come at the sharpshooters just as thick as before, and they were trying to return fire as best they could, even with their ammunition running perilously low. When a sudden wave of shot came from their flank and rear, they knew that the fleeing men had spoken the truth. Somehow the rebs had found a way to outflank the entire Union force, and the sharpshooters were in danger of being cut off from the rest of II Corps. As the men started to take aim at targets in front of and behind them, the bugler sounded the call to fall back.

Webster, with only a few more rounds left in his cartridge box, nodded to some of the nearby sharpshooters and got ready to beat a hasty retreat. However, just as they started to make their move, Joseph Lyman from Machias, Maine, was struck down. Webster had known him for three years, and he scurried over to help him up, but the young man's wounds were fatal. Webster did his best to comfort him; there was nothing else he could do. At the sudden scrotum-tightening shriek of a massive rebel yell coming from beyond their position to the west, he looked up to see if he could spot their advance, but the thick gun smoke made that impossible. When he glanced back down at Lyman, he was already dead. Crouching close to the body, he took aim at where he expected the advancing forces to come. He knew it was now too late to get away from the wave of rebel counterattackers about to flood the area in pursuit of the retreating Union Army, and he was prepared to fight to the end.

And while most men would have been numbed into inaction, Zachary Webster's survival instinct only heightened. There was no time to mourn Joseph Lyman, so he quickly rifled through the dead man's cartridge box and grabbed the extra rounds. Then he scanned his surroundings to find a better spot to mount his desperate defense. The nearby battered stub of a dead tree offered a small space within the trunk where he could hide. He had only a few rounds left for his rifle, but he had his bowie knife, his reb revolver, and his battle-tested skills—and these were all he had ever needed to make his way back from behind enemy lines in all of the previous battles. His breathing slowed and his mind became peaceful and still. He felt the power that comes from the certainty one feels when they know it is not their time to die, and he crawled into his hidey-hole to wait. He was ready for whatever might come his way.

When he saw the tattered uniforms of the small group of Confederate soldiers coming near to him, he recognized that they were skirmishers, and he knew his chances of survival were suddenly much improved. Instead of sending their reinforcements blindly in and risking the chance that they would stumble right into the defensive positions of the Union forces or get bottled up with their own flanking forces, the rebel leadership had sent skirmishers to probe the enemy first. This meant that the real force was being resupplied and rested before they mounted their counteroffensive. If Webster could take care of these first few skirmishers, he had a good shot at getting back to his unit.

The skirmishing line spread out and moved forward carefully but quickly. Three men advanced directly toward Webster's location, so he breathed slowly and let his body prepare to react lethally when they got close. When two of the men went to the blind side of the tree, he jumped out and thrust the butt of his rifle into the head of the lone soldier on his side. He had put his body weight behind the blow, and the sound of squashed skull bones was followed by the man crumpling to the forest floor. Then, swinging the gun end around, he bayonetted the throat of the closest soldier on the other side of the tree and pulled the trigger. The shot blew the man's throat apart, and the bullet traveled into the other soldier right behind him, hitting him in the shoulder and knocking him to the ground.

Webster did not hesitate. The rifle shot had alerted the other skirmishers in the area of his presence, and he needed to finish the job and keep ahead of their response. With the fluid movements of a dancer, he left his rifle and bayonet in the dead reb soldier while he leaped over this body, unsheathed his bowie knife, and grabbed the other wounded soldier's hair. The man was too dazed from the rifle shot to fend off his attacker, and Webster drew the knife blade across the man's throat with such speed and strength that he nearly decapitated him.

Turning quickly, he jerked his rifle from the neck of the dead reb and turned back toward the Union lines to make his break. That was when the revolver shot hit him in the left arm above the elbow. The bullet entered in the back of his arm, glanced off the bone, and exited through his bicep muscle. He didn't even glance at the wound, but spun instead and hurled his bowie knife into the chest of the soldier he had initially rifle-butted. Mortally wounded, the reb continued to stand unsteadily with his revolver pointed at Webster. Slowly the man's legs gave out and he sat down heavily like he was tired from doing too much labor. As his consciousness continued to ebb, the reb sat back and lay down on the forest floor with a loud sigh.

With his enemy dispatched, Webster went over to gather up his rifle. The pain of gripping it reminded him that he'd just been wounded, so he glanced down to see how bad his arm was. It seemed to be a flesh wound that could be patched up at a field hospital, so he rushed over to retrieve his knife before making his retreat. But as he bent down and pulled the knife out of the reb, the man's hand with the revolver lifted up off the forest floor like some kind of cobra and aimed at Webster. That was when he noticed the pistol had two barrels, and in that instant he recognized the weapon as a LeMat, a favorite of Confederate soldiers. Below the main rifled barrel, the small pistol also had a smooth-bored shotgun barrel. This now discharged in a bright flash and blew a hole through Webster's left leg, right above his ankle. The force of the shot spun him around, and he landed on his back with a thud, and his world went white with pain. The gravely wounded Confederate soldier now attempted to level the LeMat at the Yankee sharpshooter's head to finish the job, but he was too weak from blood loss and his hand shook wildly.

Webster opened his eyes and calmly looked over at the man. He wasn't ready to die, but he had known this day would come eventually, and he'd made his peace. But he refused to be shot with his eyes closed, and he stared defiantly at the reb and waited for the kill shot to come. His knife had fallen onto the forest floor too far away to get it quick enough, his rifle was empty, and his Confederate revolver was pinned beneath him in the back of his belt, so in fact, Webster was dead to rights.

A shot suddenly rang out and the rebel skirmisher's head blew apart. Surprised, Webster shifted his stare toward where the shot had come from. There stood Captain Wentworth with his revolver still pointed at the dead skirmisher.

"You came back for me, Captain?" Webster croaked.

The captain inhaled sharply, shook his head, and said in a hoarse whisper, "Not quite, Mr. Webster. When the call came for the retreat, I must have tripped on a root and fallen down and was left behind by the rest of the men. From the current useless state of my ankle, I'm guessing I've broken it. I must have lost consciousness for the briefest of moments, and when I awoke, all the other men in our unit were gone. When I tried to stand up, it became clear that I'm completely unable to put weight on my foot. That's when I saw your acts of savagery."

Another wave of intense pain hit Webster, and he clenched his jaw against it. Then the severity of the situation reasserted itself and he forced himself to sit up. He looked down at his wound and saw that the closeness of the pistol barrel had neatly cauterized the wound. It was bleeding, but not as profusely as he would have expected. He shook his head and said, "Well, two half-men can become one whole, I guess, sir. We can help each other—"

When he saw that the captain was now aiming his revolver directly down at his head, he coughed. "Excuse me, Captain Wentworth, but we don't have time for theatrics."

"Oh, Mr. Webster, this surely is not theatrics. When I assumed command, I was forced to read Captain Small's logs. Even though they were filled with your heroics, I could read some of the fear behind his words as he described the violence of your actions. I began to have an inkling as to what type of man you are, but now that I've actually seen you with my own eyes, I know you are not a man—you are a monster!"

Webster opened his arms wide and snarled, "Captain, look at the carnage around us. None of us are men anymore, we're soldiers! We kill; that's what we do. There are no differing levels of civilization allowed in warfare. Whenever I have killed, it's been because I've been ordered to do so or to ensure my survival. But look at my leg, sir. My fighting days are over. And I'd much prefer to spend the rest of the war with friends and family than in some rebel prison! Be reasonable! Holster your weapon and let us help one another escape. We have no time—"

"*You* have no time, Mr. Webster. Now that I know what kind of godless savage you truly are, I'm going to do something about it! Like a farmer who must put down an unhealthy animal, I deem you to be a creature who needs to die. So I will do the deed."

Webster's temper flared. "You're a pompous moron and a drunk. If you're the leadership that's supposed to guide the Union Army to victory in this war, I want no part of it."

"Oh, don't worry, you won't have a part in any of it."

The captain took aim and drew in a breath, but before he could pull the trigger, his head split open and he fell forward, pinning Webster to the forest floor.

With survival still uppermost in his mind, Webster fought the urge to wipe away the gore from the captain's exploded head and move to avoid the warmth of the dying man's urine dripping down over his thighs. Clearly, a nearby Confederate sharpshooter had just shot the captain, and now, with the dead man draped over him and his own face looking bloody, his only salvation lay in playing dead. Surreptitiously, he moved his arms to hide his Sharps rifle under him and make sure his bowie knife was safely tucked next to his ribs. Then he closed his eyes, froze his movements, and slowed his breathing to appear dead.

With his eyes shut, he only could listen for whatever might happen next. He heard the footfalls of the Confederate soldiers swarming past his location in pursuit of the retreating Union forces. They were too focused on what lay ahead, and barely took notice of the vast numbers of dead and dying bodies they passed. When Webster heard unabated gunfire to the east, he knew that the two forces had found each other again and his ruse had worked.

He had avoided detection by this first round of the counterattacking enemy, but he knew that the most dangerous times for him were about to begin. If the rebs could hold their new position, they would begin to set up supply lines to support the pressing brigades, and it would be the men of these units who might have the time to check the dead for weapons and other salvageable items. Webster had seen firsthand the nearly naked corpses on the battlefields, stripped of anything useful by marauding and needy soldiers, and he knew that one of these scavengers might discover him. He could only hope they would wait until nighttime and that he could stay alive long enough to figure out his next move.

Chapter Fifty

Jedediah had never seen anything that equaled the horrible sights he was witnessing. After recovering dead and dying Union soldiers throughout the night, using handheld torches and the screams and groans of the wounded to locate them in the abysmally dark and entwining woods, he had asked for the chance to rest his unit at the field hospital in preparation for the next action. His request had been granted, and the men had slept for a few hours under the wagon. The insects were horrendous, but the inside of the wagon was saturated by the drying blood of injured soldiers, and since none of the men wanted to be covered with it more than they already were, they chose to sleep outside. The sheer horror of the day haunted them all, however, and they were unable to close their eyes without seeing, hearing, or smelling what they had just lived through.

The first rays of dawn came without fanfare at the field hospital. Big fires and lamps had burned throughout the night to keep the facility operating, and the vast sea of wounded and dead seemed as large in the exposed farmyard as it had when the sun had set. The sounds of far-off gunfire signaled the start of renewed fighting, and the surgeons, their eyes leaden and gray with fatigue and their leather aprons coated with coagulated blood, looked in that direction and sighed with disgust before heading back into the surgery tent to resume their endless work. Meanwhile, the exhausted nurses and stewards flitted through the throngs of wounded like bumblebees in their constant attempt to provide support to the worst off and to manage the overflowing numbers of those who could be saved.

A Union officer came over to Jedediah and asked bluntly if his gravediggers could be trusted to work without their white leaders present. The number of dead bodies at the hospital had made it necessary to start digging graves right there on the farm, but their wagon was still needed for the continued transport of the wounded. Jedediah looked at the man to analyze his intentions, but he seemed genuinely in need of the extra help, so he nodded his assent. When he announced this decision to the men, they glanced over at the corpses and closed their eyes to the unpleasantness that lay ahead. They assured Jedediah that they would give the brave dead men a proper burial.

It was just before he and Tom Buck embarked toward the Union lines at the junction of Brock Road and Orange Plank Road that Jedediah Stiller and Catherine Brandford saw one another for the first time. She was staring directly at him when their eyes met and locked, but his mind was sluggish with disbelief. When uncertainty turned into recognition, his facial expression changed from a neutral glance to a small, knowing grin. Catherine's face, however, remained blank as she watched him drive away from the hospital in the wagon with the black crow painted on its side.

•　　•　　•　　•　　•

For the rest of that day, the gravedigger wagon was in constant motion. Jedediah and Mr. Buck lost track of how many trips they made to and from the battlefield. As soon as they pulled up to the Federal entrenchments, stretcher-bearers and wounded soldiers filled the back of their wagon to capacity. There seemed to be no one in charge to supervise this process, and the wounded went into any available vehicle to get to the hospital as quickly as possible. When Jedediah's laden wagon arrived back at the field hospital, he and Tom Buck helped the stewards unload the contents with the same breakneck speed. But they both noticed that the unloading area was moving farther and farther away from the main tents of the hospital as the ever-increasing numbers of wounded occupied more of the ground outside the surgical tents. As soon as their wagon was emptied, it was immediately sent back out for another load, and Jedediah caught only the merest glimpses of both his gravediggers and Catherine Brandford throughout the remainder of that day.

Jedediah and Mr. Buck were at the front as the forest suddenly began spewing Union forces in retreat. As the wave of blue-uniformed men fled from the trees, ran across Brock Road, and jumped behind the log breastworks, the apparent collapse of the Union line threw the entire area into mayhem. The flurry of action and gunfire caused the horses and mules of the waiting wagons to attempt to bolt from their restraints. Jedediah held tight to his reins, but his mules were nearly unstoppable in their desire to flee. Only their fatigue from pulling the wagon for days on end enabled him to hold them.

The pandemonium was further heightened when a group of green-tunic-clad sharpshooters came out from behind the trunks of the trees, firing at the unseen enemy pursuing them. Just as these men made it to safety with the rest of the Union soldiers, the woods across the road erupted with a volley of Confederate muzzle fire. Jedediah struggled to get his wagon safely away from the action and back on its way to the hospital, but now he knew the battle line had been pushed back to the road. And although it initially appeared the defenders had the advantage behind their built-up protection, he saw that the vicious attack had ignited fires behind them and along their wooden defenses. He yelled at his mules, hit them hard with the reins, and let their natural fear fuel their hurried pace, for he had a kernel of apprehension in his gut that the whole battle was lost and he and his gravediggers were now in dire danger.

Chapter Fifty-One

Webster had remained absolutely still for what seemed like hours, and his body ached from the effort. The wound on his leg now throbbed and burned like nothing he had ever felt in his life, and his left arm was as stiff as a piece of pine. He kept waiting for enemy soldiers to investigate the area, but it seemed that this section of the forest was no longer of much interest to anyone. From the gun and cannon reports off to the east and the new sounds of movement to the north, he had to assume that the Confederate attack had pushed forward enough for them to use Orange Plank Road as the main avenue of their resupply and reinforcement. If that were so, he might get the chance to start moving and get away. Unfortunately, he was unsure exactly where he could escape to. The line of rebels facing the Union forces were blocking his pathway to freedom, and he'd have to somehow circumnavigate them if he wanted to reach any kind of safety. Exactly how he was going to do this on one leg and with serious wounds he wasn't sure, but he was a survivor, and he had to try.

When he reopened his eyes for the first time, the brightness of the daylight nearly blinded him. He lay completely still to let his pupils adjust, and when he could make out the leaves in the treetops again, he knew it was time to survey his surroundings. He turned his head both ways to see if there was anyone lurking nearby that he could not hear, but there were only dead bodies. He slowly pushed up on the leaden weight of Captain Wentworth's corpse, and his wounded arm rebelled with pain. He tried again with more force from his right arm until the body rolled off of him. The sound of it rustling onto the ground seemed outlandishly loud, and

Webster froze with fear that the noise had just given away his position. He waited for any sign that he'd been spotted, but nothing happened. After resting for a few minutes, he realized he didn't need to be so vigilant, for there were, in fact, no enemy soldiers anywhere near him.

He sat up and immediately vomited. Overwhelmed by the pain of his wounds, the dead captain's grotesquely gaping head wound, and the tension of the moment, his body had responded involuntarily, and he was angry at himself for succumbing to such weakness. He looked again at Captain Wentworth. Due to the startling physical resemblance between the two of them, seeing the dead captain was unnervingly like looking down at a dead version of himself. As a matter of fact, if the rebel sharpshooter hadn't dispatched the captain when he did, the man would have pulled the trigger and made Webster's face look identical to the one that now stared lifelessly up at him. This grim irony made him initially chuckle with black humor, but then a thought that had buried itself in his psyche began to dig its way out. As his eyes now quickly made their way down to the shoulder straps on the captain's tunic, the two pairs of bars within the golden rectangular patches shone with a blinding brilliance that made him smile. His plan was starting to take shape.

Getting his own coat off was far more difficult than he thought it would be. His wounded left arm made the work painful and awkward, and he kept stopping to listen for anyone approaching. Finally, he had it off and could examine the entrance and exit wounds on his arm. The bleeding from them had nearly stopped, and although the surrounding skin was horribly discolored with bruising, he knew it wouldn't kill him. He leaned over and started working on unbuttoning the captain's tunic. Removing a jacket from a dead man while being confined to the ground by his own wounds proved to be a laborious chore, but Webster was resolute in his desire to remain calm throughout the endeavor. With this finally completed, he needed to lie back and rest.

He continued to listen intently for any sounds in his vicinity, but could hear only the noise of the ferocious battle in the distance and the massive efforts to resupply Lee's army along the road. As soon as he felt strong enough, he sat up and started putting on the captain's tunic. Even though he knew it was dangerous to expend the energy, he then took the time to put his coat onto the dead captain. And by doing so, the transformation was irrevocably complete. Zachary Webster had been killed while Captain Ellison Wentworth III was gravely wounded and currently missing in action.

The exertion of this was almost too much, so he lay back and rested again for a moment. When he'd caught his breath, he sat up to take a look at his leg wound. He knew it was severe, but his initial glimpse of the blown away and burned flesh, the exposed and shattered leg bone, and the useless foot dangling by a thick cord of skin made him gasp. It wasn't strictly necessary, but he took off the captain's belt and made a tourniquet above the wound on his leg. He needed to remain conscious as long as possible, and he knew that any further loss of blood would make that harder. With some effort, he cut thin strips from the nearest dead reb's shirt and wrapped the wound with them. The rough cloth blotted up his blood. He looked around and found several branches on the ground that were the right length to provide some support and act like a splint. All this activity was exhausting, but the sight of a longer piece of wood energized him enough to crawl over to it. As he reached for his new crutch, the rich and fertile odors of the springtime earth filled his nostrils and took his mind away from the grim realities and off to better memories of life on the farm before the war.

He sheathed his knife and put the leather rifle sling over his head so that the rifle rested on his back. Then, using his crutch, he stood up and rested his weight on his good leg. Again he listened for nearby sounds, and when he heard nothing to worry him, he started the awkward process of hobbling through the woods. According to his calculations, he had just over a mile to go to get back to the Union lines, and at this pace, that would take him several hours.

He'd gone about fifty feet before he needed to stop and rest. He carefully leaned against a tree trunk and took several deep breaths. Before continuing on, he turned to look one last time at the dead bodies he was leaving behind, especially that of Zachary Webster. With the assurance that his movements had not been detected by anyone, he hobbled onward. He knew how to use the terrain to his advantage, even if he was tired beyond hope and woozy from his wounds, and he worked from tree to tree, thicket to thicket as he cautiously headed toward the rumblings of the pitched battle to the east.

Making his way in this manner proved to be maddeningly difficult. The unevenness of the land, the tangle of tree roots and brush, and the snagging of his crutch tip on the obstacles made his forward progress slow to a snail's pace. Between rest breaks, stopping to listen for the sounds of the battle, and constantly disentangling himself from the brambles, Webster was not at all surprised to notice that the treetops were beginning to darken with the impending nightfall. He continued to use the closest reports of gunfire as his compass, and as he limped painfully toward those sounds, he came across areas that were littered with evidence of the day's fight.

Pockets of silent and misshapen dead bodies lay close by struggling wounded soldiers, who called out to no one and begged for mercy. He came upon piles of empty ammunition crates and little caches of personal effects discarded by the attacking and retreating soldiers, and all of this told him he was headed in the right direction. He knew he should probably stop to comfort those wounded men still alive or search for usable items in the debris, but the onset of darkness urged him to keep moving. With nightfall, there would be a cessation of fighting, and this meant not only the loss of his ability to find his way through these bewildering woods, it would also usher in the time when soldiers wanting to procure new boots or more ammunition, or to pocket some small personal riches, would commence their grim nocturnal search.

He came to a slough of fresh water, and lowered himself down to drink from it. The act of sitting was a challenge, and in the end, he flopped heavily onto the damp soil. He looked around before rolling onto his belly to drink like an animal. As he drank his fill, his senses were on high alert. His ears scanned for footsteps and his eyes looked for movement. Once sated, he fought the urge to sit against a nearby rock to rest. He knew he was racing time, so he dragged himself up again, maneuvered around the small pool, and continued on his way to get as close to the Confederate lines as was safe. With those in sight, he figured he could stop to rest and come up with a plan for getting to his own forces alive. He knew his chances for success were quite slim, but he quickly and quietly loaded his rifle with one more shot, for he needed to be prepared to fight his way out of this mess.

Chapter Fifty-Two

When the sun finally rose on the third day of the battle, the situation at the Carpenter Farm had improved only slightly from the day before. The grounds were still littered with the bodies of the wounded, but because other Union Army hospitals had opened in nearby Fredericksburg, the unending flood of ambulances had abated. The hospital staff now had a medical team assessing the wounded right at the battle line, and only those who needed immediate surgery or those who could be patched up and returned to their units were now being sent to the field hospital. The rest were transported directly to the more permanent facilities in the east. Even some of the unfortunate souls who had been waiting on the lawn of the farm for the last day and a half were now being reloaded into wagons and joining those caravans to receive some long overdue medical care.

The morning revealed another marked difference, but it took Catherine a while to figure out exactly what it was. Then she noticed the songbirds again. Now that the fighting had died down, their heavenly warbling melodies filled the morning air even louder than the groaning and crying of the men awaiting surgery. Only intermittent musket fire could be heard far off in the distance, and after the frenzied killing of the last two days, the world seemed to Catherine to be catching its breath.

But she knew better. Word had come down from the Union headquarters that General Grant was ordering his generals to prepare their men to march south that very night in an attempt to catch Lee unawares in Spotsylvania. The staff members at the field hospital were to begin preparations to move to another location closer to the impending next rounds of battle. Not only were the logistics of such a move dizzying, what with the processing of all the men still on the farm grounds, repacking, and moving to the new location, but after the horrors of the most recent fighting, the peacefulness of the morning was addictive. Catherine found herself standing in the warm dawning sunlight with her eyes closed as she listened to the beauty of the bird songs, but the moment was dashed when a gruff steward brusquely told her to report to the surgery tent to get her orders for the day.

There, Catherine was told that the medical team at the battle line along Brock Road had worked continuously throughout the night, and they needed to be relieved. She was assigned to report there, posthaste, to be part of the relief staff. The chance to see where the actual fighting took place scared her, but being nearer to Jedediah Stiller and his wagon of death was more frightening to her. She'd seen his gravedigger wagon several times as he ferried injured soldiers from the battle while the black men of his unit tirelessly worked to bury the dead on the edges of the farm's fields. Whenever she'd been unlucky enough to make eye contact with the tattooed giant as he unloaded his cargo, she'd felt her face flush every time he grinned wickedly in response to her gaze.

Now that she'd seen the sea of dead coming from this battle, Catherine had very little hope that Zachary Webster had survived unscathed. She knew he was a veteran of such infamous battles as Antietam, Chancellorsville, and Gettysburg, but she could not let herself believe that any of those battles had been as bloody and violent as this one. That she hadn't seen him come into the hospital yet gave her a tiny glimmer of hope, but if he had survived the horrific fighting, that only meant that he was still alive for Jedediah Stiller to hunt down and kill.

But as Catherine and her team took their position in the processing station behind the earthworks along Brock Road and began the overwhelming task of evaluating the scores of wounded there, the true scope and cost of this battle hit her. Because the forest in front of her was only one of the two major battlefields of the Battle of the Wilderness, as they were calling it now, she was suddenly and painfully aware of the true magnitude of death and destruction. The number of men maimed or killed in this three-day battle was almost inconceivable, and as Catherine tried to recollect how many battles there'd been up to this point and guess how many were yet to be fought, a sour anger seeped into her stomach as she wondered when the country would ever come to its senses and stop the bloodletting long enough to end this ridiculous war. The mangled and irreparable men flowing from the battle and to the hospital made her pessimistic about what would be left of the country that was fighting so violently to reunite itself. And if that nation ended up broken by the very war being waged to save it, what sane person would be able to say it had all been worth it?

The occasional reports of muzzle fire up and down the line temporarily broke the fragile peace along the earthworks, but most conceded that the real fighting was now over. The two armies had come to another stalemate, and it appeared the Confederate leaders were pulling their soldiers away and southward to regroup. Courageous Union soldiers continued to drag wounded men from the no-man's-land between the two armies, and although they had their rifles trained on one another, both sides refused to fire on the recovery parties even though they were easy targets. Instead, the soldiers amused themselves by shooting lost ramrods at one another. These slender steel rods were jammed into the gun barrels with the tulip ends protruding and then shot at the opposing line. As they whipped through the air, they hissed like artillery shells and usually landed harmlessly in the woods behind the defensive positions. With each salvo, the men of both sides laughed and cheered at the macabre humor of it all.

While the medical team examined yet another wounded soldier, Catherine sniped with frustration, "Just how many men are still trapped in those thickets, behind the enemy line, dying slowly of their wounds?"

One of the soldiers standing nearby shook his head. "Would be a terrible way to go, Miss, that's for sure. You'd hope the rebs would take care of 'em, one way or another, so that them men didn't have to suffer anymore, but that ain't likely. But some of them wounded get themselves out on their own. Matter of fact, a green-jacketed captain came crawling out of them woods just a few minutes ago. His foot was near blown off, but he crawled across the road to safety!"

Catherine's stomach knotted with a sudden foreboding. "What? Where is this man now?"

"I saw a small wagon take him and another wounded man to the hospital in Fredericksburg. Damnedest thing I've seen! He come right out from the trees next to the reb positions like he was some kind of shadow, and they never even seen him till it was too late!"

The wounded man that the doctor was examining began to thrash about, and he called for help from the stewards and Catherine, but she remained standing and looked around for the wagon that the other soldier had just mentioned. She couldn't see it in the endless traffic on the road, but a small commotion did catch her eye. The familiar wagon with a black crow on the side was speeding away amid a shower of verbal abuses hurled by the men who'd expected it to stop to be loaded with the wounded. The wagon's mule team was not in a full gallop, but they were racing faster than the other wagons—as if the driver was pursuing someone. Instantly, Catherine knew that Jedediah Stiller had seen Zachary Webster being taken away in the cart and was chasing him down. Ignoring the shouts of the doctor in charge, she looked around frantically for some way to join in the chase.

When another ramrod came in low, hitting one of the nearby wagon drivers and knocking him off his seat, Catherine saw her opportunity. She sprinted to the ramshackle ambulance with the faded blue spade of II Corps on it and hopped up onto the bench. The men around the wagon were too preoccupied laughing at the wounded driver to stop her, and she slapped the reins furiously on the horses' backs. They bolted forward with a surge of power as she struggled to control them. Sounds of disbelief and anger echoed behind her, but she kept her eyes on the target up ahead and let the horses run. She was now in pursuit of Jedediah Stiller's wagon, which meant that she was right behind her Zachary.

Chapter Fifty-Three

It had been the lack of any kind of symbol on the wagon's canvas covering that first alerted Jedediah to its presence. He didn't know what all of the insignias meant, but the absence of one was rare. In the heat of the moment near the front, no one else seemed to notice the small wagon's lack of identification, and after it was loaded with two wounded soldiers, it was quickly sent on its way. Jedediah watched with interest as it calmly took its place among the others on the road, but he was careful not to attract too much attention by staring. Just before he'd seen the wagon, he'd heard the soldiers around him talking excitedly about the brave sharpshooter captain who had crawled out from behind the enemy's line. Without ever hearing a name, he knew it had to be Zachary Webster. Only a snake of a man like him could have slithered out of a deadly situation like that and survived. With no warning, Jedediah had thrown all caution to the wind and taken off after the emblemless wagon.

He now slowed his pursuit because he couldn't just catch up and kill the man with so many witnesses around—not if he wanted to escape and survive. And he did want that. He wanted to finish what he had come to do and then return safely to Ezra and Miryam. He had witnessed enough of this accursed war to want nothing more to do with it, and he saw it clearly for what it was—an insatiable devourer of youth. It was a soulless consumer of young boys and fresh ideals, and it was gorging itself on everything it touched. So even though he was eager to get his revenge and go back to the peacefulness of the salt marsh, he had to keep himself calm enough to wait and see where the little wagon was going before he made his move. If he could follow it to just the right location, he knew he could overtake it, kill Zachary Webster, leave the gravedigger unit in the moderately capable hands of Tom Buck, and then head northward to home.

A commotion behind him abruptly drew his attention away from the small wagon for a moment. An out-of-control ambulance was barreling toward him—not an uncommon occurrence at the lines, as teams of horses and mules often panicked from the gunfire and broke away. But this wagon seemed to have only one small person aboard it, and they were frantically trying to get control over the team. When he could see the driver better, he was shocked to realize it was none other than Catherine Brandford. He smiled wryly; the young woman's spunk and determination continued to amaze him. Not only had she somehow become a nurse and gotten down to the battlefield, but now she had correctly figured out that Zachary Webster was in that little wagon and had procured an ambulance to give chase. Jedediah shook his head at her sheer bravery and perseverance—but then again, he thought, Jonathan sure could pick 'em!

The memory of his dead younger brother empowered him to finish his task, and he turned his attention back to the unmarked wagon.

But it was not there. The steady train of wagons stretched out in front of him as far as the eye could see, but the little cart he was looking for was no longer in its place. He looked around but saw only Catherine Brandford quickly catching up to him with a mounted soldier in pursuit behind her. She was going to have to explain her actions when she got caught, and Jedediah knew that would stop her for a while. No one seemed overly worried about *his* flight anymore, so he just needed to remain calm and figure out where the hell that little wagon had gone.

Chapter Fifty-Four

Although Webster thought he was awake, his vision was blocked by what felt like an impenetrable curtain of darkness. With no vision, his nose and ears began to process what was around him. However, his brain was working too sluggishly to correctly interpret the information. He could smell coffee brewing, the aromas of roasting meat, and the thick smoke of a wood fire. He could hear the fire crackling nearby, and wherever he was, it was quite warm. There seemed to be a rough woolen blanket over him, and it was chafing his skin. Gut-wrenching waves of pain wracked his body periodically, and these were growing in intensity. He could hear people shuffling over a dirt floor and the hushed tones of their talking, but in the midst of his haze, their voices sounded more like the buzzing and humming of insects. He wanted to see where he was and who was nearby, but when he tried to open his eyes, they felt like they were glued shut. The sense of panic was growing, and he tried to bring his hands up to his face to force his eyes open, but he was tied down to the frame of the bed. The effort tired him enough that he needed to stop and rest for a moment.

The smells, sounds, and sensations of his situation suddenly transported him to the kitchen of his childhood house in Augusta. His parents were both there, and he was eagerly waiting for dinner while warming himself by a large fire in the hearth. He saw Elijah carving a small figurine out of a block of cedar, and the young boy was focused so intently on his task, he didn't look up. His father came over and patted him firmly on the shoulder, and he felt warm pangs of love for the man... And with that, he knew he was dreaming. His father was dead and in the family barn.

But even though he knew the visions were unreal, he wanted to relive the memories of his father being alive and his family together and happy, and a part of him fought to stay in that comfortable dreamworld—to be young and untainted by this war.

Ironically, it was the unmistakably sweet residual odor of ether in his nostrils that brought him to his senses. Once he identified the smell, he knew he was in a hospital, and the realities of his situation came flooding back. He'd been wounded when that rebel skirmisher had shot him through the leg with the LeMat revolver. After he'd made his way through the woods behind the enemy and then clawed his way to safety at the Union lines with much fanfare, he had a faint recollection of being loaded into a small wagon before everything went dark. Because of the ether smell, he figured he must have been taken to the field hospital for treatment of his wounds.

His left foot suddenly produced a completely new sensation. At first it felt like tingling pinpricks, but then it became a harsh and fiery pain that pulsed up his leg and smothered those other initial feelings. Because of his bindings, he could not reach down to touch it, so he tried to wiggle his toes. As soon as he did this, he knew. There was no foot attached to his left leg anymore—it had been amputated. Since none of the veteran soldiers had an optimistic view of surviving a visit to a Union field hospital, he grimaced heavily at his situation. He'd always figured it was better to die on the battlefield because, at least there, you usually died whole. In a hospital, you were just as likely to die with parts of you in bins, buckets, and piles on the ground. Webster envisioned his own foot lying atop the other bodiless limbs near the surgery tent, and he gritted his teeth with pain and anger over his loss.

He desperately wanted to see, so he forced his eyes open. As his vision adjusted to the faint light of his surroundings, he saw that he wasn't inside of a hospital tent. Instead, he was in a crudely built cabin. As he scanned his surroundings, the face of a woman appeared over him. She was not very pretty, but she was smiling. She reached down to stroke his cheek, and he could see the filth between her fingers and around her wrist. Surely this meant she wasn't a nurse, and he now fully comprehended that he was not, in fact, in a hospital. He began to writhe against the restraints.

"Yo, Yankee, stop your squirmin'!" A man's southern drawl sliced through the darkness.

Webster turned his head to look at the speaker. In a battered chair sat a man in a tattered and ill-fitting Union uniform. He spoke angrily. "Hey! Stop your squirmin' before I put a bullet in your head! If it weren't for my sister here, you'd already be dead, Yank, and that's the God's honest truth. But she's got a sweet spot for ya in her...heart."

The woman grinned, showing a mouth filled with browned and missing teeth. "Oh, that's so true, lover. I've got big plans for you!" She reached down and grabbed Webster's crotch through the blanket. "And they're gonna get even bigger with some help, right, my sweet?"

Webster struggled to understand. "Where am I? Who are you?"

The man stood up and mock-bowed. "Ah, forgive me, I ain't mindin' my manners, am I? Welcome to Oakleaf. Or what's left of it, I should say. I am Sir Jeffery and this is Lady Amanda."

The woman giggled and curtsied awkwardly.

Webster was still confused. When another wave of pain made him roll his eyes, the man thrust a finger at him. "Oh, so you don't think we look like sophisticated and cultured Southern planters, huh, Yankee? Well, I gotta tell ya a secret—we ain't. Before the war, we were just lowly servants workin' for the Wellington family who owned this-here farm. My sister helped Mrs. Wellington run the main house, and she was the nanny who took care of the wee Wellington tykes. Me, I was the one in charge of their livestock. Mr. Wellington relied on me to manage all the siring, birthing, mending, and slaughtering on the farm. Mind you, I ain't sayin' it was a perfect life, but we were happy, weren't we, Sister?"

"Oh, yes!"

"But war changes everything, don't it, Yank? Mr. Wellington, it turns out, was a man who could see the future with great clear-sightedness, and he knew exactly what was gonna happen to this place during the war. So he made arrangements for his family to go somewhere safe, far away from here. His wife and young children were sent down to her mother's family plantation south of Richmond, while he enlisted as a major in the Confederate Army. But he insisted that my sister and me stay and keep the place runnin' as long as we could. Knowing what I know now, though, I guess he thought we were expendable."

"Naw, Brother, I cannot allow myself to believe that. I do not think Mr. Wellington could foresee the pure hellishness that was gonna descend upon this place! No one could! I think he thought we were gonna be safe here."

The man looked at her and cocked his head. He started to say something, but then turned back to Webster. "Ya see, my sister and I've been stuck in the very middle of this bloodsucking war from the moment the first shooting started. In the beginning, it was our own Confederate Army that needed all the farm's livestock and supplies for their war effort. It didn't matter to them that they were leavin' us with nothin' to eat and we were sure to be facing starvation. We had the foodstuffs and they wanted it; they wanted it all. I guess they thought us loyal Southerners would jump up and down with happiness when they took everything useful or edible. Then the Yankee Army came stormin' through here on their way south. They was all swelled up with untested bravado, and they even set up headquarters in the manor house to plan their first doomed offensive. And them Yankee generals lived like Southern planters while they tried to figure out how to defeat General Lee, and they let their soldiers take anything they wanted, including my sister. Ah, them Yankees loved my sister. Raped her raw, they did.

"Then, when the mighty Union Army got its arse kicked and had to run with its tail between its legs like a beaten dog back north, they decided to burn down the manor house and the fields to punish us. There's nothin' left of it but a pile of ashes. That's all the Union Army left us to live on—ashes. Things looked mighty bleak for my sister and me, and I weren't too sure how we were gonna make it.

"But when them soldiers kept comin' back for what's between my sister's legs, she and me came to the quick conclusion that we couldn't give the milk away for free. After all, if there's a need and you got exactly what fills that need, you're obligated to give what you got, but at a reasonable rate, ain't that right? As Amanda's...uh...manager, it's my job to make sure nobody wears her out...down there. I mean, even in them children's stories she used to read to the little Wellingtons, it was clear it takes some effort to keep that goose that's layin' them golden eggs from runnin' dry. Why would my sister be any different?

"Then the proud men of the South pushed the Yankees clear out of this part of Virginia, and we thought we'd be in better straights. But it turned out that them 'gentlemen soldiers' had the same basic need as the Yankees. I guess they all just wanted to get away from the horribleness of the fightin' by bein' with the sweetness of my sister. And sure enough, business was good during those days, even as our humble abode was overrun by both sides at different times. Truth be told, me and my sister weren't never sure who she was servicing till they come to pay us. Once we had a handful of 'greenbacks' or 'graybacks,' we'd know who our customers were! And I do so hate bein' given the latter—they ain't fit to paper the outhouse these days!"

Webster tried to sit up. "But what am *I* doing here? I didn't come for any of that. You two snatched me up in your wagon and brought me here. Why?"

The woman giggled. "Well, darlin', at first you were supposed to be our supper."

"*What?*"

The man pointed his finger at him like a pistol. "With you Yankees stealin' everything or the Confederacy borrowing whatever we foraged, nobody left us a damn thing to eat! What were we supposed to do, just twiddle our thumbs while we starved to death? We couldn't eat dirt, and we got nothing *but* dirt and ashes around here. We sure as hell couldn't live off of that! But after the battle at Fredericksburg in '62, this whole area was awash with the dyin', and me and my sister knew we had the answer to our prayers. When you're starvin', Yank, ya don't got the luxury of a bellyful of ethics to feed ya—you hafta just eat whatever is available. So we turned to what was at hand, which in our case turned out to be all of them wounded soldiers. And that's how we survived."

Webster couldn't disguise his shock and disgust. Even with everything he'd seen and heard on the battlefields, this was by far the worst. "So you two are nothing but dirty whores and cannibals?"

The woman caressed his cheek. "Ooh, those are such ugly terms, don't ya think? What we are, Mr. Yankee, are survivors. You know what that means, 'cause you're one, too. We heard how ya made your way behind enemy lines. Now, did ya happen to kill anyone on your way? Did ya hurt anybody? Maim anybody? 'Course ya did. You did whatever ya had to do to survive. So, ya see, you ain't no better than us."

"That's right, Yank, you ain't in no position to judge none."

"But you *are* in the position for some fun, honeycakes!" Amanda purred.

"The only reason you ain't dead and in the smokehouse with that other soldier with the slashed throat right now is 'cause my sister took a shine to ya. So I wouldn't be disrespectin' her none, if I was you, Yankee."

The woman tittered. "That's right! Through our own guile, my brother and me have put food on the table and money in our pockets, and we've survived in a world that's been so upheaved it ain't recognizable no more. But whenever it's all put right again, I know we'll go back to our normal ways. Sure, we may look back at these times with a smattering of shame, but who cares? The fact is, we will have survived."

"Naw, Sister, I ain't gonna have no shame. Not me. We lived through this hell and we done what we had to—I ain't got no regrets."

She gave her brother a look of contempt. "'Course not, Brother. I've been doin' most of the dirty work."

The man's eyes grew large and menacing, but he did not speak for a while. Then he said, "Let's not get into this now—not in front of our guest and your new boyfriend."

Webster fought the restraints, but the ropes were tied tight and the bed frame felt too strong to break. The pain in his leg thumped with ever-increasing intensity. When he spoke, his voice came out tight through his clenched teeth. "It doesn't sound like I have much of a future to ponder, anyway. I figure you're gonna kill me and eat me eventually."

The man chuckled. "Well now, Yank, you ain't wrong about none of that—your days are truly numbered. But all of our days are like that from the time we're birthed, ain't they? At least ya know you have the chance to die with a smile on your face. After all, my sister is gonna give herself to ya for free. It's true that whenever she gets bored of you, we'll have to make some decisions about your fate, but oh, what a pleasurable stretch you're in for before that time! Many a man would want to be in your place right now."

The woman suddenly leaned closer to Webster and put her hand on his chest. She started moving it down his body, pushing the blanket away as she went. When she got near his belt line, she licked her lips suggestively. "Oh, we're gonna have so much fun, you and me! I'm gonna leave ya breathless, my young lover. But we need to build up your strength a little before you and me can really play. My brother, as skilled as he is with doctorin' cattle and horses, ain't no trained medical doctor. His surgery to take your foot was good enough, but you and me may be pressed to fully enjoy our time together. While Jeffery is doin' chores, we'll get the privacy we need. I promise you the ride of your life, boy! But ya need to get your strength...up! Hee-hee!"

She stood up, went over to a table in the shadows, and came back holding a battered metal plate with some food on it. Webster could see a few pieces of meat and half a potato covered with a gray gravy that resembled wallpaper paste. He shook his head. "I am not eating that."

The woman smiled faintly. "Oh, darlin', yes you are. If ya don't eat what I offer, I will reach right down to your stump and make it *really* hurt. I will twist it and bang on it till you vomit from the pain. And I will keep doin' that till you eat this or you die. So ya see, you *will* eat this. You will eat whatever I give ya!"

She pulled up a chair next to the bed and sat down. Her face took on the expression of a tender nurse, and she cooed, "Come on, lover, eat somethin'. It will all be worthwhile, I promise!" She grabbed a piece of meat with her grubby fingers and brought it to his mouth.

He didn't want to eat it, but his stomach heaved at the thought of her inflicting more pain upon him. He parted his dry lips to make a small slot, and she slid the morsel inside. As soon as it touched his tongue, he tasted an unfamiliar tang. He pursed his lips to spit it out, but she wagged her finger at him.

"Don't you dare spit it out! If ya do, I swear I'll make ya beg for your momma! Chew it up and swallow it. I need ya to have your strength. Eat it!"

He looked into her eyes, and the craziness in them convinced him that she would do what she was promising, and he knew he could not endure such torture, so he did as instructed and chewed the meat enough to swallow it. He closed his eyes and willed his stomach to accept the putrid offering. When he opened his eyes again, another piece of meat was coming toward him.

The madwoman said soothingly, "See? That wasn't so bad, was it? You just need a couple more bites, and we can get to the fun stuff, lover. Come on, just a couple more bites."

Suddenly, the man started laughing mockingly in the shadows. His cackling even made the woman turn toward him in annoyance. "Don't say a word, Jeffery! Not yet. Let the boy get his sustenance before you have your cruel fun."

The man's laugh was now almost hysterical, and he shook his head at his sister. "I'm just tryin' to imagine what's goin' through that Yankee's mind right now. It sure don't taste like anything else you ever ate, huh? It's got a most distinctive flavor, don't it?"

"Brother!" the woman hissed. "Shut thy mouth!"

But the man seemed unable to stop laughing. "Oh, Sister, let's show him what he's eatin'! I want to see his face when he sees it."

The woman sprang to her feet, nearly knocking over the plate of food she was holding. "Take yourself outside, *now*! I will not have my moment of enjoyment ruined by you. Let me have this one, Brother. Let me have one moment to savor life again on *my* terms!"

The man stopped laughing as suddenly as he had started. He lifted his chin and said, "But what if I don't *want* you to savor this Yankee? What if it's unpleasant for me to think about that?"

Now the woman laughed. "Oh, Jeffery, please don't tell me you're jealous!"

The man shrugged and his face twisted in anger. "What does it matter anyway? You want him and don't care nothin' about my feelings. Well, I don't care none about yours neither!"

He reached around, grabbed something out of a cast iron pot on the table, and held it up for Webster to see. It took a moment for his eyes to adjust enough to discern what the man was holding, but then it came into focus. It was a cooked human foot and ankle. *His* foot and ankle. And as it dripped its heinous gravy onto the table, the truth of what he had just eaten hit Zachary Webster like a bolt of lightning.

The woman saw the look of revulsion on his face and shrieked insanely, "Damn you, Brother!"

Just then, the door to the cabin burst open and exploded off its hinges as though blasted with dynamite. Blinding daylight streamed in behind the giant who filled the doorframe.

There stood Jedediah Stiller with a heavy but beautifully carved

Hawaiian knuckle-duster in his right hand. He was stripped to the waist, and the tattoos on his body and face pulsed with a powerful ferocity.

After working hard to find the wagon tracks that led to this tiny cabin on the decimated plantation, Jedediah had prepared his plan for revenge. He would smash right in and kill Zachary Webster on the spot. But the conversations from within the cabin had intrigued him enough to stand outside and listen to what was being said. Now that he had made his assault, he was not surprised to see Webster tied to a bed with the other two people standing over him.

He said in a hollow voice, "Even though I find you two to be absolutely deplorable, I don't have any quarrel with you. I do, however, have something to settle with that man right there on the bed. He killed my younger brother Jonathan, and I've come to make him pay for that."

The tattooed giant was terrifying enough, but he was also gripping some kind of wooden weapon with vicious shark teeth facing out and a long, sharpened spike on the end of it. His body was heavily scarred from earlier battles, and his posture and tone of voice were just as threatening as the weapon in his hand.

However, the woman was defiant. "Naw, mister. This Yankee's mine to do with what I want. Maybe you should wait your turn till I've had mine."

Jedediah waved her off. "I've gone through innumerable trials and tribulations, woman, and I will wait not one second more to get what I came for."

The brother seemed to find his own confidence, and said, "I don't know what kind of monstrous creature you are, but you cannot dictate what will happen to this Yankee."

"I beg to differ. I will do exactly what I want. If you want to live past today, you'll both just get out of my way and stand back. After all, I'll be doing you two a favor. Just think of me as your own personal butcher. After I dispatch him, you two vultures can feast on his carcass. Like I said, I ain't got no issue with you. I'll leave you two alone in peace and head on my way once vengeance is mine."

There was a momentary silence in the cabin before the woman smiled down tenderly at Webster. "Sorry, lover, but I ain't got enough invested in ya to stand in the way of a monster such as this one. I sho' didn't make it this far in life just to die over some piece of arse. And, whilst I'm more than a little disappointed to miss my ride with ya, it's better to live another day and let the giant have his satisfaction from killin' ya."

"Well, that ain't the way I see it!" the brother yelled.

"Jeffery? What in damnation are you doin'?" the woman asked with a tremor in her voice. "Just let him kill the Yankee and be on his way. What do we care?"

"Yes, Jeffery, listen to your sister and be a good boy. Back away."

"Nay, I will not! Soon as I let one man—even such a diabolic one as you—come into my home and do whatever he wants, I lose control of my own affairs. When I allow that to happen, I'm completely lost."

Jedediah took a step forward. "If you don't let me kill this man, there will be nothing left of you to be lost."

The cocking of a revolver made everyone freeze. The brother had the pistol aimed at Jedediah. He smirked. "Not today, monster. Sister, get the blunderbuss under the bed."

But she remained frozen in place. "What're you doin', Jeffery? Let him kill the Yank and leave us in peace."

"Naw, I think not. Grab that damn gun from under the bed and let's kill this monster. Look at him! He's got a fair bit more meat on him than your scrawny Yank there, so we could live lively with him and the other soldier in our smokehouse till you're done havin' fun with your soldier boy. Besides, we need a resupply. This way, we both win, see?"

The woman glanced at Jedediah with a more appraising eye, then smiled down at Webster as she bent over to reach under his bed.

Jedediah Stiller moved so fast the brother had no chance to react other than with a panic shot at the place where the giant had just been standing. In a blur of movement, he raked the shark teeth of his weapon across the bent-over woman's exposed throat. When she stood up and instinctively raised her hands to the vermillion gash, Jedediah thrust the wooden blade up under her ribs with such force that he lifted her feet from the dirt floor. The brother screamed a garbled word of anguish and fired wildly. Jedediah spun the dead sister's body as a shield until the gun clicked empty. As the man continued dry-firing the revolver, Jedediah threw the woman's body toward him and turned to finish off Zachary Webster on the bed. But he was gone.

During his furious rush toward the woman, Jedediah had unwittingly overturned the bed with such force that it broke into pieces on the floor. And even though he was terribly wounded and dazed, Webster had seized the moment to scramble free of the ropes that bound him and crawl out the gaping doorway of the cabin.

Now, as Jedediah took a step toward the door to find his quarry, another shot rang out from behind him and burned a furrow along his shoulder blade.

"Did you really think that a man with my responsibilities would only have one goddamn weapon at my disposal, you vile monster? After I dispose of you, I'm gonna eat your goddamn heart for killin' my beloved sister!"

The brother came forward, empowered by the small two-shot derringer in his hand, and aimed the weapon directly at Jedediah Stiller. The lack of fear in the advancing man's eyes and his solid hold on the gun were clear indicators that he was not bluffing, and Jedediah felt the ache that came with the realization that he would never see his Miryam again. He opened and closed his fingers on the handle of his weapon and inhaled deeply to savor his last breath before he charged.

The brother stopped moving forward, squared his stance, and leveled the pistol at Jedediah. His eyes were filled with tears of rage as his mouth turned into a snarl. "You goddamn bastard!"

A shot rang out and the brother's head exploded in pink mist. The noise of the shot in the small space was deafening, and it took Jedediah a moment to recover before he could locate its source.

There, in the doorway, stood Zachary Webster with his Sharps rifle still aimed at the spot where the man had stood. He slowly lowered the butt of the rifle to the ground and leaned against it. His face was pale and sweaty from the effort. The smell of brimstone filled the cottage. Jedediah was so stunned that his voice came out more akin to a breathless whisper, "You came back?"

Webster grimaced in pain and then nodded feebly. "I did."

"But why? Why come back for me? Why save me? I came here to kill you! If these two abominations hadn't interfered, you'd already be dead. I was not going to have any mercy for you, so why come back and save me?

Why have mercy on me?"

Webster looked down at the ground and when he spoke his voice had the dull tone of a broken drum. "I thought about leaving you with that vile creature, but that would not have been right. I've given it some thought lately about what this war has done to me. It has transformed me into a cold-blooded killer because it needed me to be that. Well, I cannot be what it needs me to be no more. I'm done with this war. I need to find my humanity again. So, after your attack on that witch gave me the chance to escape, my plan was to just keep going and disappear. But then I knew that, if I really did want to find myself again, I needed to come back and help you."

"I don't think it's at all inappropriate to say that I am grateful you did."

"Lucky for you, those two left my rifle in their wagon with one last shot in it. That being said, I'm now out of bullets and I'm powerless to stop you from killing me. So, if you still aim to get your revenge for your brother's death, I'm at peace with that."

Jedediah saw the way Webster was struggling in the doorway to stay standing and he heard the weakness in his voice, and he knew that the man was telling the truth. Killing Zachary Webster now would be easy as snapping a twig for kindling. With such a simple act, Jedediah's quest for vengeance would be over and he could head back to Miryam and Ezra immediately, free from any burdens. But the other truths that Webster had just uttered were now echoing in his head as well. He, too, sought to find his humanity. In fact, what he chose *not* to do might possibly give him the chance to rediscover a piece of his own soul. After all, killing this man would not bring his brother back. He shook his head and asked, "Do you admit to killing my brother, Jonathan Stiller?"

"I do. But I've killed many, many men these last three years."

The giant tensed as he asked his next question. "Do you have regrets or remorse about killing my brother?"

"No more than any of the other men I've killed in this war."

This answer angered Jedediah, and he took a forced step forward and raised his weapon higher in the air. "But my brother was innocent! He was not an enemy soldier on the battlefield, he was a man buying supplies in town."

Webster replied weakly, "There is nothing innocent left in this here world anymore, Mr. Stiller. Nothing."

"Jonathan was! He was just a simple farmer from Augusta."

"He fell in love with the wrong woman. Mine. That made him guilty of something."

"But you killed him and walked away from his body as if he didn't matter. How can you justify that?"

Webster coughed and this pained him. "I saw what you just did. You dispatched that crone without another care in the world. And that look in your eyes right now tells me you're ready to kill me and walk away like I don't matter. From your scars and fighting skills, I can tell you've killed your share of people, too. Were they all guilty of something? Do you have regrets or remorse about any of them?"

Jedediah drew back a little. "No, I don't. But that's different. I did what I did to stay alive."

"Aye, we all do whatever it takes to stay alive. The truth is, this world can be the most unforgiving of places," Webster said with a faint nod. "I'm done played out from all this standing here on one leg and talking about things done, so I'm gonna go out and sit there by that tree. If you still have a mind to kill me, Mr. Stiller, you'll have to come out there and do the deed. All I ask is that you make it quick."

Webster backed out of the doorway and slowly hopped over to the nearby tree. He started to put his weight on his rifle as he prepared to sit down, but as he started this painful process he heard someone softly calling out his name. When he turned, he saw his Catherine standing there. As soon as the recognition happened, he smiled faintly at her as she rushed up to support him. "Well, how in the world did you get *here*, Catherine Brandford?"

She ran her hand over his feverish forehead and through his hair. "Oh, Zachary, I've been chasing after you since you left Maine. I was trying to get to you before you and Jedediah Stiller killed each other, but now I can see that I am too late and my horrible ordeal was for naught."

Just then, Jedediah Stiller came out of the ramshackle structure into the light. In one hand was his fearsome weapon and in the other was a crude flaming torch he'd made from a piece of the broken bed. He looked down and smiled at Catherine. "Hello, Miss Brandford. I must say, you certainly are a very determined young lady! I now understand why you caused such deadly trouble between this man and my brother."

Catherine hissed at Webster, "So you didn't kill him?"

"No, he didn't. As a matter of fact, he just saved my life."

She gasped. "And now you aim to kill us both as your reward?"

"No, I think we are done with this business of killing. I think it's time for Mr. Webster and me to be square. I think it's time to get away from this accursed war and embrace whatever future befalls us."

Webster nodded weakly and then lowered himself against the tree until he was sitting on the ground. Catherine knelt down to comfort him, but could not take her eyes off the items in the giant man's hands. Jedediah looked down at them now and said, "Oh, these. I still have this weapon in my hand because it's sentimental to me. It's a symbol of my past, my present, and, I guess, my future. And I'm holding this torch because this cabin has such depths of pure evilness that it can only be cured by the cleansing power of the flame."

As he said this, he tossed the torch inside. The dry wood of the furniture and walls instantly caught fire. As they heard the whoosh of the growing flames within, Jedediah shrugged. "Well, I think we should all be headed away from this place now."

"Where will you go?" Catherine asked.

"I'll head back to the field hospital to check on my burial unit and make sure Mr. Buck understands that, as the new leader of those black gravediggers, he is required to act with the utmost dedication to their continued safety and well-being. Once I am sure of this, I will slip away quietly and head east to the new Union supply port at City Point. I'll offer my skills on a steamer headed northward. I know from experience that the captains are having trouble filling their rosters, and I can help with that. I have a new family waiting for me in a salt marsh in Delaware, and I want nothing more than to be reunited with them. What about you two?"

Catherine could see that Webster was about to lose consciousness. "Well, I need to get Zachary to the field hospital to get his wounds looked at by someone more qualified than me. After that, I'm not sure what we will do. We cannot head home to Maine, for obvious reasons, so we'll have to go somewhere else. I'm sure we'll be able to figure out what to do once

Zachary's healthy enough to travel again."

Webster suddenly spoke with a renewed strength, "First off, my name is Ellison Wentworth the Third. *Captain* Ellison Wentworth! Zachary Webster is dead. He was killed in that battle back there in those nefarious woods. Secondly, after you patch me up, Catherine Brandford, we're headed west to San Francisco. You see, I own a shipping company there, and you're more than welcome to come and run it together with me, my dear. I mean, if you want to do that."

"Oh my, he's delirious."

"Naw, say it! Say that my name is Captain Ellison Wentworth the Third! Say it, Catherine!"

"All right. Captain...Ellison...Wentworth...the Third," Catherine stuttered uneasily.

With that, Jedediah Stiller scooped Zachary Webster up onto his shoulder and carried him to the cannibals' small wagon, where he placed him almost gently in the back. He turned to Catherine. "I know it sounds strange to hear me say it, but I do wish you two good luck on your journey, wherever it takes you. Whoever survives this horrible war will form the new world, and God help us all, we'll be the ones leading it into the future."

Catherine climbed onto the driver's bench and said, "Good luck to you, too, Mr. Stiller. I pray the good Lord sees fit to heal all of our wounds and lets us enjoy whatever future He deems to give us."

Webster sat up suddenly and started waving his good hand feebly. "Come out to San Francisco, Stiller, and I'll set you up with a good-paying job! We're gonna need men like you."

Catherine slapped the reins and the small wagon lurched ahead and continued onto the rutted path. Jedediah watched it head off before turning to face the burning cabin again. The entire structure was now aflame, and billowing gray smoke was spewing out the door. The crackling fire was taking on a life of its own, and Jedediah spit contemptuously on the ground. He wished the whole world could be cleansed so easily, but he knew it couldn't. Everything and everyone was now permanently stained, and no fire could ever burn that away.

Something inside the cabin caused a small explosion that blew flame into several branches of a nearby tree, and these quickly arced with the ecstasy of the inferno. The fire was hungry and the forest dry, and Jedediah knew that this blaze would eventually consume everything in the area, so he turned quickly and walked toward the gravediggers' wagon. A group of crows began cawing loudly in the surrounding trees and Jedediah stopped to look at them for a moment. With the giant's glare upon them, the birds went eerily quiet, which allowed the crackling sounds of the vigorous flames to become loud again.

Jedediah continued walking to the wagon, for he wanted nothing more than to get on his way back to Ezra and Miryam. As he stepped up onto the driver's bench, he offered up a quick prayer to Manito and Okee for a safe journey home.

The End

View other Black Rose Writing titles at www.blackrosewriting.com/books and use promo code **PRINT** to receive a **20% discount** when purchasing.

BLACK❀ROSE
writing™

CPSIA information can be obtained
at www.ICGtesting.com
Printed in the USA
FFOW02n2025220618
47167469-49798FF